BLACK
HEART,
IVORY
BONES

Other Fairy Tale Anthologies Edited by
Ellen Datlow and Terri Windling

SILVER BIRCH, BLOOD MOON
BLACK SWAN, WHITE RAVEN
RUBY SLIPPERS, GOLDEN TEARS
BLACK THORN, WHITE ROSE
SNOW WHITE, BLOOD RED

Black Heart, Ivory Bones

Ellen Datlow & Terri Windling

AVON BOOKS NEW YORK

Copyright notices for each story appear opposite on page v, which serves as an extension
of this copyright page.

Excerpt from "Journal of the Frog Prince" from *The Water Inside the Water* by Susan
Mitchell, copyright © 1983 by Susan Mitchell. Reprinted by permission of HarperCollins*Publishers*, Inc.

AVON BOOKS, INC.
An Imprint of HarperCollins*Publishers*
10 East 53rd Street
New York, New York 10022-5299

Copyright © 2000 by Ellen Datlow and Terri Windling
Cover illustration by Thomas Canty
Published by arrangement with the editors
ISBN: 0-380-78623-0
www.harpercollins.com

Library of Congress Cataloging in Publication Data:
Black heart, ivory bones / edited by Ellen Datlow and Terri Windling.
  p. cm.
  1. Fantasy fiction, American. 2. Fairy tales—Adaptations. I. Datlow, Ellen.
II. Windling, Terri.
PS648.F3 B515 2000
813'.0876608054—dc21   99-050293

First Avon Books Trade Paperback Printing: March 2000

AVON TRADEMARK REG. U.S. PAT. OFF. AND IN OTHER COUNTRIES,
MARCA REGISTRADA, HECHO EN U.S.A.

Printed in the U.S.A.

RRD 04 03 02   10 9 8 7 6 5 4

Contents

CONTENTS

"Why is your forehead so cool and damp?" she asks.
Her breasts are soft and dry as flour.
The hand that brushes my head is feverish.
At her touch I long for
the slap of water against rocks . . .

. . . "What are you thinking of?" she whispers.
I am staring into the garden.
I am watching the moon
wind its trail of golden slime around the oak,
over the stone basin of the fountain.
How can I tell her
I am thinking that transformations are not forever?

SUSAN MITCHELL
From the *Journal of the Frog Prince*

Introduction

Once upon a time there were two girls who dearly loved fairy tales . . . and as they grew, they never lost their taste for magical, mythical stories. The girl with hair as black as night loved the dark and tragic tales best—the ones where birds weep tears of blood, the wicked dance in red-hot shoes, and poor little match girls die in the cold embrace of winter. She grew up to be an editor of horror fiction, and lived in a New York City apartment filled with cats and stones and polished bones and art by Edward Gorey. The girl with hair as light as day loved bright tales of transformation—where seal maidens dance on moonlit shores and stubborn girls weave coats of nettles for men turned into swans. She grew up to be an editor of fantasy fiction, and lived in a thatched-roof English cottage covered with roses red and white, like an Arthur Rackham painting come to life. Ten years ago these women discovered they shared a love of fairy tales—the old versions, sensual and dark, before modern children's books and cartoons turned them simple and saccharine—as well as a love for adult literature based on fairy tale themes. They decided that the time had come to rescue fairy tales from the nursery and bring them back to adult readers—and so, along with artist Thomas Canty (whose beautiful painting graces this book), they created a six-volume library of stories inspired by classic tales. The first volume in the series was *Snow White, Blood Red*, published in 1993. It was followed by *Black Thorn, White Rose; Ruby Slippers, Golden Tears; Black Swan, White Raven;* and *Silver Birch, Blood Moon*. The final volume, *Black Heart, Ivory Bones*, you now hold in your hands.

In this series, some of the finest writers of mainstream, horror, fantasy, and children's literature gather together to explore the many pathways, dark and bright, leading to enchantment. The diversity and range of their wonderful tales demonstrates our central premise: that classic folktale motifs still have much to offer fiction writers, and readers, today. Fairy tales speak in a deceptively simple, richly archetypal language; their symbols have proven to be as potent in the hands of modern fiction writers as they have been to generations of poets, playwrights, and storytellers in centuries past. The very words "once upon a time" evoke a shiver, a frisson of expectation. The oral and literary traditions meet in those words . . . and create sheer magic.

As we move between one century to the next, it is interesting to note that the current popularity of fairy tale literature echoes the fairy tale renaissance that occurred at the turn of the last century. In Europe the art nouveau movement covered buildings in Paris, Prague, and Vienna with nymphs, fairies and goddesses—and inspired magical design in ceramics, metalwork, jewelry-making and other crafts. Composers brought old folk music themes into new classical orchestral works, and "fairy" music for the classical harp became a popular trend. The Victorian genre of "fairy painting" contained adult and rather salacious imagery, as did the perverse fairy worlds drawn by Aubrey Beardsley and Harry Clarke. The mythic dreams of the Pre-Raphaelite painters and poets were enclosed in the briars of fairy tales, as were the bittersweet stories of Oscar Wilde and the poems of William Butler Yeats. In our own fin de siècle, adult fairy tale imagery has been most thoroughly explored in women's literature and art. We find fairy tales on the "mainstream" shelves in the fiction of Angela Carter, Margaret Atwood, A.S. Byatt, Sara Maitland, Marina Warner, Berlie Doherty, Alice Thomas Ellis, Elis Ni Dhuibhne, and Emma Donaghue; as well as in the literary fantasy of Jane Yolen, Patricia A. McKillip, Tanith Lee, Robin McKinley, Delia Sherman, Sheri S. Tepper, and Lisa Goldstein; in the poetry of Anne Sexton, Sylvia Plath, Lisel Mueller, Olga Broumas, Sandra Gilbert, and Gwen Strauss; and in the visual arts of Paula Rego, Leonor Fini, Yvonne Gilbert, Becky Kravetz, and Wendy Froud. Many women today—as in seventeenth century France, where the term "fairy tale," *conte de fée*, was coined—have discovered that the startling, even brutal imagery to be found in older versions of classic tales provides useful metaphors for the challenges we face in modern life. These tales come from an oral tradition passed on for hundreds, perhaps thousands, of years primarily by women storytellers—and their themes are as relevant today as they were in centuries past. Modern life is still full of wicked wolves, neglectful or even murderous parents, men under beastly spells, and beautiful women hiding treacherous hearts. We still encounter dangers on the dark and twisty paths leading through the soul, as well as fairy godmothers and animal guides to light the way.

In the pages that follow (as in the previous five books of this series) we welcome writers of both genders and from all areas of the literary arts to explore those paths and to see what new twists and turns they have to offer. We invite you to join us on this last excursion into the enchanted forest . . . laying a trail of bread crumbs and stones to bring us safely home, one last time.

—*Terri Windling*
Devon, England

—*Ellen Datlow*
New York City

Rapunzel

TANITH LEE

Tanith Lee lives with her husband John Kaiine by the sea in Great Britain and is a prolific writer of fantasy, science fiction, and horror. Her most recent books are Faces Under Water *and* Saint Fire, *the first two of a quartet of novels set in a parallel Venice (Venus);* Islands in the Sky, *a children's novel; and* White As Snow, *for Terri Windling's series of fairy tale novels for adults.*

Lee's dark fairy tales have been collected in Red as Blood, *or* Tales From the Sister Grimmer—*and have been included in* Forests of the Night, Women as Demons, *and* Dreams of Dark and Light.

Rapunzel

Not for the first time, a son knew himself to be older than his father.

Urlenn was thinking about this, their disparate maturities, as he rode down through the forests. It was May-Month, and the trees were drenched in fresh young green. If he had been coming from anywhere but a war, he might have felt instinctively alert, and anticipatory; happy, nearly. But killing others was not a favorite pastime. Also, the two slices he had got in return were still raw, probably inflamed. He was mostly disgusted.

It was the prospect of going home. The castle, despite its luxuries, did not appeal. For there would be his father (a king), the two elder sons, and all the noble cronies. They would sit Urlenn up past midnight, less to hear of his exploits than to go over their own or their ancestors': the cap-ture of a fabulous city, a hundred men dispatched by ten, the wonderful prophecy of some ancient crone, even, once, a dragon. There may have been dragons centuries ago, Urlenn judiciously concluded, but if so, they were thin on the ground by now. One more horror, besides, was there in the castle. His betrothed, the inescapable Princess Madzia. The king had chosen Madzia for Urlenn not for her fine blood, but because her grandmother had been (so they said) a fairy. Madzia had thick black hair to her waist, and threw thick black tempers.

After the battle, Urlenn let his men off at the first friendly town. The deserved a junket, and their captains would look out for them. He was going home this way. This *long* way home. With luck, he might make it last a week.

After all, Madzia would not like—or like too much—his open wounds. They ran across his forehead and he had been fortunate to keep his left eye. Doubtless the king would expect the tale of some valiant knightly one-to-one combat to account for this. But it had been a pair of glancing arrows.

Should I make something up to cheer the Dad?

No. And don't call him "the Dad," either. He's king. He'd never forgive you.

Urlenn found he had broken into loud, quite musical song. The ditty was about living in the greenwood, the simple life. Even as he sang, he mocked himself. Being only the third son had advantages, allowing for odd lone journeys like this one. But there were limits.

Something truly odd happened then.

Another voice joined in with his, singing the same song, and in a very decent descant. A girl's voice.

The horse tossed its head and snorted, and Urlenn reined it in.

They sang, he and she (invisible), until the end. Then, nothing. Urlenn thought, *She's not scared, or she would never have sung.* So he called: "Hey, maiden! Where are you?"

And a laughing voice—you could tell it laughed—called back, "Where do you think?"

"Inside a tree," called Urlenn. "You're a wood-dryad."

"A *what?* A dryad—oh, Gran told me about those. No I'm not."

Urlenn dismounted. There was, he had come to see, something gray and tall and stone, up the slope, just showing through the ascending trees.

He did not shout again. Nor did she. Urlenn walked up the hill, and came out by a partly ruined tower. Sycamores and aspens had rooted in its sides, giving it a leafy, mellow look. A cottage had rooted there, too, a large one; also made of stones, which had definitely been filched from the tower.

Before the cottage and tower was an orchard of pear and apple trees just losing their white blossom. Chickens and a goat ambled about. The girl was hanging up washing from the trees.

She was straight and slim, with short yellow hair like a boy's. And yes, still laughing.

"Not a dryad, as you see, sir."

"Maybe unwise, though, calling out to strangers in the wood."

"Oh, you sounded all right."

"*Did* I?"

"All sorts come through here. You get to know."

"*Do* you?"

"Sometimes I fetch the animals, and we hide in the tower. Last month two men broke into the cottage and stole all the food. I let them get on with it." She added, careless, "I was only raped once. I'd been stupid. But he wished he hadn't, after."

"That's you warning me."

"*No.* You're not the type, sir. You looked upset when I told you. Then curious."

"I *am.* What did you do, kill him?"

"No, I told him I loved him and gave him a nice drink. He'd have had the trots for days."

Urlenn himself laughed. "Didn't he come back?"

"Not yet. And it was two years ago."

She looked about seventeen, three years younger than he. She had been raped at fifteen. It did not seem to matter much to her. She had a lovely face. Not beautiful or pretty, but unexpected, *interesting*, like a landscape never seen before, though perhaps imagined.

"Well, maiden," he said. "I'm thirsty myself. Do you

have any drinks without medicine in them? I can pay, of course."

"That's all right. We mainly barter, when I go to town." She turned and walked off to the cottage. Urlenn stood, looking at the goat and chickens and a pale cat that had come to supervise them.

The girl returned with a tankard of beer, clear as a river, and cold from some cool place, as he later learned, under the cottage floor.

He drank gratefully. She said, "You're one of the king's men, aren't you, sent to fight off the other lot?"

The other lot. Yes.

He said, "That's right."

"That cut over your eye looks sore."

"It is. I didn't want it noticed much and wrapped it up in a rag—which was, I now think, dirty."

"I can mix up something for that."

"You're a witch too."

"Gran was. She taught me."

Presently he tethered the horse to a tree and left it to crop the turf.

In the cottage he sat watching her sort and pound her herbs. It was neither a neat nor a trim room, but—pleasing. Flowering plants burst and spilled from pots on the windowsills, herbs and potions, vinegars and honeys stood glowing like jade and red amber in their jars. A patchwork curtain closed off the sleeping place. On the floor there were baskets full of colored yarns and pieces of material. Even some books lay on a chest. There was the sweet smell of growing things, the memory of recent baking—the bread stood by on a shelf—a hint of damp. And her. Young and healthy, fragrant. Feminine.

When she brought the tincture she had made, and applied it to the cuts, her scent came to him more strongly.

Urlenn thought of Madzia, her flesh heavily perfumed, and washed rather less often. He thought of Madzia's sulky, red, biteable-looking mouth.

This girl said, "That will sting." *It does*, he thought, *and I don't mean your ointment.* "But it'll clean the wound. Alas,

I think there'll be a scar. Two scars. Will that spoil your chances, handsome?"

He looked up and straight in her eyes. She was flirting with him, plainly. Oh yes, she knew what she was at. She had told him, she could tell the good from the bad by now.

I don't look much like a king's son, certainly. Not anymore. Just some minor noble able to afford a horse. So, it may be me she fancies.

Her eyes were more clear than any beer-brown river.

"If you don't want money, let me give you something else in exchange for your care—"

"And what would you give me?"

"Well, what's on the horse I need to keep. But—is there anything you see that you'd like?"

Was *he* flirting now?

To his intense surprise, Urlenn felt himself blush. And, surprising him even more, at his blush she, this canny, willful woods-witch, she did, too.

So then he drew the ring off his finger. It was small, but gold, with a square cut, rosy stone. He put it in her palm.

"Oh no," she said, "I can't take that for a cup of ale and some salve."

"If you'd give me dinner, too, I think I'd count us quits," he said.

She said, without boldness, gently, "There's the bed, as well."

Later, in the night, he told her he fell in love with her on sight, only did not realize he had until she touched him.

"That's nothing," she said, "I fell in love with *you* the minute I heard you singing."

"Few have done *that*, I can tell you."

They were naked by then, and had made love three times. They knew each other well enough to say such things. The idea was he would be leaving after breakfast, and might come back to visit her, when he could. If he could. The talk of being in love was chivalry, and play.

But just as men and women sometimes lie when they say they love and will return, so they sometimes lie also when they believe they will not.

They united twice more in the night, while the cat

hunted outside and the goat and chickens muttered from
their hut. In the morning Urlenn did not leave. In the morning she never mentioned he had not.

When she told him her name, he had laughed out loud.
"What? Like the salad?"

"Just like. My ma had a craving for it all the time she
carried me. So then, she called me for it, to pay me out."

The other paying out had been simple, too.

"In God's name—" he said, holding her arm's length,
shocked and angry, even though he knew it happened frequently enough.

"I don't mind it," she said. He could see, even by the
fire and candlelight, she did not. *How forgiving she is—no,
how understanding of human things.*

For the girl's mother had sold her, at the age of twelve,
to an old woman in the forests.

"I was lucky. She was a wise-woman. And she wanted
an apprentice not a slave."

In a few weeks, it seemed, the girl was calling the old
woman "Gran," while Gran called *her* Goldy. "She was better than any mother to me," said the girl. "I loved her
dearly. She left me everything when she died. All this. And
her craft, that she'd taught me. But we only had two years
together, I'd have liked more. Never mind. As she used to
say, 'Some's more than none.' It was like that with my hair."

"She called you Goldy for your hair."

"No. Because she said I was 'good as gold and bad
as butter.' "

"*What?*"

"She was always saying daft funny things. She'd make
you smile or think, even if your heart was broken. She had
the healing touch, too. I don't have it."

"You did, for me."

"Ah, but I *loved* you."

After an interval, during which the bed became, again,
unmade, the girl told Urlenn that her fine hair, which would
never grow and which, therefore, she cut so short, was better
than none, according to Gran.

"It wasn't unkind, you see. But pragmatic."

She often startled him with phrases, words—she could read. (Needless to say, Gran had taught her.)

"Why bad as butter?"

"Because butter makes you want too much of it."

"I can't get too much of you. Shall I call you Goldy— or the other name?"

"Whatever you like. Why don't you find a name for me yourself? Then I'll be that just for you."

"I can't name you—like my dog!"

"That's how parents name their children. Why not lovers?"

He thought about the name, as he went about the male chores of the cottage, splitting logs, hunting the forest, mending a scythe. Finally he said, diffidently, "I'd like to call you Flarva."

"That's elegant. I'd enjoy that."

He thought she would have enjoyed almost anything. Not just because she loved him, but because she was so easy with the world. He therefore called her Flarva, not explaining yet it had been his mother's name. His mother who had died when Urlenn was only six.

Urlenn had sometimes considered if his father's flights of fantasy would have been less if Flarva had lived. The Dad (*Yes, I shall call you that in my head*) had not been king then. Kingship came with loss, after, and also power and wealth, and all the obligations of these latter things.

Other men would have turned to other women. The Dad had turned to epics, ballads, myths and legends. He filled his new-sprung court with song-makers, actors and story-tellers. He began a library, most of the contents of which— unlike this young girl—he could not himself read. He inaugurated a fashion for the marvelous and magical. If someone wanted to impress the Dad, they had only to "prove," by means of an illuminated scroll, that they took their partial descent from one of the great heroes or heroines—dragon-slayers, spinners of gold, tamers of unicorns. Indeed, only four years ago the king had held a unicorn hunt. (It was well attended.) One of the beasts had been seen, reportedly, drinking from a fountain on the lands of the Dad. Astonishingly, they never found it. Rumors of it still circulated from time to time. And those who claimed to have seen it, if they told their tale just in *that* way, were rewarded.

Was the king mad? Was it his brain—or only some avoiding grief at the reality of the brutal world?

"Or is it his genius?" said the girl—Flarva—when he informed her of his father's nature. "When the dark comes, do we sit in the dark, or light candles?"

How, he thought, *I love you.*

And strangely, she said then, "There, you love him."

"I suppose I do. But he irks me. I wish I could go off. Look at me here. I should have got home by now."

He had not, despite all this, yet revealed to her that the Dad was also the king. Did she still assume his father was only some run-down baron or knight? Urlenn was not sure. Flarva saw through to things.

"Well, when you leave, then you must," was all she said in the end.

He had been up by now to the town, a wandering little village with a church and a tavern and not much else. Here he found a man with a mule who could take a letter to the next post of civilization. From there it would travel to the king. The letter explained Urlenn had been detained in the forests. He had only one piece of paper, and could not use it up on details—he begged his lordly sire to pardon him, and await his excuses when he could come home to give them.

Afterward, Urlenn had realized, this had all the aura of some Dad-delighting sacred quest, even a spell.

Would he have to go to the king eventually and say, "A witch enchanted me?"

He did not think he could say that. It would be a betrayal of her. Although he knew she would not mind.

There was no clock in the cottage, or in the village-town. Day and night followed each other. The green thickened in clusters on the trees, and the stars were thinner and more bright on the boughs of darkness. Then a golden border stitched itself into the trees. The stars waxed thicker again, and the moon more red.

Urlenn liked going to the village market with Flarva, bartering the herbs and apples and vegetables from her garden plot, and strange patchwork and knitted coats she made, one of which he now gallantly wore.

He liked the coat. He liked the food she cooked. He liked milking the adventurous goat, which sometimes went calling on a neighbor's he-goat two miles off and had to be brought back. He liked the pale cat, which came to sleep with them in the hour before dawn. He liked woodcutting. The song of birds and their summer stillness. The stream that sparkled down the slope. The gaunt old tower. Morning and evening.

Most of all, he liked her, the maiden named first for a salad. Not only lust and love, then. For liking surely was the most dangerous. Lust might burn out and love grow accustomed. But to like her was to find in her always the best—of herself, himself, and all the world.

One evening, when the lamp had just been lit, she straightened up from the pot over the fire, and he saw her as if he never had.

He sat there, dumbfounded, as if not once, in the history of any land, had such a thing ever before happened.

Sensing this, she turned and looked at him with her amused, kindly, *feral* eyes.

"Why didn't you tell me, Flarva?"

"I was waiting to see how long you'd take to notice."

"How far gone is it?"

"Oh, four months or so. Not so far. You haven't been too slow."

"Slow? I've been blind. But you—you're never ill."

"The herbs are good for this, too."

"But—it must weigh on you."

"It—*It*—"

"He, then—or she, then."

"They, then."

"*They?*"

"Twins I am carrying, love of my heart."

"How do you know? Your herbs again?"

"A dowsing craft Gran taught me. Boy and girl, Urlenn, my dear."

He got up and held her close. Now he felt the swell of her body pressing to him. *They* were there.

She was not fretful. Neither was he. It was as if he knew no harm could come to her. She was so clear and wholesome and yet so—yes, so *sorcerous*. No one could know her and think her only a peasant girl in a woods cottage. Perhaps it was for this reason, too, he had had no misgivings that he abused, when first he lay down with her. He a prince. She a princess. Equals, although they were of different social countries.

However, what to do now?

"I've grasped from the beginning I'd never leave you, Flarva. But—I have to confess to you about myself."

She looked up into his eyes. She had learned she had two children in her womb. Perhaps she had fathomed him, too.

"Have you? I mean, do you know I am—a king's son?

She smiled. "What does it matter?"

"Because—"

"If you must leave me, Urlenn, I've always left open the door. I'd be sorry. Oh, so very sorry. But perhaps you might come back, now and then. Whatever, love isn't a cage, or if it is, a pretty one, with the door undone, and the birds out and sitting on the roof. I can manage here."

"You don't see, Flarva. Maybe you might manage very well without me. But I'd be lost without you. And those two—greedily, I want to know them as well."

"I'm glad. But I thought you would."

"So I must find a way to bring you home."

"Simple. I shall give this cottage to our neighbor. The goat will like that. The neighbor's good with fruit trees and chickens, too. As for the cat, she must come with us, being flexible and quite portable."

"No, my love, you know quite well what I mean. A way to bring you into my father's castle, and keep you there. And selfishly let you *make* it home for me at last."

They sat by the fire—the evenings now were cooler than they had been. Side by side, he and she, they plotted out what must be done. The answer was there to hand, if they had the face, the cheek, for it.

*   *   *

It had been a harsh, white winter. Then a soft spring. Now flame-green early summer lighted the land.

Amazed, the castle men-at-arms, about to throw Urlenn in the moat, recognized him.

"I'm here without any state."

"*In* a state," they agreed.

But then some of the men he had led in the war ran up, cheering him, shaking his hand.

"Where on God's earth have you been? We searched for you—"

"A wild weird tale. Take me to the king. He must hear first."

Urlenn had been driving a wagon, pulled by two mules, and his war-horse tied at the back. One or two heard a baby cry, and looked at one or two others.

Prince Urlenn went into the king's presence just as he was, in workaday colorful peasant clothes, and with two white scars glaring above his shining eyes.

The king (who did not know he was the Dad) had been on a broad terrace that commanded a view of the valleys and the distant mountains that marked his kingdom's end. The two elder sons were also there, and their wives, and most of the court, servants, soldiers, various pets, some hunting dogs, and Princess Madzia, who, for motives of sheer rage, had not gone away all this while.

Urlenn bowed. The king, white as the paper of Urlenn's last—and only second—letter, sprang up.

They embraced and the court clapped (all but Madzia). Urlenn thought, *I've been monstrous to put him through this. But surely I never knew he liked me at all—but he does, look, he's crying. Oh, God. I could hang myself.*

But that would not have assisted the Dad, nor himself, so instead Urlenn said, "Will you forgive me, my lord and sire? I was so long gone on the strangest adventure, the most fearsome and bizarre event of my life. I never thought such things were possible. Will you give me leave to tell you the story of it?"

There followed some fluster, during which Princess Madzia scowled, her eyes inky thunder. But these eyes dulled as Urlenn spoke. In the end they were opaque, and all of her gone to nothing but a smell of civet and a dark red dress. Years after, when she was riotously married elsewhere, and cheerful again, she would always say, broodingly (falsely), "My heart broke." But even she had never said that Urlenn had been wrong.

Urlenn told them this: Journeying home through the forests, he had come to an eerie place, in a green silence. And there, suddenly, he heard the most beautiful voice, singing. Drawn by the song, he found a high stone tower. Eagerly, yet uneasily—quite why he was not sure—he waited nearby, to see if the singer might appear. Instead, presently, a terrible figure came prowling through the trees. She was an old hag, and ugly, but veiled in an immediately apparent and quite awesome power which he had no words to describe. Reaching the tower's foot, this being wasted no time, but called out thus: *Let down your hair! Let down your hair!* And then, wonder of wonders, from a window high up in the side of the tower, a golden banner began unfolding and falling down. Urlenn said he did not for one minute think it was hair at all. It shone and gleamed—he took it for some weaving of metal threads. But the hag placed her hands on it, and climbed up it, and vanished in at the window.

Urlenn prudently hid himself then more deeply in the trees. After an hour the hag descended as she had gone up. Urlenn observed in bewilderment as this unholy creature now pounced away into the wood.

"Then I did a foolish thing—very foolish. But I was consumed, you see, by burning curiosity."

Imitating the cracked tones of the hag, he called out, just as she had done: "Let down your hair!"

And in answer, sure enough, the golden woven banner silked once more from the window, and fell, and fell.

He said, when he put his hands to it, he shuddered. For he knew at once, and without doubt, it had all the scent and texture of a young girl's hair. But to climb up a rope of *hair* was surely improbable? Nevertheless, he *climbed*.

The shadows now were gathering. As he got in through the window's slot, he was not certain of what he saw.

Then a pure voice said to him, "Who are you? You are never that witch!"

There in a room of stone, with her golden tresses piled everywhere about them, softer than silken yarn, gleaming, glorious, and—he had to say—rather untidy—the young girl told him her story.

Heavy with child, the girl's mother had chanced to see, in the gardens of a dreaded, dreadful witch, a certain salad. For this she developed, as sometimes happens with women at such times, a fierce craving. Unable to satisfy it, she grew ill. At last, risking the witch's wrath, the salad was stolen for the woman. But the witch, powerful as she was, soon knew, and manifested before the woman suddenly. "In return for your theft from my garden, I will thieve from yours. You must give me your child when it is born, for my food has fed it. Otherwise, both can die now." So the woman had to agree, and when she had borne the child, a daughter, weeping bitterly she gave it to the witch. Who, for her perverse pleasure, named the girl after the salad (here he told the name) and kept her imprisoned in a tower of stone.

"But her hair," said Urlenn, "oh, her hair—it grew golden and so long—finer than silk, stronger than steel. Was it for this magic, perhaps imparted by the witch's salad, that the witch truly wanted her? Some plan she must have had to use the hapless maiden and her flowing locks? I thwarted it. For having met the maid, she and I fell in love."

Urlenn had intended to rescue his lover from the tower, but before that was accomplished, he visited her every day. And the witch, cunning and absolute, discovered them. "You'll realize," said Urlenn, "she had only to look into some sorcerous glass to learn of our meetings. But we, in our headstrong love, forgot she could."

"Faithless!" screamed the witch, and coming upon the girl alone, cut off all her golden hair. Then the witch, hearing the young man calling, *herself* let the tresses down for his ladder. And he, in error, climbed them. Once in the tower's top, the witch confronted him in a form so horrible, he could not later recall it. By her arcane strengths, however, she flung him down all the length of the tower, among great thorns and brambles which had sprung up there.

"Among them I almost lost my sight. You see the scars

left on my forehead. Blinded, I wandered partly mad for months."

Beyond the tower lay an occult desert, caused by the witch's searing spells. Here the witch in turn cast the maiden, leaving her there to die.

But, by the emphasis of love and hope, she survived, giving birth alone in the wilderness, to the prince's children, a little boy and girl, as alike as sunflowers.

"There in the end, sick, and half insane, I found her. Then she ran to me and her healing tears fell on my eyes. And my sight was restored."

Love had triumphed. The desert could not, thereafter, keep them, and the prince and his beloved, wife in all but name, emerged into the world again, and so set out for the kingdom of the prince's father.

He's crying again. Yes, I should hang myself. But maybe not. After all, she said I might make out her Gran was wicked—said the old lady would have laughed—all in a good cause. A perfect cause. They're all crying. Look at it. And the Dad—he does love a story.

"My son—my son—won't this evil sorceress pursue you?"

Urlenn said, frankly, "She hasn't yet. And it was a year ago."

The king said, "Where is the maiden?"

Oh, the hush.

"She waits just outside, my lordly sire. And our children, too. One thing . . ."

"What is it?"

"Since the witch's cruel blow, her hair lost its supernatural luster. Now it's just . . . a nice shade of flaxen. Nor will it grow at all. She cuts it short. She prefers that, you see, after the use to which it was last put. By her hair, then, you'll never know her. Only by her sweetness and her lovely soul, which shine through her like a light through glass."

Then the doors were opened and Flarva came in. She wore a white gown, with pearls in her short yellow hair. She looked as beautiful as a dream. And after her walked two servants with two sleeping babies. And by them, a pale stalking cat which, having no place in the legend, at first no one saw. (Although it may have found its way into other tales.)

But the king strode forward, his eyes very bright. Never, Urlenn thought, had he seen this man so full of life and fascinated interest. Or had he seen it often, long ago, when he was only three or four or five? In Flarva's time . . .

"Welcome," said the king, the Dad, gracious as a king or a father may be. "Welcome to the wife of my son, my daughter, Rapunzel."

Tanith Lee says of her story, "My only other assault so far, on the story of 'Rapunzel' "— 'The Golden Rope,' in Red as Blood, *1983—"tried to explore, as I normally do, intricacies within intricacies, the convolutions under already complete knots and windings. This time a preposterous simplicity suggested itself. Perhaps it was just the time for it, for me. Any supernatural myth or folktale could have a similar base, and some maybe do. . . . What endeared this debunking to me so much was that the deceptions sprang from love. And love, of course, the pivot of so many fairy tales (along with the darker avarice, rage and competitiveness) is itself one of the magic intangibles. Invisible as air, only to be seen by its effects, love remains entirely and intransigently real."*

The Crone

DELIA SHERMAN

Delia Sherman is the author of numerous short stories, and of the novels Through a Brazen Mirror, The Porcelain Dove *(which won the Mythopoeic Award), and* The Freedom Maze. *She is the co-author of "The Fall of the Kings" in* Bending the Landscape *(nominated for a World Fantasy Award) with fellow fantasist and partner Ellen Kushner, and co-editor of* The Horns of Elfland: An Anthology of Music and Magic. *Sherman is also co-editor, with Terri Windling, of* The Essential Bordertown. *She is a contributing editor for Tor Books and a member of the Tiptree Awards Motherboard.*

The Crone

I sit by the side of the road, comfortably planted
On a stone my buttocks have worn silky.
My garments are a peeling bark of rags,
My feet humped as roots, my hands catch
Like twigs, my hair is moss and feathers.
My eyes are a bird's eyes, bright and sharp.
I wait for sons.

They always come, sometimes twice a day
In questing season, looking for adventure,
Fortune, fame, a magic flower, love.
Only the youngest sons will find it:
The others might as well have stopped at home
For all the good I'll do them.

It's the second sons who break my heart,
Anxious at their elder brothers' failure,
Stuck with the second-best horse, the second-best sword,
The second-best road to disaster. Often I wish
A second son would share his bread with me,
Wrap his cloak around my body, earn
The princess and the gold.

That's one wish. The second (I'm allowed three)
Is that a daughter, any daughter at all—
Youngest, oldest—seeking her fortune,
A kingdom to rule, a life to call her own
Would sit and talk with me, give me her bread
And her ear. Perhaps (third wish) she'd ask
After my kin, my home, my history.
Ah then, I'd throw off my rags and dance in the road
Young as I never was, and free.

*The old crone is a familiar fairy tale figure found in stories around
the world. In "quest" and "boy-in-search-of-fortune" fairy tales,
the hero encounters an old woman on the road and must treat
her with courtesy or suffer the consequences. In courtly French
fairy tales she is usually a beautiful fairy in disguise, but in
German and French peasant folk lore, the crone sits mysteriously
at the edges of the story, encouraging children to be kind to
poverty-stricken old ladies.*

Big Hair

ESTHER FRIESNER

Esther Friesner lives in Connecticut with her husband, two children, two rambunctious cats, and a fluctuating population of hamsters. She is the author of twenty-nine novels and over one hundred short stories, in addition to being the editor of four popular anthologies. She is also a published poet, a playwright, and once wrote an advice column. Besides winning two Nebula Awards in succession for Best Short Story (1995 and 1996), Friesner won the Romantic Times Award for Best New Fantasy Writer in 1986 and the Skylark Award in 1994. She is currently working on an epic fantasy and is also editing the third in the Chicks in Chainmail anthology series, called Chicks and Chained Males.

Big Hair

Mama took her to all the pageants, Mama kept the boys away. No one got near Ruby except the judges and the newspaper folks and the TV people unless Mama said. Even then, not too many of those got through. Mama told Ruby that a woman's greatest attraction was staying just out of reach, and she was there to see to it that Ruby learned that lesson even if she had to keep her locked up in her hotel room the whole time to make sure she did.

Ruby disagreed, especially about the reporters. "What's wrong with a little extra publicity?" she asked Mama that night as they drove down the mountain, headed for Richmond and the next competition.

Mama's skinny fingers knotted tight on the wheel. She didn't answer Ruby's question, not directly, not at all. "Who you been talking to?" she wanted to know.

Ruby mumbled something under her breath, tuckii[
sweet, round little chin down into the collar of the butt[
up trench coat Mama always made her wear, hot or cold,
rain or shine. Mama pulled the car over to the side of the
road and killed the engine and the headlights too, even
though there was a storm following them down out of the
mountains, roaring and grumbling at their backs like a hungry bear.

"What did you say?" Mama demanded.

"Other girls." Ruby still mumbled, but she got the
words out loud enough to be heard this time.

"I thought so." Mama sat back stiff and tall against the
driver's seat, making the old plastic covers creak and groan.
There weren't any lights on this stretch of road except what
the car carried with it, and those were out, but there were
little licks of lightning playing through the cracks in the sky.
One of them dashed across heaven to outline Mama's face
with silver, knife bright, her chin like a shovel blade, her
nose like a sailing ship's prow.

"Now you listen to me, little girl," Mama said out of
the pitch-black that always followed mountain lightning.
"Anything those other girls tell you is a lie. Don't matter if
it's got two bushel baskets full of facts behind it, don't matter if they say the sun rises up in the east or that air's the
only thing fit to breathe, it's still a lie, lie, *lie*. And why?
Because it came out of *their* mouths, God damn 'em to hell.
Which is the place I'll toss your raw and bloody bones if I
ever again hear you mouth one word those 'other girls' say.
Is that clear?"

"Yes, Mama."

" 'Yes, Mama.' " Mama mocked the soft, mechanical
way that Ruby spoke. "Don't you even want to know the
proof behind what I'm telling you?"

"No, Mama. You told me. That's good enough."

Mama reached over and jabbed her finger into Ruby's
hip, a place where the bruise wouldn't show even in the
bathing suit part of the competition, not even if the suit was
one of those near-indecent high-cut styles. That place was
already pretty mushed over with blues and greens and yel-

lows, generations of hard, deep finger-pokes done by an expert hand. Mama knew her merchandise.

"You lie," she said. "You want a reason. You always do, these days, whether you come right out and say so, like an honest soul, or whether you follow your blood and lie. Ever since you grew titties, you've changed. Used to be you'd take my word and all, no questions, no doubts, but not now. You're getting to be more like your mother every day, so I know what's coming, if I let it come."

Ruby didn't say anything. Ruby didn't know quite what to say. Whenever Mama talked about Ruby's mother, it was like she was daring Ruby to find the breath to speak. Ruby couldn't, though. It was like cold wax was clogging up her throat, coating the roof of her mouth with its crackling shell. Sometimes the silence was enough to make Mama let go and give Ruby back her breath.

Sometimes it was enough, but not now.

"Your mother." Mama said the words like a curse woven out of dead things and dark places. "All her pretty promises about how we'd be more of a family with a child to raise, and the hell with what folks'd say. No more sneaking, no more lies about two old maids keeping house together to save on costs like we'd been saying. Even said how she'd be the willing one, glad to make the sacrifice of lying under as many men as it took to stick you in her belly. And when you rooted and grew, what didn't I do for her when she was carrying you? Anything she asked for, any whim that tickled that bubble she called a brain, I broke my back to fetch it. I gave up all the sweetness of the woods and the brightness of the stars for a set of overpriced rooms in a city I hated, just so she could stay in walking distance of fancy restaurants, movies, stores. The night her pains came on, who was it drove her to the hospital? I held her hand, made her breathe, caught your slime-streaked body, cut the birth cord. When she looked at you that first time, all wrinkly red, and turned her head away because you weren't pretty enough to suit her, I held you close and felt you nuzzle into my chest looking for what she wouldn't give you, and I wept because I would've given it to you if I could."

In the dark, Ruby heard Mama's voice catch on a dry, half-swallowed sob. Tears were smearing her own face, but she never made a sound. This was the longest Mama'd ever gone on about Ruby's mother. Usually all she harped on was the night that woman had run off, never to return, leaving the two of them behind. Mama was saying some things Ruby knew, but there was fresh knowledge jutting itself up out of the dark like a sprouting hedge of thorns. Each new revelation drew a drop of blood from somewhere that would never show, not even during the part of the contest where the judges asked you things. Ruby let the tears flow down. It wasn't like they'd hurt her makeup; she never wore any between pageants. Mama said not to. Ruby sat tight and bruised and bleeding, waiting in silence for Mama to be done.

"There is one decent road out of these mountains, and I've put your feet on it," Mama said. She wasn't talking over tears anymore. She was in charge of everything and heaven. "One road that won't lead you into treachery or shame, like the one *she* chose, the whore. All the things you want, all you hope to own, all waiting for you to call them in just like magic, once you've won your proper place in this world. Beauty's place, with no limits to it. People pay attention to looks. People give up the earth for beauty."

"Yes, Mama," said Ruby, small. Mama didn't even hear. Mama was too taken up treading the word-web of her own weaving.

"God knows you could get by with less, but I'd be lying if I told you I believed that'd content you," Mama said. "I know you too well. I've known you from the womb. You're a hungry one, greedy like she was, only difference being now I know how deep the greed runs in your guts. I'm not losing you too, girl. She took too much from me. You're mine, now till it's over and beyond. I'm too old and homely to find someone new, and I'm damned if I'm dying alone. I'll feed your hungers until you haven't a one left, and then you'll stay. You'll have to. What'd there be left to lure you off if you got everything?"

"I ain't going anywhere, Mama," Ruby said, soft and

pleading, the way she'd learned the judges liked to hear a girl speak.

The key turned in the ignition, the car stuttered to life. "So you say." Mama's face flashed grim in a shot of lightning, but then it vanished as the dark clapped down.

They drove out of the mountains and into the city, right up to the door of the big hotel where all the contestants were supposed to stay. Mama made Ruby sit in the car in the garage under the hotel until after she got them registered and had the key to the room in her hand. Then she went down to the car and had Ruby ride up in the service elevator so no one'd get to see her.

That's how she always did it. That's how it'd always worked before.

This time he was watching, and Mama, who always seemed to know everything, never even knew.

He'd heard about Ruby, seen the tapes of all the other pageants. At first he told himself he was just doing it for the story—"Secrets of Mystery Glamour Queen Revealed!"—but the splinter of his soul that still believed he was a real writer told him another story.

He'd seen the tapes: the judges, almost evenly divided between the ones who looked ready to let their next yawn send them all the way off to dreamland and the ones who devoured the girls with their eyes; the audience, papered over with politic-perfect neutral smiles, playing no favorites, putting their own faces on the runway bodies or else imagining those bodies in their own beds; the girls themselves, shining, bouncing, gleaming for their lives. And her.

No hope, once she took the stage, no hope for anyone at all to take it back again. She'd always come in wearing whatever it was the contest demanded—bathing suit or business suit, evening gown or kitschy cowgirl outfit, furs, sequins, fringes, fluff, leather, lotion, vinyl, sweat—it didn't matter. She wore them all, always with that one accessory that didn't belong but that she could no more forget to wear than her bright bloodred lipstick.

All it was was a scarf. Just a wispy chiffon scarf the

color of a summer garden's heart, a scarf she wore wrapped tightly around her head like a turban.

Not for long. He'd seen the tapes. She'd make her first appearance in the pageant with the scarf tied around her head, go one-two-three across the stage to deadliest center, reach up, give the tag end of it the merest twitch, the slightest tug, and then . . .

BAM! Hair. Roils and curls and seething clouds of hair erupting anywhere you'd think it could be and a whole lot of places you never imagined. Down it came, all the waves of it, the golden spilling wonder of it, the flash flood of thick, endless, unbound tresses that drenched her from head to toes in impossible glory, bright as a polished sword. Hair that mantled her in the ripples of a sun-kissed sea, remaking her in the image of a new Venus, born from the heart of the foam. Hair that boiled down to hide the swell of her breasts, the jut of her ass, and every tantalizing curve of her besides just enough to say, *It's here, baby, but you can't have it, and oh my, yes, I know that only makes you want it more.*

Hair that was the sudden curtain rung down over the beauty of her body, a sudden, sharp HANDS OFF sign that made the half-slumbering judges wake up to the realization that they'd missed out, made the ravenous ones howl for the feast that had been snatched away from their eyes. And while they all gasped and murmured and scribbled their thwarted hearts out on the clipboards in their hands, she did a quick swivel-turn, flicked her trailing mane neatly, gracefully aside, out from under spike-heeled foot, and made her exit, clipping a staccato one-two-three from the stage boards, each jounce of her hair-swathed hips nothing more than a whisper, a promise, a deliciously wicked little secret peeping out from under the glimmering veil.

Sometimes the other contestants raised a fuss, but what could they do? Nothing in the rules against a girl wearing a scarf in, on, or over her hair; let them wear their own if they wanted.

As if that'd give them more than a butterfly's prayer in hell! *He* knew. He'd seen the tapes, and once—just once, by the sort of accident that slams a man's legs out from under him and smashes a fist through his heart—he'd seen her. A reporter's supposed to cover police calls, but when it's a false alarm about a stickup at the box office of the auditorium where the pageant's happening, well, what's a man to do? Toss it all up and go home when there's something else worth seeing? Of course he stayed to see her. He'd seen the tapes, but this was something else again.

And how. Seeing her pull that stunt with the scarf in person burned all the tapes to ash in his memory. He stood there, at the back of the auditorium, and felt the air conditioner dry his tongue as he gaped, blast-frozen in an impact of hair and hair and *hair*. Down it came, every strand taking its own tumbling path through spotlight-starred air, even the tiniest tendril of it lashing itself tight around his heart.

That night he dreamed about her and woke up in a tangle of love-soiled sheets. That morning he went in to see his editor and asked to leave the crime beat for just the shortest while to dog a different sort of story.

He pitched it hard and he pitched it pro. Human interest, yeah, that's the ticket! Everyone knew about this girl but nobody really knew a goddamn thing. Shame if the state's next Miss America shoo-in got to hold onto her secrets. There were no secrets anyone could hold onto once she headed for the big-time, the biggest pageant of them all, and wouldn't it be a shame if the honest citizens of this great state got left with egg on their faces in case this girl's secrets were of the sort that smeared the camera lens with slime?

His editor bought it and bit down hard. He set his hook and ran before second thoughts could intrude. That was how he'd come to be down there, waiting in the shadows of the hotel's underside, standing watch over the elevators in a borrowed busboy uniform, pretending to fix the cranky wheel of a food service cart. He'd done his homework, he'd checked out all the talk about how no one ever saw her before the pageant. He knew she had to get into the hotel somehow, that you couldn't just pluck that much woman out of thin air. Simple, really, the way it was done. He didn't waste much time thinking over why it was done at all.

Her mama never even noticed him when she came down in the service elevator to fetch Ruby from the garage. He was the "help," invisible to her until called for. Women of a certain age would sooner give a nod of recognition to a potted plant than to the man he was pretending to be. When the two women came out of the garage and he managed the supposed miracle of fixing the food service cart just in time to share a ride up with them, he saw the old bitch's mouth go a tad tight, but she never so much as acknowledged his presence in the elevator.

He punched the button for five, she punched twelve. "Oops." He grinned and punched fifteen. That prune pit mouth hardened even more, but that was as far as the hag would go to admitting his existence. A fat lot he cared! He'd seen what he'd come to see . . . nearly.

Braids. God damn it all to hell, she was wearing braids.

Mama hung up the phone and snorted, mad. "Of all the nerve."

"What is it, Mama?" Ruby came out of the bathroom, dewy and glowing from a hot shower, her wet hair trailing down her back, a golden serpent sinking into the sea.

"Can you believe the gall of those petty-minded creatures?"

"Who?" Mama was so upset she didn't even bother yelling at Ruby to put a towel around her nakedness.

"The judges. They want to know why you can't room with one of the other contestants."

Ruby's big blue eyes opened wide and melting-sweet with hope. She looked just like a dog that sees a house door left just a crack ajar and all the wide world beckoning sunlit beyond. "Room with . . . ? Oh! That a part of the official rules, Mama? I wouldn't mind doing it, if that's so. I wouldn't want to get disqualified just for—"

"I know what you wouldn't mind." Mama was a thin slice of steel, edged, flying down straight to cut off all foolish notions. "I've made it my business to study the contest rules. There is no such a one. Most likely one of the judges has a favorite—some little chippy who's not too particular about who she does to win what's *your* rightful crown. Only thing is, the judge must've seen your past wins, he *knows* his pet whore hasn't got a prayer going up against you honestly,

how she can't begin to compete with what you've got to
show. So he wants the two of you shoved together so she
can check out your weak spots."

"Do I have any weak spots, Mama?"

"None that show with your mouth shut." Mama had a
look that could shoot cold needles right through Ruby's put-
on innocence. "But then, what's to stop the bitch from making you some? Accidents happen. Hair doesn't bleed."

Ruby's mouth opened, red and wet, but she could
hardly breathe. "You mean . . . ?" She hugged her damp
hair to her breasts, a mother cradling her babe out of sight
while the monster passes by. "Oh! You mean one of them
would actually—actually—" She couldn't say it. She could
only make scissors of her fingers and tremble as they
snipped the air.

Mama nodded. "Now you're getting smart." She headed
for the door. "Don't worry, child. I'll soon set them right.
Could be all they're fretted up about is me sharing this room
for free. Stingy old badgers. I'll pay my share, if that's what
it takes, but I'll never leave you to anyone's keeping but
mine." She touched the door. "And put on a robe!" Then
she was gone.

Ruby was still alone in her room when he knocked on
the door. "Room service!" She hadn't ordered anything, but
she figured maybe Mama'd done it while she'd still been in
the shower.

Sitting on the edge of the bed, the TV on to *Seinfeld*,
Ruby didn't know what to do. Mama always told her not
to open the door for anyone or anything. The knock came
again, and the voice. She stole across the room to peer out
through the peephole. Such a good-looking young man!

Ruby told herself that if Mama came back and didn't
find her room service order laid out and waiting for her,
she'd be mad. Mama'd been mad enough all the long drive
here, mad over the message from the judges, no sense in
riling her more. Ruby reasoned that a bite of food would
be just what Mama'd need when she came back from setting
those judges straight, but all the little angels blushed to
know that Ruby only conjured up those kindly reasons for

letting that young man inside well *after* she'd opened the door.

He almost died when he saw her. His hands clenched tight to the handle of the room service wagon he was pushing, his face abruptly hot with more than just the steam rising from the two steak dinners he'd brought up with him to complete his disguise. She was wearing the old-lady-style nightie and robe set Mama'd bought her for her birthday—plain blue cotton the color of a prisoner's sky—but she owned the power to turn such stuff indecent just by slipping it on. He saw her and his breath turned to broken glass in his throat and suddenly he knew he wasn't here for just the story.

Things moved fast after that. So long alone, so long instructed in her own unworthiness to be anything but Mama's beautiful, dutiful daughter, Ruby had never dreamed she'd ever hear another human being tell her she was all things lovesome. First thing he did was beg her pardon for having sent her mama off on a wild goose chase—the judges didn't give two shits about how Ruby roomed; he'd been the one to make the call that cleared the way in here for all his desires, known and unknown both. Almost in the same breath that he confessed his subterfuge, he turned it from a journalist's ruse to a masquerade of the heart.

"I saw you and I fell in love." It was too simply said for someone like her to do anything but believe it.

"I think . . ." she began. "I think I kind of love you too, I guess."

He didn't seem to care about how many qualifiers she tacked on to her declaration. He had her in his arms and time was flying faster than the hands he plunged into the damp warmth of her hair.

She let him. All her life she'd lived walled up behind a thousand small permissions. For once it felt so good, so very good to strike out against them all, sweep them away, deny they'd ever had any power to keep her in. He asked, she gave, and giving split her high stone tower wide open to the sun. And if the swiftness of it all seemed to smack of once-upon-a-time implausibility, the fact that it *did* happen just that fast wasn't anything a rational body could deny. He was handsome and in love, she was beautiful and alone, and neither one of them knew when her mama might return. Things that happened that fast fell out the way they did because what other choice did they have? Anyhow, it takes longer to make lunch than to make love.

He didn't leave it at her hair, but he was skilled and gentle and she was flying way too high to feel the pain when he broke her somewhere that the judges wouldn't see the blood but the chambermaids would. He laughed, then he moaned over her, falling away still tangled in her hair. That was the only time he hurt her, when he yanked it like that, never meaning to, too caught up in his own sweet joy to pay anything else any mind.

Maybe that was how Mama managed to come in on them like that, with neither one of them able to hear the click of the door opening or see her standing over them, the lightning flash from the mountain storm frozen across her face.

They heard her scream all right, though. It gurgled up out of her from deeper than her throat and smashed itself shrill against the ceiling. Then it wound itself up into a banshee's howl that went on so long they neither one of them had the power left to notice that she'd got one of the steak knives in her hand.

Down it came, sharp and clean, slicing across the hand he held up to fend it off. His cry wasn't much more than a yelp from a kicked dog, and she did kick him, hard and where he'd remember it. She had to jab him off the bed, off Ruby, to do it, but it was a lesson to see how easy an old woman could herd a young man where she'd have him go as long as she held a knife. She only let him stand beside the bed a second before she jerked her foot up sharp between his legs and laid him down.

He was curled up on the floor at her feet, holding himself tight, blood from his hand striping him, belly and balls, when she went after Ruby. Ruby's screams brought folks, but by that time it was much too late. By the time anyone came from the other rooms on that floor or from the front desk or from the pageant authorities, Mama'd got her forearm wrapped with as much of Ruby's hair as she could twist 'round it, until it looked like she'd grown herself a shining gold cocoon from elbow to wrist. Then she sawed down with the blade.

It was thick hair but easy cutting, almost like such a mane was spun of dreams and had only been allowed to exist in the real world on the sufferance of someone with a witch's power over impossible things. It cut right off clean at the touch of the steak knife and it trailed down limp from Mama's arm while she stood there panting and the newspaper man lay there groaning and Ruby sobbed and sobbed into the stained sheets of her bed.

They were asked to leave the hotel right after that, all three, no surprise. Mama didn't even raise a peep of protest. She was satisfied. As soon as they told her to get out, she just started packing up her stuff, smug, and snapped at Ruby to do the same. Hotel security came to urge the newspaperman back into his clothes and down to the nearest police station to answer charges. Ruby was so taken up in too many different colors of grief that it was an hour at least before she found the strength to look after packing her things. The room door was closed but she could still hear the elated whispers of the other girls out in the hall, their giggles of delight. Even if she'd been able to deafen her ears to those sounds, there was still Mama.

"Happy?" the old witch hissed in her ear, and oh, her breath was cold on the back of Ruby's naked neck! "Was it worth it, what you did, what you threw away? Don't tell me your answer now, little girl; not just yet. We're going home. You can wait to tell me then, after you've taken any job you can find, waiting tables at the diner, standing on your feet all day at the Wal-Mart, packing boxes full of car parts at the factory. Or maybe what you'll have to do is spread your legs again and land a man who'll stuff you full of his brats and slap you around when you won't mind him just the way he wants. And you can all come visit dear old Granny at Christmastime. Oh yes, that'll do for me if you wait til then to tell was it worth it tonight."

And she kept on like that at Ruby until . . .

In all the fuss, in all the screaming and running and

calling for the police to come, no one thought to call Room Service back and have them take away the cart. There were two steaks on that cart, two steak knives. Ruby didn't have any trouble laying her hands to the second one when Mama turned her back on her and had herself a good, long laugh.

That, too, happened fast.

Ruby's man got himself all bailed out in time to hear the story come in to Police HQ; he stuck around to see them bring her in. He was waiting for her there, threw himself into her arms so quick that the arresting officers couldn't shoulder him off before he whispered urgently in her ear for her to shut up, say nothing, hold on until his paper scared her up a lawyer. Crime of passion, that's what it was, and they played up that angle big at the trial. Provocation more than any human soul could bear. All it took was one look into those big, teary eyes of hers, one glance at the sawed-off ruin of her hair, and the jury was at her feet. It didn't hurt any that she still knew how to work a crowd.

They let her off with a light sentence, and she married her man before she went through the prison doors. It wasn't the kind of prison a mama'd fear to let her daughter go in, not that Ruby had anything like that to worry about anymore. She got her high school diploma while she was inside, and she got an agent to book her on all the right talk shows when she got out and her husband got a book out of it and her hair grew back—maybe not as long or thick, but still pretty as you please. She thought it was pretty enough, anyhow.

When it was halfway down to her ass again, she went back on the pageant circuit, took the Mrs. America crown like it'd been waiting for her in a bus station locker all that time. Then she retired, sold Mary Kay, had kids—Bobby, Jim, and Angel—lived happily ever after even if her man sometimes did stare at her hair and say how it's too bad it never did grow back *all* the way to how it was. Ruby was kind of sad that she couldn't please her man as much as she'd done that first time. Mama never did think she was too smart, but Ruby knew that if she put her mind to it, she'd think of something.

Angel's got her mama's hair; Angel's three. Angel goes to all the pageants, Daddy keeps the boys away. Ruby runs a brush through Angel's hair and tells her daughter that if she's beautiful, everything will be just fine.

Esther Friesner says that "Big Hair" is the product of the fairy tale "Rapunzel" and one too many attacks of being extremely fed up with stage mamas and beauty pageants. And oddly enough, she was not thinking of the JonBenet Ramsey murder when she wrote the story.

The King with Three Daughters

RUSSELL BLACKFORD

*Australian writer Russell Blackford works as a
senior lawyer in the international firm Phillips
Fox. He has published numerous stories, articles,
essays, and reviews, mainly in Australia, but also
in Great Britain and the U.S. His work has appeared in collections, anthologies, and reference
books, and in a diverse range of journals and
magazines that includes* Aurealis, Australian
Book Review, Australian Law Journal, Eido-
lon, Foundation, Journal of Popular Culture,
Metascience, *and many others. His longer publications include a fantasy novel,* The Tempting
of the Witch King, Hyperdreams: The Space/
Time Fiction of Damien Broderick, *and*
Strange Constellations: A History of Australian Science Fiction *(with Van Ikin and Sean
McMullen).*

The King with Three Daughters

Trolls are dreadful things, and I am a troll-slayer. What I have seen and done, you can only imagine.

My name is Jorgen. On a spring afternoon I entered the town of Tromsdal, which stood above cold Atlantic breakers. Here, a King maintained his citadel on a sheer promontory, exposed to the sea's icy winds.

I'd become a wanderer. I thought myself seasoned—a veteran—and there was some truth in that. My hunting bow and broadsword, my strong right arm, had provided me with kings and chieftains to accept my service.

Before dark I reconnoitered the town, checking the narrow, zigzag path to the stony citadel, then found an inn called the Wolf's Get, built on a low piece of land beside a crossroads. Here I spent my copper coins prudently, for I had no surety that any lord or chieftain of the place would care to employ me.

My supper was a fish stew, accompanied by tough-skinned apples, rindy cheese, and three grainy pieces of black bread. As I finished, the innkeeper approached. Close by my side he stood, a fussy man with gray hair and a stubbly beard. His fat thighs pressed against the edge of the table. Finally, he spoke in a conspirator's tones. "Are you seeking an audience?"

"Eh?"

"With the King?" He refilled the wine in my goblet, pouring it out from a long-necked clay flagon, then sat beside me on my bench, appraising me unashamedly. What he saw was a windburnt man with glossy brown hair, becoming matted. My face was bony under an ill-trimmed beard—I'd grown wild on the long road. "Perhaps you can settle here."

My resigned sigh gave away my feelings. "Here, in this town? In Tromsdal?"

"Why not? What more are you seeking?"

So I told him my name—and, with it, the truth. "Tomorrow, I'll go up to the citadel, and crave audience of the King's officials."

There was no reason for a prosperous ruler, one whose kingdom embraced miles of sea and fjord, mountain and forest, to speak with me in person, but wise officials could discern my worth. The wine made me more garrulous, though I was far from drunk on the watery stuff.

"I spent this winter in the battles on the other side of the mountains." I hesitated for a moment, remembering. "The campaign ended in peace—in peace and disgrace. Can you understand that? I had to move on. The chieftains I served fought and lost. They don't want me anymore, not me, nor any who did their bloody work." I silenced my tongue. A trained warrior, I thought, was always worth his keep. I finished the last of my bread. It was grainy in my mouth, but sweet with butter.

"Have you heard about the King's daughters?" the innkeeper said, still speaking softly, and scratching his beard. "A man like you may be useful."

*   *   *

As I listened, I had no thought of trolls, of their kingdoms in dark woods, the deep earth, the high mountain ice. I had no thought, as yet, of the blood-feud between trolls and the Bright Ones.

The innkeeper gave me the sparse details of King and Queen, which he seemed to deliver by rote, then the arbitrary prophecy and the magical births, the oddities of enchantment and loss. How many times did I hear this story? Next day, I had it from the King's chamberlain, a powerful official whom I dared not interrogate, then a briefer version from the King himself, and still other variants from underlings within the citadel. Of course, it piqued my curiosity, this story of a proud and handsome king with three missing daughters, blasted from his sight on an enchanted snowdrift when, by inadvertence, he disobeyed a crone's prophecy. It made me want to know more—about the daughters, the land, about a king whom such events might befall.

The innkeeper became confused, hopelessly vague, as I questioned him more closely. "You mentioned a Queen," I said, "a Queen who bore the three daughters. Does she still live?"

"No," he said uncertainly. He paused to consider it, looking pained with the effort. "There is no queen in Tromsdal."

"Well, then, what became of her?"

"The Queen?"

"Yes," I said. "What became of the Queen?" I was long finished with eating, but the innkeeper kept refilling our stone goblets. As I said, it was watery, but it washed away some of my patience.

"There *was* a queen."

"I know that."

"Of course, there was a Queen. She, yet more than the King, wished for children to inherit the kingdom and carry on the royal line." He finished with a "so there you have it" manner about him, as he leaned away from me, comfortable with the safety of his tale.

"Well, what became of her?" We had been talking quietly, like thieves, but now I spoke aloud. "Is she still alive, my friend? Is she beautiful, as queens should always be? Tell me something about her." As I watched his discomfort, I laughed suddenly, scarcely knowing what I did. I raised my goblet and tossed back a mouthful. "To the Queen!" Diners in the inn exchanged glances. There were angry looks my way from sealers and prosperous-looking fur merchants.

The youngest daughter, so the innkeeper had said, was of scarcely fifteen years, assuming that she still lived. Even if the Queen had died in childbirth, I reckoned, that was not so long ago, yet this middle-aged man, who (so he told me) had lived in Tromsdal all his life, could not distinctly remember the Queen, nor her fate, nor a time without the current King, or before the Princesses. I shrugged it off as a trick of the mind, for there are men—and women, too— with strange afflictions that way. I went to my lumpy bed, unsatisfied with the tale, but full of zest for the morrow.

As the innkeeper told me, and then a fat-hipped woman next day in the crowded, salt-smelling fish market, the King had sworn a vow—anyone who found the Princesses alive should be granted half the kingdom and choose as a wife whichever Princess he liked.

"They are all very beautiful," the woman said. There were coarse hairs on her chin, and her mouth curved downward, like a fish's. "Each is more beautiful than the others."

I suppressed my barbed retort at so foolish an expression. "And is the Queen beautiful?"

She became as vague as the innkeeper. "The Queen?"

"Is *she* beautiful? Come now, does she hide her face from her subjects?"

The woman looked baffled.

"What's wrong with you?" I said.

"She . . . was beautiful. I think." She walked to another customer, a boatsman by the look of him, with his front teeth missing. Her back was now toward me.

"What happened to her?"

"I . . . can't remember." She faced me for a moment, but her gnawed thumb and fingers made a small sign to avert witchery. I muttered excuses and left.

When I walked the steep road to the citadel, men at arms challenged me at the gate, but the chamberlain granted me audience. He was old and white-headed, with a thin, whispery voice, his dry hands shaking unless he controlled them. I could see the frustration in his face, the intensity of character and will that told me he was once a man of great presence. He told me the story, the fullest account I heard from anyone. This is how it started.

The King and Queen had been childless. Year in, year out, it wore away at their happiness, like ocean breakers on the cliffs.

One day in early spring, when the sky remained bleak and cold, but the snow had melted from trees and meadows, the King stood high on his keep, the citadel's innermost tower, with a hooded falcon on his wrist—for he loved all things of the sky. He looked westward over wild ocean, its deep blue water as far as the eye could see, then turned his gaze to the town and fields of Tromsdal, to the long line of coast with its deep fjords, then the untamed forests—and, finally, to the foot-worn road that passed to the east through fields and forests, into a brooding line of mountains. Satisfied in a fashion, but heavyhearted, he released the falcon, watching it climb and dive and wheel in the wide, gray sky. The voice of a crone spoke from behind him. "Why so sad, great King?"

He turned to her—heaven knew where she had come from. How could she have penetrated the citadel's outer walls and baileys, then entered the keep and climbed its spiral of narrow stairs, without being challenged? The King put such thoughts aside, for he perceived that the crone who stood before him, dressed in beggar's rags, must be some kind of witch-woman. "You can't do anything to help me," he said, "so why should I tell you?"

"I'm not so sure of that. I know your thoughts, my King."

"Then tell them. But get it right, or you'll anger me."

"No fear of that," she said with a knowing laugh, then closed her eyes, seeming to look inside herself.

"I'm waiting," the King said.

"You are saddened because you have no heir to your crown and kingdom."

"You're a witch. Should I suffer you to live?"

"I am what I am," the witch-woman said. "Now hearken to me. The Queen will have three daughters. And yet, great care must be taken with them. See that they do not come out under the open heavens before they are all fifteen years old. Otherwise, they will be taken from you."

"What nonsense is this?"

"Heed my words."

In disgust, he averted his eyes—only for a second. When he looked again, she was gone. He searched the sky for his falcon.

My knees hurt on cold tiles. The King remained seated in his high-backed, granite throne.

How do I describe the man, convey his majesty, the vast power that I felt in his presence—power that resided deep in his spirit and body? His hair was like spun gold beneath his jeweled crown. His eyes were deeper gold, set beneath a broad, high forehead. He wore silk robes of fiery red and sky blue, inlaid with runes. When I saw him, I knew straightaway that the King's veins flowed not merely with the blood of ancient royalty, but with that of the Bright Ones. Well, so we all can say—those beings taught men and women the arts of civilization that made us a match, or more than a match, for the wild beasts. They mingled their blood with ours, lifting us toward the rank of celestials— part of their own strange quest for redemption, which will see them depart one day, to whatever sky they fell from.

Such is the nature of humankind, but that is not my meaning. The King was not like you or me. He was something higher. Yet, even as I wondered at him, I reflected that he could feel loss. "You're a fighting man?" he said. "You're a warrior?"

"If you will use me so."

"Very good." With a gesture of his palm, he bade me stand, then rewarded me with a smile that left his golden eyes cold, like mountain ice. "You must find my daughters. Your manner gives me confidence."

"Thank you, my liege."

"I want to trust you, warrior."

As we conversed, I kept my gaze to the floor, concentrating upon a scraped tile near his austere throne. But, now and then, I met his eyes directly—long enough to catch his expression or to speak. "Depend on me," I said clearly. "I won't disappoint you."

"I should hope not." He made a flicking motion, like brushing away a fly. "Many have set out, and failed. None have heard word of my daughters."

I bent my head further, though my bearing was proud enough.

"You'll thrive in my service," he said, "an able man like you."

"I trust that I am as able as Your Highness believes."

Again, I dared glance at him, and he gave the ghost of a grin, mostly to himself. "I can recognize ability. Be prudent and loyal, Jorgen. You'll find my daughters."

That night, as I slept on a hard pallet in the citadel, I had a dream of trolls in palaces beneath the earth. This was a dream like no other I had known, and I awoke resolved to follow it. Before we departed, I sought out the chamberlain, still thinking of such places—crevices, caves, and pits in the earth—and I asked for a length of strong climber's rope. Then, as the sun climbed the morning sky, we left with heavy wallets on our shoulders, packed with provisions.

Three of us set out. One of my companions was lean, a bony captain of the royal guard. He had a balding head and a great bristling mustache. Long ago, he'd fought as a sea-raider, and still he had a predatory look—piercing gray eyes, a nose like a hawk, and a weak chin that made him seem more beaky. The other was a stout young lieutenant with a bushy red beard. He was stiff in one leg from an old fall on horseback, but he limped along heartily, as fast as my normal pace. The chamberlain ordered us outfitted with rations, fine new bows and broadswords, fresh shirts and leggings, and tough, warm boots.

There are pretty tales about our quest; some have returned to my ears from across the icy sea. A man may flee vengeance or wrath, but not the distortions of his legend.

On the first day, I left the forest road, taking a deeper path among the ancient trees, sensing—as my dream had suggested—that this was the way to the enchantments that we sought. "Where are you going?" the captain said, standing with his long arms akimbo, head thrust forward and legs planted wide apart. The lieutenant stood at his side, resting his weight on a long, gnarled climbing stick. A bird flapped by, a jet-black crow the size of an eagle. It landed on a yew branch above us, watching and preening.

"Follow me or not," I said, "this is the path to the King's daughters." The crow cawed as if in agreement. I told my dream, and my companions agreed to join me. We pushed on, deeper into the forest and the mountains, encountering many strange beings. There were hairy, black spiders larger than cats, but they scuttled from our path. Wolf howls followed at a distance, those and the lonely cries of a beast I could not name, something huge, I thought, by the loudness and depth of its voice. We saw leathery creatures like bats, with evil teeth set in the faces of men. The songs of birds were all about us, some melodious, others far more harsh.

Many times, we came to long, narrow bridges over deep scars in the land, and these we had to cross—else turn back defeated. Oh, there were adversaries: three bridges were guarded by saber-toothed lions the size of horses; another three by shaggy, grizzled bears as big as small trolls. Finally three dwarfs, each with diabolical vigor and strength, each more powerful than the last. But always we prevailed. I could tell a tale of sinew and iron and blood, of the foes we slew before I faced the trolls.

We hate trolls. They call to the terrors in our souls—perhaps to our guilt, for their crude enchantments have not saved them from our cunning, our engines, from the enigmatic help of the Bright Ones. Fewer and fewer of the lumbering brutes are seen.

The third dwarf was a tiny, bald-pated man, no taller than my hip bone—but he fought like a demon or a wildcat, armed with a double-bladed ax. Finally we overcame him. I sheathed my broadsword, but plucked up the ax, where it fell from his hands under the weight of our blows. Lifting it took a terrible effort. "I'll split your skull," I said fiercely. "Tell me where the Princesses are."

"Spare my life. I'll tell you." I made no reply, but stayed my hand. He made a desperate movement, pointing to a narrow winding path that was barely recognizable as such. "There is a bare mound at the end. Atop the mound is a shapeless stone, and under that a pit." He chuckled to himself, like one demented. "Let yourself down, and you'll come to another world. There you will find the Princesses."

I lowered the ax, easier than raising it, and his bald skull split like an eggshell.

The path was long, and always it continued upward. At the end of three days we came to a derelict structure, a stone house, and here we took shelter for the night, while a storm raged in the woods around us. Next morning, the storm had passed; we woke to bird song. My companions hunted for game, while I stayed to guard our wallets, with what was left of our rations. We ate rabbit, cooked over a fire while the lieutenant sang bawdy songs in a fine bass voice and the captain told of journeys on long ships, tales of far lands that he'd seen and plundered. We stayed a second night, then a third, and naught disturbed us.

Finally we set off, at my insistence. I walked in front, then the lieutenant, half walking, half swinging his body around the climbing stick. Last came the captain, guarding our rear, eyes narrowed and sword drawn. After some thousands of paces, we came to the mound, and I cursed the time we'd lost.

Seldom was I glad of my comrades, for often they had fancies of their own—but our battles with lions, bears, and dwarfs were the exceptions. This time was another: the shapeless lump of black star stone was so heavy that it took all our combined strength to roll it over, and then with much grunting and resting and starting again. We grew stinking and short-tempered. It was lucky we were strong. When he peeled his shirt from his sweaty torso, the lieutenant was like a wrestler, with a deep chest and powerful limbs, no matter the crablike tendency in his gait.

Late in the day we finally shifted the stone. Where it had been was a dark pit, deeper than our eyes could see. "Measure it," the captain said, so I took my length of rope and lowered it into the pit with a cubit of old tree root knotted to its end. Only when we played out the entire length did it reach the bottom.

We retrieved the rope, and anchored it beneath the star stone's edge. The captain tried it first, putting his foot through a strongly knotted loop that we tied. Minute by minute we played out the rope, lowering him into the pit. We'd agreed to pull him up if he tugged three times. As he descended, we played out far more rope than I had brought with me, but *still* he descended, even as we wondered at it. His voice grew faint: "Further, yet," he said. Time passed, the sun low in the sky. Then there was a firm tug at the rope—and two more—so we pulled him up, the lieutenant a fine man for that heavy job. When we dragged the captain out of the pit, he was soaked through and shivering. His thin hair and blond mustachios dripped. "It's cold and dark." He wrapped his arms about his chest, rubbing himself desperately for warmth. "It smells of ancient dead things—but that's not the worst of it. The rope seemed to grow longer with every touch I made against the side of the pit. Then, finally, I came to a lake of freezing water with drifts of ice. In I went with a splash, as far as my neck, then further, and never touched bottom."

We returned to the deserted house, where we made a crackling fire to warm him, wondering what to do now. There were no bawdy songs that night. The lieutenant and I ate dried beef from our wallets, tough to chew, yet tasty, while the captain tossed and cursed in his sleep.

Next day, he was fit and recovered, something I would never have believed. Encouraged, the lieutenant wanted to try the pit. He passed me his climbing stick, and stripped to make a swim of it. Though he left behind his broadsword, he carried a dagger in his teeth. We lowered him with great difficulty, for he was so heavy, and the captain, wiry and tough though he was, lacked the lieutenant's burly strength.

As the sun journeyed upward, we persevered, and I wondered where all this rope had come from. Then there was a tug at it, and two more.

Glumly, we commenced the still more difficult job of hauling up the lieutenant, cursing the weight. "Heave," the captain said with each effort, speaking through gritted teeth and putting his back into it. "Heave." Eventually, the lieutenant's head emerged—red hair and beard all wet and plastered to him. As he struggled into the noon light, he spit out the dagger on the ground, then his teeth were chattering, his face ashen. Almost, he collapsed when he planted his bad leg.

He revived before the hearth, though his sleep was fevered.

On the third day it was my turn, for we had no other plan. Unlike the lieutenant, I stayed fully clad, with the broadsword at my side and my wallet on my back, trusting in whatever enchantments had guided us. I put my foot in the loop of rope and they lowered me quickly.

Down I went, counting to myself, minute after minute, knowing that the rope I had brought could never be so long. It seemed that hours passed. The pit became colder, and even darker, until my comrades let out a great length of rope at once, and I plunged without warning into thin ice and freezing water, gasping desperately before I sank. Down, down in the water I went—the cold clawing at my heart—spinning on the rope like a child's top, able to see nothing in the pitch-black, peer though I might. All the while, I held my breath, till my lungs were bursting for air. Suddenly, I was through; my bones were miraculously warm as if in the friendly glow of a fire, and my boots slapped against firm land. It was not so dark now, and far away in the distance, like the first chord of dawn, was a gleam of brilliant light, so I headed in that direction, patting myself in disbelief—at my dry shirt and leggings, my trusty engine in its scabbard. Before long the way grew lighter still, and then I saw a golden sun rising in the sky—yet here I was, leagues (as it seemed to me) below the ground. Soon everything about me was bright and beautiful.

I came to a herd of fat brown cattle, lowing disquietly

as I passed, and then to a palace like nothing I'd ever seen.
It was larger by far than the citadel in Tromsdal, like a
crystal mountain, with steep, straight walls of gleaming yellow quartz. The entrance was unguarded, and I crossed an
emerald bridge that arched above a clear, narrow stream. I
entered the crystal halls without hearing a sound or meeting
a soul. The doorways and ceilings were built for a giant
twice my height, and piles of gold nuggets were hoarded
in random corners; I wondered at the wealth hidden away
in this other world. Finally, I heard the hum of a spinning
wheel. When I entered the high-ceilinged chamber, a beautiful young woman was sitting there, dressed all in silk and
surrounded by amber light with no specific source. Against
the far wall was a great couch with round, satiny pillows,
but the woman sat on a polished wooden stool; she was
spinning copper yarn. Tall as she was, she seemed scarcely
more than a child; her neck was like a swan's, while her
white skin looked softer than down—surely this was one of
the King's daughters.

"What are you doing here?" the Princess said. "What
do you want?"

"The King, your father sent me. I've come to set you
free."

She ceased her spinning and looked about, her breast
heaving with emotion. "If the troll returns, he'll kill you."

I was speechless when she mentioned a troll, but not
exactly afraid, for I thought my life was charmed.

"He's a wood troll, larger than a bear. He has three
heads."

"I've journeyed all the way from Tromsdal," I said. "I
don't care how many heads it has."

She told me to creep behind a big brewing vat that stood
in a hall outside.

When it came in, the troll walked so heavily that the
solid quartz floor seemed to shake beneath my feet, even a
room away, though this must have been an enchantment,
for nothing is that weighty. "I smell human blood." Its voice
was like a lion's roar. I could hear its noses sniffing away
at the air. "Human blood and bone," it said with a different

voice, like a honking bird. The third voice was more human, but viciously accusing. "What are you hiding from me?"

"Please, dear," the Princess said, "don't be angry. A crow dropped a bone with the flesh still on it. Everything is tainted. When I threw it out, the crow dropped it back. I had to bury it in the rose garden. I fear it's an ill omen."

The troll growled suspiciously in a discord of voices, and sniffed some more.

"Lie in my lap," she said. Her sweet voice was like a songbird's. Who could resist? "Let me scratch your heads."

Again the troll growled.

"You know how you like it, and the smell will be gone when you awake."

Finally, the troll did as she offered. When I heard its three heads snoring in unison, I came out from behind the vat, and into the chamber. As I did so, the Princess freed herself from the couch, bolstering the troll's heads against a pile of pillows. For long seconds I observed the knuckly, hairy creature. The chamber was full of its musky scent, not wholly unpleasant. I noticed that a great sword rested now against one of the crystal walls, sheathed in a jeweled scabbard, and I walked to it, thinking it a more adequate engine than my own broadsword for what I must do. With all my strength, I tried to lift the troll's sword, but it was too heavy. Then the Princess kissed me on the lips, and I seized up the murderous engine from its scabbard, swinging it more mightily than I could have imagined. I severed the troll's three necks in one blow, and its blood flew everywhere. I staggered back—amazed at what I'd done—as the troll twitched, and fell like a tree. Then I caught my breath and examined the monstrous corpse.

It was shaped roughly like a man, though many times larger, with its ugly tusked heads like grotesque masks where they had fallen. One head's eyes were open, as if to accuse me for my guile. The troll's gnarled feet and hands were overly big, even for its giant size. It went naked, save for a sword-belt of black leather, but its body was covered with reddish hair half a cubit long. Beneath that its hide was thick and wrinkled, and armored with knobs of iron-wood and sinews like tough vines.

No blood had clung to the Princess. She threw her arms about me and covered my face with more kisses. For one moment I held her close to me, feeling the flutter of her heart, the softness of her breast swelling against mine. We'd faced danger, and triumphed. And yet, for a warrior, there was something unseemly about this, slaying a foe in his sleep, however little choice I had of it—for a fair fight would have been unequal; I'd never have stood a chance.

And so, my friends, I became what you see, a troll-slayer.

We humans have reveled in the deaths of trolls. We've been more thorough, more zealous than the Bright Ones who gave us the fire, the blades of stone—then the copper, the bronze, the iron and steel—to slay whatever we found threatening or unwanted or ugly. A troll will prey on human flesh when it can. Every village has its story of a three-headed man-eater that hid in the ice, the rocks, the dark forest, stalking the fringes at night, catching children in their beds, until some hero ended its reign of terror.

Yet, more trolls than humans have died.

"We must rescue my sisters," the Princess said.

"Yes."

She guided me across a courtyard with a lush garden of roses in full bloom, then along many crystal corridors, and through another huge doorway, this one framed by blocks of amethyst—it led to a high-ceilinged chamber, where the second Princess sat on her stool, tall and fair and beautiful, spinning silver yarn. "What do you want?" she said, sounding fearful and looking about.

"I've come to kill the troll," I said. "We'll set you free and return you to the King, your father."

"Hide behind the brewing vat, both of you." She pointed to the hallway outside. "I'll deal with the troll."

Soon, there was a noise like thunder, and the troll entered, a six-headed monster this time, larger than the first. It roared its displeasure, three or four of its voices speaking at once. "I smell human blood."

Strangely, the second Princess told the same story: "Yes,

dear. Don't be angry. A crow dropped a human bone, with flesh still on it. Everything is tainted. When I threw it out, the crow dropped it back. I had to bury it at last."

The troll sniffed and growled suspiciously, but she persuaded it to rest its heads in her lap, then let her scratch them. When the brute was asleep and snoring, she carefully bolstered its heads against a pile of pillows as she freed herself. The first Princess and I watched anxiously, having entered the chamber to finish the task. It was no use trying to lift the troll's sword until both Princesses kissed me on the lips. Although the sword was even heavier than the first troll's, I swung it mightily, cutting off the six heads in one bloody stroke, like harvesting stalks of wheat. I leant on the sword then, panting, before I lowered the engine to the floor beside its former master. Beneath its hair, the troll's body was half flesh, half stone; the heavy, razor-sharp blade had sliced right through the stony parts of its necks.

Then the second Princess remembered the third sister. "She is the youngest. We'll take you to her."

They led me across another gardened courtyard, through still more corridors, to the largest chamber yet, where the youngest of the King's daughters sat spinning golden yarn. "Get out," she said, looking around her. "The troll will kill you all."

When we insisted on saving her, she ordered us to hide behind the brewing vat just outside. Soon, the troll came in, and I peeked at an angle from the vat to the Princess's chamber. This troll was a nine-headed beast the size of a house, far bigger than the first two. At its side was a sheathed sword larger than a rowboat, and it dripped with icy water as it walked and grumbled, hooted and howled, growled and roared, all of its voices speaking in unison. "I smell human blood."

She told the same story as her sisters, and soon persuaded her troll to unloose the scabbard from its belt and let her scratch its heads till it slept. After one kiss from each of the Princesses, I could swing the troll's sword easily. And yet, I am a warrior; perhaps it was honor that marred my stroke. Perhaps.

"I smell human blood," each of the trolls had said.

What about the Princesses? What sort of blood did they have?

Closing my eyes, I swung the sword. My blow cleaved eight heads from the troll but missed the ninth, whose bleak eyes opened at the same moment as mine.

The troll lumbered to its feet and it rose far above me, like a storm nimbus, howling at me—a strangely plaintive howl, full of loss, full of anger, pain, and sorrow—and something *changed* inside me, something *shifted.* My unnatural strength was gone, and I dropped the huge sword, leaping aside where it fell. For the first time, I knew terror.

As the chamberlain told me the story, the Queen bore the King a girl-child one year after his encounter with the witch-woman. The year after that she had another, and the third year also. The King rejoiced, but never forgot the crone's words. He kept the Princesses locked within the keep, with a watch of soldiers at the doors.

As they grew up, the three daughters became as I saw them, beautiful, tall, and clever. The King provided them with tutors and playmates, but always these must come to the keep, and the daughters' only sorrow was that they were not allowed to play under the wide heavens, not even to stand in the open air upon the citadel's ramparts. For all that they begged and wept, the King resisted: he would never allow evil to fall them. Until even the youngest was fifteen years old, his beloved Princesses would never stand in the open air.

Only weeks before I arrived in Tromsdal, mere days before the fifteenth birthday of the youngest Princess, the King was out riding, and the Princesses stood at a window in the keep. Spring had come early. The fields were green and beautiful, alive with thousands of tiny wildflowers, and the three daughters felt they must go out and play beneath the sky, come what evil may—they begged and entreated and urged the seneschal.

"On no account," he said.

At least, they said, he could let them stand on the highest rampart, under the open sky, where they could best view the sea, the fields and flowers, the rugged coast, the woods and mountains of the kingdom. "Surely," said the youngest, "no harm can befall us here in the center of my father's stronghold. Please be reasonable." It was such a warm and pleasant day, the Princesses were so beautiful and spoke so sweetly, and it was so palpably safe. The King need never know.

"For one minute," he said. "Only one minute. You must be quick in case your father returns."

They looked about the kingdom—the dark sea and darker forest, the fields and meadows, the mountains with their distant caps of white-blue ice—safe, as it seemed, from all the dangerous world, and the seneschal congratulated himself. Suddenly, out of nowhere, there came a great drift of snow, hard enough to fling him off balance, so dense that he could not see. In that moment he knew and repented his mistake. The snow swirled, and time seemed to stop. When he regained his footing, the snow had carried the Princesses away.

So I was told it by the beetle-browed chamberlain. Such are the pretty stories they tell in Tromsdal.

"What happened to the Queen?" I said.

But he gave a papery laugh. "They executed the seneschal. The King demands obedience."

We are pawns for the Bright Ones, human and troll alike; we are merely pawns.

The stumps of the troll's necks bled icy water, some of it descending on me like bitter rain, while scabs of ice formed about the edges of its wounds, not quickly enough to prevent the outward gushing of life. "You'll pay for this," it said. There was darkness in its voice. Imagine a sharp-toothed wolf, like the demon Fenrir who will eat this world. Imagine that a wolf could talk.

The enchantment had fallen from us, but that was of no comfort, for the troll lunged with leathery hands that would have snapped me like a dry twig. I drew my broadsword from its scabbard, but I might as well have used a hairpin. Then the troll howled again, as it staggered and fell, crumbling like a cottage beneath a fallen oak tree. I stepped well back, the Princesses behind my stiffly outstretched arms, as the gargantuan creature went through its death throes. When the troll was finally still, I examined it. Beneath its long, coarse hair, the naked body was more ice than flesh, and the ice began to melt, pooling on the crystal floor of the chamber. The Princesses smothered me with kisses; but it meant nothing, for my heart had frozen against them.

I needed to get out of there, but my terror had gone, and my cunning returned. In one of the rose-scented gardens I found a wooden bucket, three feet high, held together with iron bands—this I filled with as many gold nuggets as I could carry. To haul me up with these, the lieutenant would need all his strength. The Princesses tried to amuse me with sweet talk, but I was silent as we returned to my climbing rope where it still hung in near darkness between two worlds. The first Princess placed her ruby-colored slipper through the knotted loop, we tugged the rope three times, and the captain and lieutenant pulled her up to the surface far above us. We repeated this for each of her sisters, but then I became afraid. I realized that my companions now had the Princesses but no reason to rescue me from the troll world. To test them, I attached my bucket of troll gold to the rope. I scraped handful after handful of damp, loamy-smelling soil into the bucket, adding to its weight, then stepped aside and tugged the rope thrice more, wiping my soiled hands against my leggings as I waited for what might happen.

They lifted the bucket far above me, into the inky darkness, but then they cut the rope. At first I could not see, but heard a bumping and scraping against the pit's side. Down came the bucket from the region of water and ice, falling at my feet with an awful *crack!*, hitting so hard that the wood split, and I would have died if it had been me. Now the captain and the lieutenant had their choice of the Princesses, and only two men, not three, need share half the kingdom.

I laughed aloud as I peered in the dim light, feeling around for three big nuggets of the gold. Into my wallet they went. I *had* to laugh, for the clouds had cleared from my mind's eye. There was no Queen in Tromsdal. There was never a Queen. These Princesses could not be threatened, for how do you harm the sendings of the Bright Ones, creatures spun from the sky and never born of womankind, creatures that can enchant a mighty troll.

For hours or days, I don't know how long, I wandered in that underworld, searching for a way out. I returned, at last, to the crystal palace, looking from hall to hall, until I lay down and slept on the ice troll's bed, ignoring the residue of its smell. In my dream I heard a large rustling sound, greater than the noise of a thousand wings, and I awoke.

Through corridor after corridor, I ran—outside to the field with the cattle herd. There I saw a huge, black crow, vaster in body even than the great, nine-headed ice troll, and with wings one hundred feet across to bear it up. Its feathers had a greenish shine, its eyes were like golden topazes, and it smelt stale, like horse sweat. "You called me in your dream," it said to me in a mocking voice, harsher than thunder, like cutting through iron with a hardened steel saw. "I've come, Jorgen. But you must feed me."

"If it's food you require, you could slay an ox." For such a being, with talons as long as scimitars, this would be the easiest of tasks.

The crow shook its head. "I shall not kill. Yet, I feast on the strength of my enemies. Where are the trolls?"

I finally understood. "I have slain them all, just as you wished."

"Butcher them for me." It lifted its head and laughed. "I *will* not taint myself."

I fell on my knees. "I have not disappointed you, Bright One," I said. "The Princesses are safe with the captain and the lieutenant."

"Stand."

My companions would threaten the Princesses with their swords, demanding that the King's "daughters" say they—the captain and the lieutenant—were the ones who slew the trolls. Poor fools, poor fools; no human engines could harm those Princesses.

There was a wrenching of being, and I could see right through the crow as it became ethereal, a twisting thing of smoke, sucking inward, as though time itself ran in reverse—smoke returning to its source in the fire. In a moment the King stood before me. I still knelt, flabbergasted.

"Stand," he said again. "Please stand." When I did so, he overtopped me by more than a head, unburning flames dancing across his garments. "So you *are* an able man."

"What will you do?" Whatever monstrous form he took, he would not endure the taint of killing me directly, but nor could I harm him. He could leave me there to rot, if such were his caprice. "What will happen to my companions?"

"They proved to be treacherous, as I foresaw. I shall order them executed." How brave to enchant a kingdom with tales of queens and daughters; how fine to become a king!

"And me?"

"You would marry one of my daughters?"

I shook my head. "No." His creatures, his sendings— whatever they were—for all their beauty, I had no desire to marry one.

"And half my kingdom?"

"I renounce any claim. Will you leave me here?"

"You have served me well. But now I crave troll flesh. Butcher me the trolls, and I will take you wherever you wish. This I vow."

"You will have your meat," I said.

"So I foresaw."

It was a messy business, butchering trolls with my broadsword. Their carcasses contained much bloody flesh, but also hair, bone, gristle, wood, and stone. The icy parts had melted away. As the King, again in crow form, ate his fill of meat, I climbed upon his back. I was covered, by now, in troll blood.

If I return, my death awaits me—some indirect and expedient form of death. There is a sea-dragon in the west of your kingdom, so I was told by a raggedy innkeeper's daughter. "It's as big as a ship," she said. "It's got ruby flames and emerald scales." I want no part in its slaying. They say that gold appeases it—well, I have two troll nuggets. The third I converted to coin, to meet my modest needs.

One day, trolls and dragons will be words for nurses to frighten little children. Each season, a human child has less cause to fear the old terrors—the harshness and mystery of forest and mountain, of ice and salt sea, and the wild beasts. Something is always lost.

I climbed on the giant bird, and it spread that hundred-foot span of wings. With a single hop, it took to the air. Higher and higher it flew, speaking no more. We met no resistance from the rock and earth above us. Soon we were over the woods, then the wide, foamy sea, heading for the liquid sun. Westward we traveled, and south.

As twilight dimmed, the crow departed, leaving me— here, with my blood and gold, on a far, dark shore. I had become a witness and a mourner of something lost, something strange to tell—of the terror and the pity, of the ugliness and splendor, of trolls.

In Norse fairy tales the usual enemies are not witches, wolves, or wicked fairies, but trolls—powerful, brutal, semihuman creatures who embody the grim and dangerous aspects of nature. In such tales as "The Three Princesses in the Blue Mountain," on which "The King with Three Daughters" is based, trolls are deceived and slain with no compunction or sympathy whatsoever. The relationship of humankind to the natural world appears very different at the turn of the third millennium, after a history of ecological devastation; hence, Blackford has depicted a troll-slayer who comes to see his victims in a new light.

Boys and Girls Together

NEIL GAIMAN

Neil Gaiman is a transplanted Briton who now lives in the American Midwest. He is the author of the award-winning Sandman *series of graphic novels, co-author (with Terry Pratchett) of the novel* Good Omens, *and author of the novel and BBC TV series* Neverwhere. *He also collaborated with artist Dave McKean on the brilliant book* Mr. Punch. *In addition, Gaiman is a talented poet and short story writer whose work has been published in a number of earlier volumes of retold fairy tales, in* Touch Wood: Narrow Houses 2, Midnight Graffiti, *and several editions of* The Year's Best Fantasy and Horror. *His short work has been collected in* Angels and Visitations *and* Smoke and Mirrors.

Boys and Girls Together

Boys don't want to be princes.
Boys want to be shepherds who slay dragons,
Maybe someone gives you half a kingdom and a princess,
But that's just what comes of being a shepherd boy
and slaying a dragon. Or a giant. And you don't really
even have to be a shepherd. Just not a prince.
In stories, even princes don't want to be princes,
disguising themselves as beggars or as shepherd boys,
leaving the kingdom for another kingdom,
princehood only of use once the ogre's dead, the tasks are
    done,
and the reluctant King, her father, needing to be convinced.

Boys do not dream of princesses who will come for them.
Boys would prefer not to be princes,

and many boys would happily kiss the village girls,
out on the sheep-moors, of an evening,
over the princess, if she didn't come with the territory.

Princesses sometimes disguise themselves as well,
to escape the kings' advances, make themselves ugly,
soot and cinders and donkey girls,
with only their dead mothers' ghosts to aid them,
a voice from a dried tree or from a pumpkin patch.
And then they undisguise, when their time is upon them,
gleam and shine in all their finery. Being princesses.
Girls are secretly princesses.

None of them know that one day, in their turn,
Boys and girls will find themselves become bad kings
or wicked stepmothers,
aged woodcutters, ancient shepherds, mad crones and
    wise-women,
to stand in shadows, see with cunning eyes:
The girl, still waiting calmly for her prince.
The boy, lost in the night, out on the moors.

*Neil Gaiman has been making his way through a rereading of all
the Andrew Lang fairy books, and so his poem take elements from
throughout the whole fairy tale corpus.*

And Still She Sleeps

GREG COSTIKYAN

Greg Costikyan designs games and writes novels, short stories, and articles about the games industry. His most recent games include Fantasy War *and* Seven Wonders, *an historical graphic adventure game. His most recent novel is* Sales Reps From the Stars.

He lives in New York with zero TVs, one guinea pig, three cats, four computers, two children, and a redhead.

He asserts that he is not a Romantic.

And Still She Sleeps

" **'O**w'd ye like to kiss them smackers, eh?" said the fellow in the queue ahead of me—cloth cap, worn tweed trousers, probably his only shirt. I gave him a stern look, and he, suitably chastened, turned away.

There she stood in her glass case; they had dressed her in someone's idea of Medieval garb, a linen dress at least four centuries wrong. Slowly, her breast rose and fell; slowly enough to show that this was no mortal slumber.

I forbore from saying that I had indeed kissed her, poor dear. To no avail, to no avail.

I found her, after all. Well, to be literal about it, one of von Stroheim's diggers found her, but von Stroheim was away at the time. I was in charge of the excavation.

We were in the Cheviot Hills, not far from the village

of Alcroft in Northumberland. It was a crisp October day, a brisk breeze off the North Sea some miles to our east, the sky pellucid; a good day to dig, neither cold enough to stiffen the fingers nor hot enough to raise a sweat. I had been with von Stroheim in Mesopotamia, and this was far more pleasant—though the stakes were surely smaller, a little Northumbrian hill fort, not a great city of the Urartu. Still, it was a dig; while many of my profession prefer less strenuous scholarship—days and nights spent with cuneiform and hieroglyphs—I enjoy getting out in the field, feeling the dust of ages between my fingers, divining the magics and devices the ancients used.

This, indeed, is my dear Janet's despair: that I am forever, so she says, charging off to Ionia or Tehran or the Valley of the Kings, places where a woman of refinement is unlikely to find suitable accommodation. Ah, but the home-comings after such forays are sweet; and truthfully, they are not so common, a few months out of each year. And between times, there is our little Oxford cottage, the rose garden, the faculty teas; a pleasant enough life for a man of scholarly bent and a woman of intelligence, a serene and healthful environment for our children. Far better this than the life of many of my classmates, amid the stinks and fumes and poverty of London, or building the Empire amid ungrateful savages in some tropical hell a thousand miles from home.

When I told Janet that von Stroheim proposed to excavate in Northumberland, she was pleased. She and the children could accompany us; after all, it was in England. What was the difficulty?

So I had let a little house in Alcroft, and rode up each morning to join von Stroheim and his men.

I brought Clarice with me that morning, she riding behind me, small arms about my waist, a picnic lunch in the panniers. I doubted she would want to come with me often, as there is not much to excite a child at a dig; but she could play on the lea, pet the sheep, wander about and plague us with questions.

The encampment made me glad that I had taken the

house in Alcroft; the tents were downwind from the jakes, today, the sheep browsing amid them. The diggers were breaking their fast on eggs and kippers, while our students dressed in their tents. De Laurency was missing, I saw—my prize pupil, but a bit of a trial, that man.

While Clarice happily chased sheep, I went up the hill. The diggers—rough men in work shirts and canvas trousers—and such of the students as had completed their toilet came with me. They resumed excavation along the lines von Stroheim had marked out with lengths of twine, while I pottered about with a surveyor's level, an enchanted pendant, a dowsing rod of ash.

It was while I was setting up my equipage that de Laurency appeared, striding up the hill, burrs in his trouser legs, his hair windblown and wild, a gnarled old walking stick in one hand. "Where the devil have you been?" I asked him.

He smiled vaguely. "Communing with the spirits of the moor," he said.

"Damme, fellow," I told him. "There's work to be done. And hard work, too; you can't expect to gad about the countryside all night and—"

"Bosh, Professor," he said gently. "I'll dig like a slavey, never you fear."

I returned to my equipment; if it weren't for his brilliance, I'd shuck de Laurency off on some other don. Dig like a slavey indeed; the man was slight and prone to sickness. He'd be exhausted by midday, I had no doubt, and wandering Northumberland in a mid-October night is a good way to become consumptive.

But to work. My task was to delineate the ley lines, the lines of magical force that converged on this site. They were the reason we had chosen to dig here; in this part of Northumbria, there was no site so propitious for ritual. That, no doubt, was one reason a fort had been built here; another was its defensibility and its capacity to dominate the region. From the hilltop, one could see as far as Woolet to the north, to the peak of the Cheviot to the west.

There was not much left of the old hill fort: a hummock of sod marking where walls had run. It was one of a series of forts built by the Kings of Northumbria along these hills, defenses against the Picts, though by the eighth century it was well within the Northumbrian borders, for the kingdom stretched north as far as the Firth of Forth.

Still, it was the prospect of magic that had drawn us here. We knew so little about the period, really; we knew the Romans had bound the Britons with powerful spells, had tamed the wild Celtic magic of their precursors. We knew the Anglo-Saxons had brought with them their own pagan power; and we knew the Church preserved much Roman knowledge through the fall, magic well used by the Carolingians in their doomed attempt to re-create the Empire. But how much exactly had survived, here in Britain? What was the state of the art in the eighth century? We could not ask the question in the south, for modern works have masked so much of the past, but here in sparsely inhabited Northumberland we had a better chance to find some answers.

My first surprise of the morning was to discover that the ley lines were active; power was drawing down them, from a line up the Cheviot in the direction of Glasgow. A spell or spells were active still, buried somewhere in this fort.

Lest this sound everyday to you, let me emphasize that the fort was eleven centuries old. The last mention of it—Castle Coelwin, it was called—was in the chronicles of the reign of Eadbehrt of Northumbria, who abdicated in 765. I have seen working spells as old, and older—in Rome, and Athens, and China—but who in miserable, divided, warring eighth century England could perform a ritual so strong, so binding?

It was while studying my equipment, dumbfounded at this discovery, that one of the workers ran up to me, out of breath. "Professor Borthwick," he said, "best coome quick. We've found a gel."

Indeed they had. They had dug a trench about two feet deep in what we termed the Ironmongery, a location toward the center of the fort where we had expected to find a forge, a common feature of fortresses from the period. The rusted remnants of several tools or weapons had already been found there, and the diggers had abandoned spades for trowels and brooms, lest some artifact be damaged by digging. And well that they had, for I shudder to think what a spade might have done to her fair flesh.

About her was loam, evidence of rotted wood; de Laurency, a curious look of epiphany on his face, crouched over her, tenderly brushing away loose dirt with his bare fingers. He had uncovered a hand and a part of an arm.

Her femininity was obvious through the narrowness of the hand. Her fingernails were long, inches in length; God knows when they had last been trimmed.

I cannot count the number of times I have carefully whisked the dirt from a skeleton, uncovering evidence of past violence or disease, looking for artifacts or skeletal damage to learn something of the corpse's fate. *But this was no corpse.* It was a living body, clad in flesh—cool to the touch, but with a slow, slow pulse—buried in the cold earth and yet somehow holding on to life.

Gently, we uncovered her; her hair and nails were preserved along with her body, but her hair was matted and filthy, her poor flesh besmirched with a millennium's dirt.

De Laurency worked by me; the diggers stood back, the other students stood aside to give us room. He said, low enough that I think only I heard him:

"How long hast thou rested in England's clay?
How long since the sun on thy tresses played?
How long since thy tender lips were kiss'd?
What power hast brought thee to this?"

I glanced at him, askance; there are times when I greatly appreciate von Stroheim's brutal practicality. Romanticism is all very well in poetry, but this is science. And *that*, I believe, was doggerel.

We had uncovered her head and shoulder when von Stroheim appeared, returning from an errand.

"Mein Gott," he muttered when he saw her, and turned to me with excitement. "Well, Alistair. Another puzzle, eh? What shall we make of this?"

It took a good two hours to dig her cautiously from the earth. And then we put her in a litter and carried her down to the encampment.

Clarice was fascinated, and with her little hands helped us to bathe and barber the girl. Though her hair was golden, it was far too matted and filthy to leave; we were forced to cut it off. For the nonce, we covered her with a simple canvas sheet; we had no women's clothing with us.

She appeared to be about sixteen; blond-haired and, when an eyelid was held back, blue-eyed. She was a scant five feet tall—probably large for the period—and just under a hundred pounds. She was well-formed, and her skin fine, though faint scarring gave evidence of a bout with smallpox. She breathed shallowly—a breath every five minutes or so; her pulse ran an impossibly slow beat every thirty seconds. Apparently, she had received enough oxygen, filtered through the soil, to survive. Since her discovery, she has never made water, nor passed stool; never eaten nor drunk. Yet her fingernails and hair slowly grow.

Clarice looked up at me with shining eyes. "It's Sleeping Meg," she said.

Out of such things are discoveries fashioned: a peculiar magical fluctuation, an unexpected finding in the dirt, the words of children.

An intelligent child, Clarice, my sweetheart; eight going on twenty, her mother's dark curls and laughing eyes.

She took me to the house of her playmate, Sybil Shaw, a local girl whose widowed mother eked out a living taking in cleaning and letting out rooms. Mrs. Shaw was a stout, tired-looking woman in her forties, hands reddened with her washing, wispy curls of blond turning gray escaping her cap. She greeted us warmly at the door and offered tea; behind her, I could see irons warming before the fire, petticoats laid out for goffering.

"If you would be so kind, Mrs. Shaw," I told her, a cup of tea balanced on a knee, "I would very much appreciate it if you could tell me the story of Sleeping Meg."

"Och aye," she said, a little mystified. "Sleeping Meg?

'Tis but a children's tale, ye ken, a story of these parts. What mought a scholar like you to do with tha'?"

And so, patiently, I explained what we had found at Castle Coelwin, and Clarice's words.

Mrs. Shaw snorted. "I misdoubt it has owt to do wi' the tale," she said, "but that's as may be."

I shall set out the story here in plainer language, for Mrs. Shaw (good heart though she has) possesses a thick North Country accent—and a meandering style—that would simply obscure it.

It seems that in the days when Arthur and Guinevere were still much in love, the Queen gave birth to a daughter whom they named Margaret. She was the darling of Arthur's knights, and as a child was dandled on the knees of the likes of Gawain and Lancelot. And at sixteen she was betrothed to the King of Scotland, whose armies had several times ravaged towns along England's northern border, and with whom by this marriage Arthur hoped to cement the peace.

But Morgain heard of this, and saw in it a danger to her son, Mordred, Arthur's bastard; a legitimate daughter, wed to the Scottish monarch, would have a better claim to Arthur's throne. With whispers and magic, she turned the King of Scotland against the proposal.

When Arthur and the Scottish King met in Berwick to seal the marriage, the Scot demanded all of Northumberland as a dowry. To this Arthur could not agree; and the King of Scotland took this as confirming Morgain's words against Arthur. Enraged, he enlisted the sorceress's aid to wreak his revenge; and she cast a mighty spell on Margaret, that she should sleep and never waken till betrothed to a Scottish prince, the betrothal sealed with a kiss.

In horror, Arthur went to Merlin, who could not directly unweave so mighty a spell; but he altered its terms, so that but a kiss by her own true love would awaken Margaret.

They built her a bed in Camelot, and covered her floor with flowers; many a knight essayed her awakening, but though many loved her, they loved her as a child and not a woman. And dark times soon befell Arthur and his knights; and what became of Margaret none could say, though perhaps she sleeps somewhere still, awaiting her true love's lips.

"What," said von Stroheim, feeding a stick to the campfire under the starry October sky, "are we to make of this old wive's tale?"

"I've asked about, and it's not just Mrs. Shaw's; it seems to be common in the region."

"It's merely a variant on Sleeping Beauty," von Stroheim said. "My own mother told me that story when I was a child."

"I'm sure she did," I told him. "As did mine. But there is often a nugget of truth in legends, as von Schliemann showed at Troy, what? Perhaps rather Sleeping Beauty is a variation on Sleeping Meg. A happier ending, at any rate; surely I would alter the tale in such fashion, if I were to rewrite it."

"Yes, very well," he muttered impatiently. "But Arthur? Centuries off, and problematic in any event, as you well know."

"It's common for stories to become conflated with others," I pointed out. "Suppose the true story goes something like this: Eadberht offered his daughter to one of the Pictish kings to seal a truce. For whatever reason, the deal broke down and a spell was cast. She fell into a slumber, from which she never recovered."

Von Stroheim scowled. "Ach, incredible," he said. "Eleven centuries and no one falls in love with her?" He looked toward the tent where she now lay, properly dressed in my wife's own clothes, guarded by de Laurency. "I'm half in love with her myself."

I grinned at him. "Well, kiss her, then," I told him.

He looked at me startled. "Why not you?"

I raised an eyebrow. "I, sir, am a happily married man."

He snorted. Von Stroheim is a cynic on the subject of marriage. "Very well. And why not?"

We entered the tent. The girl slept on a pallet of straw; de Laurency sat by her, gazing at her fair face by the light of a kerosene lamp. He looked up as we entered.

Von Stroheim went directly to the pallet, knelt, and kissed her: first on the forehead, then on the lips.

De Laurency sprang to his feet, a flush on his pale cheeks. "What the devil are you doing?" he demanded of von Stroheim.

Von Stroheim raised a bushy brow and stood to face the student. "That's 'What the devil are you doing, *Professor,*' " he said.

De Laurency flushed. "Do you often attempt to kiss women to whom you have not been introduced?" he demanded.

The two were silent for a moment, standing in the flickering yellow light under the low canvas roof. It is an image that has stayed with me; the young, sickly Romantic attempting to defend the honor of the girl; the older, bearlike man of science astounded that his simple experiment should rouse such antipathy.

"Be serious," he said at last, and ducked to leave the tent.

De Laurency sat, fists still clenched. "He had best leave her be," he said.

"Simmer down, boy," I told him. "It was an experiment, nothing more. If the story has any truth, it is a kiss that will awaken her."

"Not a kiss from the likes of him," said de Laurency fiercely.

Outside the tent von Stroheim was gazing at Orion, hands in his pockets against the chill. "It is all nonsense, anyway," he said. "You have erected an enormous structure of conjecture on an amazingly small investment of fact."

"Yes, Herr Doktor Professor," I said, a little sardonically, amused at this change in mood. "It is time we telegraphed the Royal Thaumaturgical Society."

Janet sighed when she heard the news from London, sitting on the chaise in the parlor with me, her arm about my waist and her thigh against mine; the children were asleep, coal burned in the fireplace, we sipped hot cider before retiring. "How long?" she said.

"No more than a week," I said. "Sir James has promised

to investigate directly we arrive, but I wish to be present for at least the preliminary examination. I do want to return as soon as I may; it is important that we find out as much as we can at the dig, before cold weather sets in."

She laid her head on my shoulder. "And is that the only reason you want to return quickly?" Her lips were on my neck.

"No, dearest," I whispered in her ear. "Neither the only nor the most important."

She kissed me, and I tasted the cider on her tongue.

The trip to London—de Laurency insisted on joining me— was, as usual, quite dull. But Sir James Maxwell made us quite welcome at the Thaumaturgical; after a cursory examination of Meg in his laboratory, he joined us in the society's lounge.

I was not insensible of the honor. While I have a modest scholarly reputation, Sir James outshines me by several orders of magnitude; it was he, after all, who through his discovery of the field equations, put thaumaturgy on a firm mathematical and scientific footing.

Ensconced in leather armchairs, we ordered Armagnac and relaxed.

"Precisely what do you hope from me?" Sir James inquired.

"Two things, I think," I said after a pause for consideration. "First, a spell clearly binds her; it would be useful to learn as much of it as we can, to cast light on the state of magical knowledge during the period. Second, it would be marvelous if we could awaken the girl; wouldn't it be grand if we could talk to and question someone who had actually lived a thousand years ago?"

De Laurency rather darkened at this, and muttered something into his brandy. I glanced at him. "Speak up, Robert," I said.

"She is a freeborn Briton," he said, rather defiantly. "If she should waken, you would have no right to keep her, study her, like some kind of trained ape."

" 'Briton' in the period would mean 'Celt,' " I pointed out. "She is Anglo-Saxon."

"Pedantry," he said.

"Perhaps. But I take your point; she would be a free woman. However, I suspect that learning to live in the modern age would be difficult, and that she would be grateful for our assistance. Surely we can expect cooperation in return?"

De Laurency coughed, a little apologetically. "I'm sorry, Professor," he said. "I'm sure you mean her no harm. But we must remember that she is a person, and not an . . . an artifact."

Sir James nodded sagely. "You are quite correct, sir," he said, "and we shall take the utmost caution."

Sir James promised to begin his studies on the morrow, and we parted.

I had taken rooms at the Chemists, my own club and not far from the Thaumaturgical. The next morning—a fine, brisk autumn day, the wind whipping London's skies clean of its normally noxious fumes—I walked back toward the RTS. And as I did, I heard the omnipresent cries of the street hawkers:

"*Globe, Wand, Standard, Times!* Getcher mornin' papers 'ere, gents. Sleepin' Beauty found in North Country. Read hall about it."

"Blast," I muttered, handing the boy a few pence for a *Wand*—one of the yellower of Fleet Street's publications. The article, and the illustration that accompanied it, was rather more fallacy than fact; but it contained the ineluctable truth that our discovery was now at the Royal Thaumaturgical Society.

I fully comprehend the utility of publicity when the need to solicit funds for research arises; but I feared, at this juncture, that public awareness of Meg could only serve to interfere with our investigation.

My fears proved immediately well-founded. While I checked my coat at the Thaumaturgical, a man in a rather loud herringbone suit spied me and approached.

"Dr. Borthwick?"

"I am he," I responded, wondering how he knew me; I caught the eye of the porter at the front desk, who looked down slightly shamefacedly. A little bribery, I supposed.

"I'm Fanshaw, of Fanshaw and Little, promoters," he said, handing me a card. It bore a picture of a Ferris wheel and an address in the East End. "Wonder if we might chat about this Sleeping Beauty girl you've got."

"I fail to see—"

"Well, sir, you see, I read the papers. Can't always believe what they say, but this is a wondrous age, ain't it? Magic and science, the Empire growing, strange things from barbarous lands. *That's* me business."

"Your business appears to be sideshow promotion," I said.

"Dead right, sir. Educational business, educational; bringing the wonders of seven continents and every age to the attention of the British public. *That's* me business. Though the gentry may view us askance, we serve a useful function, you know, introducing the common people to the wonders of the world. The *Wand* says she'll be awoken by true love's kiss, is that right? Can't believe what you read in the *Wand*, of course, but you could make such a spell, could be done, I understand."

Wondering how to get rid of the fellow, I said, "A variety of theories have been propounded to explain the young woman's state, and this is indeed among them. But until further research is performed—"

"Oh, research, yes, of course," he said. "Research costs money, indeed it does; a shame, that exploration of the wonders of the universe don't come cheap. And *that's* me business."

"Beg pardon?"

"Making money. For all concerned, all concerned; business ain't worth much unless all walk away from the table happy, eh? Now, sez I to meself, be nice to wake up the girl, eh, find out what life was like back in those days, eh? Sez I, bet Dr. Borthwick would be keen on that."

"It would be desirable to be sure, but until we better understand the magic that has so long sustained her—"

"Well now, look here. A kiss to awaken her, eh? But has to be her own true love. Where d'ye find her own true love?"

"Even should the theory prove meritorious, I'm at a loss—"

"Precisely! Impossible to say. So then, kiss her a lot, eh? Many folk. True love bound to burgeon in some young man's breast eventually, eh?"

I blinked at the man. "Precisely what are you proposing?"

"Consider the possibilities. 'Will you be the one to wake up Sleepin' Beauty? Are you her prince?' A shilling a peck, I imagine; bit of a sum, for a sideshow, but this is high-class stuff, Sir James Maxwell investigated, a princess of the ancient world, eh? Bit of pelf for me, bit of pelf for you, bit of pelf for research, eh? And maybe one of the marks wakes up the bint."

I restrained the urge to smite him on his protuberant and rather rugose nose. "Get out of here," I told him, raising my voice, "or I shall have you forcibly ejected."

"Right ho," he said cheerfully. "Jimmy Fanshaw don't stay where he's not wanted. Further research required, and all, maybe the proposition's a little premature. But you've got me card; if you lose it, just remember, Fanshaw and Little, easy to find us, we're big in the business. Once you've finished looking her over, what're you going to do with her, eh? Research costs money, we could make a pretty penny, you and me. And *that's* me business."

Two porters, looking rather worried, were approaching across the marble floor; Fanshaw saw my eyes on them and turned.

"Oh yes, yes," he said, "just going, keep calm, lads," and he strode off toward the big brass doors.

I was glad de Laurency wasn't with me; I didn't fancy a fistfight in the lobby of the RTS.

And what a ludicrous notion! That the poor girl's "own true love," whatever such a thing might mean, might be found in a horde of carney marks nicked at a shilling a head! I'd sooner use her as a hat stand. It would be more dignified.

Some days later I stood with Sir James in his laboratory, at the stroke of noon when white magic is best performed; it was a clear day, despite the lateness of the year and the smokes of London, sunlight spilling through the large French doors and across the pentacle inlaid in the wooden floor. A brazier wafted the scent of patchouli through the air.

Within the pentacle pale Meg lay atop a silver-metaled table, clad in a shift of virgin linen, her arms crossed over her breast; the lines of the pentacle shone blue with force. Sir James's baritone raised in invocation to the seraphim, the Virgin, and (I thought oddly, but perhaps appropriately under the circumstances) the great Boadicea.

The brazier produced a little smoke, enough to show the beams of light shining from the windows—as well as a line of energy stretching northward from Meg's body, across the space demarcated by the pentacle, disappearing through the wall of the laboratory.

Slowly, Sir James touched that line with a wand of ash, then brought the wand toward a manameter, a device of glass and mercury.

The wand touched the manameter. Mercury boiled suddenly over its top, and its glass shattered. The pentacle snapped cold, its blue glow disappearing.

Sir James looked a little shaken. "Well over a kilodee," he said to me. "That answers one of your questions, at any rate."

"It does?" I said.

"*Someone* had a good grasp of magical principles in the eighth century," he said. "As good as a competent Roman mage, at any rate. That is a good, strong spell."

"Could you shield her from that line of power?" I asked.

He nodded warily. "Aye," he said, "but would that waken or kill her? She is more than a thousand years old; magic must sustain as well as suspend her."

As I bent to swab up the mercury with a rag, there was a knock at the door. It was one of the society's porters, a little agitated, bearing a salver with a card. "A . . . a gentlemen has asked to speak with you, Sir James," he said.

Sir James took the card, raised a brow, and handed it to me. It said:

H.R.H.
THE PRINCE OF WALES

Edward, Prince of Wales, is a large man. Large in many ways: large in girth, large in stature, and large in appetites. We bowed, of course.

"Maxwell!" the Prince bellowed. "You look well, man. Haven't seen you at the theater lately."

"Mmm, no, Your Highness. Press of work, you know."

"Ah well, work. Smokes, fumes, and explosions in the lab, eh? Good smelly fun, for a chap like you, I assume. I may smoke in here, may I not?"—this while brandishing a cigar.

"Of course, Your Highness."

"Well sit down, dammit," he said, clipping off the end of the cigar and running a lit lucifer down its length. "Can't smoke at Windsor, you know, Mater won't have it. Can't at any of her residences. Reduced to wandering about the gardens in the most beastly weather just for a smoke. Caught Count von Hatzfeldt, the German ambassador, in his pajamas with his head up the chimney once, can you imagine? Just wanted a cigarette, caused the most dreadful ruckus. I hear you've made quite a discovery, Dr. Borthwick."

I cleared my throat. "An interesting one, certainly, Your Highness," I said.

"Oh, call me Wales, all my friends do," he said, waving the smoke away from his neatly trimmed beard. "Beautiful girl, I understand. Shan't wake till kissed by a Scottish prince."

Sir James cleared his throat. "This is an hypothesis," he said. "We have verified that the binding spell is Scottish in origin, but the rest is speculation based on local legend."

His Royal Highness snorted in amusement. "Trust scientists and wizards for excessive qualification," he said. " 'Hypothesis . . . speculation.' Well, you deal with hypotheses by testing them, what?"

Sir James and I exchanged glances.

"What do you propose, Your Highness?" I inquired.

"Wales, Wales," he said, waving his cigar before his cummerbund. "Ah, case in point; my most important title, to be sure, Prince of Wales. But you know, I've got scads of them—Earl of this and Commander of that. I'm a Rajah, too, did you know? Several of them. In any event, I am also Thane of Fife, as well as Earl of Dumfries and Galloway.

Since the Act of Union, I'm the closest thing you'll find to a Scottish prince. And I can't say I object to kissing a pretty girl."

Sir James chuckled. "I've never known you to," he said. "You propose to assist us with our inquiries, I suppose?"

The Prince of Wales gave us a bristly smile.

As we climbed the stairs toward the laboratories, I wondered what the Princess Alexandra would think; but Edward's wife, I suppose, must have inured herself to his infidelities by now, of which this was far from the most egregious.

He bent over her drawn form, her lips almost blue with the slowness of her circulation, her cheeks lacking the blush of life but somehow still alive, her shorn hair now reshaped into a more attractive coiffure than we had first given her, there in the Cheviot Hills. He bent his stout waist, planted one massive hand to the side of her head and, with surprising tenderness, kissed her through his beard.

She never stirred.

He looked down at her for a long moment, with three fingers of one hand inserted in the watch pocket of his vest. "Poor darling," he said. Then after a moment he turned back to us. "Not much fun if they don't kiss back, eh, lads?"

When I told de Laurency we were to leave Meg with Sir James and return to Alcroft, we had a bit of a tiff. He didn't want to leave her; I believe he felt he could protect her better than the RTS—which, to my certain knowledge, has stronger magical wards than anything in Great Britain with the possible exception of the Grand Fleet's headquarters at Scapa Flow. Eventually, he stomped off into an increasingly bitter night, not reconciled to the decision yet knowing it was mine to make.

He met me the following morning at Paddington Station, reeking of Irish whiskey; I imagine he was out with his radical friends, a passel of socialist trash. Cambridge men mostly, thank God, though we get our share at Oxford. Ten minutes out of the station, he opened the window to vomit down the side of the train, admitting quite a quantity of ash and cinders into the car. Filthy things, trains. He slept for a time thereafter.

Still hours out of Berwick, he awakened, and I told him of the visit by the Prince of Wales. He was appalled. "You let that vile lecher kiss her?" he demanded.

"You *are* referring to your future monarch, you realize."

He snorted. "Lillie Langtry," he said. "Lady Brooke. Mrs. George Keppel. And those are merely the ones that are public knowledge. The man is a scoundrel."

"And was it not you who, scant weeks ago, was lecturing me on the morality of free love?"

He subsided slightly. "That's different," he said. "He married the Princess Alexandra, did he not? Does he owe her nothing?"

"I hadn't heard that she objected to his, um, extracurricular activities," I pointed out.

"Tcha," went de Laurency. "Would you? In her position?"

"See here," I said, "there was no harm done. And how could I have stopped the man in any event? He *is* the Prince of Wales."

"Yes he is," said de Laurency, "and God help England."

As the train sped northward, I contemplated de Laurency's words while he sat quietly on the opposite bench, reading poetry. Byron, of course.

Did I owe Janet, my own dear wife, nothing? On the contrary, I owed her a great deal. But not because a minister said words over us. I am a good C of E man, and believe in the sanctity of the sacrament of marriage; but what I owe her I owe her because she is *my* own true love.

True love. A silly concept, in a way; the stuff of penny novels and Italian opera. God's love, the love of a parent for a child: more tangible and, in a way, more comprehensible. There is love between man and woman: could I deny it? Yet the proximate cause of my love for Janet, and hers for me, was no great fluxion in the celestial sphere, no fated union of souls, no great internal singing when first our glances met. The proximate cause—not the ultimate, you understand, nor the only, but the proximate—was a silly conversation we had one evening at a Christmas party at her father's house. The details are otiose, and we disagreed; but she is one of the very few women I have ever met in whom intelligence, grace, and beauty are united.

She was waiting at Alcroft station.

It was an eternity before the children were at last in bed.

And hours later, studying her sleeping profile by the half-moon's light, her black hair curling in rings across the pillow, her sweet bosom rising and falling beneath the sheets, I realized that however beautiful she might be, I would surely have never fallen in love with her if we had never had that silly conversation about Bentham, Gladstone, and the Suez Canal. How could I have loved her, never knowing her? And how could I have known her, merely looking?

We stayed in Alcroft a scant few weeks; the weather was turning cold. I spent our remaining time performing such magics as lie within my skill, to try to understand what had transpired here; helping the diggers at their work, laying out plans for future excavation. We found precious little of any value: a few bronze implements, a few Frankish coins, a nicely preserved drinking horn, and various shards.

De Laurency was less a help than a hindrance. He never seemed to be about the dig, and soon lost any interest in keeping his journal notes up to date. I often spied him atop the Cheviot, a small dark figure at such a distance, striking a pose and staring into space. I suspect when he wasn't mooning about the moor, he was imbibing too much of the local ale.

God send me sturdy, even-tempered students!

Soon enough the first frost came, and we decamped to Oxford.

"I've brought Meg back to you," said Sir James, standing in my office and warming his hands before the coal grate. De Laurency moodily fiddled with the fire irons.

"So your cable said you would," I said. "I'm honored that you made the trip yourself."

He sighed, and sat in the armchair to the side of my desk. De Laurency remained standing, staring into the blue flames. "Well," said Sir James, "I felt it incumbent to report in person, though of course I shall be writing up my findings for the Transactions."

"I appreciate that, sir. And what, if I may, have you discovered?"

Sir James cleared his throat. "Precious little, I fear," he said. "The symbology, alas, is foreign."

I blinked. "I don't—"

"Magic is symbolic manipulation, yes?"

"Quite so."

"By noting the effects of a spell cast by another, you can frequently deduce much about the symbolic elements used therein, and possibly re-create the spell yourself—perhaps not in very detail, to be sure, but close enough."

"I have done so many times as an exercise."

"And you have studied Roman magic?"

"Yes, and Mesopotamian."

"And does not the symbology differ from our own?"

I blinked as I came to understand what he was getting at. "Certainly," I said. "They had whole different systems of worship, of color association, of folk tradition; therefore, the symbolic elements used differ greatly from our own. Untangling a Greco-Roman spell is not particularly difficult, since so much has come down to us in both languages, but of the Mesopotamian we have scant understanding."

Sir James nodded. "And this spell was cast by a wild Pictish mage of the eighth century A.D., possibly a Christian but still greatly influenced by pagan traditions. If I were a scholar of the Medieval Celts, I might conceivably be able to untangle the spell better, but as it is, I can really only report on its effects. Which is of dubious utility, as its effects are evident: she sleeps."

De Laurency broke in. "*Why* does she sleep?"

Sir James looked mildly at him. "She is ensorcelled, of course."

De Laurency snorted. "That much is obvious. Can you say nothing of the manner of her ensorcellment, nor how she may be released? Is Professor Borthwick's 'Sleeping Beauty' theory proven or disproven?"

Sir James sighed. "The spell clearly contains a release, a

means of ending. I believe, but cannot prove, that the release is tied to love, in some fashion; a strong emotion, love, and it somehow flavors the spell. What further qualifications attend the release, and whether it must be effected by a kiss, I cannot say. As for Dr. Borthwick's theory, it is consistent with the facts as we know them; but it is far from definitively demonstrated."

De Laurency scowled and made a small noise expressive of impatience.

Sir James frowned and said, "Young man, as a scientist, you must learn to be comfortable with a degree of ambiguity. As a system of epistemology, science relies on theories tested and not yet disproven; but even the solidest theory is grounded on quicksand by comparison to the only two things that we can truly know, in the strong philosophical sense of 'to know.' "

"And those are?"

"I know that I exist, because I experience my existence," replied Sir James. "And I know that the Creator exists, through faith. And some would argue with the latter as an adequate proof."

"Is there no hope for her?" I said.

Sir James turned to me. "Oh certainly," he said. "There is always hope. Perhaps her true love will find her. And perhaps as the state of magical knowledge advances, some future wizard, cleverer than I, will untangle the Gordian knot of her spell and release her from slumber."

For some days I left poor Meg sitting in my guest armchair, her head cushioned by a pillow, as I pondered what to do with her. De Laurency was right; she was a free woman, and any experimentation more intrusive than Sir James's gentle exploration was inappropriate. Yet she seemed to need our care not at all; she required no greater sustenance, it seemed, than the very air.

One snowy December afternoon I returned from high table in the company of von Stroheim, with too much capon and a bit of port under my belt. Somewhat to my surprise, we discovered a small, elderly, dark-complexioned gentleman sitting at my desk chair, gloved hands on walking stick, gazing at her visage. He was outlandishly garbed: green velvet pants, paisley vest, silver-buckled shoon. He wore rings on both ring fingers, over the outside of his mole-skin gloves.

"Good afternoon, my Lord Beaconsfield," I said, von Stroheim glancing at me in startlement; he had not recognized Disraeli, but I had, of course. I am, to be sure, a life-long Tory. "To what do I owe the honor?"

He glanced up at me. "Dr. Borthwick, I presume? And can this be Professor von Stroheim? Please forgive an old man's intrusion. I read of your young charge and had wished to see her. I trust I may be forgiven."

"I believe England may forgive you anything, sir," I said. Von Stroheim grinned a sardonic grin at me from behind Beaconsfield's back; he has often accused me of shameless flattery.

Disraeli chuckled. "Well, it seems the public loves me now that I am retired," he said, "but it has not always been so. Nonetheless, I take the compliment in the spirit in which it is offered. Is this fairy tale true?"

"Wholly bosh," said von Stroheim. "The maunderings of old wives and the wistful fancies of middle-aged men."

"My conjecture has not been falsified, Helmut," I said. "You must forgive us, my lord; the disagreements of scientists must sometimes seem like the quarrels of old couples."

"I rather hope the story is true," said the Earl of Beaconsfield. "I came . . . well, it's a peculiar thing. I'm working on a novel, you know; I haven't had time for fifteen years, but now I do. And, as in all novels—well, most—love plays a role. But the devil of it is that I know so little of love; I came to it so late, and in so untidy a fashion. I had thought somehow I might gain an insight from the young lady's plight."

"That is the problem with novels," von Stroheim said. "They revel in pretty lies."

"Late and untidy, my lord?" I said.

"As a young man," said Beaconsfield, "I was too enraptured with my own prospects to pay much heed to 'pretty lies,' if it please you, Professor. 'Woman was to him but a toy, man but a machine,' if I may quote my own *oeuvre*. I

married not for love, but for money; Mrs. Lewis was fifteen
years my senior, rich and well-connected, when I asked her
hand. I did so neither from passion nor affection, but out of
cold political calculation, for my modest inheritance had
been squandered, my novels did not suffice to keep me in
the style to which I had become accustomed, and I desperately needed funds to continue my political career."

"You, my lord? Act from cold, political calculation?"
said von Stroheim—a trifle sardonically.

The Earl chuckled. "It is so. Yet I came to love her; she
soon let me gently know that she understood my motiva-
tions, but loved me nonetheless. And as time passed, a true
affection ripened between us. The proudest and happiest
day of my life was not when the Queen granted me the title
of Beaconsfield, nor when I acquired the Khedive's shares
in the Suez Canal, nor yet when I browbeat old Derby into
sponsoring the Reform Act; it was in sixty-four, when I ob-
tained for my darling the title of Viscountess."

"Some men give jewelry," von Stroheim said.

Disraeli laughed out loud. "A Prime Minister can do
better than that," he said. He sobered, and reached out a
gloved hand to trace the line of her jaw. "I found love so
unexpectedly; surely this poor creature is as deserving as I?"

"Ach, it is incredible," said von Stroheim. "Eleven centuries! The world is full of idiots. Surely one falls in love
with her. Has de Laurency kissed her yet?"

"I haven't the vaguest idea," I said.

"Is it that easy?" Beaconsfield said. "*True* love, as the
story goes?"

"*True* love," said von Stroheim incredulously. "*Vas ist?*"

"Yet it exists," said I.

Von Stroheim looked me up and down. "Well," he said
at length, "you and Janet almost make me believe it is so."

"You too, my lord," I said, "came to love only after
acquaintance."

Disraeli shrugged.

"Is there no hope for her, then?" I asked.

The Earl stood up abruptly. "Perhaps none," he said.
"Some stories are tragedies, you know. A fact that presses
against me, as the end of my own tale draws near."

He died last year, did you know? But he left us one last novel.

Was it that very night? I think not; the next, perhaps. Certainly within a few days.

I was working late by gaslight; after putting the children to bed, I had found myself wakeful and, begging Janet's pardon, had returned to Balliol to continue my fruitless attempt to decipher the Linear B. I found the shutter to my office window unlatched; sleet and cold wind dashed through it. Cursing, I latched it shut and, fingers shaking with the cold, lit a fire in the grate.

As I crouched before the fender, hands held out to the burgeoning flame, I heard a tenor keening; the drone of words, as faint as an insect buzz. I cocked my head, wondering what on earth this could be, then realized the sound came from up the flue.

I went to the window, threw open the shutters, and peered up at the roof.

My office is on the top floor of the hall; its window is a dormer. About it, and upward, slope slate shingles, slick that night with the freezing rain. And there, atop the curved Spanish tiles that run the length of the roof's peak, clutching the chimney, stood de Laurency, sleet pelting his woolen greatcoat, a scarf about his neck, his lanky hair plastered against his skull.

Into the sleet he said, in a curiously conversational tone of voice:

> *"Farewell! if ever fondest prayer*
> *   For other's weal availed on high,*
> *Mine will not all be lost in air,*
> *   But waft thy name beyond the sky.*
> *'Twere vain to speak, to weep, to sigh:*
> *   Oh! more than tears of blood can tell,*
> *When wrung from guilt's expiring eye,*
> *   Are in that word—Farewell!—Farewell!"*

I was tempted to shout, yet I feared to dislodge him from his unsteady perch. I forced my voice to a conversational tone. "What the devil is that?" I demanded.

He blinked down the slick roof at me. "Byron," he said.

I snorted. "No doubt. And what the devil are you doing up there?"

De Laurency gave me a quick smile; a smile that departed as quickly as it had come. "In a moment," he said, "I propose to step onto these tiles and slip to my death on the cobbles below."

I was tempted to tell him to try to hit head first, as he might otherwise simply be crippled.

"And why," I asked, "should you want to do that?"

He closed his eyes, and with real pain in his voice said, "I am unworthy! Truly I love her, and yet I am not her true love!"

"Ah! Kissed her at last, did we?"

He blinked down at me, with some hostility.

"About bloody time," I said. "Mooning about like a silly git. All right, you've had your smoochie, didn't work, carry on, eh? Come on in and I'll fix you a brandy."

"Is it you," he said bitterly, "your age, or *the* age? The age of machines and mechanical magic, all passion and glory a barely remembered palimpsest? Or you, a dried-up old didactic prune with no remembrance of what it is to love and be loved in the glory of the springtime moon? Or were you always a pedant?"

I looked up at him at a loss for a time. Finally, I said, "Oh, I was a pedant always; an insufferable youth, I fear, and barely more tolerable in middle age. And yes, this is a practical age. But I, I know more of love than three of you, de Laurency; for I have three to love, who love me dearly in return."

De Laurency looked at me incredulously. "You?" he said. "You have three lovers?"

"Oh yes," I said. "My darling Janet, my sweet Clarice, and littlest Amelia."

"Oh," he said with dismissal. "Your children."

"My children, yes," I said. "And will you know what that is like if you dash your fool brains out on the cobbles below?"

He straightened up, scowling. "Know this," he said. "I love Meg truly; I have worshiped her since first I saw her,

gloried in the scent of her golden hair, longed to see the
light of her eyes. I have felt her slow, shallow breath; in
dreams have I seen her life amid the court of Northumbria,
the gallant knights who served her, the adoration of her
royal father." Here I could not restrain a snort; you'd think
a prospective archaeologist would better understand the
misery of such a primitive and barbaric life. "And I feel we
have communed, one spirit to another! And so I gathered
my courage, my every hope, and with my lips I gently
kissed her! And still she did not stir!"

"Yes, well, so did von Stroheim and the Prince—"

"They did not love her!"

"And you do? You puppy! You pismire! You love yourself rather more than you love her! What vanity, striding
about the moor and reciting Byron! I'll wager you spent
more time contemplating what a Romantic figure you cut,
against the heather, with your windblown hair, then considering the beauties of nature or the nature of beauty! Love!
What do mean by that? *Agape* or *eros*? Do you know the
difference? Do you care?"

He stared at me, thunderstruck. "Of course I know! Do
you think me ignorant? And *agape*, of course; I would hardly
dare to desire her, to—"

He sobbed, and swayed, barely holding onto the
chimney.

It occurred to me that the lad badly needed a rogering
by some down-to-earth, buxom lass. But I dared not suggest
such a course.

Love, indeed.

"Come in, Robert," I said at last. "The night is cold, the
lady sleeps, and I have brandy waiting."

And to my surprise, he did.

And, oh dear, what was I to do with her? The finest minds
of magic could not help her. If ever she had had her own
true love, he was centuries dead, and to love without knowing is an impossibility. She would sleep, sleep on, and sleep
forever, if I had my guess.

Hire her out for a shilling a peck? Pshaw.

Leave her be on my guest armchair? Well, you know. I rather need the space.

De Laurency said once that she was a person, not an artifact. True, in its fashion; but she might as well be an artifact, you know. A fine specimen of Medieval English maidenhood, 765 A.D. (est.), Kingdom of Northumbria. You could tie a tag to her toe and stick her in a case.

And why not?

The great and good of England had shown up to gawk at her; and if they, why not the masses? Edify the people of England, preserve the specimen for future study. That is the function of a great museum.

After I packed de Laurency off home, I looked down at the poor dear, and kissed her.

On the forehead, not the lips; I am a happily married man. And though I love her, in a fashion, I have already my own true love.

And the next day I sent a telegraph the British Museum.

Poor darling Meg; I hope she is happy here, 'tween Athene and Megatherium; surely happier, at any rate, than buried in Alcroft's clay.

Greg Costikyan says: " 'And Still She Sleeps' was the first short story I wrote after a three year hiatus that resulted from severe depression. Depression is sometimes a treatable psychiatric condition, and sometimes a completely normal response to external events—in my case, the collapse of my marriage. One shouldn't put too much emotional freight onto a story that is fundamentally wry and rather light in tone, but 'And Still She Sleeps' is, in some sense, an attempt to grapple with the nature of love—a matter of obvious concern, given my immediate experiences, and a subject I still can only claim to have the haziest grip on. The story of 'Sleeping Beauty' is one of the ur-stories that shapes our society's notion of Romantic love—and thinking about it, and what's wrong with the image of love it presents, was the proximate cause of the urge to write this piece."

Snow in Summer

JANE YOLEN

Jane Yolen lives part of the year in Hatfield, Massachusetts, and part of the year in St. Andrews, Scotland. She has won the World Fantasy Award, the Nebula Award, three Mythopoeic Society Awards, a runner-up for the National Book Award, and other medals, statuettes, plaques, and medallions too numerous to mention. Yolen has over two hundred published books; her best known include The Devil's Arithmetic; Owl Moon, Briar Rose; Sleeping Ugly; *the Commander Toad books; the Pit Dragon Trilogy; and the novels about White Jenna.*

Snow in Summer

They call that white flower that covers the lawn like a poplin carpet Snow in Summer. And because I was born in July with a white caul on my head, they called me that, too. Mama wanted me to answer to Summer, which is a warm, pretty name. But my Stepmama, who took me in hand just six months after Mama passed away, only spoke the single syllable of my name, and she didn't say it nicely.

"Snow!" It was a curse in her mouth. It was a cold, unfeeling thing. "Snow, where are you, girl? Snow, what have you done now?"

I didn't love her. I couldn't love her, though I tried. For Papa's sake I tried. She was a beautiful woman, everyone said. But as Miss Nancy down at the postal store opined, "Looks ain't nothing without a good heart." And she was staring right at my Stepmama when she said it. But then

Miss Nancy had been Mama's closest friend ever since they'd been little ones, and it nigh killed her, too, when Mama was took by death.

But Papa was besot with my Stepmama. He thought she couldn't do no wrong. The day she moved into Cumberland he said she was the queen of love and beauty. That she was prettier than a summer night. He praised her so often, she took it ill any day he left off complimenting, even after they was hitched. She would have rather heard those soft nothings said about her than to talk of any of the things a husband needs to tell his wife: like when is dinner going to be ready or what bills are still to be paid.

I lived twelve years under that woman's hard hand, with only Miss Nancy to give me a kind word, a sweet pop, and a magic story when I was blue. Was it any wonder I always went to town with a happier countenance than when I had to stay at home.

And then one day Papa said something at the dinner table, his mouth greasy with the chicken I had cooked and his plate full with the taters I had boiled. And not a thing on that table that my Stepmama had made. Papa said, as if surprised by it, "Why, Rosemarie . . ." which was my Stepmama's Christian name, "why, Rosemarie, do look at what a beauty that child has become."

And for the first time my Stepmama looked—really looked—at me.

I do not think she liked what she saw.

Her green eyes got hard, like gems. A row of small lines raised up on her forehead. Her lips twisted around. "Beauty," she said. "Snow," she said. She did not say the two words together. They did not fit that way in her mouth.

I didn't think much of it at the time. If I thought of myself at all those days, it was as a lanky, gawky, coltish child. Beauty was for horses or grown women, Miss Nancy always said. So I just laughed.

"Papa, you are just fooling," I told him. "A daddy has to say such things about his girl." Though in the thirteen years I had been alive, he had never said any such overmuch. None in fact that I could remember.

But then he added something that made things worse, though I wasn't to know it that night. "She looks like her Mama. Just like her dear Mama."

My Stepmama only said, "Snow, clear the dishes."

So I did.

But the very next day my Stepmama went and joined the Holy Roller Mt. Hosea Church, which did snake handling on the fourth Sunday of each month and twice on Easter. Because of the Bible saying, "Those who love the Lord can take up vipers and they will not be killed," the Mt. Hosea folk proved the power of their faith by dragging out rattlers and copperheads from a box and carrying them about their shoulders like a slippery shawl. Kissing them, too, and letting the pizzen drip down on their cheeks.

Stepmama came home from church, her face all flushed and her eyes all bright, and said to me, "Snow, you will come with me next Sunday."

"But I love Webster Baptist," I cried. "And Reverend Bester. And the hymns." I didn't add that I loved sitting next to Miss Nancy and hearing the stories out of the Bible the way she told them to the children's class during the Reverend's long sermon. "Please, Papa, don't make me go."

For once my Papa listened. And I was glad he said no. I am feared of snakes, though I love the Lord mightily. But I wasn't sure any old Mt. Hosea rattler would know the depth of that love. Still, it wasn't the snakes Papa was worried about. It was, he said, those Mt. Hosea boys.

My Stepmama went to Mt. Hosea alone all that winter, coming home later and later in the afternoon from church, often escorted by young men who had scars on their cheeks where they'd been snakebit. One of them, a tall blond fellow who was almost handsome except for the meanness around his eyes, had a tattoo of a rattler on his bicep with the legend "Love Jesus Or Else" right under it.

My Papa was not amused.

"Rosemarie," he said, "you are displaying yourself. That is not a reason to go to church."

"I have not been doing this for myself," she replied. "I thought Snow should meet some young men now she's becoming a woman. A beautiful woman." It was not a compliment in her mouth. And it was not the truth, either, for she had never even introduced me to the young men nor told them my true name.

Still, Papa was satisfied with her answer, though Miss Nancy, when I told her about it later, said, "No sow I know ever turned a boar over to her litter without a fight."

However, the blond with the tattoo came calling one day and he didn't ask for my Stepmama. He asked for me. For Snow. My Stepmama smiled at his words, but it was a snake's smile, all teeth and no lips. She sent me out to walk with him, though I did not really want to go. It was the mean eyes and the scars and the rattler on his arm, some. But more than that, it was a feeling I had that my Stepmama wanted me to be with him. And that plumb frightened me.

When we were in the deep woods, he pulled me to him and tried to kiss me with an open mouth and I kicked him in the place Miss Nancy had told me about, and while he was screaming, I ran away. Instead of chasing me, he called after me in a voice filled with pain, "That's not even what your Stepmama wanted me to do to you." But I kept running, not wanting to hear any more.

I ran and ran even deeper into the woods, long past the places where the rhododendron grew wild. Into the dark places, the boggy places, where night came upon me and would not let me go. I was so tired from all that running, I fell asleep right on a tussock of grass. When I woke there was a passel of strangers staring down at me. They were small, humpbacked men, their skin blackened by coal dust, their eyes curious. They were ugly as an unspoken sin.

"Who are you?" I whispered, for a moment afraid they might be more of my Stepmama's crew.

They spoke together, as if their tongues had been tied in a knot at the back end. "Miners," they said. "On Keeperwood Mountain."

"I'm Snow in Summer," I said. "Like the flower."

"Summer," they said as one. But they said it with softness and a kind of dark grace. And they were somehow not so ugly anymore. "Summer."

So I followed them home.

*   *   *

And there I lived for seven years, one year for each of them. They were as good to me and as kind as if I was their own little sister. Each year, almost as if by magic, they got better to look at. Or maybe I just got used to their outsides and saw within. They taught me how to carve out jewels from the black cave stone. They showed me the secret paths around their mountain. They warned me about strangers finding their way to our little house.

I cooked for them and cleaned for them and told them Miss Nancy's magic stories at night. And we were happy as can be. Oh, I missed my Papa now and then, but my Stepmama not at all. At night I sometimes dreamed of the tall blond man with the rattler tattoo, but when I cried out, one of the miners would always comfort me and sing me back to sleep in a deep, gruff voice that sounded something like a father and something like a bear.

Each day my little men went off to their mine and I tidied and swept and made-up the dinner. Then I'd go outside to play. I had deer I knew by name, gray squirrels who came at my bidding, and the sweetest family of collared doves that ate cracked corn out of my hand. The garden was mine, and there I grew everything we needed. I did not mourn for what I did not have.

But one day a stranger came to the clearing in the woods. Though she strived to look like an old woman, with cross-eyes and a mouth full of black teeth, I knew her at once. It was my Stepmama in disguise. I pretended I did not know who she was, but when she inquired, I told her my name straight out.

"Summer," I said.

I saw "Snow" on her lips.

I fed her a deep-dish apple pie, and while she bent over the table shoveling it into her mouth, I felled her with a single blow of the fry pan.

My little men helped me bury her out back.

Miss Nancy's stories had always ended happy-ever-after. But she used to add every time: "Make your own happiness, Summer dear."

And so I did. My happiness—and hers.

I went to the wedding when Papa and Miss Nancy tied the knot. I danced with some handsome young men from Webster and from Elkins and from Canaan. But I went back home alone. To the clearing and the woods and the little house with the eight beds. My seven little fathers needed keeping. They needed my good stout meals. And they needed my stories of magic and mystery. To keep them alive.

To keep me alive, too.

When Jane Yolen was a child living in New York City, her mother always warned her never to open the door to strangers. So when she read "Snow White," she assumed—little tartar that she was then—that Snow White got what she deserved, letting that old witch in. So in "Snow in Summer" Yolen feels that she has finally written the Snow White she was meant to write, way back then.

Briar Rose and Witch

DEBRA CASH

Debra Cash is a poet whose work often draws on images from traditional literature, including the Hebrew Bible and liturgy. She lives in Boston, Massachusetts, where she runs an international consultancy in workplace analysis and design. She has also been a dance critic for the Boston Globe *for a number of years.*

Briar Rose

A hundred years of dreams—
I would not have given up an hour
of those shifting landscapes, the tower, the lagoon
the rough roses making a cradle around my bed.

Everything stops
for me and for everyone I know
while behind my wincing eyelids I absorb
my parents' recklessness.

We wanted the best for you, they'll tell me:
all those girlish virtues
a pretty face and figure, kindness to the poor
the ability to sing and play the spinet.

Inviting the colors of the rainbow to my christening,
spraying me with holy white light,
they locked out one color of the spectrum
the darkness that absorbs it all

and I blame my father. Maleficent came to his birth
just as surely as she did to mine:
the difference is that everyone knew her then
when her name was Poverty and Need

and the guests all bowed their heads. In our day
my birthday, no one expected her.
Evil, they called her. I call her
Resentment, Fury. Locked away, I dream

and no one tells me what to do.
No one breaks in. And when a stranger offers me a spindle
glistening, sexual, I sink into the pillows
and remember the worst has already happened:

I have survived death and turned it into sleep
and a dream lasting one hundred years.

When I wake
I will know my lover's face.

Witch

If I were really cruel I would have turned them into frogs
   and snakes
and squirmy insects with brittle legs
not gingerbread and oatmeal raisin—
and I would have hid them under stones
not set outside as lawn ornaments.

O my house is my only safety
hidden in the deep, dark forest
where animals know to stay away
and children drift in like leaves falling
from parents who neglect them
and tell them they are bad.

I am so ugly I want to bay at the moon
my heart feels like a cinder
the wicked, wicked witch
my heart gnawed like the shrinking night.

One day I will get lucky and a girl will push me in the oven
its raw bricks making walls without windows
a house square, solitary, exploding.
I long for it, to be baked like they were baked
become sweet and sweet-smelling as the minutes tick.
I am waiting for some pigtailed Gretel,
loyal and clever and loving
to give me a shove, headfirst—
and she will be the next witch in the forest
turning the children back into children.

*Although "Witch" and "Briar Rose" were not written as a pair,
they both expose silences at the heart of their respective tales: in
one case, the unexplored private pain at the heart of evil, and in
the other, the mysterious fluttering pictures that enable a sleeping
beauty to wake renewed and aware.*

Chanterelle

BRIAN STABLEFORD

Brian Stableford lives in Reading, England, and is the author of more than forty novels including Empire of Fear, Young Blood, *and* Inheritors of Earth. *His most recent publications include* Teach Yourself Writing Fantasy and Science Fiction, Yesterday's Bestsellers, Glorious Perversity: The Decline and Fall of Literary Decadence, The Dictionary of Science Fiction Places, *and the novel* The Black Blood of the Dead. *His short stories have been published in* Interzone, OMNI Internet, *and* Sirens and Other Daemon Lovers. *Stableford is also the editor of* The Dedalus Book of Decadence (Moral Ruins), Tales of the Wandering Jew, *and* The Dedalus Book of Femme Fatales.

Chanterelle

There was once a music-loving carpenter named Alastor, who fell in love with Catriona, the daughter of a foundryman who lived in a Highland village near to the town of his birth. Catriona was known in the village as the Nightingale, because she had a beautiful singing voice. Alastor loved to play for her, and it was while she sang to his accompaniment that she fell in love with him.

When Alastor and Catriona were married, they left the Highlands for the Lowlands, taking up residence in the nation's capital city, where Alastor was determined to make a living as a maker of musical instruments. Their first child, a son, was born on the first Monday after New Year's Day, which is known throughout Christendom as Handsel Monday.

A handsel is a gift made to celebrate a new beginning,

as a coin might be placed in the pocket of a freshly tailored coat. Alastor knew that his son might be seen as exactly such a gift, bestowed upon his marriage, and he was determined to make the most of him.

"Should we call him Handsel, do you think?" Alastor asked Catriona.

"It is a good name," she said.

Every choice that is made narrows the range of further choices, and when the couple's second child was due, Alastor said to Catriona: "If our second-born is a girl, we must not call her Gretel. There is a tale in which two children so-named are abandoned in the wild forest by their father, a poor woodcutter, at the behest of their stepmother. The tale ends happily enough for the children, but we should not take chances."

"You are not a woodcutter, my love," Catriona replied, "and we live in the city. We left the wild forest behind us when we left the Highlands, and I am not sure that we should carry its legacy of stories and superstitions with us."

"I think we should," said Alastor. "There is a wealth of wisdom in that legacy. We may be far away from the haunts of the fairy-folk, but we are Highlanders still. There have been those in both our families who have had the second sight, and we have no guarantee that our children will be spared its curse. We should be careful in naming them, and we must take care that they hear all the stories we know, for whatever their guidance might be worth."

"Here in the city," said Catriona, "it is said that children must make their way in the real world, and that stories will only fill their heads with unreasonable expectations."

"They say that," admitted Alastor, "but the city-dwellers have merely devised a new armory of stories, which seem more appropriate to the order and discipline of city life. I would rather our children heard what *we* had to tell—for they are, after all, *our* children."

"What name did you have in mind?" Catriona asked him.

"I hope that our son might choose to follow me in working with his hands," Alastor said. "I would like him to master the grain of the wood, in order that he might make pipes, harps, fiddles, and lutes. I hope that our daughter might complement his achievements with a singing voice the equal of your own. Let us give her a name which would suit a songstress."

"Ever since I was a girl," said Catriona, "I have been nicknamed Nightingale—but if you mean what you say about the wisdom of stories, we should not wish *that* name upon our daughter. No sooner had it been bestowed upon me than I was forced to listen to the tale of the little girl who fell into the care of a wicked man who knew the secret of training nightingales to sing by day. Even today I shudder when I think of it."

"She was imprisoned in a cage by a prince, was she not?" said Alastor. "She was set to sing in the depths of the wild forest, but suffered misfortune enough to break her heart, and she refused to sing again, until she fell into the clutches of her former master, who—"

"Please don't," begged Catriona.

"Well," said Alastor, "we must certainly avoid the name that was given to *that* girl—which was Luscignole, if I remember rightly. I wonder if we might call our daughter— if indeed the child you are carrying should turn out to be a daughter—Chanterelle, after the highest string of a musical instrument?"

"Chanterelle is an excellent choice," said Catriona. "I never heard a story about a girl named Chanterelle. But what if the baby is a boy?"

There is no need to record the rest of the conversation, for the child *was* a girl, and she was named Chanterelle.

When Handsel and Chanterelle were old enough to hear stories, Catriona was careful to tell them the tales that were popular in the city as well as those she remembered from her own childhood in the Highlands, but it was the Highland tales that they liked better. Although there was not the faintest trace of the fairy-folk to be found in the city, it was the fairy-folk of whom the children loved to hear tell.

Handsel, as might be expected, was particularly fond of the tale of Handsel and Gretel. Chanterelle, on the other hand, preferred to hear the tale of the foundryman who was lured away from his family by a fairy, until he was called back by the tolling of a church bell he had made, which had fallen into a lake. Catriona told that story to help her children understand the kind of work her father did, although she assured them that he was not at all the kind of man to be seduced by a fairy, but it was Alastor who told them the story of the little girl whose wicked guardian knew the secret of making nightingales sing by day. Catriona could not tell that story without shuddering, and she did not altogether approve when her husband told the fascinated children that *she* had once been nicknamed Nightingale, even though she had always been able to sing by day.

"In actual fact," Catriona told her children—using a phrase she had picked up in the city—"nightingales are not very good singers at all. It is the mere fact of their singing by night that is remarkable, not the quality of their performance."

"Why can we not hear them?" Handsel asked. "I have never heard *any* bird sing by night."

"There are no nightingales in the city," she told them. "They are rare even in the forests above the village where I was born."

"As rare as the fairy-folk?" asked Chanterelle.

"Even rarer, alas," said Catriona. "Had more of my neighbors heard one, they might have been content with my given name, which comes from *katharos*, or purity."

As Alastor had hoped, Handsel soon showed an aptitude for woodwork, and he eventually joined his father in the workshop. He showed an aptitude for music too, and was soon able to produce a tune of sorts out of any instrument he came across. Chanterelle was no disappointment either; she proved to have a lovely voice. She sang by day and she sang by night, and on Sundays she sang in the choir at the church that Alastor and Catriona now attended.

All was well—until the plague came.

"It is not so terrible a plague as some," Alastor said to Catriona, when Handsel was the first of them to fall ill. "It is not as rapacious as the one in the story of the great black spider—the one which terrified and blighted a Highland village, infecting the inhabitants with fevers that sucked the blood and the life from every last one. This is a disease which the strong and the lucky may resist, if only fortune favors them."

"We must do what we can to help fortune," Catriona said. "We must pray, and we must nurse the child as best we can. He *is* strong."

The instrument-maker and his wife prayed, and they nursed poor Handsel as best they could—but within a week, Chanterelle had caught the fever too.

Alastor and Catriona redoubled their efforts, praying and nursing, fighting with every fiber of flesh and conviction of spirit for the lives of their children. Fortune favored them, at least to the extent of granting their most fervent wishes. Handsel recovered from the fever, and so did Chanterelle—but Catriona fell ill, and so did Alastor.

The roles were now reversed; it was the turn of Handsel and Chanterelle to play nurse. They tended the fire, boiled the water, picked the vegetables, and cooked the meat. They ran hither and yon in search of bread and blankets, candles and cough-mixture, and they prayed with all the fervor of their little hearts and high voices.

Catriona recovered in due course, but Alastor died.

"I was not strong enough," Handsel lamented. "My hands were not clever enough to do what needed to be done."

"My voice was not sweet enough," mourned Chanterelle. "My prayers were not lovely enough for Heaven to hear."

"You must not think that," Catriona said to them. "Neither of you is at fault."

They assured her that they understood—and it seemed that Handsel, perhaps because he was the elder, really did understand. But from that day forward, Chanterelle refused to sing. She would not join in with the choir in church, nor would she sing at home, by day or by night, no matter how hard Handsel tried to seduce her voice with his tunes.

Catriona and Handsel tried to complete the instruments that Alastor had left unfinished. They even tried to begin more—but Handsel's hands were only half grown and his skills

less than half trained, and Catriona's full-grown hands had
no woodworking skill at all. In the end, Catriona and her
children had no alternative but to sell the shop and their
home with it. They had no place to go but the Highland
village where Catriona's parents lived.

The journey to the Highlands was long and by no means
easy, but their arrival in the village brought no relief. The
plague had left the highest parts of the Highlands untouched, for no fever likes to visit places that are too high
on a hill, but it had insinuated itself into the valleys, descended on the villages with unusual ferocity. When the
exhausted Catriona and her children finally presented themselves at the foundry, they found it closed, and the house
beside it was dark and deserted.

Neighbors told Catriona that her mother had died, and
her mother's sister, and her father's brother, and her father's
brother's wife, and both their sons, her only cousins.

The catalogue of catastrophe was so extended that Catriona did not notice, at first, that her father's name was not
included in it—but when she did, the flicker of hope that
burst forth in her frightened mind was quenched within
a minute.

"Your father," the neighbors said, "was driven mad by
loss and grief. He fled into the wild forest, determined to
live like a bear or a wolf—for only bears and wolves, he
said, know the true joy of unselfconsciousness. Before he
went he cast the bell that he had made for our church into
the tarn, declaring that the spirits of the lake were welcome
to roll it back and forth, so that its echoes would toll within
his heart like the knell of doom. He had heard a story, it
seems, about another founder of bells who went to dwell in
the wild forest, among the fairy-folk."

"He told me the story half a hundred times, when I was
a child," Catriona admitted. "But that was a tale of vaulting
ambition, about a man who sought unprecedented glory in
the mountain heights because he was seduced by a fairy. If
what you say is true, my father has been stolen rather than
seduced, by demons and not by fairies."

"We are good Christians," the neighbors said piously.
"We know that there is no difference between demons and

fairies, no matter what those with the second sight may say. The house is yours now, by right of inheritance, and the foundry too—you are welcome to make what use of them you will." Perhaps that was honest generosity, or perhaps the villagers thought that the foundry and house were both accursed by virtue of the death and madness to which they had played host. In either case, the donation was useless; if Catriona and Handsel could not run a workshop in the city, they certainly could not run an iron-foundry in a Highland village.

"There is only one thing to be done," Catriona told the children. "I must go into the wild forest to search for my father. If only I can find him, I might make him see sense. At least I can show him that he is not alone. Pray that the idea of meeting his grandchildren for the first time will persuade him that it is better to live as a human than run wild as a bear or a wolf."

"Will he not be a werewolf, if he has been away too long?" Handsel asked. "There is a story, is there not . . . ?"

"You are thinking of the tale in which an abandoned boy became king of the bears," Catriona told him, firmly, although she knew that he was thinking of another blood-curdling tale of Alastor's. "He called upon their aid to reclaim his inheritance, if you remember, and they obliged. What I must do is help my father to reclaim *his* heritage."

"But what shall we do," Chanterelle asked, in the whisper that was now her voice, "if you are lost, and cannot return? What shall we do if the fairy-folk take you away, or if the werewolves eat you? What will become of us then?"

"I *will* return," said Catriona, even more firmly than before. "Neither fairy nor werewolf shall prevent me." She knew even as she spoke, however, that there were too many stories in which such promises were made and never kept— and so did Chanterelle.

Handsel had sense enough to hold his tongue, and wish his mother well, but Chanterelle was too frightened to do anything but beg her not to go. Handsel had enough of the city in him to know that stories were not always to be taken literally, but Chanterelle—perhaps because she was younger—did not. Catriona could not comfort her, no matter how hard she tried.

Catriona realized that when *she* had been a child she had known the reality of the wild woods as well as the stories that were told about them, while Chanterelle knew only what she had heard in stories. Alastor had overlooked that point of difference when he had insisted that the children must be told the stories that he had known when he was a boy.

"Please don't be afraid, Chanterelle," Catriona said, when she finally set out. "The fairy-folk never harmed me before."

"But they will not remember you," said Chanterelle. "You're a stranger now. Don't go."

"I must," said Catriona. "What earthly use is an iron-foundry without an iron-master?"

The two children found that the charity of their new neighbors lasted a full week. At first they were able to go from door to door, saying: "We are the grandchildren of the village iron-master and our mother has gone to search for him in the wild forest. Could you spare us a loaf of bread and a little cheese, or perhaps an egg or two, until our mother returns?"

As the days went by, however, the women who came to the door when they knocked began to say: "We have fed you once; it is someone else's turn"—and when the children pointed out that everyone in the village who was willing had taken a turn, the women said: "We have no guarantee that your mother will ever return, and even if she does, she has no means to repay us. The parish has its own poor; you are strangers. We have done all that we must, and all that we can."

When ten days had gone by without any sign of their mother, Handsel and Chanterelle went to the village church and said to the priest: "Advise us, please, as to what we should do. We have prayed long and hard, but our prayers have not been answered."

"I am not surprised, alas," said the priest. "Your grandfather was a good man once, but in casting the bell intended for our church into the dark waters of the tarn he committed an act of sacrilege as well as an act of folly. There is a story, you see, about an iron-master who was seduced away from faith and family when a church-bell he had founded was lost in a lake. Your grandfather was knowingly putting himself in that man's place, asking for damnation. It is good of you to pray for his return, but if he does not ask forgiveness for himself, one can hardly expect Heaven to grant it, and even then—"

"Yes," said Handsel, "we understand all that. But what shall we *do?*"

"There is no living for you here, alas," said the priest with a sigh. "You must go into the forest in search of your mother, and pray with all the might of your little hearts that *she* can still be found. It is possible, after all, that she is still alive. The forest is full of food, for those bold enough to risk its hazards. It is the season for hazelnuts, and brambleberries, and there are always mushrooms. It is time to commit yourself to the charity of Heaven, my little darlings. I know that Heaven will not let you down, if you have virtue enough to match your courage. There is a story about a boy named Handsel, as I recall, and his little sister, which ended happily enough—not that I, a priest, can approve of the pagan taint which such stories invariably have. In the final analysis, there is only one *true* story, and it is the story of the world."

"That isn't so, sir," said Chanterelle. "There are hundreds of true stories—perhaps thousands. I only know a few, but my grandfather must be old enough to know far more."

"You are only a child," the priest said tolerantly. "When you are older, you will know what I mean. If your grandfather can recover his lost wits, he will be wise to forget all the stories he ever knew, except for the one which holds the promise of our salvation. I wish you all the luck in the world, little Gretel, and I am sure that if you deserve it, Heaven will serve you well."

"My name is Chanterelle, not Gretel," Chanterelle corrected him.

"Of course," said the priest serenely, "and you can sing

like a nightingale, Chanterelle, as your mother could when she was young and lovely?''

"My mother is lovely still," Chanterelle replied, with unusual dignity in one so young, "and she can still sing— but I have never heard a nightingale, so I don't know which of them is better."

"When we say that a human sings like a nightingale," the priest said, with a slightly impatient smile, "we do not mean it *literally*. That is to say, we do not mean it *exactly*."

"Thank you," said Handsel, taking his sister's hand. "We shall take your excellent advice." Even Chanterelle could tell by the way he said "excellent" that he did not mean it *exactly*—but the advice was taken nevertheless. On the morning of the next day, Handsel and Chanterelle set off into the wild forest to search for their mother. Their new neighbors waved goodbye to them as they went.

The priest had told them the truth, at least about the season. There were indeed hazelnuts on the hazel-trees and ripe brambleberries on the brambles. The only problems were that hazel-trees were not easy to find among all the other trees, none of which bore any edible nuts, and that brambles were equipped with ferocious thorns that snagged their clothing and left bloody trails on their hands and arms.

There were mushrooms too, but at first the two children were afraid to touch them.

"Some mushrooms are poisonous," Handsel told his sister. "There are death-caps and destroying angels, and I do not know how to tell them apart from the ones which are safe to eat. I heard a story once which said that fairies love to squat on the heads of mushrooms, and that although those which the good fairies use remain perfectly safe to eat, those which are favored by naughty fairies become coated with an invisible poisonous slime."

Even Chanterelle did not suppose that this story was entirely trustworthy, but she agreed with Handsel that they ought to avoid eating mushrooms, at least until the two of them became desperate with hunger. By the end of the first day they were certainly hungry, but by no means desperate, and it was not until they had been searching for a second day that desperation and its cousin despair began to set in. On their first night they had slept long and deep, but even though they were exhausted they found it more difficult to sleep on the second night. When they finally did go to sleep, they slept fitfully, and they woke up as tired as they had been when they settled down.

Unfortunately, the wild forest was not consistent in its nature. Although the lower slopes were host to hazel-trees and brambles, such plants became increasingly scarce as the two children went higher and higher. Their third day of searching brought them into a region where all the trees seemed to be dressed in dark, needlelike leaves and there was nothing at all to eat except for mushrooms. They had not yet found the slightest sign of their mother, their grandfather, or any other human soul, even though Handsel had shouted himself hoarse calling out to them.

"Well," said Handsel as they settled down to spend a third night in the forest, bedded down on a mattress of leaf-litter, "I suppose Heaven must be on our side, else we'd have been eaten by wolves or bears before now. If we're to eat at all tonight we must trust our luck to guide us to the most nourishing mushrooms and keep us safe from the worst."

"I suppose so," said Chanterelle, who had been keeping watch on all the mushrooms they passed, hoping to catch a glimpse of a fairy at rest. She had seen none as yet, but that did not make her any happier while they made their first meal of mushrooms, washed down with water from a spring. They found it difficult to sleep again, and tried to comfort one another by telling stories—but they found the stories comfortless and they slept badly.

They made another meal of white mushrooms, which settled their hunger after a fashion and caused their stomachs no considerable upset. As the day's journey went higher and deeper into the forest, however, they found fewer and fewer of that kind.

Handsel continued to shout occasionally, but his throat was raw and his voice echoed mockingly back at him, as if the trees were taunting him with the uselessness of his attempts to be heard. Chanterelle helped as best she could, but her voice had never been as strong as it was sweet, even when she sang with the choir, and it seemed much feebler now.

When darkness began to fall yet again, and the two of them were badly in need of a meal, Handsel proposed that they try the red mushrooms with white patches, which were much commoner in this region than the white ones they had gathered on the lower slopes. Chanterelle did not like the look of them at all and said that she would rather go hungry.

"Oh well," said Handsel, "I suppose the sensible thing to do would be for *one* of us to try them, so that their safety can be put to the proof."

Again they found it difficult to go to sleep, but they decided to suffer in silence rather than tell discomfiting stories. The forest, of course, refused to respect their silence by falling silent itself; the wind stirred the branches of the trees restlessly—but tonight, for the first time, they heard another sound.

"Is that a nightingale?" Chanterelle asked her brother.

"I suppose so," Handsel replied. "I never heard of any other bird that sings at night—but it's not as sweet a singer as the birds that were kept in cages by people in the city. They had at least a hint of melody about their songs."

"It may not have much melody," said Chanterelle, "but I never heard a song so plaintive."

"If it *is* a nightingale," said Handsel, "I can't begin to understand why the old man in the story thought the secret of making them sing by day so very precious."

"I can," whispered Chanterelle.

When she finally fell asleep, Chanterelle dreamed that an old man was chasing her through the forest, determined to make her sing again, even if he had to do to her what the old man in the story had done—first to the nightingales, and in the end to Luscignole. Usually, such nightmares continued until she woke in alarm, but this one was different. In this one, just as the old man was about to catch her, a she-wolf jumped on his back and knocked him down—and then set about devouring him while Chanterelle looked on, her anxious heart slowing all the while as her terror ebbed away.

When the wolf had finished with the bloody mess that had been the old man, she looked at Chanterelle and said: "You were right about the mushrooms. They'd been spoiled by fairies of the worst kind. You'll have a hard job rescuing your brother, but it *might* be done, if only you have the heart and the voice."

"Mother?" said Chanterelle fearfully. "Have you become a werewolf, then? Is Grandfather a werewolf too?"

"It's not so bad," said the she-wolf, "but Grandfather was wrong to think he'd find the solace of unselfconsciousness in the world of bears and wolves. Remember, Chanterelle—*don't eat the mushrooms.*"

Having said that, the she-wolf ran away into the forest— and Chanterelle awoke.

Handsel was already up and about. He appeared much fitter than he had been the previous day, and he was much more cheerful than before, but he seemed to have lost his voice. When he spoke to Chanterelle, it was in a hoarse and grating whisper.

"You must eat *something*, Chanterelle," he told her. "We must keep our strength up. The red-capped mushrooms are perfectly safe, as you can see. I've suffered no harm."

Had Chanterelle not had the dream, she might have believed him, but the dream made her determined to leave the red-capped mushrooms alone.

"Did you dream last night?" Chanterelle asked her brother.

"Yes I did," he croaked, "and rather frightening dreams they were—but they turned out all right in the end."

"Was there a wolf in your dream?"

"No. There were other monsters, but no wolves."

"I can't eat the mushrooms," Chanterelle told him. "I just can't."

"You will," he said, "when you're hungry enough. You'll need all your strength, I fear, because I can't raise my voice at all. It's up to you now. You have to sing out loud and clear."

"I can't do that either," said Chanterelle, her voice falling to a whisper almost as sepulchral as his. She was afraid that he would become angry, but he didn't. He was still her brother, even if he had eaten mushrooms enslimed by naughty fairies.

"In that case," she said, "we'll have to hunt for mother without calling out."

That was what they did, all morning and all afternoon. The forest was so gloomy now that even the noonday hours hardly seemed daylit at all. The dark-clad branches of the pines and spruces were so dense and so extensive that it was difficult to catch the merest glimpse of blue sky—and where the sun's rays did creep through the canopy they were reduced to slender shafts, more silver than golden. For four days they had wandered without catching sight of any predator more dangerous than a wildcat, although they had seen a number of roe deer and plenty of mice. That afternoon, however, they were confronted by a bear.

It was not a huge bear, and its thinning coat was showing distinct traces of mange, but it was a great deal bigger than they were, and its ill-health only made it more anxious to make a meal of them. No sooner had it caught sight of them than it loped toward them, snuffling and snarling with excitement and showing all of its yellow teeth.

Handsel and Chanterelle ran away as fast as they could—but Chanterelle was smaller than Handsel, and much weaker. Before they had gone a hundred yards she was too tired to run any farther, and her legs simply gave way. She fell, and shut her eyes tight, waiting for the snuffling, snarling bear to put an end to her with its rotten teeth. She felt its fetid breath upon her back as it reached her and paused—but then it yelped, and yelped again, and the force of its breath was abruptly relieved.

When Chanterelle opened her eyes she saw that Handsel had stopped running. He was snatching up cones that had fallen from the trees, and stones that had lodged in the crevices of their spreading roots. He was throwing these missiles as quickly as he could, hurling them into the face of the astonished bear—and the bear was retreating before the assault!

In fact, the bear was running away. It had conceded defeat.

"He wasn't hungry enough," Handsel whispered when the bear had gone. "Are *you* hungry enough yet, Chanterelle?"

"No," said Chanterelle, and tried to get up—but she had twisted her ankle and couldn't walk on it. "It'll be all right soon," she said faintly. "Tomorrow, we can go on."

"If the bear doesn't come back," Handsel said hoarsely. "When it's hungry enough, it might. If we can't search any longer, you really ought to sing. A song might be heard where shouting wouldn't."

"I can't," said Chanterelle.

Handsel said no more. Instead, he went to gather red-capped mushrooms. When he came back, his shirt was bulging under the burden of a full two dozen—but all he had in his hands was a tiny wooden pipe.

"I found this," he murmured. "It couldn't have been hollowed out without a proper tool, and the finger-holes are very neat. Mother had nothing like it, but I suppose it might be Grandfather's. Perhaps Father made it for him long ago, and gave it to him as a parting gift when he took Mother away to the town. If it's not Grandfather's, it's the first real sign we've found of the fairy-folk. I think I have breath enough to play. Perhaps, if you have a tune to follow, you'll be able to sing."

So saying, Handsel sat down beside his sister and began to play on the little pipe. He had no difficulty at all producing a tune, but it was as faint as his voice if not as scratchy. It was pitched higher than any tune she had ever heard from flute or piccolo.

"It *must* be a fairy flute," said Chanterelle anxiously. "All the stories say that humans must beware of playing elfin music, lest they be captured by the fairy-folk."

Handsel stopped playing and inspected the pipe. "I could have made it myself," he croaked. "Smaller hands than mine might have made it as easily, I suppose."

"Elfin music loosens the bonds of time, in the tales that Mother used to tell," said Chanterelle, "and time untied has weight for no man . . . whatever that's supposed to mean."

"I think it means that while a fairy flute plays a single song, years may pass in villages and towns," said Handsel.

"I only wanted to help you sing, Chanterelle—but now the dusk is falling and the darkness is deepening. I couldn't see a bear by night, Chanterelle. I couldn't hurt his nose and eyes with pinecones. If the bear comes back, it will gobble us up. *Are you sure you cannot sing, even if I play a tune?*"

"Even if you play a tune, dear Handsel," Chanterelle told him, "I could not sing a note. Even if you were to do what the old man in the story did—"

"I never understood how that was supposed to work," Handsel said, his voice like wind-stirred grass. "On nightingales, perhaps—but what good would it do to run red hot needles into poor Luscignole's eyes? Will you eat some mushrooms, Chanterelle? I fear for your life if you won't."

"A she-wolf warned me against them," said Chanterelle. "I dare not—unless she comes to me again by night and tells me that I may."

Handsel would not press her. He set about his own meal quietly—but he was careful to show her that he had only eaten half the mushrooms he had gathered, and would save the rest for her.

When night fell, Chanterelle tried to sleep. She wanted to see her mother again, even if her mother had to come to her in the guise of a wolf. Alas, she could not sleep. Hunger gnawed at her stomach so painfully that she soon became convinced the bear could have done no worse. She tried to fight the pain, but the only way she could do that was to call up a tune within her head, and the only tune she could summon was the tune that Handsel had begun to play on the wooden pipe which had somehow been left for him to find.

It was an old tune, perfectly familiar, but she had never heard it played so high. Chanterelle was afraid that it might be the key in which a tune was played that made it into elfin music, rather than the tune itself. At first, when the tune went round and round and round in her sleepless mind, there was nothing but the sound of the pipe to be "heard," but as it went on and on it was gradually joined by a singing voice: a voice that was *not* her own.

Eventually, Chanterelle realized that although the sound

of the pipe was in her head, conjured up by her own imagination, the voice was not. The voice was real, growing in
strength because the singer was growing closer—but how
could it be, she wondered, that the imaginary pipe and the
real voice were keeping such perfect harmony?

Chanterelle sat up and began to shake her sleeping
brother, who responded to her urging with manifest
reluctance.

"Let me sleep!" he muttered. "For the love of Heaven,
let me sleep!"

"Someone is coming," she hissed in his ear. "Either we
are saved, at least for a while, or lost forever. Can you not
hear her song?"

The singer was indeed a female, and when she came
in view—lit by the lantern she bore aloft—Chanterelle was
somewhat reassured, for she was taller by far than the fairy-
folk were said to be. The newcomer wore a long white dress
and a very curious cape made from bloodred fur, flecked
with large white sequins. She had two dogs with her, both
straining at the leash. They were like no dogs Chanterelle
had ever seen: lean and white, like huge spectral grey-
hounds, each with a stride so vast that it could have out-
sprinted any greyhound in the world.

"*Bad* dogs," said the lady, who had stopped singing as
soon as her lantern revealed the two children to the inspection of her pale and penetrating eyes. "*This* is not the prey
for which you were set to search. These are children, lost in
the wilderness. Were you abandoned here, my lovelies?" As
she spoke she looked down at Chanterelle. Her eyes seemed
strangely piercing; it was as if she could look into the inner
chambers of a person's heart. Chanterelle hoped that it was
a trick of the lantern-light.

"We came in search of our mother," said Chanterelle.
"Have you seen her?"

"I've seen no one, child," the lady replied. "I'm hunting
a she-wolf which has plundered my birdhouse once too
often. I thought that Verna and Virosa had her scent, but it
seems not. What are your names?"

"I'm Chanterelle, and this is my brother Handsel."

"Why are you whispering, child?" the lady asked, although her own voice was low and her singing had been soft, in spite of the notes she had to reach.

"Misfortune and too much shouting have weakened our voices," Handsel explained. "Have you bread, perchance— my sister will not eat the mushrooms which grow here- abouts, because she fears they have been poisoned by the fairies."

"Those old wives' tales are best forgotten," the lady said, "but I have bread at home, and meat too, if you can walk as far as my house."

"I can," whispered Handsel, "but Chanterelle cannot. She twisted her ankle while fleeing from a bear."

"Well,"' said the lady, without much enthusiasm, "I suppose I can carry her, if you will hold the lantern and my dogs—but you'll have to be strong, for they can pull like the Devil when they're of a mind to do so."

"I can do that," said Handsel.

The lady gave the lantern and the two leashes to Hand- sel, and bent to take Chanterelle in her arms. For a fleeting instant the warmth of her breath reminded Chanterelle of the bear, but it was sweeter by far—and the lady's slender arms were surprisingly strong.

"Who are you?" Chanterelle asked as she was borne aloft.

"My name is Amanita," the lady said, turning around to follow the dogs, which had already set off for home with Handsel in tow.

"I hope your house is not made of gingerbread," mur- mured Chanterelle.

"What a thing to say!" the woman exclaimed. "Indeed it is not. Whatever made you think it might be?"

"There is a story about a boy named Handsel, who was lost with his sister in a wild forest," Chanterelle told her. "They found a house of gingerbread and began to eat it— but the witch who owned it caught them and put them in a cage."

"It's exactly as I said," the lady observed. "Old wives' tales are full of nonsense, and mischief too. Do you think I'm a witch?"

"You were singing a song," said Chanterelle uneasily.

"I was remembering a tune, and your song fitted the tune. If that's not witchcraft, what is?"

"You poor thing," said the lady, clutching Chanterelle more tightly to her, so that Chanterelle could feel the warmth of the bloodred fur from which her cape was made. "You've been sorely confused, I fear. Don't you see, dear child, that it must have been my song that started the tune in your head? Your ears must have caught it before your mind did, so that when your mind caught up it seemed that the tune had been there before. But you're right, of course; if there's no witchcraft there, there's no witchcraft any-where—and that's the truth."

Chanterelle knew better than to believe it. She had heard too many stories in her time to think the world devoid of magic. She knew that she would have to beware of the lady Amanita, whatever her house turned out to be made of.

The sleep that Chanterelle had been unable to find while she lay on the bare ground, fearful of the bear's return, came readily enough now that she was clasped in Amanita's arms. The lady did not carry her quite as tenderly as her mother would have, but the warmth of the red cape seemed to soak into Chanterelle's enfeebled flesh, relaxing her mind. In addi-tion, the lady began to sing again, albeit wordlessly, and the rhythm of her voice was lullaby-gentle and lullaby-sweet.

In such circumstances, Chanterelle might have expected sweeter dreams, but it was not to be. This time, she found herself alone by night in a vast and drafty church—vaster by far than any church in the town where she had lived, let alone the village whose priest had advised them to search for their mother in the forest. Its wooden pews formed a great shadowy maze, and Chanterelle was searching that maze for a likely hiding place—but whenever she found one, she would hear ominous footsteps coming closer and closer, until they came so horribly close that she could not help but slip away, scurrying like a mouse in search of some deeper and darker hidey-hole. She never saw her pursuer, but she knew well enough who he must be and what he must be holding in his gnarled and arthritic hand. She knew, too, that no she-wolf could come to her aid in such a place as this—for werewolves cannot set foot on consecrated ground, no matter how noble their purpose might be, nor how diabolical the schemes they might seek to interrupt.

When Chanterelle awoke, she realized that she was in a bed with linen sheets. When she opened her eyes she saw that the bed had a quilt as red as Amanita's cape, patterned with white diamonds as neatly sewn as any she had ever seen. It was obvious that the lady Amanita was an excellent seamstress—which meant, of course, that she must possess a sharp, sleek, and polished needle.

Bright daylight shone through a single latticed window the shape and size of a wagon-wheel. Handsel was already up and about, as he had been the morning before. As soon as he saw that his sister was astir, he rushed to her bedside.

"Isn't this wonderful?" he said, gesturing with his arm to indicate the room in which they had been placed. As well as the bed on which Chanterelle lay, it had a number of chairs, one of them a rocking-chair; it also had a huge wooden wardrobe, a chest of drawers, a wooden trunk, and a tiny three-legged table. The walls were exceptionally smooth, but their gray surfaces were dappled with black, and the curiously ragged shelves set into them were an offensive shade of orange.

"No gingerbread at all?" Chanterelle whispered.

"None," said Handsel, who had obviously recovered the full use of his voice during the night. "I'll bring you some *real* bread. It's freshly baked."

Handsel left the room—passing through a doorway that was far from being a perfect rectangle, although the door fit snugly enough—before Chanterelle could ask where a woman who lived alone in the remotest regions of the Highland forest could buy flour to bake into bread. When he returned a few minutes later, Amanita was with him, carrying a tray that bore a plate of what looked like neatly sliced bread and a cup of what looked like milk.

Alas, the bread had neither the odor nor the color of wheaten bread, and the milk had neither the color nor the viscosity of cow's milk.

"I can't," said Chanterelle weakly.

"Of course you can," said Handsel.

"It's not poison," said the lady Amanita—but Chanterelle did not believe her.

"You're a bad fairy," said Chanterelle to Amanita.

"You're a silly fool," said Amanita to Chanterelle.

"This is pointless," said Handsel, to no one in particular. "We can't go on like this—and if we don't go on, how will we *ever* find our mother?"

"You won't," said Amanita. "This isn't like one of your stories, you know. This is the real world. Your mother never had the slightest hope of finding your grandfather, and you don't have the slightest hope of finding your mother. They'll both be dead by now—and you ought to count yourselves very lucky that you're not dead yourselves. You will be, Chanterelle, if you won't eat."

"Poor Chanterelle," said Handsel, who seemed even fitter and bolder today than he had when he drove off the bewildered bear, and was in far better voice. "Can't eat, can't walk, can't sing, can't do anything at all. How can we save you, little sister?"

"Find Mother," Chanterelle replied. "Leave me, if you must, but *find Mother.*"

"Handsel won't go on without you, Chanterelle," said Amanita. "If you won't get better, he'll stay with you until you die." *And after that*, she didn't add, *he'll stay with me.*

"Find Grandfather," whispered Chanterelle. "Please leave me, Handsel. Find Grandfather, because he can't find himself. The bell in the tarn can't toll, you see. Its chimes can't echo in his heart like the chimes of conscience, drawing him back to his hearth and home. Find Mother, before she loses herself entirely. Find them both, I beg of you. If you love me, go."

"You'll regret it if you do," said Amanita to Handsel.

Handsel seemed to agree with her; he shook his head.

"One more day, Handsel," whispered Chanterelle. "If you'll search for just one more day, I'll eat something. That's a promise. Even if you fail, I'll eat—but *you have to try.*"

That argument worked, as Chanterelle had known it would. "If you're sure you'll be all right," Handsel said dubiously, "I'll go." Even as he said it, though, he looked at Amanita. It was as if he were asking her permission.

Amanita shrugged her shoulders, whose narrowness was evident now that she was no longer wearing the speckled cape. "You might as well," she said, "although I'm sure that there's nothing to find. I'll lend you Verna and Virosa if you like. If there's anything out there, they'll track it down—but you'll have to be strong if you're to hold on to them."

"No," said Chanterelle quickly. "Don't take the dogs. Don't take that little pipe either. Your voice will be enough, now that you've got it back. Search *hard*—you have to find them today, if they're to be found at all."

Again Handsel looked at Amanita, as if for permission. Again Amanita shrugged her narrow shoulders.

"Look after my sister," Handsel said to the white-clad lady. "If anything were to happen to her—"

"Nothing will," said Amanita. "She's safe here. Nothing can hurt her, if she doesn't hurt herself—but if she won't eat—"

"She will," said Handsel firmly. "She will, if I keep my part of the bargain." And having said that, he left.

When the door closed behind him, Amanita looked down at Chanterelle for a full half minute before she put the bread that wasn't wheaten bread and the milk that wasn't cow's milk on the three-legged table. Then she sat down in the rocking-chair, tilting it back so that when she released it she moved gently to and fro. She never took her eyes off Chanterelle, and her brown eyes were exactly as piercing now as they had seemed by tricky lantern-light.

"That was very brave of you, my dear," the lady said at last, "if you really believe what you said about my being a bad fairy."

"I do," said Chanterelle, "and I'm *not* a silly fool."

"That," said the lady, "remains to be seen."

Chanterelle tested her injured ankle by stretching the toes and turning it to the left and the right. The pain she felt made it evident that she still wasn't able to walk, and wouldn't be able to for quite some time. The pain nearly brought tears to her eyes—but the anguish wasn't entirely unwelcome, because it distracted her attention from the awful hunger that felt as if it were hollowing out her belly with a fork.

The fake bread and the fake milk were beginning to seem attractive, in spite of the fact that they were not what they seemed to be. Handsel had obviously eaten them, just as he had eaten the red-capped mushrooms, but Chanterelle couldn't be certain that Handsel was still what he seemed to be.

"I wish you would eat, my dear," said Amanita after a long silence. "If you don't eat, you'll never recover your strength. If you do, you might even recover your voice. You mustn't let stories make you afraid—and in any case, you can see readily enough that my house isn't made of gingerbread."

Chanterelle put out a hand to touch the wall beside the bed. It was softer than she had expected, and warmer. It had a curious texture unlike any wall she'd ever felt before. It wasn't brick or stone, and it wasn't wood or wattle-and-daub.

"It's a mushroom," whispered Chanterelle. "The whole house is a gigantic mushroom. How did it grow so big? It must be magic—*black* magic."

"Magic is neither black nor white, my dear," said Amanita. "Magic either *is* or *isn't*."

"The witch in the house of gingerbread tried to fatten Handsel for the cooking-pot," Chanterelle observed. "She wanted to eat him. Bad fairies and witches are much of a muchness, in all the stories I ever heard."

"Did the witch succeed?" asked Amanita.

"No," said Chanterelle. "Gretel—Handsel's sister, in the story—put an old stick in the witch's hand every time she reached into the cage to see whether Handsel was plump enough to eat yet. The witch was nearsighted, and couldn't tell that it wasn't Handsel's arm. When the witch finally grew impatient and tried to cook Gretel instead, Handsel pushed her into her own oven and cooked *her*. Then the children took the witch's hoard of gold and jewels back to their father, so that they would never be poor again."

"I see," said Amanita. "I fear, dear child, that I am not nearsighted. Were I what you suspect me to be, you'd have no chance at all of escaping me. In any case, it would do you no good if you did bundle me into my own oven. I have no hoard of gold and jewels, and you have no father. Your brother told me *another* story, about a little girl with a marvelous singing voice, who lost the will to sing when her heart was broken—but she was found by the old man who'd kept her when she was a child, who knew the secret of making nightingales sing by day. You know that story, of course."

"I know," whispered Chanterelle fearfully.

"Well," said Amanita, "that's nonsense too. All you need to set *your* voice free is a little bread and milk."

"The bread isn't wheaten bread and the milk isn't cow's milk," said Chanterelle. "The bread is baked from mushrooms and the milk is squeezed from mushroom flesh."

"That's true, as it happens," admitted Amanita. "As you've observed yourself, there's not much food fit for children growing wild in *this* part of the forest. There are insects a-plenty, and animals which eat insects, and animals which eat animals, but children can't hunt. Fortunately, the mushrooms with the red caps *do* make nourishing food. Handsel is as bold and strong as he ever was, don't you think? *He* isn't afraid to eat my bread and drink my milk."

"Handsel will find Mother today," whispered Chanterelle, "and Grandfather too. Then we shall all go home."

"Go home to what?" asked Amanita. She stopped the chair rocking and leaned forward to stare at Chanterelle even more intently than before. "To an empty foundry, which had failed long before the plague came and your grandfather tipped the unfinished church-bell into the tarn? Do you know why no one can hear it tolling in the dark current, least of all its maker? Because it has no tongue! It cannot ring, dear child, any more than you can sing."

"Mother will know what to do," said Chanterelle, so faintly that she could hardly hear herself.

"When Handsel returns," Amanita told her coldly, "you'll understand how foolish you are. Remember your promise, Chanterelle. When Handsel returns, you must eat and drink."

Having said that, Amanita got up and stalked out of the

room, her white skirt swirling about her. The rocking-chair was thrown into violent motion by the abruptness of Amanita's abandonment, and it continued rocking back and forth for what must have been at least an hour.

Chanterelle tried to stay awake, but she was too weak. When she drifted off to sleep, however, the pain in her ankle made it difficult for her to sleep deeply. She remained suspended between consciousness and oblivion, lost in a wilderness of broken dreams.

She dreamed of mournful she-wolves and decrepit bears, of ghostly hunting-dogs which bounded through the forest like malevolent angels, of sweet-smelling loaves of bread which broke to reveal horrid masses of blue-green fungus, of cups of milk infested with tiny worms, of long ranks of club-headed mushrooms which served as cushioned seats for excited fairies, and of wizened old men who knew the secret of making nightingales sing by day.

When she woke again, the room was nearly dark. The patch of blue sky that had been visible through the latticed window had turned to velvet black, but the stars were out and the moon must have been full, for the room was not *entirely* cloaked in shadows.

At first Chanterelle couldn't tell what it was that had awakened her—but then she realized that the door had creaked as it began to open. She watched it move inward, her heart fluttering in dread because she expected to see Amanita.

When she saw that the person coming into the room was Handsel, not Amanita, Chanterelle felt a thrill of relief, which almost turned to joy when she saw the excited expression on his face. For one delicious moment she read that excitement as a sign that he must have found their mother—but when he came closer, she realized that it was something else.

"Oh, Chanterelle!" Handsel whispered as he knelt down beside the bed and put his head on the pillow beside hers. "You've no idea what a day I've had."

"Are you hoarse from shouting," she whispered back, "or are you afraid of waking Amanita?"

"Amanita's not here," Handsel said in a slightly louder voice. "She must have gone out again with those dogs of hers to hunt the she-wolf. I shouted myself hoarse all morning, as I knew I must, but no one answered. Then I stopped to pick and eat more mushrooms. Then I began to shout again, but it was no use at all. I had lost my voice—*but I had gained my sight!*"

"You never lost your sight," said Chanterelle faintly.

"I never *had* my sight, dear sister. I always *thought* that I could see, but now I know that I never saw clearly before today. I had never seen the trees, or the earth, or the air, or the sun.

"Today, for the first time, I saw the life of the trees, the richness of the earth, the color of the air and the might of the sun. Today, for the first time, I saw the world as it truly is. I saw the fairy-folk about their daily business. I saw dryads drawing water from the depths and breathing for the trees. I saw kobolds churning the soil to make it fertile. I saw sylphs sweeping the sky and ondines bubbling the springs.

"Oh Chanterelle, you were right about the mushrooms—and yet so very wrong! The fairy-folk swarm about them, hungry for pleasure, and make them grow tall and red, but there's no *poison* in them. There's only nourishment, for the mind as well as the body. Those who eat of the mushrooms tended by the fairy-folk may learn to see as well as growing strong. You must not be afraid of eating, Chanterelle. You must not starve yourself of light and life."

"I *am* afraid," said Chanterelle, and shut her eyes for a moment. She knew that the sight Handsel had discovered must be the *second* sight of which the stories told, which was sometimes a blessing and sometimes a curse. She had always thought that if either of them turned out to have the second sight, it would be her, and she felt a sharp pang of jealousy. She, after all, was the one who could sing—or *had* been able to sing, before grief took the melody out of her voice.

When she opened her eyes again, Handsel was no longer there—or, if he was, he was no longer Handsel. Kneeling beside her bed was the strangest creature she had ever seen. It was part human, having human legs and human arms, but it was also part insect, having the wings and head of a hawk-moth. Where the human and insect flesh met and fused, in the trunk from neck to hip, there was a soft carapace mottled with white stars. Even in the dim light, Chanterelle could see that the color of the carapace was crimson, exactly like Amanita's cape.

The huge compound eyes looked at Chanterelle with what might have been tenderness. The principal part of the creature's mouth was a pipelike structure coiled like a fern-leaf, which gradually uncoiled and stiffened, so that the tip reached out to caress her face.

When the creature spoke to her, its words sounded as if they were notes produced by some kind of flute, and every sentence was a delicate musical phrase.

"The sweetest nectar of all is fairy blood," the monster informed her, "but the fairy-folk offer it willingly. Human blood is bitter, spoiled as anything is spoiled that is kept for far too long. Iron bells are hard and cold, and their voices are the tyrants of time. The bells of forest flowers are soft and beautiful, and their voices can unloose the bonds of the hours and the days. When humans go mad, they usually become bears or wolves, but find neither solace nor liberation. The fairy-folk are forever mad, forever joyous, forever free. Children may still be changelings if they choose. While the true sight has not quite withered away, children may find the one true path. While the true voice is not yet lost, children may soar on wings of song."

If only the monster had chosen its words more carefully, Chanterelle thought, it might have contrived a melody of sorts—but she had heard the songs of the skylarks and thrushes that the city-dwellers kept in cages, and she knew full well that even they had little enough talent for melody. Nightingales, for all their fame, were merely plaintive.

Chanterelle shut her eyes again and counted to ten. When she opened them, the monster was gone and Handsel was himself again.

"What did you say?" asked Chanterelle, in a voice as faint as faint could be.

"I said that we might be safe and happy here," murmured Handsel, in a voice that was not quite lost. "If we can only persuade Amanita to take us in, we might live here forever. She must be lonely, must she not? She has no husband, and no children of her own. She might accept us as her children, if we promise to be good. Wouldn't you like to live in an enchanted forest, sister dear?"

"I would rather find my mother," said Chanterelle.

"We have tried and failed," said Handsel sadly, "and must make the best of things. Would you rather starve than eat? Would you rather go down to the valley, where no charity waits us, than stay in the wild forest and live as the fairy-folk live? You promised, did you not, that you would eat Amanita's bread and drink her milk if I could not find our mother or our grandfather in one more day of searching? I have tried, and failed; I have lost my voice, but I can see. Will you eat, dear sister, and live—or will you break your promise, and die?"

"I will eat and drink in the morning," whispered Chanterelle. "If Mother has not found us by then, I will eat Amanita's mushroom-bread and drink her mushroom-milk."

Handsel stood up and turned toward the door.

"Don't go!" said Chanterelle.

"I have my own room now," said Handsel, "and my own bed."

No sooner was Chanterelle alone than the room grew noticeably darker. A cloud must have drifted across the face of the moon. Chanterelle moved her injured foot from left to right and back again, and then she stretched her toes. The result was agony—but it was the kind of agony that chased sleep away, and delirium too. Her mind had never been sharper.

Because she had no voice, Chanterelle cried out silently for her mother and her grandfather. *If you don't come by morning*, she thought with all the fervor she could muster, *you will come too late. If you don't come by morning, I shall be lost.*

In stories, she knew, such silent cries sometimes brought results. In stories, panic was sometimes as powerful as prayer. She prayed as well, though, in the hope that even if her mother and her grandfather could not help her, Heaven might.

As before, the pain could not keep sleep at bay indefinitely, but the sleep to which Chanterelle was delivered was shallow and turbulent.

She dreamed that she was running through the forest yet again, still pursued by an old man who carried a long needle in each hand. All night long his footsteps grew closer and closer, until at last she sank exhausted to the ground and waited for the inevitable.

The old man had no chance to use the needles; he was knocked flying by the paw of a bear, which then limped away into the forest with its ancient head held low. When the old man attempted to rise again, he was confronted by a she-wolf whose gray coat was flecked with blood. For a moment or two it seemed that he might try to defy the she-wolf, which was limping almost as badly as the bear, but when she showed her bright white teeth, he thought better of it and ran off, taking his needles with him.

"Thank you," Chanterelle whispered to the she-wolf.

"Don't thank me," said the wolf, sinking down beside her. "I can't help you. I can't even help myself." The wolf began licking at her wounds. Both her hind legs had been bitten, and her belly too. It was obvious that the hounds had almost brought her down.

"Who will help me if you cannot?" asked Chanterelle. "Must I trust in Heaven?"

The she-wolf stopped licking long enough to say: "Heaven is a poor ally to those still on Earth, else plague would have no power to consign us to damnation. Had you kept your promises, you'd be beyond help already—and those who are less than honest can hardly look to Heaven for salvation."

"Then what will become of me?" asked Chanterelle.

The wolf was too busy feeding on its own blood to give her an immediate answer, but when her fur was clean again she looked the child full in the face with sorrowful eyes.

"I wish I knew," the wolf said. "I can't even tell you the answer to your other question."

"What other question?" asked Chanterelle.

"Why the girl sang again when she was captured for a second time by the man who knew the secret of making nightingales sing by day. I don't know the answer. All I know is that there's no more joy in being a wolf than there is in being a bear. I have to go away now. If I stay in this part of the forest, the hounds will have me for sure—and a wolf shouldn't have to live on mice while there are sheep in the valleys."

"Please don't go," begged Chanterelle. "If only you could save me, I think I *might* be able to sing again."

"It's too late," said the wolf as she disappeared into the darkness of the forest.

"It's too late," said Amanita, as Chanterelle woke to morning daylight. "You must eat now, or it will be too late."

Amanita was sitting no more than an arm's reach away from Chanterelle's head, having drawn a chair to the side of the bed—not the rocking-chair, but one of the others. The white-clad woman was holding a bowl full of steaming soup, which had the most delicious scent. The soup was thick and creamy, with solid pieces of a darker hue half submerged beneath the surface.

"Mushroom soup," said Chanterelle very faintly.

"The best mushroom soup in the world," said Amanita. "Not all mushrooms are alike, you know. These are the very best. They're called chanterelles—did you know you had a mushroom's name, my dear? I had to hunt far and wide to find them for you, but I knew that I'd have to find them even if it took all night. Luckily, the moon was full. Only eat this, and you'll be yourself again—or perhaps for the first time ever."

"I don't want it," whispered Chanterelle.

"But you don't have any choice," said Amanita. "You promised Handsel that you'd eat if your mother and grandfather were still lost. You don't understand what's happening here. You don't understand who and what you are. When your father named you Chanterelle, he thought it was a safe name for a nightingale, but he forgot the other meanings of the word. He knew that the highest string of a musical instrument was a chanterelle, but he *should* have known that a chanterelle is the most delicious kind of edible mushroom, and an imitation bird used to draw others into traps.

Fate plays these little tricks all the time, you see. You thought you were supposed to be a singer, but you never knew how to find your voice, or how to use it, until you came to me. All children are kin to the fairy-folk, dear Chanterelle, but only a few have the chance to cross over, to see the world as *we* see it, with the *second* sight. You have that chance, but you must seize it. You must welcome it, because the cost of refusal will be more terrible than you imagine."

"Where's Handsel?" asked Chanterelle. "I must see Handsel."

"In the hope that he can seize me and throw me in my own oven, to burn me alive? In the hope that you and he can run away, laden down with gold and gems? Handsel can *see* now, my darling. Handsel will be my lover now, my darling boy, the sweetest of the sweet."

"I must see Handsel," whispered Chanterelle.

Amanita called out to Handsel to come and see his sister—and Handsel came. He stood beside Amanita, with his arm about her shoulder and his cheek next to hers.

"You must eat, Chanterelle," he said. "If you can't eat, you'll never sing."

"Can't you see that she's a wicked fairy?" Chanterelle asked in a voice so faint as hardly to be there at all.

"I *can* see," said Handsel. "I never could before, but now I can. I never want to be blind again. I couldn't stand it."

"The poor girl thinks that she's a nightingale," said Amanita, softly and sadly. "She can't believe what she really is, and she's starving herself to death because of it. But you know—don't you, darling Handsel?—how nightingales can be taught to sing by day. Tell me what the secret is, darling Handsel."

"The old man trained the nightingales to sing by day by running hot needles into their eyes," Handsel said calmly. "Afterward, they thought eternal night had come, and that was their idea of Heaven—so they sang, and sang, and sang in celebration. When Luscignole first saw what the old man did, she ran away, but that was because she didn't understand her true nature and her true destiny. She lost her voice when her heart broke, and the only way she could find it again was to find Heaven where she had never been able to look before: in eternal darkness."

"We don't need to do anything nearly as unkind as that," said Amanita. "Chanterelle will find her voice if she'll only eat the chanterelles. Eat, dear child, and discover what you truly are!"

Chanterelle could not believe that what was being done to her was any kinder than what had been done to Luscignole. She opened her mouth and tried to scream, but no scream came out. Instead, a spoon went in, bearing a full load of the impossibly delicious soup.

Chanterelle would have swallowed the soup if she had not gagged and choked, but the reflex saved her, and sprayed the contents of the spoon all over the bosom of Amanita's white dress, flecking it with gray and brown. So astonished was Amanita that she dropped the bowl and howled with anguish as the hot liquid flooded the thin fabric of her skirt.

Chanterelle, fearful for her very life, threw back the crimson coverlet that had kept her warm for two nights and a day and made her bid for freedom. She flew across the room to the open window, beating her wings with all the force and skill of long-frustrated instinct, and soared into the welcoming sky.

Some months later, on the first Monday after New Year's Day, Handsel and Amanita were walking in the wild forest by the light of the full moon. Their two ghostly hunting-dogs were beside them, neither needing a leash.

Amanita wore her favorite cape of bloodred fur, flecked with silver sequins. Handsel wore a fur cloak cut from the hide of a brown bear, trimmed along the edges with the silkier fur of a gray she-wolf. The body of the fur was a trifle mangy in places but the cape was warm in spite of the spoiled patches.

"How beautiful the sylphs are as they dance on the moonbeams," Handsel said, "freshening the air with their agility."

"Indeed they are, my love," said Amanita.

"I like the dryads even more," said Handsel. "'They

know the very best of elfin music, and they love to play their pipes when the wind blows. I was a piper myself once, and a plucker too, but I was never very good. One should leave the exercise of such arts to those who know them best."

"Indeed one should, my darling," said Amanita.

"There is another song in the air tonight, is there not?" said Handsel, pausing suddenly and cocking his ear. "There is another voice, even more distant and more plaintive than the dryad pipes. I have heard it before, but never by day and always very faint. What is it?"

"It is the song of a nightingale," said Amanita. "There is a way to make one sing by day, if you remember—but you would have to snare it first, and hold it very still. Would you like me to do that, Handsel? I think I can sing a song which will tempt it from the tree, if you wish. Birds are silly creatures, easily lured by artifice."

Handsel remained where he was for a moment longer, considering this proposition. He frowned as he listened to the plaintive voice, redolent with loss. It seemed, somehow, to be trying to lure him away from Amanita—but he was not the kind of creature who could be tempted by a song.

"What would be the point?" he said. "The poor thing cannot hold a melody at all."

Brian Stableford started with the story structure of "Hansel and Gretel," incorporating significant embellishments borrowed from two modern "art fairy tales": the novella "Luscignole" by Catulle Mendes, and the play "The Sunken Bell" by Gerhardt Hauptmann. The link between fairies and magic mushrooms was appropriated from Maureen Duffy's book on The Erotic World of Faery.

Bear It Away

MICHAEL CADNUM

Michael Cadnum lives in northern California and is a poet and novelist. He is the author of St. Peter's Wolf, Ghostwright, Calling Home, Skyscape, The Judas Glass, Zero at the Bone, Edge, The Lost and Found House, *and other novels. He has also published an illustrated book based on Cinderella called* Ella and the Canary Prince, *and a novel about Robin Hood and the Sheriff of Nottingham. His most recent collection of poetry is* The Cities We Will Never See.

Bear It Away

I never liked the woodland, even in my youth, but the forest here has never been one of your lowly hoar-wilds, all crag and moss. It was really very pleasant, a happy mix of pinecones and little red ants, dock and nettles. You wouldn't want to muss your skirt, going on a picnic in the cockleburs. But it was nice wood, little yellow flowers when the snow melted, and mushrooms shaped like willies. Some of our more prominent watercolorists traveled here to set up their easels, and botanists collected herbs along the streams.

A maiden could go berry picking with the silversmith's son, or slip off to meet the young professor from down-valley, and if she ran across a bear, it would be one of the old traditional bears, little eyes, big rumps, snuffling the air, trying to see if you were trouble or something to eat. If a bear said anything at all it was in antique bear-tongue, not

much to it, really, just *good-bye* or *go away*, all a bear needed
to know.

From time to time a typical bear fracas broke out. A sow
bear killed a miller down by the well, for example, when
he stepped on a cub, it being night and the miller having
lost his spectacles in the inn. The she-bear threw him over
her shoulder and left him by the quarrymen's privy quite a
boneless puddle. But what did we expect? It was reassuring,
in a way, having bears to worry about. Kids afraid of the
dark were easier to quiet down. A sudden gust or a scuttling
acorn on the roof and Mom and Dad would roll their eyes
and whisper, "A bear looking for children who won't eat
their cabbage!"

Gentlemen of rude humor would disguise a burp by
muttering, "Must've been a bear, growling in the glade,"
and if things got boring on a long summer's day, the villagers would unpen the hounds, run down a granddad bruin,
and pen the bear in a sand pit. It was sport, all fair-play,
joy under a summer's eve. Bets would flow hand to hand
on the question which would expire first, bear or dog. Life
was simple. Mosquitoes and holidays, ale and bear skins.

But it changed.

Some people say it was better nutrition, trout multi-
plying as the rivers ran clear. The weather changed, the
magnetic poles shifted—we all had our theories. I don't
know how, but it happened. One day we had dumb bears
rolling logs to gobble worms, and the next we had bears in
the vicarage library. They were wood-bears, still, and kept
off to themselves, when they weren't stocking up on rhym-
ing dictionaries. But a revolution was underway.

It could be overlooked for a while. Bears still slept half
the year and they still had trouble seeing. But when a boar-
bear lumbered into the fletcher's wife one afternoon and
offered effusive apologies for treading on her toe, we all
knew something profound had happened to bear nature.
The bears rushed her to the surgeon, stood around waiting
for news of her recovery. Mrs. Fletcher regained her health
and sanity, until she stepped out a week later to take some
medicinal sun. A bear made way from the midden, dainty-
like, a she-bear, and said, "I hope I see you well."

Which killed the fletcher's dame. She died of the shock. Many of us understood exactly. I didn't mind a bit of sass from a bluejay or the tinsmith's mutt, but I did think that this was more than mortal humans need endure, a curtsy from a bear wearing a bonnet.

Myself, I was blond, and if the glazier liked the look of me as well as the joiner, why, let them all have an eyeful, was how I always felt. I was charitable with my smiles, but when a bear asked how I was on this finest of mornings, and held the post office door open for me, I hurried right past and never said a word.

A long era of tranquillity was underway: bears writing essays, offering opinions on the likelihood of rain, bears making excellent neighbors. And most humans liked this, an age of peace. But I never got used to bears reading haiku, bears laughing at our human jokes. Months went by, entire seasons, and a bear never ate a single human. Not one. There was bear laughter and bear song, noon and night.

I had a plan.

I wanted a hunter, one of those always just in time to drill a musket shot through a wolf's lights. And if he was fine of leg and loin, I wouldn't mind parting the bracken a bit with such a man, not being quite so young as I had been, and looking for the right sort to share my winter nights. Although this was not the point-entire. I wanted to teach the bears why they shouldn't weave rugs and write plays, and give them a lesson they'd never forget.

I wanted to teach them to keep their bear-talk to themselves. And if the cottage-dwelling men were too weak-kneed to educate the bears, I'd find myself a red jacketed crack shot and make him mine.

And so I did. He was a square-jawed elk-hunter from the vale to the east. His red jacket was sappy-brown along the sleeves, and he smelled of brandy, but he showed me how he double-powdered both barrels and blew twin holes in my mum's quilt hanging out to dry—and he paid gold florins for a new one.

He was perfect.

I recall that early morning well, how I tickled him

awake. I tugged him from the bed, red-cheeked, unshaven. I remember the dawn as if it were a week ago, although these days I'm the only one alive who can sing the words to a single bear madrigal. I led my hunter to the woods, mist in the tulips, wood smoke in the thatch. I filled him with my scheme, and before I let him yea-or-nay, I kissed him wide-awake and said, "Follow me."

Bears are fond of walking—or they were, our wise bears used to be. They walked, they slept. Peripatetic brethren, as the priest would say, they were always cooking their oats, howling when the porridge scalded, and using the excuse for another ramble, up one trail and down the next. My hunter and I spied a family, dad, mam, and wee one. They ambled off, blinking in the sunlight, happy as cows to be out in the grass, the little one hopping, rabbit-like. "Stay here," I whispered to my gunner.

I hid behind a berry bush. I waited, and when the family vanished up the trail, I scurried into the cottage. I violated their breakfast bowls, hot and cold, and made sure they would see the mess when they returned to table. Spoon and finger, I tasted, scooped, and splattered. (It was delicious— just the right amount of honey.) I did what I could with the furniture, the chairs and settles too stout for the likes of me to break. All I could manage was a high chair in the corner, one the bear-lad must have just outgrown.

I broke that into kindling, and left it sowed around the nook. I took myself upstairs. I flung wide the shutters so Redcoat would hear me shriek when the time came, and I settled myself in the largest of the three beds. This mattress was packed with straw so coarse it was like sprawling in a thicket. So I tried the middle bed, just my size, but it was so cratered by the weight of Mistress Griz that I climbed up and down the bedding, clinging to the edges.

Finally I escaped the bed and found the laddie's bunk, and slept. Why did you fall asleep, moon-calf? I would demand of myself in years to come. And I have no retort. No clever answer to myself. I lay, I slept. Not one to stoop to excuses, but mayhap the hunter's nip, that brandy wine he said was courage, overdid my wakefulness. "Just a taste," he had said, tasting some himself.

I never heard them on their way. When the three ram-
bled back into the cottage, I had no inkling they were home,
peering at their porridge, aghast at the broken high chair,
nosing the air. Or perhaps I had a hint of what was happening, in one part of my mind.

Step by step, they ascended to the bedroom. The oak
door creaked. Their heavy steps were slow, the floorboards
groaning. Only then did I hear them, words as clear as any
tinker's. "What's this—my pillow all mussed," said the
father.

"And here, my mattress half in, half out," said mum-
bear, nearsighted, nose to her bed. "And me, and me!" cried
the pup-bruin. "My bed too!" he cried.

I am now the only one in the land who knows, how
like to our own speech it was, this language, this Bear
tongue. "Mine too," he stammered, "and she is still—still
here!"

I didn't have to feign my horror, yelling from the window, tangled in a sheet, screaming, bellowing. I called out,
"What are you waiting for?" But my huntsman was lying
in plain sight, sound asleep, sunlight in the green grass
gleaming off his gun.

"She's here, she's here!" cried the cub. Both parents trying to make me out, blinking in the bright morning light
through the open window.

I ran home.

In my haste I soaked my skirts in the ford, dragged
them in the thistles, muddied them and tore them, all the
way to hearth and safety. I was scolded by my mum, and
I sobbed into the shot-rent quilt, swearing virtue, good
deeds, and chastity to God.

I kept my visit secret. And a perfect secret it was too.

Except that the silence fell.

No ursine gardeners peddled roots from door to door.
No kindly bear held the pasture gate to let a goodwife pass.
No bear song drifted from the meadow. Nine days later a
pigeon-hunter accidentally uncovered the powder horn, one
weather-glazed hunter's boot, and one sap-stained quarter
of a jacket.

"A mishap," said the magistrate, eyeing the tooth marks

in the shoulder of the scrap. "A lamentable misadventure," he said with sadness. "A mystery." Anyone could see the nature of the hunter's sudden end, but the sheriff said it was beyond us all, what might have taken place. Because the bears were loved, and loved in return, in their bluff, like-human way.

But all the bears had vanished. Their cottages stood dark. No one knew what caused this blight, or where the speaking grizzlies repaired to, why they left our woods.

No one except myself.

The last time I saw a bear beside a creek, not a fortnight past, she stood on her two hind paws and listened while I bid her a good evening. "And good health to you," I said. She turned away and left me alone, the stream beside me running like a song.

Only I know, and I keep it to myself. But I see too clearly what happened. I know exactly how the huntsman leaped to his feet, face red with sleep and drink. I see too well in the eye of my mind how the redcoat brandished his double-shotted gun.

I see him drawing aim upon the cub, and in my waking dream I see what a bear can eat for breakfast, when she has to on a sunny morn.

While not originally a part of the folk tale canon, "Goldilocks and the Three Bears" (an English story from the nineteenth century) has entered the oral tradition to become a treasured piece of our cultural lore. With its depiction of domestic bears, with favorite chairs and porridge for breakfast, and the daring and dangerously innocent Goldilocks, the story continues to intrigue generations of children and adults. Cadnum says that he loves to take a traditional story and turn it upside down, or inside out, to see the tale with new eyes.

Goldilocks Tells All

SCOTT BRADFIELD

Scott Bradfield was born in California but now lives in the United Kingdom. He has published both mainstream and genre fiction, including the novels The History of Luminous Motion, What's Wrong with America, *and* Animal Planet. *His stories have been collected in* Dream of the Wolf *and* Greetings From Earth. *He is currently writing screenplays in Hollywood and reviews in London.*

Goldilocks Tells All

"I definitely didn't know what I was getting into," Goldy told the crowd of demographically diverse audience-participants. "I certainly never thought it would go so far. Imagine yourself in my place, just a kid really, lost in the Enchanted Forest for weeks now, and no familiar paths in sight. All of a sudden—winds howl, owls hoot, the woody noose tightens. Which is when you smell porridge bubbling in a big iron pot, and after heeding your nose for a mile or so, find it. What looks like salvation. But what turns out to be something completely different."

Goldy paused long enough to hear the high-ceilinged studio hum: cameras, audio-processing equipment, boom mikes, even the agitated curls of Goldy's Dolly Parton–style wig.

"Bavarian modern, baby," Goldy continued. "With

cotton-candy smoke burbling from a candy-cane striped chimney, and all the doors wide open. So what would *you* do, ladies? Maybe what I did—climb in through one of those convenient, Hobbit-style windows, pull yourself up to the porridge bowl, and after a good hard dose of victuals, eventually fall asleep dreaming of feathery opulence in a just-right lacy bed. I felt like a million bucks. I thought I'd died and gone to heaven. A warm home, warm food, cool sheets, all the things I'd ever dreamed about and more. Little did I realize that fast fate was already hastening toward me through the hoary woods. Little did I know, ladies, what Papa Bear had in store for me when *he* got home."

Goldy let the sentence hang, establishing eye-contact with every working-age woman in the studio audience. I am your sister, Goldy's glance affirmed. And I wouldn't say it if I didn't mean it.

"We've all got a Papa Bear in our lives, ladies, even though we may call him by different names. I'm talking about that guy who comes home late every night stinking of pretzels and beer, slamming all the kitchen cabinets, enacting his plans for world domination on our soft, life-affirming bodies. Which brings me, ladies, not-quite-so-coincidentally, to the subject of my new book—"

Goldy held up a bright laminated glare to the camera. The assembled studio audience blinked.

"It's my latest," Goldy concluded, "my best, and the one which the *New York Times* recently described as 'thrilling, sad, heartbreaking' and 'packs a huge wallop.' Entitled *The Goldilocks Syndrome*, it's currently available in the lobby at a today-only discount of $21.95. And if you act *now*, I'll sign and date this sucker at no extra charge."

Goldilocks hated book tours. She hated the silent-time in chauffeur-driven stretch limos when the cellular phone didn't beep. She hated the articulated virtual-landscape of acoustically muffled hotel corridors and velour-scented penthouse restaurants. She hated predawn wake-up calls, the hard crack of ice machines in the night, and hasty publicity girls going ballistic over memos. In fact, the only things Goldy *did* appreciate about book tours were hotel room-

service and movie people. Because both entered and departed her life on perfectly fitted steel casters. And both
always made just enough of a fuss to let her know that they
really *cared*.

"We love you, Goldy," Sid Croft said. "We love everything about you. We love the way you look, the way you
write, even the way you comb your hair. When Barbara and
I first read your book, we couldn't help it, we both said,
'Wow.' Isn't that right, Barbara? When we first read Goldy's
book, what's the first thing we said to each other, huh?"

Barbara looked up from her blue loose-leaf notebook
and finished biting the eraser off her Number 2 Ticonderoga.

"I'm not sure, Sid. But didn't we both say something
like, I don't know, like 'Wow'?"

Barbara looked like she had spent most of her life on
an IV drip. About the only weight and buoyancy in her
entire body was confined to her pointy breast-implants.

"That's it! That's *it!*" Sid was bouncing up and down
on the flexible toes of his beige penny-loafers as if he were
preparing to return a particularly wicked volley. "We said,
'Wow.' We said '*double*-Wow.' And what's more, Goldy—
we meant every word of it."

Goldy was perched in front of her vanity mirror, gaug-
ing the depth of her own reflection. Goldy loved moments
like this. Moments when everybody else waited for *her*.

"So what is it, Sid?" she asked finally, applying a modi-
cum of blush to each cheek. "I've got a conference call at
five, and a TV gig at five-thirty."

Sid was as short, round, and immovable as a mailbox.
With an almost audible pop, a bright bead of sweat broke
from his receding forehead and slalomed down the right
side of his face.

"We love the anti-male thing," Sid said, exchanging a
rapid semaphore of glances with Barbara. "We love the
woman-striking-out-on-her-own thing. We really, well,
we're really *intrigued* by the three bears in the gingerbread
house thing, but maybe we can talk about that, okay? I
mean, couldn't they be reindeer, or lions, or even East Ger-
mans? Think about it, Goldy. I've got Sandra Bullock's agent
on the line, and he just doesn't go for this *bear* thing at all."

Goldy's unmascaraed eyes pinned Sid's reflection to the mirror like a butterfly to a killing tray.

"So what are we talking about, Sid? Because if we're not talking contract, I've got better places I need to be."

Sid, with a long expiring exhalation, wiped his forehead with a monogrammed silk handkerchief and smiled.

Ahh, Sid thought. Take a deep breath. Now another. This is the moment when Goldy waits for *you*.

Sid reached into the left breast pocket of his white linen sport jacket, withdrew the folded legal documents, and slapped them perfunctorily onto Goldy's vanity table like a summons.

"Of course we're talking contracts, babe. Guild deal, pay-or-play, mega-points, your script until you lose it. But not until you've gotten us signed releases from all three bears, especially Papa. We're asking primary rights, subsidiary rights, foreign rights, you name it. Those bears don't go to the bathroom we don't own the rights to it, get me? You deliver what we need, Goldy, and we're ready to make heap-um big medicine on this one. We're gonna make you the deal you've been waiting for all your life."

Even Papa Bear couldn't remember what really happened anymore. He had rationalized events in his mind, then re-rationalized them, then re-re-rationalized them again. He told Mama Bear one version of events, Baby Bear another, and himself alone in his bed at night still another. He woke from cold sweats dreaming about what might have happened. What probably didn't happen. What never happened but seemed like it had. The most frightening thing of all, though, was that he couldn't escape one firm unalterable version of his own history. And that, of course, was Goldy's version—available in trade-paper, CD-ROM, and audio-cassette.

"You ruined the best years of my life!" Goldy screamed, appearing from her long sleek limousine in a thigh-length sable coat, pearl-drop earrings and a sequined raw-silk blouse from agnès b. "And maybe if you hadn't made me lose so much confidence in myself, I could've developed into a more stable, nurturing-type personality, and gotten married and raised my own family, instead of ending up like *this*. You know what I mean, Papa Bear. Totally fucked up!"

"Why don't you calm down, Goldy," Papa Bear said without inflection. "Then maybe for once we could talk things over without getting so, you know, emotional all the time."

Mama Bear stood in the kitchen doorway, wiping her sudsy paws on the hem of her white cotton apron. Oh Papa Bear, she thought simply. When will you learn to keep your big mouth *shut*?

It began as less than a whisper. And ended as more than a roar.

"Me?" Goldilocks replied. "You want *me* to stop being *emotional*?"

As Goldy's heat gathered, Papa Bear gazed out the frosty window at her limo in the driveway. Its density belongs to a different world than this one, Papa Bear thought. Somewhere cleaner, perhaps. With firmer lines and harder surfaces.

"You *ruin* my life and I'm not supposed to get *hysterical*? You chase me out of my adopted *home* at the most defenseless and impressionable age for a young woman, and I'm not supposed to be *hostile*! What kind of animal are you, Papa Bear? Don't you ever think about anybody but yourself?"

Giving under the weight of an exclamatory little stamp, Goldy's left stiletto heel broke with a resounding crack. Goldy staggered—but, as usual, she didn't fall.

"You bastard!" she shouted at Papa Bear. "You hairy ball-less honey-sucking *bastard*!"

The words didn't make an impact so much as clear space in the room. Then, from the upstairs landing, Papa Bear heard it, a soft assembling presence like rain gathering behind dark clouds. Footsteps, a slamming door, an aimless cry in the dark.

"I can't stand it! I can't stand it anymore!" Baby Bear screamed from the summit of stairs. He was wearing his sloppiest Varsity sweat suit and a pair of buzzing stereo headphones. As he pounded the floorboards with his hairy adolescent feet, lamps toppled from tables and windows rattled in frames.

"All I ever hear about is *you you you!*" Baby Bear cried. "But what about *my* feelings? Why doesn't anybody stop for a minute to think about *me*?"

When things finally settled down again, Mama Bear fixed everybody porridge. Hot and lumpy for Papa Bear. Tepid and slightly mushy for herself. And in-between for Baby Bear and Goldy, who, like all good children, preferred to drive straight down the middle of roads so they didn't veer too dangerously toward either side.

"You can sleep in your old room," Mama Bear bossed abstractly as she pottered at the sink. "And Baby can sleep on the convertible sofa in the den. It'll be just like old times again, won't it? Goldy and her three bears. Arguing about every little thing, but living their lives just the way they're supposed to. Together—and happily ever after."

Goldy dipped steadily into her porridge with the just-right-sized silver teaspoon. Meanwhile, Baby Bear sniffled into his checkered linen napkin, and kept close tabs on how much of *his* porridge was being eaten by *her*.

"I'm telling you, Sid," the chauffeur said discreetly into the hall phone. "Take a left on Enchanted Forest Boulevard and drive straight past 7-Eleven. Get your butt over here and see for yourself."

It's all so futile, Papa Bear thought. All four of them sitting around the table just like old times, nursing their private hurts and grudges, learning a lot of complicated ways not to tell each other anything. Papa Bear felt it blossom in the pit of his stomach like gastritis. So much for so long. He couldn't stand to hold it back another minute.

So Papa Bear *roared*.

Causing everybody to jump at least three feet higher than the backs of their chairs. Except, of course, Goldy. Who simply stared into Papa Bear's eyes and smiled.

"I knew it," Goldy said. "I knew he'd raise his voice eventually. When Papa Bear can't persuade people by means of superior reason, he threatens to use force instead. It's such a goddamn dick-thing it makes me want to puke."

Papa Bear took a slow moment to catch up with his own impact. It didn't seem right somehow.

But I'm the one who's scared, he thought finally. And I don't know any way to tell you but this.

"We gave you a bed to sleep in," Papa Bear pleaded. "We gave you food to eat and clothes to wear. And believe me, I *tried* to be patient and put up with your endless constant complaining. 'This cereal is too cold,' or 'This bed is too hard,' or 'You can't have red wine with fish—whatever happened to that nice little Chablis Papa Bear was saving in the cellar?' I *tried* to be a good foster-father, Goldy, but okay, maybe I didn't do a very good job. Eventually I couldn't take it anymore and I chased you the hell out of my house. I chased you into the dark woods and you never came back. Jesus, Goldy, I'm sorry, I really am. I'm sick about it nearly every night, I can't sleep, I can't enjoy a decent bowel movement. Please, Goldy. I'm begging you. Help me make amends."

As Papa Bear talked, Goldilocks grew increasingly out of breath, as if she were performing a weird act of ventriloquism. She stood with her tiny fists planted on her overgrown hips, her large round face flushed and damp. She had been waiting for this moment all of her life.

"You want to make it up to me, Papa Bear? You want to make everything all right again?"

Papa Bear breathed silently for a moment.

"Yes, Goldy," he said softly. "Anything. I'll do anything I can."

Goldilocks permitted her frozen expression to lapse into an equally frozen smile. Then she removed the tidy white rectangle of legal documents from her purse and showed them to Papa Bear the same way she might show a fly swatter to a fly.

"Well," Goldilocks concluded, "let's see what we can come up with. Okay?"

"There may not be third acts in American lives!" Sid Croft shouted through an old-fashioned plastic megaphone. "But there sure-the-hell are third acts in a Sid Croft Motion Picture Production! Let's work together, everybody! And roll on three!"

Papa Bear was so exhausted it felt like catharsis. Seated in his familiar recliner with a bottle of Weiss Bier braced between his thighs, he let Mama Bear mop his feverish brow with an ice-cool dishcloth.

"One!" Sid Croft shouted. Technicians and administrative assistants went scurrying. The high hot lights activated with a flash.

Jumping her cue, Goldilocks charged out of her dressing room, trailing a haze of anxiety and talcum.

"Where's that bitch from Continuity!" Goldilocks shouted, frantic with black eyeliner. Her artificial beauty spots were popping off her face like buttons from an overextended blouse. "I asked for forty-one minor changes to this scene and all I've counted so far are seven! Don't you guys understand comedic development around here? I can't go chasing after Papa Bear! Papa Bear's got to come chasing after *me!*"

On shooting days, Papa Bear didn't know why he bothered. Four months ago he had happily signed away every legal right he ever had just to get Goldy off his back. Now, as a result of those very same concessions, it was beginning to look like she would leave.

"I'm starting over again from two, folks!" Climbing atop the exhausted luncheon trolley, Sid stood among the pink shell-shards of King Crab and Jumbo Shrimp like a height-challenged swashbuckler. "And *you*, young lady! I'm talking to *you*, right?"

Sid Croft pointed directly at Goldy. All around her, studio technicians (especially the male ones) started to snicker.

"*You* take another look at your contract. And do it with a good lawyer, okay?"

Papa Bear retreated into a slow shrug. He felt totally alone, and, as per usual, he was totally wrong.

"First we live our lives," Mama Bear whispered, "then we get on to the equally hard job of making those lives make sense. We eat jam, drink coffee, belch, defecate, bump our heads in the night, make love, eat more jam, suffer toothaches and bad faith. Then we wake up the next morning and tell stories about what we think really happened. We call our friends on the phone. We write letters and compose poorly punctuated e-mail. We publish books, outline screenplays, adopt the latest word-processing equipment, and dream our way through a thousand endless hibernal lapses. All I'm saying, Papa, is that maybe you and Goldy aren't so different after all. She needs her anger and you need your guilt. Where would you be without each other, huh?"

Mama Bear was showing Papa Bear to his chalk mark on the polished wooden floor. Then she brushed lint from his hairy chest with a soft gray brush.

"Two!" Sid Croft shouted.

"I'm ready!" Goldy volleyed back, pulling her ringletted blond wig into place and readjusting her bosom. "Just hold your horses, Sid, I'm *ready!*"

Out of the corner of his eye Papa Bear spotted Baby Bear at the cappuccino bar, stroking the script girl's pale cheek with a tender ursine restraint. Look, I may be a bear, the stroke implied. And you may be a woman. But that doesn't mean we can't still be friends.

"Three! And that's *action*, ladies! Roll 'em! Let's go! I got an early date tonight! Look alive and I mean *now!*"

Papa Bear felt the room dilate down to the width and glossy thickness of a six-inch lens. At which point Goldilocks, with a stamp of her high-heels on the parquet linoleum, entered stage right.

"Now let me tell *you* something, Papa Bear! Nothing you say or do can ever hurt me, because I love myself too much to let you beat me down. Before I'll let your negative-sounding criticisms damage my self-image factor, I'm leaving the Enchanted Forest and never coming back! You can't throw me out of your miserable hovel, Papa Bear—because I *quit!*"

Papa Bear took a deep breath, awaiting his cue.

And from the wings, Mama Bear made a perfect round O of her lips.

"O Goldilocks," Papa Bear woodenly pronounced in Camera Two's general direction. "I stand naked before you in all my testosterone-drenched male rage. My futile penile

egocentrism withers in the all-embracing light of your het-
erogeneous female-multiplicity. Forgive me, O Goldilocks,
for the terrible indignities your brave female self has suffered in my cruel clutches! What I'm trying to tell you,
Goldy, is that you win, all-powerful woman! You win, you
win, you win, you *win*!"

Papa Bear dropped his chin to his chest. It was the closest he could bring himself to self-abasement.

"Cut!" Sid Croft shouted. "That's a wrap, kids! Let's
work together again real soon!"

Papa Bear remained on his mark, waiting. It seemed like
forever—the time that elapsed between who he was supposed to be and who he really was. When he looked across
the room at Goldy, Goldy steadfastly refused to look at him.

"Let's go, girls," Goldy told Hair and Makeup. "I'm
opening a factory outlet in Reseda at six."

Papa Bear watched the overhead arc lights flicker and
diminish with a series of foggy pops, while stagehands
coiled thick black cables and clumps of electrical wiring
around their burly forearms. Papa Bear could smell her scent
and perspiration. This was the lie he had been waiting for
all day.

"You were wonderful," Mama Bear whispered as the
studio lights dimmed. "Maybe Goldy had all the good lines.
But you definitely stole the show."

*Goldilocks was never completely an innocent, even in the original
story—she was not only a trespasser but a force of chaos as she
destroyed the property of those three sympathetic bears. In Bradfield's satire she becomes the bitch goddess of the media as she
uses her exaggerated experience as a victim to attain her fifteen
minutes of fame.*

My Life as a Bird

CHARLES DE LINT

Charles de Lint is a writer and musician who makes his home in Ottawa, Canada, with his wife MaryAnn Harris, an artist and musician. His most recent novels are Trader *(nominated for the World Fantasy Award) and* Someplace to Be Flying, *both set in the imaginary town of Newford. He has also published three Newford story collections:* Dreams Underfoot, The Ivory and the Horn, *and* Moonlight and Vines. *For more information about his work, visit his website at <http://www.cyberus.ca/~cdl>*

From the August 1996 issue of the
Spar Distributions catalog.

THE GIRL ZONE, No. 10. Written &
illustrated by Mona Morgan. Latest
issue features new chapters of "The
True Life Adventures of Rockit
Grrl," "Jupiter Jewell" and "My Life as
a Bird." Includes a one-page jam
with Charles Vess.
My Own Comix Co., $2.75
Back issues available.

My Life as a Bird

"My Life as a Bird"
Mona's monologue from chapter three:

The thing is, we spend too much time looking outside ourselves for what we should really be trying to find inside. But we can't seem to trust what we find in ourselves—maybe because that's where we find it. I suppose it's all a part of how we ignore who we really are. We're so quick to cut away pieces of ourselves to suit a particular relationship, a job, a circle of friends, incessantly editing who we are until we fit in. Or we do it to someone else. We try to edit the people around us.

I don't know which is worse.

Most people would say it's when we do it to someone else, but I don't think either one's a very healthy option.

Why do we love ourselves so little? Why are we suspect

for trying to love ourselves, for being true to who and what
we are rather than what someone else thinks we should be?
We're so ready to betray ourselves, but we never call it that.
We have all these other terms to describe it: Fitting in. Doing
the right thing. Getting along.

I'm not proposing a world solely ruled by rank self-inter-
est; I know that there have to be some limits of politeness
and compromise or all we'll have left is anarchy. And anyone
who expects the entire world to adjust to them is obviously
a little too full of their own self-importance.

But how can we expect others to respect or care for us
if we don't respect and care for ourselves? And how come no
one asks, "If you're so ready to betray yourself, why should I
believe that you won't betray me as well?"

"And then he dumped you—just like that?"

Mona nodded. "I suppose I should've seen it coming.
All it seems we've been doing lately is arguing. But I've
been so busy trying to get the new issue out and dealing
with the people at Spar who are still being such pricks . . ."

She let her voice trail off. Tonight the plan had been to
get away from her problems, not focus on them. She often
thought that too many people used Jilly as a combination
den mother/emotional junkyard, and she'd promised herself
a long time ago that she wouldn't be one of them. But here
she was anyway, dumping her problems all over the table
between them.

The trouble was, Jilly drew confidences from you as easily as she did a smile. You couldn't not open up to her.

"I guess what it boils down to," she said, "is I wish I
was more like Rockit Grrl than Mona."

Jilly smiled. "Which Mona?"

"Good point."

The real-life Mona wrote and drew three ongoing strips
for her own bi-monthly comic book, *The Girl Zone*. Rockit
Grrl was featured in "The True Life Adventures of Rockit
Grrl," the pen and ink Mona in a semiautobiographical strip
called "My Life as a Bird." Rounding out each issue was
"Jupiter Jewel."

Rockit Grrl, aka "The Menace from Venice"—Venice

Avenue, Crowsea, that is, not the Italian city or the California beach—was an in-your-face punkette with an athletic body and excellent fashion sense, strong and unafraid; a little too opinionated for her own good, perhaps, but that only allowed the plots to pretty much write themselves. She spent her time righting wrongs and combating heinous villains like Didn't-Phone-When-He-Said-He-Would Man and Honest-My-Wife-and-I-Are-As-Good-As-Separated Man.

The Mona in "My Life as a Bird" had spiky blond hair and jean overalls just as her creator did, though the real-life Mona wore a T-shirt under her overalls and she usually had an inch or so of dark roots showing. They both had a quirky sense of humor and tended to expound at length on what they considered the mainstays of interesting conversation— love and death, sex and art—though the strip's monologues were far more coherent. The stories invariably took place in the character's apartment, or the local English-style pub down the street from it, which was based on the same pub where she and Jilly were currently sharing a pitcher of draft.

Jupiter Jewel had yet to make an appearance in her own strip, but the readers all felt as though they already knew her since her friends—who did appear—were always talking about her.

"The Mona in the strip, I guess," Mona said. "Maybe life's not a smooth ride for her either, but at least she's usually got some snappy comeback line."

"That's only because you have the time to think them out for her."

"This is true."

"But then," Jilly added, "that must be half the fun. Everybody thinks of what they should have said after the fact, but you actually get to use those lines."

"Even more true."

Jilly refilled their glasses. When she set the pitcher back down on the table, there was only froth left in the bottom.

"So did you come back with a good line?" she asked.

Mona shook her head. "What could I say? I was so stunned to find out that he'd never taken what I do seriously that all I could do was look at him and try to figure out how I ever thought we really knew each other."

She'd tried to put it out of her mind, but the phrase "that pathetic little comic books of yours" still stung in her memory.

"He used to like the fact that I was so different from the people where he works," she said, "but I guess he just got tired of parading his cute little Bohemian girlfriend around to office parties and the like."

Jilly gave a vigorous nod which made her curls fall down into her eyes. She pushed them back from her face with a hand that still had the inevitable paint lodged under the nails. Ultramarine blue. A vibrant coral.

"See," she said. "That's what infuriates me about the corporate world. The whole idea that if you're doing something creative that doesn't earn big bucks, you should consider it a hobby and put your real time and effort into something serious. Like your art isn't serious enough."

Mona took a swallow of beer. "Don't get me started on that."

Spar Distributions had recently decided to cut back on the non-superhero titles they carried, and *The Girl Zone* had been one of the casualties. That was bad enough, but then they also wouldn't cough up her back issues or the money they owed her from what they had sold.

"You got a lousy break," Jilly told her. "They've got no right to let things drag on the way they have."

Mona shrugged. "You'd think I'd have had some clue before this," she said, more willing to talk about Pete. At least she could deal with him. "But he always seemed to like the strips. He'd laugh in all the right places and he even cried when Jamaica almost died."

"Well, who didn't?"

"I guess. There sure was enough mail on that story."

Jamaica was the pet cat in "My Life as a Bird"—Mona's one concession to fantasy in the strip since Pete was allergic to cats. She'd thought that she was only in between cats when Crumb ran away and she first met Pete, but once their relationship began to get serious, she gave up on the idea of getting another one.

"Maybe he didn't like being in the strip," she said.

"What wasn't to like?" Jilly asked. "I loved the time you

put me in it, even though you made me look like I was
having the bad hair day from hell."

Mona smiled. "See, that's what happens when you drop
out of art school."

"You have bad hair days?"

"No, I mean—"

"Besides, I didn't drop out. You did."

"My point exactly," Mona said. "I can't draw hair for
the life of me. It always looks all raggedy."

"Or like a helmet, when you were drawing Pete."

Mona couldn't suppress a giggle. "It wasn't very flattering, was it?"

"But you made up for it by giving him a much better
butt," Jilly said.

That seemed uproariously funny to Mona. The beer, she
decided, was making her giddy. At least she hoped it was
the beer. She wondered if Jilly could hear the same hysterical edge in her laugh that she did. That made the momen-
tary good humor she'd been feeling scurry off as quickly as
Pete had left their apartment earlier in the day.

"I wonder when I stopped loving him," Mona said. "Because I did, you know, before we finally had it out today.
Stop loving him, I mean."

Jilly leaned forward. "Are you going to be okay? You
can stay with me tonight if you like. You know, just so you
don't have to be alone your first night."

Mona shook her head. "Thanks, but I'll be fine. I'm actually a little relieved, if you want to know the truth. The past
few months I've been wandering through a bit of a fog, but
I couldn't quite figure out what it was. Now I know."

Jilly raised her eyebrows.

"Knowing's better," Mona said.

"Well, if you change your mind . . ."

"I'll be scratching at your window the way those stray
cats you keep feeding do."

When they called it a night, an hour and another half pitcher
of draft later, Mona took a longer route home than she normally would. She wanted to clear her head of the decided
buzz that was making her stride less than steady, though con-

sidering the empty apartment she was going home to, maybe that wasn't the best idea, never mind her brave words to Jilly. Maybe, instead, she should go back to the pub and down a couple of whiskeys so that she'd really be too tipsy to mope.

"Oh damn him anyway," she muttered, and kicked at a tangle of crumpled newspapers that were spilling out of the mouth of an alleyway she was passing.

"Hey, watch it!"

Mona stopped at the sound of the odd gruff voice, then backed away as the smallest man she'd ever seen crawled out of the nest of papers to glare at her. He couldn't have stood more than two feet high, a disagreeable and ugly little troll of a man with a face that seemed roughly carved and then left unfinished. His clothes were ragged and shabby, his face bristly with stubble. What hair she could see coming out from under his cloth cap was tangled and greasy.

Oh my, she thought. She was drunker than she'd realized.

She stood there swaying for a long moment, staring down at him and half expecting him to simply drift apart like smoke, or vanish. But he did neither and she finally managed to find her voice.

"I'm sorry," she said "I just didn't see you down . . . there." This was coming out all wrong. "I mean . . ."

His glare deepened. "I suppose you think I'm too small to be noticed?"

"No. It's not that. I . . ."

She knew that his size was only some quirk of genetics, an unusual enough trait to find in someone out and about on a Crowsea street at midnight, but at the same time her imagination or, more likely, all the beer she'd had was telling her that the little man scowling up at her had a more exotic origin.

"Are you a leprechaun?" she found herself asking.

"If I had a pot of gold, do you think I'd be sleeping on the street?"

She shrugged. "No, of course not. It's just—"

He put a finger to the side of his nose and blew a stream of snot onto the pavement. Mona's stomach did a flip and a sour taste rose up in her throat. Trust her that, when she finally did have some curious encounter like the kind Jilly had so often, it had to be with a grotty little dwarf such as this.

The little man wiped his nose on the sleeve of his jacket and grinned at her.

"What's the matter, princess?" he asked. "If I can't afford a bed for the night, what makes you think I'd go out and buy a handkerchief just to avoid offending your sensibilities?"

It took her a moment to digest that. Then digging in the bib pocket of her overalls, she found a couple of crumpled dollar bills and offered them to him. He regarded the money with suspicion and made no move to take it from her.

"What's this?" he said.

"I just . . . I thought maybe you could use a couple of dollars."

"Freely given?" he asked. "No strings, no ties?"

"Well, it's not a loan," she told him. Like she was ever going to see him again.

He took the money with obvious reluctance and a muttered, "Damn."

Mona couldn't help herself. "Most people would say thank you," she said.

"Most people wouldn't be beholden to you because of it," he replied.

"I'm sorry?"

"What for?"

Mona blinked. "I meant, I don't understand why you're indebted to me now. It was just a couple of dollars."

"Then why apologize?"

"I didn't. Or I suppose I did, but—" This was getting far too confusing. "What I'm trying to say is that I don't want anything in return."

"Too late for that." He stuffed the money in his pocket. "Because your gift was freely given, it means I owe you now." He offered her his hand. "Nacky Wilde, at your service."

Seeing it was the same one he'd used to blow his nose, Mona decided to forgo the social amenities. She stuck her own hands in the side pockets of her overalls.

"Mona Morgan," she told him.

"Alliterative parents?"

"What?"

"You really should see a doctor about your hearing problem."

"I don't have a hearing problem," she said.

"It's nothing to be ashamed of. Well, lead on. Where are we going?"

"*We're* not going anywhere. I'm going home, and you can go back to doing whatever it was you were doing before we started this conversation."

He shook his head. "Doesn't work that way. I have to stick with you until I can repay my debt."

"I don't think so."

"Oh, it's very much so. What's the matter? Ashamed to be seen in my company? I'm too short for you? Too grubby? I can be invisible, if you like, but I get the feeling that'd only upset you more."

She had to be way more drunk than she thought she was. This wasn't even remotely a normal conversation.

"Invisible," she repeated.

He gave her an irritated look. "As in, not perceptible by the human eye. You do understand the concept, don't you?"

"You can't be serious."

"No, of course not. I'm making it up just to appear more interesting to you. Great big, semi-deaf women like you feature prominently in my daydreams, so naturally I'll say anything to try to win you over."

Working all day at her drawing desk didn't give Mona as much chance to exercise as she'd like, so she was a bit touchy about the few extra pounds she was carrying.

"I'm not big."

He craned his neck. "Depends on the perspective, sweetheart."

"And I'm not deaf."

"I was being polite. I thought it was kinder than saying you were mentally disadvantaged."

"And you're *certainly* not coming home with me."

"Whatever you say," he said.

And then he vanished.

One moment he was there, two feet of unsavory rudeness, and the next she was alone on the street. The abruptness of his disappearance, the very weirdness of it, made her legs go all watery, and she had to put a hand against the wall until the weak feeling went away.

I am *way* too drunk, she thought as she pushed off from the wall.

She peered into the alleyway, then looked up and down the street. Nothing. Gave the nest of newspapers a poke with her foot. Still nothing. Finally she started walking again, but nervously now, listening for footsteps, unable to shake the feeling that someone was watching her. She was almost back at her apartment when she remembered what he'd said about how he could be invisible.

Impossible.

But what if . . . ?

In the end she found a phone booth and gave Jilly a call.

"Is it too late to change my mind?" she asked.

"Not at all. Come on over."

Mona leaned against the glass of the booth and watched the street all around her. Occasional cabs went by. She saw a couple at the far end of the block and followed them with her gaze until they turned a corner. So far as she could tell, there was no little man, grotty or otherwise, anywhere in view.

"Is it okay if I bring my invisible friend?" she said.

Jilly laughed. "Sure. I'll put the kettle on. Does your invisible friend drink coffee?"

"I haven't asked him."

"Well," Jilly said, "if either of you are feeling as woozy as I am, I'm sure you could use a mug."

"I could use something," Mona said after she'd hung up.

"My Life as a Bird"
Mona's monologue from chapter eight:

Sometimes I think of God as this little man sitting on a café patio somewhere, bewildered at how it's all gotten so out of his control. He had such good intentions, but everything he made had a mind of its own and, right from the first, he found himself unable to contain their conflicting impulses. He tried to create paradise, but he soon discovered that free will and paradise were incompatible because everybody has a different idea as to what paradise should be like.

But usually when I think of him, I think of a cat: a little mysterious, a little aloof, never coming when he's called. And in my mind, God's always a he. The New Testament makes it pretty clear that men are the doers; women can only be virgins or whores. In God's eyes, we can only exist somewhere in between the two Marys, the Mother of Jesus and the Magdalene.

What kind of a religion is that? What kind of religion ignores the rights of half the world's population just because they're supposed to have envy instead of a penis? One run by men. The strong, the brave, the true. The old boys' club that wrote the book and made the laws.

I'd like to find him and ask him, "Is that it, God? Did we really get cloned from a rib and because we're hand-me-downs, you don't think we've got what it takes to be strong and brave and true?"

But that's only part of what's wrong with the world. You also have to ask, what's the rationale behind wars and sickness and suffering?

Or is there no point? Is God just as bewildered as the rest of the us? Has he finally given up, spending his days now on that café patio, sipping strong espresso, and watching the world go by, none of it his concern anymore? Has he washed his hands of it all?

I've got a thousand questions for God, but he never answers any of them. Maybe he's still trying to figure out where I fit on the scale between the two Marys and he can't reply until he does. Maybe he doesn't hear me, doesn't see me, doesn't think of me at all. Maybe in his version of what the world is, I don't even exist.

Or if he's a cat, then I'm a bird, and he's just waiting to pounce.

"You actually believe me, don't you?" Mona said.

The two of them were sitting in the window seat of Jilly's studio loft, sipping coffee from fat china mugs, piano music playing softly in the background, courtesy of a recording by Mitsuko Uchida. The studio was tidier than Mona had ever seen it. All the canvases that weren't hanging up had been neatly stacked against one wall. Books were in their shelves, paintbrushes cleaned and lying out in rows on the worktable, tubes of paint organized by color in wooden and cardboard boxes. The drop cloth under the easel even looked as though it had recently gone through a wash.

"Spring clean-up and tidying," Jilly had said by way of explanation.

"Hello? It's September."

"So I'm late."

The coffee had been waiting for Mona when she arrived, as had been a willing ear as she related her curious encounter after leaving the pub. Jilly, of course, was enchanted with the story. Mona didn't know why she was surprised.

"Let's say I don't disbelieve you," Jilly said.

"I don't know if I believe me. It's easier to put it down to those two pitchers of beer we had."

Jilly touched a hand to her head. "Don't remind me."

"Besides," Mona went on, "why doesn't he show himself now?" She looked around Jilly's disconcertingly tidy studio. "Well?" she said, aiming her question at the room in general. "What's the big secret, Mr. Nacky Wilde?"

"Well, it stands to reason," Jilly said. "He knows that I could just give him something as well, and then he'd be indebted to me, too."

"I don't *want* him indebted to me."

"It's kind of late for that."

"That's what he said."

"He'd probably know."

"Okay. I'll just get him to do my dishes for me or something."

Jilly shook her head. "I doubt it works that way. It probably has to be something that no one else can do for you except him."

"This is ridiculous. All I did was give him a couple of dollars. I didn't mean anything by it."

"Money doesn't mean anything to you?"

"Jilly. It was only two dollars."

"It doesn't matter. It's still money, and no matter how much we'd like things to be different, the world revolves around our being able to pay the rent and buy art supplies and the like, so money's important in our lives. You freely gave him something that means something to you, and now he has to return that in kind."

"But anybody could have given him the money."

Jilly nodded. "Anybody could have, but they didn't. You did."

"How do I get myself into these things?"

"More to the point, how do you get yourself out?"

"You're the expert. You tell me."

"Let me think about it."

Nacky Wilde didn't show himself again until Mona got back to her own apartment the next morning. She had just enough time to realize that Pete had been back to collect his things— there were gaps in the bookshelves, and the stack of CDs on top of the stereo was only half the size it had been the previous night—when the little man reappeared. He was slouched on her sofa, even more disreputable-looking in the daylight, his glower softened by what could only be the pleasure he took from her gasp at his sudden appearance.

She sat down on the stuffed chair across the table from him. There used to be two, but Pete had obviously taken one.

"So," she said. "I'm sober and you're here, so I guess you must be real."

"Does it always take you this long to accept the obvious?"

"Grubby little men who can appear out of thin air and then disappear back into it again aren't exactly a part of my everyday life."

"Ever been to Japan?" he asked.

"No. What's that got to—"

"But you believe it exists, don't you?"

"Oh, please. It's not at all the same thing. Next thing you'll be wanting me to believe in alien abductions and little green men from Mars."

He gave her a wicked grin. "They're not green and they don't come from—"

"I don't want to hear it," she told him, blocking her ears. When she saw he wasn't going to continue, she went on, "So was Jilly right? I'm stuck with you?"

"It doesn't make me any happier than it does you."

"Okay. Then we have to have some ground rules."

"You're taking this rather well," he said.

"I'm a practical person. Now listen up. No bothering

me when I'm working. No sneaking around being invisible when I'm in the bathroom or having a shower. No watching me sleep—*or* getting into bed with me."

He looked disgusted at the idea. Yeah, me too, Mona thought.

"And you clean up after yourself," she finished. "Come to think of it, you could clean up yourself, too."

He glared at her. "Fine. Now for my rules. First—"

Mona shook her head. "Uh-uh. This is my place. The only rules that get made here are by me."

"That hardly seems fair."

"None of this is fair," she shot back. "Remember, nobody asked you to tag along after me."

"Nobody asked you to give me that money," he said, and promptly disappeared.

"I *hate* it when you do that."

"Good," a disembodied voice replied.

Mona stared thoughtfully at the now-empty sofa cushions and found herself wondering what it would be like to be invisible, which got her thinking about all the ways one could be nonintrusive and still observe the world. After a while she got up and took down one of her old sketchbooks, flipping through it until she came to the notes she'd made when she'd first started planning her semi-autobiographical strip for *The Girl Zone*.

"My Life as a Bird"
Notes for chapter one:

(Mona and Hazel are sitting at the kitchen table in Mona's apartment having tea and muffins. Mona is watching Jamaica, asleep on the windowsill, only the tip of her tail twitching.)

MONA: Being invisible would be the coolest, but the next best thing would be, like, if you could be a bird or a cat—something that no one pays any attention to.

HAZEL: What kind of bird?

MONA: I don't know. A crow, all blue-black wings and shadowy. Or, no. Maybe something even less noticeable, like a pigeon or a sparrow.

(She gets a happy look on her face.)

MONA: Because you can tell. They pay attention to everything, but no one pays attention to them.

HAZEL: And the cat would be black, too, I suppose?

MONA: Mmm. Lean and slinky like Jamaica. Very Egyptian. But a bird would be better—more mobility—though I guess it wouldn't matter, really. The important thing is how you'd just be there, another piece of the landscape, but you'd be watching everything. You wouldn't miss a thing.

HAZEL: Bit of a voyeur, are we?

MONA: No, nothing like that. I'm not even interested in high drama, just the things that go on every day in our lives—the stuff most people don't pay attention to. That's the real magic.

HAZEL: Sounds boring.

MONA: No, it would be very Zen. Almost like meditating.

HAZEL: You've been drawing that comic of yours for too long.

The phone rang that evening while Mona was inking a new page for "Jupiter Jewel." The sudden sound startled her and a blob of ink fell from the end of her nib pen, right beside Cecil's head. At least it hadn't landed on his face.

I'll make that a shadow, she decided as she answered the phone.

"So do you still have an invisible friend?" Jilly asked.

Mona looked down the hall from the kitchen table where she was working. What she could see of the apartment appeared empty, but she didn't trust her eyesight when it came to her uninvited houseguest.

"I can't see him," she said, "but I have to assume he hasn't left."

"Well, I don't have any useful news. I've checked with all the usual sources and no one quite knows what to make of him."

"The usual sources being?"

"Christy. The professor. An old copy of the *Newford Examiner* with a special section on the fairy folk of Newford."

"You're kidding."

"I am," Jilly admitted. "But I did go to the library and had a wonderful time looking through all sorts of interesting books, from K. M. Briggs to *When the Desert Dreams* by Anne

Bourke, neither of whom write about Newford, but I've always loved those fairy lore books Briggs compiled, and Anne Bourke lived here, as I'm sure you knew, and I really liked the picture on the cover of her book. I know," she added, before Mona could break in. "Get to the point already."

"I'm serenely patient and would never have said such a thing," Mona told her.

"Humble, too. Anyway, apparently there are all sorts of tricksy fairy folk, from hobs to brownies. Some relatively nice, some decidedly nasty, but none of them quite fit the Nacky Wilde profile."

"You mean sarcastic, grubby, and bad mannered, but potentially helpful?"

"In a nutshell."

Mona sighed. "So I'm stuck with him."

She realized that she'd been absently doodling on her art and set her pen aside before she completely ruined the page.

"It doesn't seem fair, does it?" she added. "I finally get the apartment to myself, but then some elfin squatter moves in."

"How *are* you doing?" Jilly asked. "I mean, aside from your invisible squatter?"

"I don't feel closure," Mona said. "I know how weird that sounds, considering what I told you yesterday. After all, Pete stomped out and then snuck back while I was with you last night to get his stuff—so I *know* it's over. And the more I think of it, I realize this had to work out the way it did. But I'm still stuck with all this emotional baggage, like trying to figure out why things ended up the way they did, and how come I never noticed."

"Would you take him back?"

"No."

"But you miss him?"

"I do," Mona said. "Weird, isn't it?"

"Perfectly normal, I'd say. Do you want a shoulder to commiserate on?"

"No, I need to get some work done. But thanks."

After she hung up, Mona stared down at the mess she'd made of the page she'd been working on. She supposed she could try to incorporate all the squiggles into the back-

ground, but it didn't seem worth the bother. Instead she
picked up a bottle of white acrylic ink, gave it a shake and
opened it. With a clean brush she began to paint over the
doodles and the blob of ink she'd dropped by Cecil's head.
It was obvious now that it wouldn't work as shadow, seeing
how the light source was on the same side.

Waiting for the ink to dry, she wandered into the living
room and looked around.

"Trouble with your love life?" a familiar, but still disembodied voice asked.

"If you're going to talk to me," she said, "at least show
your face."

"Is this a new rule?"

Mona shook her head. "It's just disorienting to be talking into thin air—especially when the air answers back."

"Well, since you asked so politely . . ."

Nacky Wilde reappeared, slouching in the stuffed chair
this time, a copy of one of Mona's comic books open on his lap.

"You're not actually reading that?" Mona said.

He looked down at the comic. "No, of course not.
Dwarves can't read—their brains are much too small to
learn such an obviously complex task."

"I didn't mean it that way."

"I know you didn't, but I can't help myself. I have a
reputation to maintain."

"As a dwarf?" Mona asked. "Is that what you are?"

He shrugged and changed the subject. "I'm not surprised you and your boyfriend broke up."

"What's that supposed to mean?"

He stabbed the comic book with a short stubby finger.
"The tension's so apparent—if this bird story holds any
truth. One never gets the sense that any of the characters
really like Pete."

Mona sat down on the sofa and swung her feet up onto
the cushions. This was just what she needed—an uninvited,
usually invisible squatter of a houseguest who was also a
self-appointed analyst. Except, when she thought about it,
he was right. "My Life as a Bird" was emotionally true, if
not always a faithful account of actual events, and the Pete
character in it had never been one of her favorites. Like the

real Pete, there was an underlying tightness in his character; it was more noticeable in the strip because the rest of the cast was so Bohemian.

"He wasn't a bad person," she found herself saying.

"Of course not. Why would you let yourself be attracted to a bad person?"

Mona couldn't decide if he was being nice or sarcastic.

"They just wore him down," she said. "In the office. Won him over to their way of thinking, and there was no room for me in his life anymore."

"Or for him in yours," Nacky said.

Mona nodded. "It's weird, isn't it? Generosity of spirit seems to be so old-fashioned nowadays. We'd rather watch somebody trip on the sidewalk than help them climb the stairs to whatever it is they're reaching for."

"What is it you're reaching for?" Nacky asked.

"Oh, god." Mona laughed. "Who knows? Happiness, contentment. Some days all I want is for the lines to come together on the page and look like whatever it is that I'm trying to draw." She leaned back on the arm of the sofa and regarded the ceiling. "You know, that trick you do with invisibility is pretty cool." She turned her head to look at him. "Is it something that can be taught or do you have to be born magic?"

"Born to it, I'm afraid."

"I figured as much. But it's always been a fantasy of mine. That, or being able to change into something else."

"So I've gathered from reading this," Nacky said, giving the comic another tap with his finger. "Maybe you should try to be happy just being yourself. Look inside yourself for what you need—the way your character recommends in one of the earlier issues."

"You really have been reading it."

"That is why you write it, isn't it—to be read?"

She gave him a suspicious look. "Why are you being so nice all of a sudden?"

"Just setting you up for the big fall."

"Uh-huh."

"Thought of what I can do for you yet?" he asked.

She shook her head. "But I'm working on it."

"My Life as a Bird"
Notes for chapter seven:

(So after Mona meets Gregory, they go walking in Fitzhenry
Park and sit on a bench from which they can see Wendy's
Tree of Tales growing. Do I need to explain this, or can it just
be something people who know will understand?)

GREGORY: Did you ever notice how we don't tell family stories anymore?

MONA: What do you mean?

GREGORY: Families used to be made up of stories—their
history—and those stories were told down through the generations. It's where a family got its identity, the same way a neighborhood or even a country did. Now the stories we share we
get from television and the only thing we talk about is
ourselves.

(Mona realizes this is true—maybe not for everybody, but
it's true for her. Agh. How do I draw this???)

MONA: Maybe the family stories don't work anymore.
Maybe they've lost their relevance.

GREGORY: They've lost nothing.

(He looks away from her, out across the park.)

GREGORY: But we have.

In the days that followed, Nacky Wilde alternated between
the sarcastic grump Mona had first met and the surprisingly
good company he could prove to be when he didn't, as she
told him one night, "have a bee up his butt." Unfortunately,
the good of the one didn't outweigh the frustration of having to put up with the other, and there was no getting rid
of him. When he was in one of his moods, she didn't know
which was worse: having to look at his scowl and listen to
his bad-tempered remarks, or telling him to vanish but
know that he was still sulking around the apartment, invisible and watching her.

A week after Pete had moved out, Mona met up with Jilly
at the Cyberbean Café. They were planning to attend the
opening of Sophie's latest show at the Green Man Gallery,
and Mona had once again promised herself not to dump

her problems on Jilly, but there was no one else she could talk to.

"It's so typical," she found herself saying. "Out of all the hundreds of magical beings that populate folktales and legends, I had to get stuck with the one that has a multiple personality disorder. He's driving me crazy."

"Is he with us now?" Jilly asked.

"Who knows? Who cares?" Then Mona had to laugh. "God, listen to me. It's like I'm complaining about a bad relationship."

"Well, it is a bad relationship."

"I know. And isn't it pathetic?" Mona shook her head. "If this is what I rebounded to from Pete, I don't want to know what I'll end up with when I finally get this nasty little man out of my life. At least the sex was good with Pete."

Jilly's eyes went wide. "You're not . . . ?"

"Oh, please. That'd be like sleeping with the eighth dwarf, Snotty—the one Disney kept out of his movie, and with good reason."

Jilly had to laugh. "I'm sorry, but it's just so—"

Mona wagged a finger at her. "Don't say it. You wouldn't be laughing if it was happening to you." She looked at her watch. "We should get going."

Jilly took a last sip of her coffee. Wrapping what she hadn't finished of her cookie in a napkin, she stuck it in her pocket.

"What are you going to do?" she asked as they left the café.

"Well, I looked in the yellow pages, but none of the exterminators have cranky dwarves listed among the household pests they'll get rid of, so I guess I'm stuck with him for now. Though I haven't looked under exorcists yet."

"Is he Catholic?" Jilly asked.

"I didn't think it mattered. They just get rid of evil spirits, don't they?"

"Why not just ask him to leave? That's something no one else but he can do for you."

"I already thought of that," Mona told her.

"And?"

"Apparently it doesn't work that way."

"Maybe you should ask him what he can do for you."

Mona nodded thoughtfully. "You know, I never thought of that. I just assumed this whole business was one of those Rumpelstiltskin kind of things—that I had to come up with it on my own."

"What?" Nacky said later that night when Mona returned from the gallery and asked him to show himself. "You want me to list my services like on a menu? I'm not a restaurant."

"Or computer software," Mona agreed, "though it might be easier if you were either, because then at least I'd know what you can do without having to go through a song and dance to get the information out of you."

"No one's ever asked this kind of thing before."

"So what?" she asked. "Is it against the rules?"

Nacky scowled. "What makes you think there are rules?"

"There are always rules. So come on. Give."

"Fine," Nacky said. "We'll start with the most popular items." He began to count the items off on his fingers. "Potions, charms, spells, incantations—"

Mona held up a hand. "Hold on there. Let's back up a bit. What are these potions and charms and stuff?"

"Well, take your ex-boyfriend," Nacky said.

Please do, Mona thought.

"I could put a spell on him so that every time he looked at a woman that he was attracted to, he'd break out in hives."

"You could do that?"

Nacky nodded. "Or it could just be a minor irritation— an itch that will never go away."

"How long would it last?"

"Your choice. For the rest of his life, if you want."

Wouldn't that serve Pete right, Mona thought. Talk about a serious payback for all those mean things he'd said about her and *The Girl Zone*.

"This is so tempting," she said.

"So what will it be?" Nacky asked, briskly rubbing his hands together. "Hives? An itch? Perhaps a nervous tic under his eye so that people will always think he's winking at them. Seems harmless, but it's good for any number of face slaps and more serious altercations."

"Hang on," Mona told him. "What's the big hurry?"

"I'm in no hurry. I thought you were. I thought the sooner you got rid of Snotty, the eighth dwarf, the happier you'd be."

So he had been in the café.

"Okay," Mona said. "But first I have to ask you. These charms and things of yours—do they only do negative stuff?"

Nacky shook his head. "No. They can teach you the language of birds, choose your dreams before you go to sleep, make you appear to not be somewhere when you really are—"

"Wait a sec. You told me I had to be born magic to do that."

"No. You asked about, and I quote, 'the trick *you* do with invisibility,' the emphasis being mine. How I do it, you have to be born magic. An invisibility charm is something else."

"But it does the same thing?"

"For all intents and purposes."

God, but he could be infuriating.

"So why didn't you tell me that?"

Nacky smirked. "You didn't ask."

I will not get angry, she told herself. I am calmness incarnate.

"Okay," she said. "What else?"

He went back to counting the items on his fingers, starting again with a tap of his right index finger onto his left. "Potions to fall in love, to fall out of love. To make hair longer, or thicker. To make one taller, or shorter, or—" He gave her a wicked grin. "—slimmer. To speak with the recent dead, to heal the sick—"

"Heal them of what?" Mona wanted to know.

"Whatever ails them," he said, then went on in a bored voice. "To turn kettles into foxes, and vice versa. To—"

Mona was beginning to suffer overload.

"Enough already," she said. "I get the point."

"But you—"

"Shh. Let me think."

She laid her head back in her chair and closed her eyes. Basically, what it boiled down to was she could have whatever she wanted. She could have revenge on Pete—not for leaving her, but for being so mean-spirited about it. She could be invisible, or understand the language of birds and animals. And though he'd claimed not to have a pot of gold when they first met, she could probably have fame and fortune, too.

But she didn't really want revenge on Pete. And being invisible probably wasn't such a good idea since she already spent far too much time on her own as it was. What she should really do is get out more, meet more people, make more friends of her own, instead of all the people she knew through Pete. As for fame and fortune . . . corny as it might sound, she really did believe that the process was what was important, the journey her art and stories took her on, not the place where they all ended up.

She opened her eyes and looked at Nacky.

"Well?" he said.

She stood up and picked up her coat where she'd dropped it on the end of the sofa.

"Come on," she said as she put it on.

"Where are we going?"

"To hail a cab."

She had the taxi take them to the children's hospital. After paying the fare, she got out and stood on the lawn. Nacky, invisible in the vehicle, popped back into view. Leaves crackled underfoot as he joined her.

"There," Mona said, pointing at the long square block of a building. "I want you to heal all the kids in there."

There was a long moment of silence. When Mona turned to look at her companion, it was to find him regarding her with a thoughtful expression.

"I can't do that," he said.

Mona shook her head. "Like you couldn't make me invisible?"

"No semantics this time," he said. "I can't heal them all."

"But that's what I want."

Nacky sighed. "It's like asking for world peace. It's too big a task. But I could heal one of them."

"Just one?"

Nacky nodded.

Mona turned to look at the building again. "Then heal the sickest one."

She watched him cross the lawn. When he reached the front doors, his figure shimmered and he seemed to flow through the glass rather than step through the actual doors.

He was gone a long time. When he finally returned, his pace was much slower and there was a haunted look in his eyes.

"There was a little girl with cancer," he said. "She would have died later tonight. Her name—"

"I don't want to know her name," Mona told him. "I just want to know, will she be all right?"

He nodded.

I could have had anything, she found herself thinking.

"Do you regret giving the gift away?" Nacky asked her.

She shook her head. "No. I only wish I had more of them." She eyed him for a long moment. "I don't suppose I could freely give you another couple of dollars . . . ?"

"No. It doesn't—"

"Work that way," she finished. "I kind of figured as much." She knelt down so that she wasn't towering over him. "So now what? Where will you go?"

"I have a question for you," he said.

"Shoot."

"If I asked, would you let me stay on with you?"

Mona laughed.

"I'm serious," he told her.

"And what? Things would be different now, or would you still be snarly more often than not?"

He shook his head. "No different."

"You know I can't afford to keep that apartment," she said. "I'm probably going to have to get a studio apartment somewhere."

"I wouldn't mind."

Mona knew she'd be insane to agree. All she'd been

doing for the past week was trying to get him out of her life. But then she thought of the look in his eyes when he'd come back from the hospital, and knew that he wasn't all bad. Maybe he was a little magic man, but he was still stuck living on the street, and how happy could that make a person? Could be, all he needed was what everybody needed—a fair break. Could be, if he was treated fairly, he wouldn't glower so much, or be so bad-tempered.

But could she put up with it?

"I can't believe I'm saying this," she told him, "but, yeah. You can come back with me."

She'd never seen him smile before, she realized. It transformed his features.

"You've broken the curse," he said.

"Say what?"

"You don't know how long I've had to wait to find someone both selfless and willing to take me in as I was."

"I don't know about the selfless—"

He leaned forward and kissed her.

"Thank you," he said.

And then he went whirling off across the lawn, spinning like a dervishing top. His squatness melted from him and he grew tall and lean, fluid as a willow sapling, dancing in the wind. From the far side of the lawn he waved at her. For a long moment all she could do was stare, open-mouthed. When she finally lifted her hand to wave back, he winked out of existence, like a spark leaping from a fire, glowing brightly before it vanished into the darkness.

This time she knew he was gone for good.

"My Life as a Bird"
Mona's closing monologue from chapter eleven:

The weird thing is I actually miss him. Oh, not his crankiness, or his serious lack of personal hygiene. What I miss is the kindness that occasionally slipped through—the piece of him that survived the curse.

Jilly says that was why he was so bad-tempered and gross. He had to make himself unlikable, or it wouldn't have been so hard to find someone who would accept him for who he seemed to be. She says I stumbled into a fairy tale, which is pretty cool when you think about it, because how many people can say that?

Though I suppose if this really were a fairy tale, there'd be some kind of "happily ever after" wrap-up, or I'd at least have come away with a fairy gift of one sort or another. That invisibility charm, say, or the ability to change into a bird or a cat.

But I don't really need anything like that.

I've got *The Girl Zone*. I can be anything I want in its pages. Rockit Grrl, saving the day. Jupiter, who can't seem to physically show up in her own life. Or just me.

I've got my dreams. I had a fun one last night. I was walking downtown and I was a birdwoman, spindly legs, beak where my nose should be, long wings hanging down from my shoulders like a ragged cloak. Or maybe I was just wearing a bird costume. Nobody recognized me, but they knew me all the same and thought it was way cool.

And I've touched a piece of real magic. Now, no matter how gray and bland and pointless the world might seem sometimes, I just have to remember that there really is more to everything than what we can see. Everything has a spirit that's so much bigger and brighter than you think it could hold.

Everything has one.

Me, too.

De Lint's story incorporates elements of "Rumpelstiltskin" and "The Fisherman and His Wife," along with other familiar fairy tale tropes—but transplants them to the modern urban setting of Newford, an imaginary North American city where legends come to life.

The Red Boots

LEAH CUTTER

Leah Cutter grew up in Minnesota and lived all over the world, teaching English (in both Hungary and Taiwan), supervising an archeological dig in England, and bartending in Thailand. She currently lives in northern California with her husband, and works as a technical writer.

She originally wrote "The Red Boots" while living in Taiwan, then rewrote it at Clarion West, which she attended in 1997. "The Red Boots" was her first sale, although another story was published first, in the anthology called Last Stop at the End of the World. *She's working on her first novel.*

The Red Boots

After driving 2295 all day, Karen decided that the larger the Texas highway number, the smaller and meaner the road. When she saw the signs for 624, she turned off gratefully. Annaville, population 5,087, was the first town she came to. Scrub oak with dirty leaves edged the town square. Mother's Café, one of the restaurants facing the square, had a sign in the window, promising fresh pies. She and her mama couldn't have afforded even a run-down small town café; the Old Lady who'd taken her in after her mama'd died would have walked by without bothering to look. Karen tried to drive by slowly, but her foot kept tapping the accelerator instead of the brake. She circled back around the square for a second look.

At the stop sign on the far corner, a young couple in jeans crossed the street in front of her. They held hands with two children; an older boy and a younger girl, in matching striped shirts. Enviously, she watched them swinging their arms and skipping. She imagined the home-cooked meal of pork chops and apple compote they would have in their cozy kitchen, passing warm biscuits around a wooden table and interrupting each other with talk about their day. Unable to join them, or any family of her own, she decided that Mother's Café was the next best thing.

Karen angled her flatbed into a parking spot half a block past the café. After she pulled to a stop, her feet danced across the pedals as if they wanted to keep driving. She ignored them. A pain shot up her shins as she stepped down from her truck. She stamped her feet, then wriggled her ankles as much as she could in her brilliant red cowboy boots. Because of her curse, she usually only ever felt physical pain for a few minutes; at most, for a few hours.

Karen walked toward the café using slow baby steps, almost on her toes. A mother with a stroller was walking the other way. The baby in the stroller started crying and fussing. The mother kept walking, reaching a hand down to casually pat the baby's stomach. Karen minced to a halt to let them pass. If only she hadn't been cursed. *She* would care for a baby better than that. Better than her mama had. Better even than the Old Lady had. Sighing, she moved on.

As she neared the café sign, she saw the border was decorated with different types of fruit; blackberries and strawberries chased each other in a cotillion, and solitary peaches with a hint of fuzz stood in the corners like wallflowers. Her feet twitched at the sight.

"Please," Karen prayed softly. "Let me stay calm enough to eat. I won't try to stop any longer than that. Mercy," she asked of any passing angel. Her feet twitched one last time, then she felt a tingling move up the front of her legs, through her shoulders, and out the crown of her head. Her French braid loosened slightly, like unseen ravens adjusting their perch on her scalp. Karen stood still, too shocked to move. What had just happened? Had an angel heard? And maybe answered?

When no other sign came, she walked the rest of the way to the café. The heavy glass door felt warm against her palms as she pushed against it. Inside, the moist heat wrapped around her face like a towel fresh from the dryer. The salty, mouth-watering smell of grilling potatoes and garlic greeted her. Luckily, no music was playing.

She paused by the door, bracing herself for the tide of conversation that always rolled away when she went anywhere to surge back. But no one seemed dazzled by the rhinestones embedded in the yoke of her satin blouse, or tsked over how tightly her jeans molded her legs, or giggled at the brilliance of her red boots. The pair of women that looked up didn't stop their own conversation but did give her welcoming smiles.

Karen smiled back, then, following the sign directing her to make herself at home, chose a table far from everyone, next to the window. Healthy looking spiked ferns, pothos and spider plants lined the low windowsill. The plastic tablecloth was stiff and yellow with age, but a real cloth napkin lay folded next to her plate. It still smelled of Ivory soap. A scratched stainless-steel vase sat on the table, holding a sprig of cheap silk fuchsia. The menu was stuck behind it: hand-lettered on green construction paper, stained and bent.

Karen had just picked up the menu when the waitress came up and asked her what she wanted.

Karen wanted to order pie, and only pie, but she needed fuel, a full meal; she was skinny as a Yankee.

"The special's awfully good tonight," the waitress said. Karen looked up, then gawked at the smiling woman. The light coming in from the picture window back-lit the waitress's frizzy hair, making it glow like a halo. Karen's eyes adjusted. The waitress's beautiful dark eyes held the light, her round cheeks and full lips hinted at liking good cooking, her small chin spoke of stubbornness. She was young, like Karen, probably only eighteen or nineteen. Her name tag read, FRIEDA.

"I'll take the special, then," Karen said. She read the menu after the waitress had walked away and discovered she'd ordered chicken-fried steak with mashed potatoes, all the gravy and biscuits she could eat, a serving of the vegetable of the day, and a bottomless glass of iced tea to wash it all down.

She put down her menu and looked at the other customers. Mostly women, women who seemed friendly with each other, who weren't giggling falsely or screeching in competition but sharing good-hearted laughter. She saw two women holding hands over a table. Isn't this a friendly place? she thought. No wonder no one had commented when she walked in. Maybe she and her best friend Angie would have been comfortable here, even though it was so run-down. All the chairs and tables looked secondhand and didn't go together. The Old Lady wouldn't have approved at all.

The waitress came back with her order quickly. The off-white platter holding her steak didn't match the small blue bowl of vegetables, but everything smelled heavenly under the blanket of gravy. Karen picked up her knife and fork immediately.

"Can I get you anything else? Ketchup? Steak sauce?" the waitress asked.

Karen forced herself to be polite and look at the waitress. An oval stain ran from her shoulder to just above her name tag. "No, thank you," she said, then, unable to hold herself back, she attacked her food.

The steak was hard to cut, and the bright highlights in the gravy turned into grease, but Karen didn't care. She sliced the meat into small bits and was nibbling on some gristle when the waitress came back.

"So how is it?"

"Best I've had since I don't know when," Karen said, hastily clearing her mouth with a gulp of iced tea.

"I'll be sure to tell Harry. My brother, the cook."

Karen nodded. They were quiet for a moment, then Frieda asked, "Where you from?"

"A long ways away."

"Just passing through?" the girl asked, shifting from one foot to the other.

"Yes," Karen said, drawing out the s a little, watching Frieda's gaze amble from her braided hair, along the slope of her neck, past the glittering yoke of her blouse, only to pause at her breasts, then continue down to her hips, and after another pause, slide back up again. A bell rang in the kitchen.

"Shame," Frieda said as she walked past Karen, her hips within fingertip-grazing distance.

A warm, floating feeling rose in her chest as she watched Frieda's shapely back. With a start, Karen pushed down the feeling and made herself look at her plate. Her mama had told her it wasn't natural to feel that way. She speared another piece of patty-pan squash and tried to eat lady-like. Her feet started tapping the patterned linoleum impatiently.

When she finished wiping up the dregs of gravy with her last biscuit, her belly felt full and solid, yet her mouth still hungered for something comforting, like pie. Through the fatty cooking smells she imagined she could smell apples and nutmeg. Her mouth began to water.

When she was a little girl, she'd watched on Saturday mornings as the Old Lady's cooking woman carried the pies out of the oven to the cooling racks; white-gold crusts topped with large grains of beet sugar, dark red fruit bubbling within. Karen had been patient then, and could sit in one place for hours. She would stare at the pies, greedily watching them cool in the sunny whitewashed kitchen, flour dust dancing in the air, the heavy combination of baking soda and cinnamon sticking to her jumper. Waiting for that first bittersweet taste of berries, buttered crust, and sugar; baked feelings of home forming her bones, making them solid.

The memory of living in a home, staying in one place, unmoving, made her full belly seem empty and hollow. Her feet jerked violently, bringing her back to the restaurant. She had to go.

When she stood up and began walking to the counter, Karen realized she'd been sitting too long. She couldn't walk regularly anymore. Her feet insisted on dancing. She tried to take gliding steps, tried to seem normal. About halfway to the counter she turned as if to check her table, to see if she'd left anything there, sneaking in a quiet pirouette in the process.

Karen handed Frieda a crumpled ten dollar bill and asked, "You know where there might be any dancing tonight?"

"I don't know if we have anything like what you're used to," Frieda said, her look appraising Karen's outfit.

"I don't dance that fancy, I just like to dance," Karen said. "With anyone," she emphasized, putting her arms around an imaginary partner and taking a few steps. Frieda stared at Karen, her eyes growing larger. Karen waltzed closer, almost touching her.

Without moving her eyes from Karen's, Frieda replied, "If that's what you're looking for, I know the place. The VFW hall. It's about two miles down Main Street. Tonight—every Wednesday night—eight o'clock."

"How do I get there? Do I go down this street?" Karen gestured, making a sweeping motion, her fingertips almost brushing Frieda's curls.

Frieda shook her head. "The street on the opposite side of the square is Main Street. It's a one-way. Just follow it past the county museum. The street'll fork at Ed's Chicken Shack. Take the left side. The hall's on your right, just outside town, before the railway crossing. There's a sign out front, but sometimes it isn't lit. You'll have to go by slow and listen for the music."

"Thank you," Karen said, and with another elaborate movement asked for her change.

Frieda placed the bills in her palm but held onto them for an extra moment and said, "If you'll be there later, I might get Harry to close up early tonight. I haven't gone dancing in a long while." She waited expectantly, one eyebrow raised while the other half of her lips lifted in a smile.

Angie had always looked at her in that same quizzical, playful way. Angie, her best friend, who smelled of Lily-of-the-Valley powder, even when she sweated. Angie, the one she wasn't supposed to love. Angie, who had cursed her.

Karen wanted to stop and touch that smile. She wanted to plant herself and be drenched in it daily. But her feet kept waltzing. She had to leave before she embarrassed herself completely.

She turned toward the door abruptly, accidentally jerking the money out of the other girl's hand. Karen looked over her shoulder at Frieda and saw her slowly moisten her top lip with the tip of her tongue, like Angie always had.

What gods were playing with her now? Or was she being given a second chance?

Her feet propelled her away, their need to move greater than her ability to stop them. But she still smiled at the other woman when she reached the door.

"See you later," Karen said.

"See you later," Frieda called out after her.

Karen rushed from the café, struggling to walk in a straight line while her feet insisted on moving from side to side. In the safety of her truck, she watched with dismay as her feet moved wildly in a heel and toe pattern across the pedals. Generally, driving, moving from place to place and never knowing a home, pacified her feet. But she couldn't curb them enough to drive now. She had to dance.

She tried to distract herself by counting all her money. She was running so low. She didn't know how much she'd have to dance, or who she'd have to outdance, before her boots gave her more money. Or if she'd get beaten up again. By the time she had counted every penny three times, her feet had slowed to the point that she could control them. A little. She checked her dashboard clock. Not quite seven-thirty. Maybe she could walk, maybe a stroll through the cool evening would dampen the fire banked inside her.

She slid out of the cab of her truck, touching the concrete cautiously, like a child testing the temperature of a lake with her toe. Her feet didn't dance away under her, so Karen left her truck and started walking.

Just beyond the town square she passed a mansion that had been turned into the county museum. Fluted pillars lined the front, painted yellow with white tops and bottoms. Gabled windows poked out from the red roof. A carriage house stood connected to the side with a leafy arch. It was only a little more grand than the house the Old Lady had lived in. Karen walked by its soft green lawns quickly, hoping no one would see her, the shame of being turned out of a place like that still burning her face.

Next came a less expensive house, with white wooden sides and black window shutters. The lawn was brown, and the front yard sprouted an abandoned car as trimming. It was like Angie's house.

Karen wondered what type of house Frieda lived in, what the kitchen looked like. She decided it would probably be poor, though not as poor as her mama's shack had been. The stove would be tiny and there wouldn't be enough counter space. But in between the permanent stains the sink would be scoured and smell like bleach. There would be room for standing and talking while Frieda cooked. Karen could see herself watching Frieda, leaning against the door to the kitchen, the buzzing, round fluorescent light in the center of the kitchen ceiling a comforting note underlying their conversations. She and Frieda would talk, and eat, and laugh, try new recipes on each other, steal bits of food off one another's plate; closer than sisters, better than friends. Maybe their friendship could be accepted here. Even if her feelings weren't normal, maybe she could fit in, here in Annaville.

The hall was much farther than two miles away—typical Texas directions. Just after the abandoned Ed's Chicken Shack she heard the first few notes. Suddenly her arms lifted, her fingers snapped, syncopated with the cicadas, and her feet started a sideways *pas de bas*.

No one was on the road, so Karen indulged herself for a few happy steps. She brought her arms around an imaginary partner, closed her eyes and let her boots move across the road without a care. The air felt soft against her cheeks. She smelled wildflowers in the fields next to her. As she danced, a partner grew out of the shadows of her dreams. The image solidified into Frieda.

Shocked, Karen opened her eyes and tried to bring her arms to her sides and walk plainly, but her boots wanted to keep dancing. Angrily, she fought for control, focusing on her feet, trying to bring them back into line. Though she couldn't restrain her arms, she could drive her nails into her palms. The shock broke her stride. Within the next few steps she suppressed her boots again. She forced her arms to her sides and wiped her sweating hands down her jeans, wincing. She had bruised her palms with her nails, but she knew they wouldn't hurt for long because her body healed so quickly.

The VFW hall sat twenty feet from the railroad tracks,

square and indistinct, the edges blurred by the evening sun.
Karen didn't see the poorly lit sign until she walked up to
it. She paid her dollar at the door (running out so fast!) and
stepped inside.

The hall looked like a thousand others she had danced
in. Overhead fluorescent lights scorched the room: on a
Wednesday night dancers wanted to see each other, not
spoon. A few couples were already moving around the floor,
dancing to "Let's Sleep on It Tonight," a medium-paced
two-step. Mostly they wore plain clothes: jeans, boots, clean
work shirts. A few of the women had flashy yokes on their
blouses. A cursory glance told Karen none of them danced
as well as she did.

In the far left corner of the hall a pair of elderly women
sat behind a table. They sold pieces of cake trapped on paper
plates with layers of cellophane, and lemonade sweating in
waxy cups. A tall, skinny man in a green and white western
shirt with a red kerchief tied around his neck stood in the
far right corner. Next to him a black portable stereo system
sang out dance music.

Karen scanned the hall for the right partner. Most of the
people standing on the edge of the dance floor appeared too
old or too taken, though a cluster of high school girls stood
close to the door, giggling. Karen decided on a gray-haired
yet vigorous-looking man who kept eyeing the door every
time it opened. He stood apart from the other couples, yet
clearly he wasn't a stranger.

He watched as she came near, a puzzled look in his eye.
Karen looked down and swallowed hard before she smiled
at him. So he wouldn't hear now nervous she was, she indicated with her hands that she wanted to dance with him.
His eyes darted to the door again. Would it make the person
he was waiting for jealous? Angry? It didn't matter. To her
relief, he nodded at her, then took her outstretched arms.

"Let's Sleep on It Tonight" slowed to an end. Karen and
her partner danced until it finished, then paused in the quiet
between the songs. Karen rocked back and forth on her feet,
waiting. The next song was faster, more bouncy, and
brought a twinkling grin to her partner's face. He bobbed
his head to the beat three times, then they started.

Karen glided across the room as if a cushion of air lay between her feet and the wooden floor. It was better than flying. The rush of adrenaline made her giddy. The people standing around the edge of the dance floor blurred into a white mass. A swift comparison with the other dancers reassured Karen she was the best. She felt her feet go faster. She wanted to throw her head back and laugh, but didn't; it wouldn't have been proper.

Her partner danced well, with an easy grace and a bit of skill. He didn't talk to her, though he smiled often. Karen knew she made him appear a better dancer than he actually was. She tried to stay in that supportive partner role, trying not to be a prima donna, but she couldn't rein in her feet as he turned her. She spun too many times, making him wait. When she looked up, a forgiving grin filled his face. After that he turned her often, pausing and subduing his dance for hers. Karen felt so grateful she could have cried. She spun faster now, like a moth when it first finds a flame.

After the proper three songs, all she could dance with any one man without giving him ideas, she pulled away and thanked him with a slight curtsy. He bowed with a large flourish in return. She hoped she could dance another set with him later.

The next song was a familiar line dance, "The Turkey Three-Step." She stood at the perimeter for a minute to watch for any local variations. A few cropped up, nothing to throw off the rhythm of the dance, so she flowed into the center, joining the steps in perfect time.

Now she could really let go. She didn't have to worry about a partner or what anyone else thought. She could discharge the energy cached in her legs and feet and toes. She added small touches—an extra kick at the turn, a couple of shakes as she moved forward, a twist of her wrist, fingers splayed, as she sidestepped—all the things she needed to do to make the dance her own. It felt good to express herself and to lose all her lonely aches in the music.

Karen barely glanced at the surrounding dancers. Sure, some of them were good, but she felt magnanimous. She didn't need to compete with anyone tonight. She would forget she had so little cash. Instead, the hall could become her temple, she, a dervish, sacrificing herself for them. She could dance until a fey light shone through her, until she was pure and clean, her sweat smelling sweet. She did still love to dance.

After the song ended, Karen heard someone close to her say hello. She jumped and turned around. Frieda was standing behind her. Impulsively, Karen took both of Frieda's hands in her own, greeting her the same way she had always greeted Angie. Frieda's hands were smaller than Karen's, and warm. When Karen felt Frieda squeeze her hands, she looked down, embarrassed. They had only just met, and it wasn't, well, normal. She dropped Frieda's hands and didn't meet her eye again before the music started.

Karen started adding her own flourishes right away. Frieda matched her step for step: as soon as Karen came up with a new twist, Frieda also started doing it, almost at the same time. The warm glow spread through Karen's belly again. They augmented each other's dance, dancing with each other in a line. When Frieda smiled the Angie smile again—one eyebrow raised while the other half of her lips lifted—Karen felt blessed. She chanced a set of syncopated finger snaps. Frieda was right with her, the rhythms piling up on top of one another. Karen let herself laugh out loud with joy.

The next song, "King of the Mountain," was a country waltz. Neither Karen or Frieda looked for other partners. They stayed in the center of the bobbing dancers, weaving around each other with slow, intricate steps and expressive arm gestures. They almost danced like a couple, moving from side to side, mirror images. Karen felt her boots running out of steam, the slow movements releasing the pressure faster than the two-stepping had. Maybe she could leave the floor with Frieda after the waltz.

Karen looked away from Frieda once. A heavyset woman with a big bosom smiled at her before her partner turned her again. Maybe Annaville was a different place, and she could be accepted here. She extended her arm to Frieda, as if she was passing a fragile glass ball to her. Frieda accepted it gracefully, then passed it back. More than once their hands almost touched.

As the music wound down, Karen reached for Frieda's hand, her fingers extended. Frieda smiled at her, and reached out her hand as well. But before their fingers met, the man in the corner switched from the soft music and started playing "So Much for Pretending," another fast two-step. Frieda turned abruptly to look at him. Karen retracted her hand. When Frieda looked back, she snapped her fingers and slapped her feet. Stunned, Karen didn't respond immediately. Frieda did another flurry of steps, heel-to-toe with her feet turned out, and threw Karen another smile.

Was it a smile of friendship? Or mocking challenge? A voice inside her head warned, *No! Don't do this. This is your chance. Walk away now!* But Karen wouldn't let herself leave, though her boots were no longer controlling her dance. She paused for another beat and swept her eyes over Frieda. The quilted yoke on Frieda's blouse was obviously hand-sewn on top of a plain shift, and her jeans showed wear down the thighs and through the knees. Her boots, too, were scuffed. Karen added a half-stag leap to her hitch-kick, spun on her heels and snapped her fingers. She wasn't about to be outdone by a simple waitress at a local café.

Frieda's smile sharpened. Fiercely they danced at each other. Sometimes they copied and changed the other's steps, sometimes they came up with new portions of dance. Even during the slow dances they didn't rest.

Within two hours Frieda's frizzy hair flattened down with sweat, her eyes closed to half-mast exhaustion. Karen thought she still looked beautiful, even though it wasn't right for her to notice that way. Soon after that, Frieda stopped challenging or bringing new flourishes to their dance. A thick core of excitement strengthened Karen's bone and fueled her feet. She felt loose and warm, ready to dance forever. She bounced on the balls of her feet with every step and spun often. The thrill made her breath come short and shallow. An intoxicating heat filled her chest, like an expanding balloon, anxious to explode. The taste of near victory, sweeter than any pie, made her forget all the empty miles between dance halls.

The man in the corner was playing "One More Last Chance" when Frieda tripped and fell. Karen didn't stop. Chin raised high, she clicked her heels in triple time and danced a fandango around the girl, clapping her hands over her head. She had won. Again. The balloon burst through her limbs, melting all her hard places, filling her with beauty. She danced on her toes, in love with the world, which must now surely love her back. For a measureless moment she danced at the top of the world. The stars moved in mere mimicry of her faultless steps. Crystal music shimmered in the soft night air, then gently carried her back to earth.

When she looked over her shoulder at Frieda, the other girl shot her a look of contempt that burned even in the night's heat.

Suddenly Karen saw Angie on the floor, fallen as she had the night they competed with each other for the red boots she now wore. It had been an endurance contest. If they'd been a true couple, they could have danced with each other, supported each other. But they had been separate dancing forces, competing against each other for a single prize, like girls were supposed to, according to her mama.

Karen and Angie had been dancing without a break for twenty-seven hours, and were the only ones left on the dance floor. Karen's lips felt swollen, her mouth was dry, her head pounded with the heat. The humid hall held her sweat against her arms and legs, making her so wet it feel like she was swimming through the air. Exhaustion drained her, so she couldn't do much more than shuffle her feet. Still, when Angie fell, and Karen knew she had won, she looked toward the ceiling and yipped, doing three quick ball-change steps in a victory dance. A burst of pride coursed through her; on top of the world, she didn't have to care about not fitting in.

When she looked down again, Angie's shocked expression drilled into her as deeply as her words had. "You don't rightly care about me, do you? No, you won't let yourself care, it isn't normal. You don't care, you can't care, about anything but that damn fine house you live in and winning those damn boots!" Angie had taken a deep breath. Karen

held out her arms to her, but it was too late. Angie had
already started her curse. "May you always have to dance,
alone, homelessly wandering without a breath of hope until
you let someone else win!"

Angie had died on the way to the hospital; no one knew
she had a bad heart. Karen hadn't ridden in the ambulance
with her, instead staying in the hall and collecting her prize.
When she first pulled on the boots, her feet tingled with
new life. By the time she heard about Angie's death, the
boots were making her dance again, each step a heartbreaking pain.

Karen looked down again and saw Frieda. She tried to
stop, but it was too late. She tried forcing her weight against
the floor so her boots couldn't lift her feet up. But her boots,
fueled by her victory, were now stronger than she was.

Karen stayed in the center of the two-stepping couples,
dancing alone, as always. When she spun, she saw Frieda
standing in the corner, talking with a young man—Harry,
she presumed—but always watching her. If only Frieda
would come back and challenge her again, she would back
down this time. Honest, she would. But her boots wouldn't
let her stop and walk over to the girl.

The hall started emptying slowly. The long, live version
of "If You Really Loved Me" signaled the last dance of the
evening. Karen knew there would be no rest for her. She
made her way out of the dancing couples. Instead of heading back to town, she two-stepped across the railroad tracks
to an empty spot nearby.

Frieda found her there, still dancing. Karen accepted her
fate when she saw the baseball bat in the other girl's hands,
the glazed look in her eyes. Frieda was under the spell of
her boots, too. Sometimes just winning wasn't enough, and
her boots wanted physical pain as well. Yet Karen found
Frieda's possessed smile beautiful.

Frieda fondled Karen's face, then slapped her with her
full arm. Karen kept her head turned away. Frieda grabbed
Karen's chin, kissed her, then punched her in the mouth.
Then she used the baseball bat as if hitting a grounder,
knocking Karen's feet out from under her. Karen landed

hard on her back but didn't try to get up. Frieda knelt and felt up her leg, then pounded on it with her fists.

With a last fingertip stroke along her cheek, Frieda stood. Karen curled up on her side, trying to protect her stomach from the other girl's kicks, her breasts from her fondling. When Frieda started using the bat again, both for caressing and for hitting, Karen put her arms over her head, but she couldn't protect her ribs. She heard them crack, one by one.

Through the choked pain in her side she heard the click of a hunting knife opening. She laughed, or maybe it was only a gurgle through the blood in her mouth, at Frieda's frustration when she couldn't slice her boots. Karen wanted Frieda to cut her feet from her legs, but she couldn't catch enough breath for the words. Before she felt anything else being cut, a soft darkness came, swooping her away.

Karen awoke in the bed of her truck, which Frieda had driven past the county line. Her body ached, but she could move; none of her bones stayed broken for long. The collar of her now clean and starched shirt pressed against her bruised cheek. Her jeans had a crease in them again, like when they were new. Her boots were a darker red, more blood-colored. She looked through her pockets. Her "prize money," awarded by the curse, was there; more than any waitress made in a month, she was sure. The beating had been worse than she'd received in other towns, and maybe she could have stayed this time. . . . Her toes twitched. She had to get going.

She stood by the side of her truck a moment, stretching her legs. The flat countryside was so empty of people. She'd forgotten that. Her ribs a solid block of pain, she didn't try to take any deep breaths.

Maybe next time she would back down. Maybe next time she would listen to that voice in her head and stop before it was too late. Maybe it could be okay to not be normal. Maybe . . . The bleakness of the Texas morning sunshine on the bluebonnets stilled her thoughts. After a quick look to make sure no one was watching, she raised her arms and started doing pirouettes down the center of the road. She knew she could dance forever down that dotted line.

"The Red Boots" is based on Hans Christian Andersen's story "The Red Shoes." Andersen's fairy tales often end cruelly and unhappily. Neither the little match girl nor the little mermaid live happily ever after in the originals. And so it is for the poor orphan, cursed by a mysterious old soldier to dance in her beautiful red shoes until she begs to have her feet chopped off.

Although Cutter's version isn't quite as brutal as the original, both demonstrate the sin of pride.

Rosie's Dance

EMMA HARDESTY

*Emma Hardesty lives in the American Southwest
and does quite a number of satisfying things, of
which writing is second to gardening. She was
surprised to learn only a few years ago that lots
of other writers have long reworked and newly
phrased all the classic fairy tales, because she's
been writing such stories since she was a kid.
This is her first published work of fiction.*

Rosie's Dance

"**C**indy's all right but her butt's too big."

They all had a really good laugh at that. I don't know why. Clyman, and most of the others, had known me about all their lives. I wasn't any kind of surprise to them. It seemed that every day of my life I had heard some boy yell "Hey, Hardcastle. Get on out here." They never meant me, of course, the only girl in a family of overgrown boys, who were also mean. Not that I would have ever answered them. I was used to hearing their stupid names for me, especially because of my wild hair, but this was a new one about my big butt. It kind of gave me the creeps because all of them were younger than me.

My name isn't Cindy. That's just something my father started calling me after he saw me down on my knees scrubbing the bathroom floor, like you-know-who, for my stepmother. My real mother named me Rose, but just about nobody remembers that. Serafima remembers it, though.

This story here is something I am ready to tell and to forget.

I finished wiping down the counter that day, while the boys were still laughing at my expense. That kitchen counter was mostly bare plywood, full of jagged holes. It was a real job to keep clean, but I always tried. I cared if the house was clean because it made me feel better, even if the boys didn't care at all. I think the only thing they ever noticed was whether their pants were zipped or not. Trying is everything, it seems to me, and I didn't mind trying anything I thought I could handle. I wiped the crud off the cracked wood, pulled all the big splinters out of the rag, and left the kitchen so those boys could make their jokes without me.

I pretty much felt sorry for Clyman, but not his friends, and I was a little bit sorry for the other two boys. I still viewed as lucky the one that had died. I didn't feel sorry for myself, though. Serafima told me I had the world on a string, but I knew that the other women in the neighborhood didn't think much would come of any of us. After being scared, twice, that I might be pregnant, and then being talked about afterward, I decided to make sure the neighborhood women were wrong. At least about me.

I wasn't as happy to stay ignorant as my brothers seemed to be. I had my mother's books, lots of books, and I got my own library card when I was seven, the year before Mama died. Books meant the whole world to me, they *were* my whole world, except for the times I gave those lover boys a tumble. But that kind of thinking is long past me now. I started reading Mama's books when I was just young. I didn't understand most of those books, but they gave me something more than my brothers had, I could see that, and it taught me the world was mean but it didn't have to be ugly, too.

The boys, Clyman, Duane, and Jeffrey, weren't really my brothers at all. My father, R.I.P., had shoved them and their mother, R.I.P., into my life, after my mama died, and we moved out here from Arkansas. It seems like I never did a thing except clean from that time on. I still like cleaning a house, I like the results, but even then I knew it had its place.

Clyman, the oldest boy, seemed like a poor creature to me. I think he missed his real father too much. His father's name was Royale. I never knew if he was really dead or still alive somewhere, because Clyman talked about him as if he was both. Clyman talked real loud, as loud as anybody could possibly talk, but he would always speak really quiet and gentle when he was around little kids. I think maybe Royale had been that way with him, once upon a time. As loud as Clyman talked, though, he didn't talk often, but every time I thought maybe he was beginning to think about his life and the fact that he wouldn't be a kid forever, he would prove me wrong and I realized he just didn't talk much.

Duane was about two years younger than Clyman but he got away with acting like they were the same age. I never trusted Duane for a minute. He did cruel things that were so bad I'm not even going to talk about them. Duane was pretty good, though, at helping me keep things fixed around the house. He did this for his own sake. He just blew up when something broke, like the water heater, and he couldn't take his hot showers. He fixed anything that directly affected his own existence, but when the old car engine sitting on the back porch fell through and splintered a bunch of wood planks, Duane didn't even notice. It didn't matter to him that it blocked the side of the house where I had my garden. He only cared about things that gave him immediate satisfaction.

Jeffrey was on his way to becoming a criminal, pure and simple. He hit or kicked everything in his path. He was only two years old when the baby was born, and he missed that little boy more than anyone when he died. I was the only one who seemed to know that. I don't even think his mother knew. Jeffrey never talked to me unless he absolutely had to, not even when Laverle was still with us.

I was oldest, having hit the big age of fourteen when Laverle left, and I'm almost nineteen now. I tried to keep the house clean. I read a lot, mostly at night. I took walks, mostly in the little forest behind the neighborhood that was later turned into a bowling alley. It wasn't really a forest, but there had been a little pond there, with bullfrogs and perch and crawdads, and all the kids loved to go there before the bulldozers came. I had a few jobs, now and then, cooking, but I didn't want the benefit checks to stop and I thought they might if I got some kind of real job. Besides, what sort of résumé could I have put together?

The boy that died was my genuine half brother, Roscoe. Laverle got pregnant right after she started going with my father. I really loved that little boy. He had the same deep brown eyes as Mama. Mama's eyes were like a dove's, an orange-brown color ringed with black. It seemed to me that Roscoe really came from her instead of being Laverle's baby. Also his name had my name in it. I believed for a long time that my loving Rocky too much is what made him die. Then my father died, and Laverle took off. I was left with those boys, and it wasn't easy. I knew what that town thought of me. I thought the same of it.

For a while Laverle's sister would come by on Laverle's birthday, and she would show up a few days after Christmas, but I can't say she was anyone I looked forward to seeing. She would always pick up the book I was reading and say, "Why do you read stuff like that?" but I never answered her.

Some social-worker-type people came around a few times at first, once with Laverle's sister. Duane and Clyman just sat there with their knees together, and lied about their ages and everything else, and I've been told I look older than I am. Jeffrey took off when the welfare folks showed up, and they didn't even seem to know he existed. I doubt that Laverle's sister remembered him either. When they asked the boys, "Are you kids going to school?" I answered for them, "Yes ma'am." I don't know why I did that but I did, and I suppose the piles of books I always had sitting around were proof enough for the social workers. That was the one and only time the boys and I were in cahoots with one another. After a few visits, the welfare folks didn't come around anymore. I was glad. There's a lot of kids around there who needed them more than we did. Besides, what they had to offer didn't look like help to me, anyway, which was probably dumb of me, but that's how it worked out at the time.

We did get money, not much, but it was regular and directly deposited into my father's account. I knew enough never to ask what that money was all about, 'cause I figured it would stop. My father and I had the same names: Frances Rose Hardcastle, that's me—people confuse Francis and Frances all the time—and those checks went right into his account and I just drew on them, little enough as it was. Being able to do that gave me some control over the boys. I can handle money. I always made sure that the lights and the gas and the water bills were paid on time. We didn't need a phone. If your gas gets turned off, they send someone out to do it, and I didn't want any strangers coming around who would notice how we were living, since we were really just kids. Besides that money, the boys were dealers and thieves, with natural good luck it seems, because they were never officially caught at those things.

It never crossed my mind to stop cooking and cleaning, and see what education I could get for myself. I was waiting for the right moment, I guess, but I knew it was all up to me. I had read enough fairy tales to know that Prince Charming was about as exciting and gainfully employed as my brothers, and also way too soft and pale for a girl like me. Besides, he didn't live anywhere near the area. That was clear.

Maybe I should feel sorry for my brothers, but I don't think so. Serafima said they had their own choices to make, just like I did. She said the hand of fate is a helping hand, no matter how hard it slaps sometimes. She said you could give that hand a high-five and laugh, and that was okay. Or you could slap it 'cause it didn't seem good enough. Or you could grab it by the wrist and pull yourself up one more notch. Serafima said no telling how many notches a person would need pulling up, but that was always better than no notches at all. Yes ma'am. Sometimes Serafima was as corny as the day is long. She said salvation comes in small packages and you needed the hand of fate to untie them. I didn't always understand her.

Serafima was my friend. She was just an old woman, I guess, but it was the biggest thing to me, just to know that there was someone like her. She called me Rosie. She was like a godmother to me, but I'm not going to say much about her 'cause she doesn't like that. Some people called her Ms. Fimmy, but her name was Serafima, and that's what I called her. Seems like everybody wanted to change your name around there. She once told me there would come a day when I would forget about her, that I would vanish, but I don't think I will ever forget her. This story is for her.

Serafima was a gardener, not the kind that goes and buys little potted plants, but the kind that has seeds growing from her grandmother, and probably the grandmother before that. Her garden was all over her yard, it never stopped anywhere, except at the ends of her lot and the little paths that ran all over so you could get by. She had the biggest yard in the neighborhood, and part of it backed onto the little forest. Serafima said her yard was all that was left of 160 acres her parents used to farm. She had comfrey plants covering the ground under her apple trees that I especially liked. The leaves were like the soft ears of a rabbit, flopped over the big rocks she had all around the yard. That's what she called those plants, her bunnies. Serafima used a shovel, and an ax, and a hoe that was made from a cow bone. That's all she had and she said it was the best. She used her hands for everything else. She pretty much smelled like fresh dirt, and I just loved that. Her flowers grew all among the vegetables and there weren't any straight rows anywhere. She used to tell me, "I'm gonna plant me a rose someday," but she never had any rosebushes. I know now that she meant me. I was her one and only Rose, and I did get uprooted and I did get replanted.

One day, long ago it seems to me now, a lady knocked on the door and gave me something she said was a ticket out of there. She was good-looking, held herself straight, but wasn't pushy about it. She didn't ask to come inside but, still, I was grateful the boys weren't around. Duane was capable of crawling up the steps and sniffing around her legs. I'd seen him do that. He didn't have a clue how to act around a real woman. The lady told me about a program

for people like me, who just needed a little help. Well, she
didn't say that, but that's what she meant. She told me that
I should put on good clothes and go to a certain place, on
a certain day, before noon. I would then have the opportunity to take a simple test. She did say that. Nobody had
ever used the word *opportunity* to me before, and hearing
that word made me listen to what she said.

She gave me a brochure and left, and I took it with me
into the kitchen. I heard Clyman's car pull up, fast, into
the yard.

We lived in an unfinished tract house that was fore-
closed before it was even finished being built. My father
and Laverle got it cheap because of that, and in fact it was
paid for. Luckily, the whole neighborhood went to pieces at
about the same time, so our house didn't stick out like the
sore thumb it really was, but the car frames scattered around
it made it a little different from the others. Clyman and his
buddies always pulled up right in the front yard, which was
just dirt and junk. The curb was chipped away and there
was too much stuff in the driveway to park there. I never
even tried to clean the yard. My garden was on one side of
the house, which was penned in by a chain-link fence in the
front and that old engine in the back. I had to get to my
garden by going through the bathroom window, which
wasn't as hard as it sounds, and it made it real private.
Every so often some smart aleck would lock me out there
and then a whole other thing would go on. There was a
mean dog on the other side of the fence, that was sometimes
out in the yard. I had to be really careful not to let it see
me, but that dog only had a dog's brain. I pretty much
thought like a cat and so I always outsmarted him.

I grew real food in that garden and I was a good cook.
When the boys got too nasty from just hanging around
doing nothing day after day, I would make lentil stew,
which I knew they hated to smell. I don't know why. They
wanted to eat meat all the time, and they hated the smell
of my stew full of celery and garlic. That was another way
I had of controlling those boys. They would whine all the
way out the door. We never talked about it.

I had my own room, right off the kitchen. It was meant

to be a laundry room, I guess, so there weren't any windows in it, but it had a metal door and I could lock it real securely when I needed to. I felt safe there and in fact I loved that little room, and that's where I read. Not one of those boys had ever been in it, but I used to read stories to Roscoe there. My bed was a big shelf I had nailed up, which went from wall to wall, and it was good enough, and cozy. On the opposite wall were more shelves running, just like my bed, wall-to-wall, and filled with books and my clothes, folded up. I had an old mirror in a black wood frame of Mama's that still had traces of gold and pink roses painted on it. It was big enough and reflected my lamp. When I was in bed with my book, I could look over and see myself reading, and I liked that. Half of the ceiling was covered with bunches of dried flowers that Serafima had given me. I really liked how the ceiling light showed through them. It smelled good in there too. Serafima was the only person besides Roscoe who had ever been all the way inside my room, but there were some mice that visited me there, regular, 'cause I fed them oats and celery, and I found out mice don't especially like cheese. I loved those little mice about like I loved Serafima, and Mama, to tell you the truth.

There was only one thing I wished for then, other than to not live there at all, and that was a picture of my real mother. She was big, like me, I knew that, but that was about all I remembered, except that she used to tell me stories about everything under the sun. The only time I had been out in the wilderness was when I was with Mama, but I can't really talk about that now. I still remember when Laverle burned all the pictures of her. I think my father started his dying from that moment, 'cause I could see he still missed Mama. I didn't much care how my father was feeling, at any time, with good reason, but I know I felt a stab in my body when I saw what Laverle had done, and I knew he felt it too.

I can kind of understand why Laverle left this family when her baby died, and I can even see why she thought it would be okay to dump her big ugly boys on me, but I can't bring myself to understand why she needed to burn the pictures of a dead woman. I hope I get over that someday.

It seems to me that forgiveness is something that you give, real easy, to the people you love, no matter what they've done, it just goes without saying, but the ones who can't be forgiven are the ones who've never said they're sorry, the ones who never asked. Laverle never asked. Neither did my father. It didn't have to be with words, but they never did. When I figured that out, I knew I must have cared for both of them more than I thought.

Clyman was someone I could forgive. He sort of helped me keep people out of my room. There were even times when he seemed to know I had reached a point with all the work I did, and with all the filth I put up with in his friends. Clyman seemed to know when that was, and he would shove all the boys out of the house. They would all leave me alone for a while, for days. Pretty soon, Jeffrey got so he seldom showed up at all, and Duane always acted any way that Clyman did, but it was an act. If Duane was sitting around, doing nothing at all, you could bet it was because Clyman was doing nothing at all either. If Clyman said something sounded like a good idea to him, Duane would say it sounded good to him too, only Duane would keep on talking about it, just to make it sound like it was his own idea all the time. If I ever find any of this funny to think back on someday, it will probably be memories of Duane copying Clyman.

That day in the kitchen, after that lady had given me the brochure, I was standing there looking through the window over the sink, knowing the boys would be barging in any minute. The window glass was held together with duct tape but it was clean. A dog I'd never seen before was chained outside. I only noticed that because my dishpan was beside it for a water dish. Jeffrey always kept a dog out there in the filth, but never for more than a few weeks at a time. I always heard him say he was training those dogs and selling them. I started to go outside and get my dishpan back when I heard the Coons stomp into the house.

Clyman and his friends were a sort of gang, and they called themselves the Coons, because they thought that was funny and because they were so hot for killing those scared little animals. But I thought it meant that someday, somebody was going to tree them all and maybe blow their heads off. Serafima said I shouldn't talk that way. She said it was very similar to a prayer to say things like that. I told her I *really* thought it was something that would be a blessing for everybody, including the boys themselves.

Clyman clomped into the kitchen that day and called out in his loud voice, "Who's that?" He must have seen the lady's truck pull away. Things often turned out better if I didn't answer Clyman at all. I waited and he said, "What's that?" and grabbed the brochure out of my hands. I knew he could hardly read, and he ended like I thought he would. "Shit," he said, "probably some religion thing."

Lately Clyman had started acting like he was the oldest, so none of this surprised me, but then he said something unusual for him. "Was he white or black?" I just looked at him and didn't say a thing. He hadn't even thought of red. He put the brochure in his dirty jeans pocket and left the room, and that was the end of that.

I didn't care that Clyman had taken my ticket to opportunity. I knew I wouldn't do anything with it anyway. I didn't believe in magic, but Clyman did. Later I saw him and Ada using rolled-up pieces of that brochure to snort coke.

The rest is pretty easy to tell. Maybe Serafima was right and I never will see her again because I am surely not going back, and I know she understands. At least I want her to know she was the one who gave me the ticket out of there.

Clyman left the house with Ada, and Jeffrey hadn't been seen in days. Duane later came in, ate something in the living room, which was also his bedroom, and left. Duane always did things sneaky so I never really heard him leave. That night the dog began to bark when it was late so I let it go. Nothing was new.

The next day nobody came home, which was a holiday for me because it meant they would probably be gone for days, so after my gardening I went over to Serafima's. We had her usual weak tea, and I told her about the lady who had come by, and about her saying I should get all dressed up, that this was an opportunity. Serafima got serious for a minute, as we both knew I didn't have any decent clothes. Then she told me, "You look in your mama's stuff." I didn't answer. I had looked through those old things before, of course. My mother's special smell was long gone, and I didn't look anymore. Her clothes were in some moldy boxes in the garage, although that was just a beat-up shed full of junk and spiders. Laverle had thought those boxes were full of outgrown things of her boys, but I always knew they were Mama's, and I didn't say anything.

Sometimes I had gotten those clothes out, but they were too big for me. I thought they were old-fashioned, but I had liked the colors and the way they moved. Mama had been a thrift-store shopper and so her clothes were even older than they might have been, but I went home and tried them on again. They fit good enough now, and I knew those old clothes were considered cool, and I knew they looked pretty good. I took a pair of pants, some shirts, and I put my own stuff into her old shoulder bag.

The clothes were wrinkled and I didn't have any iron, but I knew how to steam things in the shower to straighten them out, so I did that. One thing we had was plenty of hot water for Duane's boiling hot showers. I'd had to steam clothes in the shower when I went to my little brother's funeral, so I knew how that worked. I had figured it out. Later I hung my mother's clothes on the bar that was directly over the bed in my room.

That night, sitting on my bed, looking up at those particular clothes, it seems like I knew I had to have them ready, and I thought about that. I also cried that night but I don't know why.

A few nights later, I guess, all the boys came in around sunrise, loud and drunk, and it woke me up. Something made me get dressed fast and see what was up. They were all giggling, like they had done something bad. But they hadn't done something bad—they were getting ready to do it. I didn't like how everything felt. There were two derelicts with them I had seen before, and all of them were mighty drunk. I stood in the doorway of my room and heard Jeffrey outside yelling that somebody stole his dog. Clyman stumbled into the kitchen but he wouldn't look at me. That worried me. He didn't seem as drunk as the others, and I knew he wasn't as mean as the rest of them could be. They all sort of rolled and punched their way through the kitchen, and it filled up with the smell of mud, and beer, and pee, and noise. I saw then that the two homeless men were struggling to hold onto something alive. I heard a high-pitched whine and my stomach lurched. I felt like I needed to run, but I also didn't want to leave. I wanted to help what made that noise but I couldn't move. They had a live raccoon, a young one, and that poor, bloody creature looked right into my eyes.

They dropped the little animal on the table, its feet all tied up, knocking its backbone against the edge. I thought I was dying then because I felt everything in my body come to a stop. I heard myself saying, Oh, no, oh no, over and over. "No, Clyman, oh no." Somebody had grabbed my wrists and he was taller than I was. I looked and it turned out to be Jeffrey who was so tall. I hadn't even known that about him, he was such a stranger to me. He's the one who said to Clyman, "Let's take it outside." He didn't even look at me when he dropped my arms. I'm big, as I said, but I don't fight. Serafima had taught me how to work out life so that it wasn't necessary to do things that way, and I had seen she was right.

I saw right then that Clyman had made his choice to join in on the meanness, and in my mind I said goodbye to him, but I hope he stops that someday.

I won't tell you what happened out in the yard that night. I don't really know. I filled the dishpan full of hot water and took it into my room and bolted the door. My hands weren't shaking at all. I took off my clothes and washed up, trying not to listen to what was going on outside. They were making plenty of noise. I brushed my hair careful, back and away from my face in a way I'd never done before. I put on my mother's clothes and put some of my favorite books in her shoulder bag. I did all that, quick and smooth. I put on the most decent pair of shoes I had, opened the door and walked through the house. I felt like

I didn't have any feet at all. The house smelled bad to me, my own food smells, and I remember thinking I would never cook another lentil again, and I think that's going to be true.

I stood there in that ugly front door of Duane's bedroom, and I could smell the early morning there. I realized this was the day, the day hanging out in my memory, the day I had to be somewhere before noon, like the lady had said. I heard a police siren not too far off and I knew it had to be on its way to the house. I pulled at a box of matches that were stuck in the wax of a dusty melted candle and ran back to my bedroom. I got that box of matches blazing and threw it on my bed. I figured the clothes and books would catch fire easy, and all of Serafima's flowers. I grabbed up the little pumpkin she had grown and dried for me, and put it in my bag.

I walked through the house fast, and out the front door, and even though I lost one of my shoes on the steps, I didn't look back. I felt like I was breathing for the first time in my life, and I felt like I was floating. I remembered just exactly where the lady had said to go, and I heard later that I had a big smile on my face. I felt like I was some kind of queen. I felt like I was going to the ball.

"Reading a husky poem by Anne Sexton, and seeing a tough and tender drawing by Terri Windling, both about Cinderella, got me going on a grand consensus of the different versions of the tale that I had written over the years. I'm pretty sure Cinderella wasn't a fool."

You, Little Match-girl

JOYCE CAROL OATES

Joyce Carol Oates is one of the most prolific and respected writers in the United States. She has written fiction in almost every genre and medium. Her keen interest in the Gothic and psychological horror has spurred her to write dark suspense novels under the name Rosamond Smith, with enough stories in the genre to have published four collections of dark fiction, the most recent being The Collector of Hearts, *and to edit* American Gothic Tales. *Oates's short novel* Zombie *won the Bram Stoker Award for Superior Achievement in the Novel, and she has been honored with a Life Achievement Award given by the Horror Writers Association. Oates's short fiction has often been reprinted in* The Year's Best Fantasy and Horror. *Her most recent novel is* My Heart Laid Bare.

You, Little Match-girl

She was a lonely girl but her loneliness was hidden by her pride in her accomplishments, as a gnarled thicket can hide even the blazing sun. So she became a young woman without comprehending the depth of her aloneness. At crucial times she warned herself in a calm, reasonable voice, *If I love no one I am free. So long as I love no one, I can travel where I wish. I can become anyone I wish.*

And so it was, and so it came to be.

Already as a bright, secretive child thinking her own thoughts as her parents smiled at her, kissed and hugged her, took pride in her (for even as a very small child she was obviously intelligent, sharp-eyed, talented), as her grandmother cuddled and sang to her, she understood that she could become anyone she wished. You have only to shut your eyes, hurry down a shadowy corridor to a doorway shimmering with light—and cross the threshold. It was Grandma who sang Mother Goose songs to her, "The Fairy Ship," "Jack and Jill," "Three Blind Mice," "Humpty Dumpty"—she laughed at the comical illustration of the bland, bald, egg-faced Humpty Dumpty teetering on his wall—and, when she was very sleepy, and couldn't keep her eyes open (though trying! she'd been eager to emulate grown-ups from the cradle onward) "Rock-a-Bye Baby." It was Grandma who read to her from her favorite book, tales beginning *Once upon a time* . . . which excited and enthralled her, the stories of "Snow White," "The Frog Prince," "Little Red Riding Hood," "The Little Match-Girl," "Cinderella." One day she would learn that the tales in this book were not the original, harsh tales but tales with happy endings: *Once upon a time* would lead eventually, reassuringly, to *And they lived happily ever after.* The illustrations were vividly colored and fascinating, her favorites were Little Red Riding Hood with bouncy chestnut curls and bright red cloak, and the brave woodsman with his red shirt, bristly black beard, and up-raised ax hurrying to kill the wolf and save Little Red Riding Hood; and Cinderella in her dazzling white gown, the fairest of all the land, a glittering glass slipper on her upraised foot; and the Twelve Dancing Princesses who were so secretive and obstinate, even their father the King couldn't tell them what to do. She did not like the Frog Prince, who too much resembled a comic-strip frog with bulging eyes, nor did she like the Little Match-Girl, who was so ragged, hunched over, *sad.* You can make yourself anyone you wish, why then make yourself *sad?* Shut your eyes, run down the secret corridor, step over the threshold and you can be a princess, a queen, Puss-in-Boots, Jack climbing the beanstalk, Goldilocks who dares to enter the house of the Three Bears but wins their love and admiration anyway. You can imagine yourself anywhere, in any remote kingdom by the sea or in the mountains. Many centuries ago, or centuries into the future dwelling among a race of beings like angels. *My choice! Mine.*

Then abruptly, overnight it seemed to her family, she lost all interest in fairy tales and childish things. She began school, she discovered school books and the excitement of pleasing her teachers, no longer her parents, or Grandma. Of course she loved her parents, and she loved Grandma, who was so nice to her, but it was her teachers she admired, respected, wished to emulate. And how she succeeded!—it was like a fairy tale, how she became a "star"—and the other children, even the prettier girls, even the boys, were made to envy her. And so, one day, when she was in sixth grade, in a burst of energy she cleared out her shelves of her oldest books, most of them gifts from Grandma she hadn't glanced into in years—out went battered *Mother Goose*, out went *Favorite Fairy Tales* with the stained, warped cover that had once slipped into the bath, out went *Tales of Hans Christian Andersen*—out! Grandma was surprised and hurt, but she decided not to care. For she was on her way to growing up. *Becoming who I really am.*

Even before her twentieth birthday she'd begun to travel, to England, to Europe, to Northern Africa, to Turkey. By the age of thirty she'd traveled to the Far East, including Tibet and Afghanistan. Sometimes she traveled with companions, students like herself, but more often she went alone; or, starting out in the company of others, splitting off on her own. She was a photojournalist: her province was what was *real*. She had no patience for fantasy, for wishful thinking in any guise—political, religious, literary. She was an attractive woman, but an air of impatience and something vaguely sneering in her manner rebuffed men, and discouraged women from befriending her. *If I love no one, I am free. So long as I love no one.* Looking back upon her childhood, she felt a stab of embarrassment, and scorn. No one in her family had been educated beyond high school, not one of her relatives, including her cousins, had ventured much beyond the territory (rural Maine, west of Skowhegan) of their childhoods. She recalled the old fairy tales her grandmother had read to her, tales of people so strangely *fated*. Yet, in real life, only fools are *fated*.

By the age of thirty-five she'd realized her dream of establishing an international reputation as a photojournalist of the highest integrity and professional skill, and she liked it very much, though she was never boastful, that her work commanded the highest fees as well. She was known for her remarkable reliability: alone among her competitors, whose personal lives were often stormy, she seemed never to allow personal problems (if she had any, these were kept secret even from friends) to interfere with her work. She'd been out of contact with relatives, photographing Tibetan monks, when her grandmother had died; when her father died unexpectedly, she'd been traveling in Lebanon, and hadn't even known of his death until twelve days later; but when her mother became gravely ill, she was in Berlin as a fellow of the Berlin Institute, and easily accessible, so when she received a telegram from one of her mother's sisters she had no choice but to fly home. *What a time for this to happen. What bad luck.* Her emotions were confused—anger, fear, even a touch of panic. As if she were a high-flying bird enthralled by her natural element the sky, oblivious of Earth, caught suddenly in a net and hauled back to the ground. Her German colleagues believed that Maine must be a romantic place, like America of the nineteenth century, and she told them flatly that it was not romantic at all—"Except at a distance of thousands of miles." Yet when she arrived at the Skowhegan airport with its single runway, and was met by relatives she hadn't seen in years, and taken to the hospital to see her mother, whom she hadn't seen in years, she was astonished at the rawness of her emotion. Her mother so aged, so frail, so exhausted by her long ordeal of surgery—it was as if her heart were wrenched from her. "Mother!—Mommy." She burst into childlike tears and had to be consoled by her relatives, and even by her mother.

After her mother's death she took upon herself the task of shutting up the old house. Which she insisted upon doing alone. The farmhouse and five-acre property were hers but she wanted to prepare the furniture for storage since she intended to sell the house, and hoped to put things as much in order as possible before returning to Berlin. *To my own life. My life.* Her relatives were advising her not to sell so quickly, maybe one day she'd want to return, perhaps to spend part of a summer, but she was emphatically against this, no it wasn't a good idea, returning to Maine had no part in her plans for the future. *I will travel where I wish. Become anyone I wish.* In truth she'd been deeply moved by

the experience of returning. Deeply shaken by her mother's
death. And by the realization that she'd missed her father's
death, and her grandmother's death, as if a strange spell
had been cast over her, she'd been asleep for most of her
life. What had she been thinking of? The familiar refrain
taunted her, *If I love no one. So long as I love no one.* Never
before had she detected its flat jeering tone, like struck tin.

She was desperate to be gone. Her emotions were too
raw here. She couldn't trust herself. Her mother had been
hospitalized in mid-November, had died in early December
as the days rapidly shortened and the hours of darkness
lengthened like shadows pushing out of the snow-encrusted
earth. And it was cold, bitter cold. She'd forgotten how cold.
Almost, she felt panic at being snowed-in—stranded in the
country. As if there weren't snowplows! As if this weren't
a civilized place. As if she hadn't lived through many win-
ters here, along with everyone else. Yet she was eager to be
back in Berlin by Christmas if not earlier. The house and
property would be managed by an agent. She'd agreed to
sell for any reasonable price. She refused to listen to her
relatives. *No! I have no plans to return.* In truth she was
shocked at how distraught she'd been by her mother's
death, and memories of the past that flooded upon her, she
who'd told herself and others since college that she hadn't
been close to anyone in her family, she'd been intellectually
"estranged" from them. Yet seeing her relatives again, particularly her cousins, had been quite moving. Driving Cuttler's Mill Road into Skowhegan, those nine miles of
countryside she would not have known she'd memorized,
was hypnotic. *As if somewhere along the way I might encounter
Daddy driving our old Plymouth, with Mommy beside him,
Grandma and me in the backseat. That child-face peering from a
rear window.*

How strange, whether wonderful or ominous she didn't
know, that the countryside west of Skowhegan hadn't
changed much in the past fifteen years. Names on farmers'
mailboxes were familiar—*Cosgrove, Thorndike, Ward, Proctor.*
(She'd imagined herself in love, in her covert, distant way,
with one of the Proctor boys, her senior by two or three

years.) An older generation had passed away, her own generation had inherited and come into maturity.

But she was desperate to be gone. She wasn't a superstitious person like a surprising number of her fellow photojournalists, but she believed she must leave Maine by December 21, the winter solstice. She made flight arrangements to leave on the twentieth. She'd nearly completed packing cartons, shutting up the old house. She'd been sleeping in her old room, no other room felt quite comfortable to her, and by the morning of the twentieth she was in a state of nerves for there was a traveler's advisory against driving in central and northern Maine for the next twelve hours, the first severe blizzard of the winter was expected. Her flight didn't leave Skowhegan until four P.M. but she decided to lock up the house, throw her things into her car (her mother's car, which she would be leaving with her aunt in town) and drive out before noon. Already it had begun to snow—light, feathery snowflakes. There were patches, still, of pale blue sky. The winter sun had shone coldly and thinly that morning. Yet as she drove, she glanced anxiously upward to see clouds massed and ominous as malignancies; she felt her car rock in sporadic gusts of wind; snow by the roadside was lifted in coils and skeins, flung snakelike into the path of her car, and onto her windshield; there were few other cars on the road, their headlights looming up ghostly in the deepening dusk. Not yet midday, and already it was dusk. *If I can make it to the edge of Skowhegan at least. To that Sunoco station. Then I will be safe.* Snow burst out of the air in a delirium of faded white, if white can be faded. Even in her headlights this white looked discolored, like old ivory. She understood that her flight to Bangor in a twin-prop plane would be cancelled, but at least she'd be in town and could stay the night at a motel near the airport and fly out tomorrow. Or the next day. From Bangor she would be flying to Kennedy, and from Kennedy direct to Berlin, she'd made such careful plans, always she made such careful plans, she was a woman who'd planned her life with care, and she had made for herself a success in the vast world beyond her childhood. *That world is there, awaiting me. I'm coming!* Though the narrow road was icy in patches, and the wind had grown stronger, snow rushing thicker and more blinding into the feeble path of her headlights, she pressed her foot down harder on the gas pedal; gripped the steering wheel until her fingers seemed frozen to it. As if by such force she might hold the speeding, suddenly skidding car on the road.

She heard a cry—"No! No!" A child's hurt, incredulous voice.

For it was so unfair.

Waking in a haze of muted white, a delirium of swirling white, pain wracking her upper chest, a terrible roaring in her ears—for some dazed minutes she didn't know where she was.

Then she remembered. Her mother's car. On the way to Skowhegan.

Without the safety belt I would have been killed! My neck broken. Skull broken. Flung against the windshield. Through the windshield. As in the old days before such safety features—people must have been injured, killed, in such accidents all the time. Shaken, crushed and broken like silly dolls. This was the tale she would tell others, the tone of the tale. If you're disinclined to self-pity and feel uncomfortable speaking of a car accident in which you'd nearly died (but wasn't that an exaggeration? she hadn't nearly died), you can speak elliptically, with a dry, detached humor. For she'd broken her collarbone with her desperate driving, and her head ached so she was nearly blind, nose and mouth dripping blood that wasn't red (for it was dark inside the car, overturned in a snowdrift in a ditch) but oddly black, greasy to the touch. Her thoughts came in a blur that roared like the wind. *Oh! oh! oh. My God. What have I done?* Groping panicked in the glove compartment where the flashlight was kept, her father's old, rusted flashlight—yes, she found it, and yes, there came a beam of light when she forced the switch.

How frugal Daddy had been, they'd teased him, reluctant to part with old things like this flashlight—decades old.

She would climb out of the capsized car, get help on the road. Yet in the next instant she was overcome by drowsiness, sleep—there was some confusion about time, between the moment when she'd realized the car was skidding out of control on a curve (but it hadn't been her fault, she would insist to the insurance company it had been the wind, gale-force winds, that seemed to lift her car and fling it off the road as a vengeful giant might have done) and the moment she forced her eyelids open, in a stab of panic realizing *I will die if I sleep here: I will freeze to death.*

Maybe she was in a state of shock. Things came to her oddly, in broken pieces. Comprehending the cold, for instance. The car's motor had died, the heater was dead. Already her breath steamed, thinly. Her body temperature was dropping—was it? Before leaving her parents' house she'd walked guiltily through the downstairs rooms a final time and paused to stare out the kitchen window at the rusted thermometer beside the wild bird feeder. Seeing with a shudder that it was −12° F. And now with the ferocious wind it might have been as cold as −30° F.

So unfair! She could have wept with hurt, disappointment, rage, except she had no time. She was grunting, struggling to get the car door open. A wedge of snow, obscuring most of the window, surprisingly heavy for newly fallen powdery snow. Her chest throbbed with pain, a network of flashing pain, her heartbeat was quickened and erratic, yet by desperate force she managed to get the door open a few inches, push herself through the narrow space, and out— into more snow, swirling snow, icy stinging particles of snow like buckshot. She was gripping the flashlight. It was all she could carry from the car, her belongings would have to be left behind temporarily, even her expensive Japanese camera, her handbag with numerous airline tickets.

At least it was good luck: her mother's lightweight, compact car had listed toward its right side, leaving the driver's side relatively clear of snow. Otherwise she might have perished in the freezing dark.

But she was safe. Stumbling in the snow like a drunken woman, limping, waving the flashlight and calling, "Help? Help me?"—though there were no headlights in sight, no lights of any kind. The beam of light was stronger than she'd dared hope. With luck it would penetrate the near-opaque wall of falling snow. *If there's anyone to see it. Anyone*

for miles. She seemed to know she wasn't behaving altogether rationally but she wasn't sure what was wrong. Cupping a hand to her mouth, calling, "Help! I'm here! I've been
injured!" But where exactly was the road? Her mother's car
had skidded, slid into a drainage ditch that must have been
four feet deep at least, when not drifted with snow, but
which direction had it come from? She blinked, wiped at
her eyes—all was white, faded white, a white of shadows,
drifting driving snow like sand. She was in the Sahara during a sandstorm. She was lost in the Himalayas, in a sudden
unexpected blizzard. But no: she was on the Cuttler's Mill
Road only a few miles from the shut-up house. There was
a farm not far away—in which direction? The Cosgroves'
farm. Or was it the Proctors'? If she tried to walk to it she
might get lost, wander in circles, become desperate, panic.
For she had no seed to drop in her wake, to mark her path,
and if she had, falling snow would cover it within minutes.
She would collapse, perish in the bitter cold. Every winter
in Maine there were such tales of motorists freezing to death
in fields, wandered from their cars; or fallen within a few
yards of a house, their frozen corpses discovered beneath
drifts of snow.

She was very cold. Shivering. Trembling. Her teeth chattering. The blood on her face had frozen, like a mask. She
was wearing a black wool coat, a scarf wound around her
head, not a very warm coat by Maine standards. Why hadn't
she taken her mother's quilted goose-down coat, which had
a hood, newly purchased before her mother had taken ill,
her mother had given it to her, or tried to—*Wear it. It's
warm. It's no use to me now, dear.* But she hadn't wanted such
a coat. A coat from Sears. Though her father's old Goodyear
flashlight, purchased probably at Sears as well, was precious
to her, it would save her life. She held it at chest-level as
headlights appeared at last in the near distance, moving
with maddening slowness. Someone was coming! "Here!
Help me—" She waved the flashlight wildly but the vehicle
veered off to the left, and was gone. Dim red taillights that
vanished too, within seconds. She'd stumbled toward the
headlights, fell heavily, flailing in the snow, pushed herself
with difficulty to her feet, panting, sobbing. "Come back!

I'm here! I've had an accident! Help me!"—*I'm alone, I'm injured. Don't leave me here to die.* But now at least she had a clearer sense of where the road was, and it wasn't where she'd have thought, perpendicular to her and then veering away. She switched off the flashlight, to save the battery. There was sure to be another vehicle along soon, if she was lucky a snowplow, a tow truck. She was only about five miles from Skowhegan, though not on a highway. Still she wanted to believe that Cuttler's Mill Road was important enough to plow out in the midst of a blizzard that had only just begun. Stamping her feet which were going numb, bringing her fists together. In a sudden panic she realized that her eyelashes would freeze together, she'd be blinded if she didn't stop crying. *God help me. God, please forgive me. Why did I stay away so long?* She had the uneasy feeling that she was being punished, there was a plan to this, as in a children's story of punishment out of all proportion to blame. *Once upon a time . . .* A woman cousin had invited her to spend the night at her house in Skowhegan, near the airport, but she'd declined for she wanted to be alone on her last night in the old house, she'd had more work, more packing, more thinking to do, and possibly that had been a mistake for her cousin had wished to befriend her, and now of course she'd be in Skowhegan and safe except how could her decision have been a mistake unless her entire life had been a mistake and this possibility *I refuse to accept.*

She waited. She would be patient. For impatience, fear, panic would not save her. Standing in what she believed to be the road, waiting. How long, she could not gauge. It was too much of an effort for her to push back her coat sleeve and check her wristwatch for the time. Or perhaps she was fearful of knowing the time. How long she'd been stranded here on the Cuttler's Mill Road. Minutes were passing, the wind tore at her face, her thin wool scarf, snow encrusted her hair, eyelashes, she must resemble a snow-sculpture by this time, it was such effort to keep moving, stamping her feet, shaking her head, how sleepy she was, how powerful the urge to lie down in the snow blanketing the earth, how sweet, her eyelids heavy, closing—and just at that instant she saw, or seemed to see, another pair of headlights. This time she'd be rescued! She knew. She fumbled to switch on the flashlight. At first nothing happened, there was no light, she shook the flashlight and the light came on, though in a reduced, feeble beam. But she was stumbling toward the headlights anyway, really she didn't need the flashlight, she was crying, "Here! Help! I had an accident!" This time the vehicle came to a stop. A man's voice called, in surprise, "Hello? Is someone there?" and she was sobbing with relief, waving desperately in the blinding headlights, "Yes! Here! Help me."

She must have collapsed. Though with no memory of falling to the ground. A man was stooping over her, his breath steaming. His face was familiar but she didn't know his name. She could not have spoken his name. That creased adult face like a mask upon a boy's face, subtly disfiguring it. Yet she recognized the eyes. Her rescuer was talking to her, comforting her, his voice booming yet difficult to decipher. Yet it was her own language he spoke—the flattened nasal accent of inland Maine. He was calling her by name: he knew her! For he, too, lived on the Cuttler's Mill Road. He would drive her to Skowhegan, to the hospital. He stooped to shove his arms beneath her, lifting her with care, like a man accustomed to such emergencies, the sensation of being lifted, carried, like a child, was unnerving to her, yet wonderful—she was whimpering, sobbing with relief, gratitude. "Oh, thank you. Thank you, thank you, you've saved my life." Inside the cab of his pickup truck it was warm, astonishingly warm, she'd forgotten what warmth was, the heater was on full blast. Deftly, explaining he'd had some paramedic training, he was a volunteer fireman, he yanked off her tight stylish leather boots and rubbed her numb toes, until sensation, sharp stabs of pain that made her wince, returned. He rubbed her hands, too, briskly, and laid the flat of his warm, broad palms against her cheeks which had begun to freeze. In her weakened condition she didn't even feel embarrassment or self-consciousness as always she felt when a man touched her for the first time.

Driving to Skowhegan, through the swirling snow, at no more than ten miles an hour, her rescuer identified himself

as Burt Proctor—did she remember him? Feebly she nodded,
yes. Yes, she did. He told her that he was living on his
father's farm, though not farming, working in Skowhegan,
he had a small construction firm, they'd gone to school together, he was two or three years ahead of her, he was sorry
to hear of her mother's death, he'd heard in fact that she
was back visiting, dealing with her mother's estate, he'd
drive her to the Skowhegan hospital, she'd be all right.
Maybe she'd broken something? Her collarbone, ribs. Fingers. And her face—her face was lacerated, a little. They'd
fix her up in emergency just fine. She tried to respond,
would have liked to laugh with relief, instead of crying with
relief, she wasn't a weak woman, and how grateful she was,
*and what did it mean that Burt Proctor of all people had rescued
her*, saved her from death on the Cuttler's Mill Road where
their families had long lived, only a few miles apart. Burt
Proctor was bearded now, his coarse black beard short-
trimmed and threaded with gray; his eyebrows too were
coarse, nearly meeting at the bridge of his nose in a way
she didn't remember from when he'd been a boy; there was
a distracting, hooklike scar on his upper lip. He wore a
practical winter hat, not very clean, with prominent ear flaps
and a strap that buckled beneath his chin, and a dull-red
sheepskin jacket. His face that was no longer a boy's smooth
good-looking face but the face of an adult man who'd suffered losses. For the elder Proctors, too, had surely passed
away, she believed she'd heard this, so much time had
passed in her absence. Burt Proctor was telling her he'd been
making improvements on the old place since moving back,
he'd lived in town while married, had two kids, teenagers
now, but his family was broke-up and he didn't get to see
the boys very often now, they were living with their mother
and stepfather in Portland. The odd words *broke-up* were
poignant in her ears, she blinked back tears, felt a trickle of
moisture running down her face, and Burt Proctor smiled
at her and wiped her face with the back of his hand, gently,
as you might wipe a child's runny nose, and now she was
embarrassed for it was blood he'd wiped away, blood
smeared on his right hand, this was an intimacy she hadn't
been prepared for, and didn't know how to assess.

In Skowhegan there was the Sunoco station: bright-lit, busy, a tow truck steaming exhaust near the road. And there were vehicles on Main Street, not many, slow-moving and ponderous as ancient beasts, and a county snowplow spewing snow at the curb, red light winking on top of the cab. What relief: here in Skowhegan things were under control, the storm had been expected, emergency vehicles were in readiness, no one would perish in the cold, in drifting snow. She was in pain by now, considerable pain, now the numbness had passed from her, but she drew breath in relief seeing so much activity, lighted buildings and houses and the Skowhegan hospital (where her mother had died at 4:20 A.M. when she'd been out at the house, unable to be with her) lighted and bustling with activity. As Burt Proctor in his red sheepskin jacket like a tall huntsman carried her in his strong arms into the emergency room yet strangely asking her what had become of her pony? that beautiful little Shetland? and she smiled in confusion for she hadn't owned a pony—had she? She'd yearned for one, she'd begged her parents for years, but nothing had come of it; yet now Burt Proctor seemed to be remembering her pony fondly, describing it as pebble-gray with a finespun silver mane and flowing silver tail; a prancing Shetland upon which she'd ridden proudly as Little Snow-Drop in one of the books her grandmother had given her. *If I had no pony in my life it's only fair that I be given my pony now.* For it turned out that she'd been injured more seriously in the accident on the Cuttler's Mill Road than she would have liked to think. Lifted by emergency room attendants from her rescuer's arms, she looked back at him seeing to her horror a mask-sized imprint of blood soaked into the man's sheepskin jacket. And his bare hands, too, were bloody. He called after her words of encouragement and affection as they bore her away to save her life.

Because he waited for her, never ceased thinking of her, through the next several hours, her life was saved. She would tell him, "Somehow, I knew this. I knew you were there, and would have been at my side if they'd allowed it."

There was the confusion of the emergency room that was so brightly lit, frantic with activity, not quiet as you'd

expect a hospital; winking lights like swirling, furious snowflakes cascading out of the sky. Yet the snowflakes had been
so strangely faded. Like the discolored, faintly cracked keys
of Grandma's upright piano. Grandma had paid for her
piano lessons when her father didn't think they could afford
it, and it was at Grandma's house, of course, she'd practiced
her pieces: "Three Blind Mice," "A Fox Went Out," "Hey
Diddle-Diddle," a showy Czerny exercise in which the second and third fingers of both hands buzzed up and down
the keyboard as rapidly as you could make them go—"The
Two Bees." She'd loved Grandma's piano and she'd inherited Grandma's piano but—where was it now?

*At the old house. In the country. In the snow. With the rest
of your things.*

Her rescuer waited for her at the hospital and at last
she was discharged, leaning on his arm, walking with difficulty, tight bands of gauze and adhesive wrapped around
her upper chest so that she could scarcely breathe, and flesh-
colored bandages on her lacerated face. "Please don't look
at me, I look like a savage," she said, but Burt Proctor said,
"No. You're beautiful. Come on." Through the now lightly
falling snow they walked. He brought her to a restaurant
for a late meal, for they were both famished. She would not
have believed she could eat in her exhausted state yet she
did eat, trembling with hunger, and happiness. They sat
close together on the same side of the booth, nudging shoulders. On the table was a small vase of bright red carnations
that, inspected, turned out to be plastic. Dim funky-sweet
rock music played, out of the shadows as out of the past.
She understood that this was her past, of which she'd been
cheated. Burt Proctor was saying, "I didn't seem to realize
how much I loved my parents, while they were alive," and
she was saying, "I didn't seem to realize how much I loved
my parents and my grandmother while I was alive," then,
realizing her mistake, quickly adding, "—I mean, while they
were alive." Burt Proctor laughed at her misspoken words.
She saw the love for her in his eyes, and was stricken to
the heart and could not speak. Her hair spilled down her
back. It had come undone in the emergency room. She
hadn't had the opportunity to brush it and fasten it back up

in a crownlike braid around her head like the beautiful golden-haired princess in the tower. And her hair wasn't golden but merely dark brown. Yet Burt Proctor touched it gently with his roughened fingers. Burt Proctor touched her cheek gently. Never had she been so close to a man with a beard like Burt Proctor's: wirelike, bristly, a coarse black threaded with coarser gray hairs. And that hooklike scar on his upper lip. He was saying, "I didn't seem to realize how I loved you, when we were young," quickly adding, "—I mean, younger." She was saying, "I didn't seem to realize, either—how much I loved you. I mean—love you." It must have been the codeine they'd given her at the hospital—for her to be speaking in such a way. Yet it was the truth, she was a woman who spoke the truth, and Burt Proctor was clearly a man who spoke the truth and would not abide anything less in others. That was the way of men in Maine, men and women both, and she meant to be worthy of that heritage. Burt Proctor framed her face in his hands and kissed her, she wanted only to kiss that scar as if she might heal it, heal any hurt in this good, decent man's life as she sensed he would wish to heal any hurt in hers. They were breathless, trembling. It was all happening so quickly. *Yes, it's absurd. My heart will be lacerated. There are no fairy tales. He will hurt me simply by touching me. If I love him, I will never be free again.* Yet she was laughing like a young girl, and Burt Proctor was laughing, elated and excited, a little frightened at what was happening to them, that seemed to rush at them blurred with speed. When he asked her to come with him, to stay the night with him at a Skowhegan hotel, she said yes, and kissed him again, and walking in the clear, freezing, starlit night, leaning on his arm, she began to cry with happiness, for happiness is so simple, so obvious.

How swiftly it was decided. What my life would be!

By late morning of the next day most of Skowhegan was plowed out and reasonably navigable. There was that festive communal air she recalled from her childhood, a sense of holiday. The partly clouded sky was laced with thin cold sunshine drawing the eye upward in the childlike hope. Burt Proctor, a practical-minded man, had arranged for a tow truck from the Sunoco station to haul her car into Skowhegan and repair it. She wasn't going to fly to Bangor after all—wasn't going to fly to Berlin—impulsively she'd decided she would stay in Maine for the next several weeks at least, for Burt Proctor had begged her, Burt Proctor had opened his heart to her as no other man had done in her life, and in a haze of happiness she'd said *Yes, yes of course, my life is yours, you saved it*. This would be the tale they would tell each other through the years of their love.

She'd said yes to each of Burt Proctor's requests except one: she would have to drive back to her parents' old house one final time, alone. Burt Proctor was astonished. "What? Why? In all this snow?" She said, "Because I've left something behind. Something I must have if we're to be—married." "But what is it?" "I can't say. I'll show you." "All right. But I'll drive you, you aren't going alone." "Yes. I must go alone." "You're not thinking clearly, you're still upset from yesterday. You're in no condition to drive anywhere by yourself." "I'm fine. You can see I'm fine." She dared to kiss Burt Proctor, though he was becoming impatient, upset. He asked, "What did you leave behind, that's so damned important? That won't wait for another few days?" She smiled evasively, and did not answer.

For in truth she wasn't certain exactly what the left-behind item was, but believed she would recognize it when she saw it. Again she kissed the man who was her rescuer, and her lover, holding him in her arms so tightly her slender body throbbed with pain. Stubbornly she repeated, "I must go alone."

And so she drove back to the Cuttler's Mill Road which had been plowed out, though not very cleanly, a single icy-rutted lane between heaped banks of snow. And she returned to the old farmhouse, which she'd locked up only yesterday, with no reason to believe she would ever return. Snow had drifted across the driveway to a height of several feet in spots, she had to leave the car out on the road, stumbling and staggering to the front door. In the wan sunshine the house's tall narrow windows reflected light as if lights were burning within but in fact the interior of the house was unnaturally dark for midday, snow heaped against downstairs windows on three sides. She was both eager and hesitant to enter. "Hello? Hello? Hello?"—she spoke brightly, simply to hear her own voice. And the silence that followed, like a subtly mocking echo. How strange this house of her childhood seemed to her now, emptied of most of the old, familiar furniture, curtains removed, floorboards bare and exposed, the floral wallpaper her mother had loved, which she'd always thought attractive, stained with time as with smudged fingerprints. She was embarrassed to think that outsiders would enter this house, examine it critically, when it seemed so diminished now, so very ordinary. The dank, melancholy odor of neglect made her nostrils pinch.

Abandoned to darkness. To oblivion. Why?

She searched the downstairs rooms, finding nothing, then upstairs in her old room, of course it would be in her old room, she saw it—*Favorite Fairy Tales.* The book Grandma had given her. It was lying on the floor, as if discarded. The familiar cover was warped from having slipped into her bathwater but the illustration was surprisingly vivid, a golden-haired princess astride a prancing silver-maned horse. *He was right. He knew!* Her heart filled with joy. She smiled, ignoring the bitter cold as she leafed through the book's mildewed pages, recognizing the illustrations, tears and stains on certain of the pages, crayon scribblings. On the last blank page she'd scribbled her name in orange crayon.

When she glanced up, she saw to her surprise that the windows of her old room, though curtainless, gave little light. She went to investigate. Had the sky darkened so quickly? Was it already dusk? There couldn't be a second snowstorm already—could there?

Again, snowflakes were being blown out of a pewter-gray sky.

By the time she left the house, stumbling through the snowdrifts to her car, the wind was ferocious. Snow was being blown in a frenzy, yesterday's drifts were being reshaped. She tried not to succumb to panic. *He knows you're here. He's waiting for you, this time.* At least she had the forgotten item she'd returned for, safe in her possession. She had not failed in her reckless quest.

There was an unnerving moment when her car motor didn't start. But then, to her relief, it did start. She managed to turn the car in the road, maneuvering back and forth in a narrow space, and, at first, she was able to drive fairly steadily through the swirling snow, determined not to make the same mistake, skidding off the road a second time. For what are the odds that any event in time might repeat precisely itself at another point in time?—such odds must be astronomical. She and Burt Proctor would laugh together over this episode, this folly of hers, such a stubborn, obstinate woman she was, when convinced she was right. Today, after the ravages of yesterday's storm, there appeared to be no other vehicles on the Cuttler's Mill Road. Snowdrifts were re-forming in the road as if alive, sinuous snaky coils lunging into the path of her car, which was now barely moving, inching forward at five miles an hour. Her windshield wipers began to slow, defeated by the snow's weight. For today the snowfall was damp. She began to talk to herself, reassure herself. As, a child, she'd sometimes talked to herself, waking alone in the night disoriented by sleep and not knowing at first where she was or, what frightened most, who she was. *Anyone I wish. I can become. If I love no one.* But that was the chill wisdom of an older child, a more calculating child. That was not the child she recalled now.

The storm was worsening. Visibility was reduced to a few feet. In her feeble headlights falling clumps of snow were discolored as old ivory. The snowplow had done a rushed, careless job on this back-country road, as usual. Stretches of ice had been left untouched. *If I can make it to the edge of Skowhegan. To the Sunoco station.* She didn't want to concede that she should have allowed Burt Proctor to drive her back, for his pickup had four-wheel drive and was far better equipped to deal with such conditions; she didn't want to concede what a mistake she'd made. Yet suddenly she began to sob and curse, in frustration, in fury, pressing her foot down on the gas pedal in her impatience to get to town, gripping the steering wheel until her fingers were frozen to it. As if by force she might hold the speeding, suddenly skidding car on the road.

She heard a cry—"No! No!" A child's hurt, incredulous voice.

For it was so unfair.

Waking in a haze of muted white, a delirium of swirling white, pain wracking her upper chest, a terrible roaring in her ears—for some dazed minutes she didn't know where she was.

Then she remembered. *This time, I will know what to do.*

It was crucial to have her father's flashlight firmly in hand. She would have to leave her grandmother's book behind, the keys in the ignition. Managing to squeeze herself out of the car, nearly fainting with pain, her bloodied face beginning to freeze into an ice-mask as soon as the wind struck it. She stumbled through snow, in the direction of the road, crying, "Help! I'm here! I've been injured!"—though she knew there was no one to hear, no headlights in sight. She understood that she wasn't behaving rationally, her strength was being exhausted, but she didn't know what else to do. There was a neighbor's farm close by—in which direction? If only the snowfall wasn't so thick. The air so dark. It was hard to breathe, in such wind. She would collapse, perish in the bitter cold. But no: this time she was wearing her mother's coat, the bulky quilted goose-down coat with the hood to protect her head. *Wear it. It's warm. So very attractive on you, dear. And it's no use to me.* She set off, this time, on what she believed to be the road, in the direction of Skowhegan, or what she believed to be that direction. She was limping badly, dragging her left leg. There was the danger of wandering into a field, of wandering in circles. She was panicked, perspiring inside her clothes even as the exterior of her body was going numb with cold. Her toes were losing all sensation. Her nose, cheeks, mouth were turning to ice. Someone was waiting for her ahead—wasn't he? Someone was coming to rescue her—wasn't he? She could not recall his name but she knew he was coming if only he knew where she was. She waved the flashlight in eager, darting circles. The battery was weak, the amber light feeble. "Help! I'm here! I've had an accident." It hadn't been her fault: the wind had blown her mother's compact car off the road, into the ditch. But where exactly was the road? And where—somewhere behind her?—was the abandoned car? She fell, her left leg buckling beneath her, but managed to get to her feet. Confused, she saw only snow, dunes, and declivities of snow, through cascading falls of snow, as if earth and sky were being shaken violently together. There was no road. Yet, a short distance away, vague lights appeared—headlights? They moved with maddening slowness. She stared, wiping snow from her eyes. "Here! I'm here!" It would be the man in the sheepskin jacket, the tall man with the bristling black beard, the hook-scar in his upper lip. She was stumbling forward, waving the flashlight desperately, but, oblivious to her effort, the vehicle must have veered away to the left, and was gone. She stared after it, stunned. "Come back! Please! Don't leave me here to—" She tried to follow the vanished vehicle, not wanting to think that it might be headed in the wrong direction, away from Skowhegan, and perhaps it hadn't been a vehicle at all but a hallucination or optical illusion caused by the flashlight's beam reflected in falling snow. She could not recall her lover's name but she would know him when she saw him. She felt the strength of his arms, the warmth and kindness of his hands, a man's big-boned, roughened hands, he'd removed his gloves to caress her feet, to revive circulation in her toes which had turned to ice, how grateful she'd been, how she'd wept with gratitude and love for him, but where was he now? She shook the flashlight to strengthen the failing light. She dared not switch it off, to save the battery, for fear it would never switch on again. The cold had gotten inside her, her throat and mouth were coated in frost, her nasal passages were blocked in ice, ice-needles had penetrated her ears, inching toward her brain. Her tongue was ice. Suddenly the thought came to her, *I have dreamt him: I have dreamt my life. God help me.* She stamped her feet, shook her head, how sleepy she was, how powerful and sweet the urge to lie down in the snow, soft blanketing snow, her eyelids heavy as if stones were pressing upon them, but she held the flashlight at the level of her chest, shining its feeble beam into the night. *I have dreamed my life—is that it?* And in the next instant, mercifully, she forgot these terrible words, even as you and I.

"This story evokes what is for me perhaps the greatest possible horror, that our happiness is but an illusion, a dream generated by deprivation. The young woman of the story has invented herself as one who doesn't need love; in fact, her soul is languishing for love, as her body is languishing for warmth. Her dream of being saved and being loved is so vivid, it's difficult not to believe it isn't real (even for the author). Maybe our lives are no more than a match girl's flaring matches; we live so long as they burn, and then are gone. In the meantime, the solace of art."

Dreaming among Men

BRYN KANAR

Bryn Kanar began to write after working at two bookstores and three libraries. In 1996 he attended the Clarion West writers' workshop, and since then he has sold a number of stories. His first appeared in the horror magazine Cemetery Dance. *"Dreaming Among Men" is his second sale but his second appearance was in gothic.net. Kanar is currently working on a mystery novel.*

Dreaming among Men

Palinuro Rubio is a teller at First National. One day he comes home to find an unexpected letter in his mailbox.

He has never received a letter like this before. He had thought all his relatives were dead. He is afraid to open it.

Palinuro puts the letter on the passenger seat of his car and drives. An unaccountable forboding beats in his chest more loudly than his heart. The sky is as white and brittle as bone.

Crow flies at dusk over the foothills of the Guadalupe Mountains, over arroyos made by rivers that dried up long ago, when time was sacred and uncounted. These days, Crow reminds himself, everything is numbered. A hundred and twenty-seven wing-beats past the Pecos. How many more until he reaches his nest?

*   *   *

Palinuro wants to scream when he feels the jar of the impact. But he does not scream. He looks in his rearview mirror at the red-faced man in the car behind him. The man is yelling and waving his arms accusingly as if the accident were Palinuro's fault.

Palinuro swings his door open and approaches the man as he begins to roll down his window. He unbuckles his belt and pulls down his pants and the man begins to roll up his window again as fast as he can as Palinuro pees on it, a hot yellow stream more apt than any words.

All of Lubbock is a single wild whining stream of piss, shimmering in the sunlight, Palinuro thinks as he drives through downtown. The buildings glisten too wetly, too yellowly, for human habitation. It's a newborn bear cub whose mother has not yet licked the placenta away. It's a dawn trigger waiting, *yearning*, for someone to pull it.

Pull me, Palinuro thinks, out of this dream. Why doesn't anyone else hear the drumming coming out of the sun. Why doesn't anyone dance.

Crow lands in a chinkapin oak and combs the leftover wind out of his feathers with his beak. All around him the world is the color of sleep. He sniffs his nest before climbing in. There is an acid smell in the air.

Have you been dreaming?

Crow looks down and sees Rattlesnake curled against the base of the tree. Maybe I was, he says.

Palinuro drives to the edge of town to read the letter. He parks, and walks some distance from the road to an abandoned, half-dug drainage ditch. He sits on the clay earth and looks at the crumpled envelope.

A wind as dry as memory blows up out of the Llano Estacado and sucks the sweat from his hair. So many traps left unset. A russet sadness buried long ago where only the roots of the cactuses can reach it. Palinuro slits the envelope with his pocketknife. The letter claims to be from his older brother, an invitation to his birthday party.

*   *   *

You have the smell of men on you, says Rattlesnake.

And what if I do?

I just never thought I'd see *you* working as Coyote's carrier pigeon. That's all.

Crow flaps his wings, knocking sleeping oak moths out of the tree. They fall on Rattlesnake like snow. Be careful what you say, says Crow, or I may have to carry Coyote a message about you.

The next morning Palinuro sets out for Fort Stockton, where his brother lives, according to the letter. It's seven hours from Lubbock.

He turns west at Big Spring onto the Pecos Plains. Sunlight dances on the windshield. It spells out words in a language he thinks he should remember. The origins of temptation, of love.

In the evening a wind blows up the Pecos River valley. It crawls into the car. It picks at his limbs like children. It brings smells of death and life and water. It wants him to remember something that he can't remember. He has trouble breathing it, as if his lungs are in his legs.

Palinuro crosses the river and drives into the brown foothills of the Guadalupe Mountains. Eyes watch from shadows.

There is a banging deep inside the car. The road slows. And stops. Palinuro looks at the gas gauge. It reads empty. There must be a leak, he thinks, I just filled the tank at Odessa, but he doesn't go out and look. The far off wail of a funeral flute holds his ear in its pale hand. The breath of the world is leaking out.

As the sun sinks toward the Guadalupe Mountains the song gets louder. Palinuro is afraid. The shadows of the mesquite trees stretch down the hillside until one of them reaches the road. Suddenly, a man stands up in front of the car. He climbs onto the hood. He is playing a long white flute made from a human femur and his ears are gray and pointy like a coyote's.

Taking the instrument away from his lips, he holds it up and looks Palinuro in the eyes. Did you lose this? he asks.

Laughter rattles in the red corners of the sunset sky. The man is gone. The femur sits on the hood of the car.

Palinuro opens his door and steps out. He walks around to the front of the car. There is a human skeleton in the road. Palinuro knows beyond any doubt that it is his own. He screams and runs blindly into the hills, into the open arms of the shadows of the mesquites.

Fox runs as fast as he can through the dry arroyos but he can't outrun his fear. It's like trying to outrun the redness of his own fur.

In the direction of the rising night he smells water and veers toward it. Peace and the end of suffering. The wind's wet nose on his nose.

Panting, he plunges through the cottonwoods and into the water's dark smile. It takes him half the night to wash the dream out of his fur. Done at last, he crawls out of the river and lies down on the grass under a cottonwood tree. He closes his eyes.

He sleeps through the next day but wakes at sunset. Just in time for the party.

Coyote's younger brother is back from dreaming among men.

" 'Dreaming among Men' " was written differently than my other stories. I didn't plan it. One day I woke up from a nap with the phrase 'Coyote's younger brother' running through my head. Still half asleep, I sat down at the computer and typed for about an hour. It wasn't until the next day, when I read the document I'd created, that I realized I had written a story.

"Several months later, reading it again, I understood that it was more than that: it was a homecoming.

"I was born in Texas, but we moved away before I was three and I've never been back, 'Dreaming Among Men' reminds me that some part of myself still lives there on the shore of the Pecos River where my father played as a child, on the desert back road where my mother rolled her Chevy Corsica, in the foothills of the Guadalupe Mountains where, somewhere, Coyote dances. . . ."

The Cats of San Martino

ELLEN STEIBER

*Ellen Steiber has written and edited a number of books for children, and has recently finished her first adult fantasy novel. Her short stories and poetry have appeared in three previous fairy tales anthologies—*Black Thorn, White Rose; Ruby Slippers, Golden Tears; Silver Birch, Blood Moon*—and in* The Armless Maiden, The Essential Bordertown, *and* Sirens.

The Cats of San Martino

". . . and it had become a saying in the town, when anyone found herself reduced to her last penny: 'I will go and live with the cats,' and so many a poor woman actually did."

ANDREW LANG

"These cats were true cats, it seemed, but they had some magic powers, almost as if they'd been fairies."

KATHERINE BRIGGS

Jenny leaned against the side of the old VW bus and stared into the rain. She deliberately ignored Carl, who was gesturing wildly to the service station attendant, trying to enact the idea that he wanted to fill the gas tank. The attendant, for his part, either genuinely couldn't make sense of Carl's charades or was enjoying the show too much to let on that he understood.

"Jen, help me out here."

Jenny shrugged. "Sorry. Someone lost the phrase book."

Two days ago Carl had managed to leave it somewhere in the Vatican. "Forget it," he'd said when Jenny insisted they replace it. "We've been in Italy all summer. We'll get by just fine."

Why, Jenny wondered for the umpteenth time, hadn't she just ignored Carl and bought another book? Why did she always go along with him? It had been her idea to spend the summer in Italy. She'd wanted to take an art history course in Florence, to study the great Renaissance painters. Instead, Carl found a bargain package in Rome, and she had spent three months staring at sculpture. The problem was, she didn't like sculpture, not even Michelangelo's. Sculpture seemed fixed to her, frozen. She couldn't look at a statue without feeling sorry for the being trapped inside.

She knew now that she should never have gone to Rome. As Carl had said, it simply wasn't her city. It was mobbed, confusing, too much of a hub. Everywhere there were flocks of nuns, droves of priests. The holy city was theirs. For Jenny, who had no religion except an innate, instinctive animism, Rome was too Catholic and Catholicism too macabre. The depictions of the crucifixion, the scenes of martyrdom, the relics of the saints' bodies, all gave her nightmares. The omnipresence of the Church made her feel like an outsider. She didn't belong.

That feeling of not belonging had only intensified with the arrival of Sasha. Sasha was everything Jenny wasn't. She was tall and thin, with long, straight blond hair, perfectly sculpted features, and an icy blend of hauteur and strength that Jenny associated with the Norse Valkyries. It was easy to imagine Sasha hoisting dead warriors from the battlefield and not even noticing when her grasp loosened and they plummeted to worlds below. Sasha had come from Minneapolis, of all places, to model in Milan. Three months later, having appeared on the covers of a dozen fashion magazines, she'd decided that modeling was a bore. She'd left Milan for Rome at the invitation of a minor duke who wanted to ensconce her in his palazzo. He'd given her a French locket that had been in his family since the 1500s. It was a round disk of bright yellow gold edged with pearls, inscribed: *L'amour dure sans fin.* While the duke's love may have lasted forever, Sasha's didn't. She'd left the palazzo two weeks later on the day she met Carl on the Spanish steps. Sasha, who called Carl *Carlo,* said she'd foreseen his coming into her life in a tarot reading. She said it was karma that they'd met, that their spirits had long been intertwined, that theirs was an ancient and powerful connection. Carl said Sasha was "mystical," which Jenny translated to mean "weird but interesting." Now they were driving through Tuscany, en route to Florence, where in three weeks time Jenny and Carl would catch their flight back to the States. The hows and whys of it were a mystery to Jenny, but somehow Sasha had invited herself along.

Jenny watched as the gas station attendant removed the gas pump from the VW and informed Carl he'd given him forty-five liters of petrol that cost 65,000 lire. Carl paled and said, "Jen, I need you to cough up some *dinero* here." That was another thing about Carl. He was always broke.

Jenny reached into her pocket. She still had travelers' checks left but was running low on cash. She needed to find an open bank. She handed Carl 15,000 lire, saying, "That's all I've got right now, and it's *lire*, not *dinero*."

Carl took the money and traced the line of her cheekbone with his thumb. "*Lire, dinero, drachma, yen,*" he chanted in the voice that always made her feel like a princess favoring a pauper with her charms. "Does it really matter, Jenny-o? You know what I mean. You always do."

Jenny's irritation faded. Carl simply didn't take things as seriously as she did. He was a lighter spirit, Sasha said, something Jenny sensed yet never put words to. But she'd always known that his gift to her was that he lent her a little of his ease, a little of his unshakable belief that no matter what, things would be all right. She remembered the first time they made love—afterward lying in his arms and him whispering, "You just sleep now, Jenny-o, 'cause everything's going to work out fine"—and later waking up amazed that she actually believed it.

Carl counted out her 15,000 and raised one eyebrow. "That's only twenty-eight thou."

"Why don't you see what Sasha can cough up?" Jenny suggested.

"Good idea," Carl said, and walked around to knock on the back of the VW. Inside, Sasha had fashioned an elaborate bed for herself, covered in midnight-blue silk velvet. Carl emerged from the back of the bus a few minutes later with a handful of bills. He paid for the gas then pocketed the rest, making Jenny wonder just how much Sasha had given him.

He came around to where Jenny stood, wound a hand through her dark hair, drew her to him and kissed her on the mouth. "You feeling all right?" he asked gently. Jenny had woken up with a headache that morning.

"I'm better now," she said.

He kissed her again. "I'm glad. So . . . if you're feeling better . . . would you mind if Sasha rode up front for a while?"

It was a reflex by now to go along with whatever Carl wanted. Jenny almost said, "Sure, no problem," but caught herself. Something inside her was simmering, something she'd been ignoring for the last two weeks.

"Actually, I *would* mind," she said, and got back into the front of the bus.

She regretted her decision at once. The back of the bus may have been converted into Sasha's private bedchamber, but the front, Carl's domain, was a disaster. Carl often bragged that Chaos Theory was his moral and aesthetic code. What this actually meant was that he couldn't be bothered to clean up after himself. Jenny, on the other hand, was meticulous by nature, a devotee of order. She took this difference between them to be a sign that she was Carl's perfect mate. She might not be beautiful or artistic; she certainly didn't have Sasha's gift for exotic ennui; but she kept things organized. Without her, Carl wouldn't find his way into his own vehicle. Despite her frequent attempts to clean it, the front of the bus was filled with Carl's dirty laundry, remnants of yesterday's lunch, and an assortment of maps, none of which even seemed to show the road they were on. The VW stank of cigarette smoke, damp socks, and overripe cheese. The smell was beginning to make Jenny queasy.

Carl got in beside her and pulled out onto the road. Sometime while they'd been at the filling station, dusk had turned to darkness. Jenny remembered how the rain had started earlier that day as they'd driven through a small walled village. She'd marveled at how the evergreen of the cypress trees became gray-green in the rain; how the red-tile roofs went dark as carnelian, and the sun-faded stone walls of the *castello* took on the grainy silver-brown of sand beside the sea. She'd never seen the Tuscan hills in sunlight. In the rain everything seemed deep and vibrant, as if the land leached color from the sky.

Carl turned on the windshield wipers. "The rain's getting worse," he said.

Jenny sat silently, grateful that he was driving. The road bent back on itself in a hairpin turn, and Carl remained calm as a Fiat barreled toward them then swerved out of their lane at the last possible moment.

"If you don't mind telling me," he said, "what have you got against Sasha?"

Jenny considered the question. She and Carl had been going out for two years, living together since last Christmas when Carl was kicked out of his dorm. Jenny assumed that they'd marry, probably next year, as soon as they graduated. They were total, complementary opposites. Yin and yang, they needed each other. Then Sasha had draped herself across their lives like a beautiful filmy curtain, and something had changed. He'd never said so, but Jenny knew that Carl now saw her through the curtain of Sasha; even more unnerving, Jenny had caught glimpses of herself through that same veil.

"Why is she coming to Florence with us?" Jenny asked. She waited for his answer, wondering how he'd phrase the inevitable evasion.

Nothing could have prepared her for Carl's blunt answer. "I asked her to come. I think I'm in love with her."

Jenny shut her eyes, suddenly nauseatingly sick. Her head was pounding, and there was a giant hollow space between her ribs that felt as if it had been eaten away by acid.

Carl kept driving, his eyes on the red taillights ahead of them. "Look," he said at last. "It's not that I don't care for you. You're a wonderful woman, better than I deserve, and we've had some good times—"

"But—"

"But . . ." His voice trailed off.

"There's Sasha now," Jenny said helpfully.

"It's not Sasha. It's you and me."

Jenny knew that what she was about to say sounded

like the lyrics of a bad country-and-western song, but she couldn't stop herself. "I thought we loved each other. What was all that affection? Did I imagine that?"

Carl spoke in a perfectly even tone. "Of course you didn't imagine it. What we had was real. It's just that we're so . . . different. I mean, we couldn't have lasted."

"We couldn't?" Jenny's voice had become an embarrassing croak. Princess into frog, the transformation was easier than anyone would have guessed.

"There's . . . stuff I can't get past with you."

Jenny wondered if he was fed up with her need to keep things clean and orderly. Or maybe he was tired of her ragging on him for being so irresponsible about money. And she *had* gotten bitchy about Rome. Carl, who was raised Catholic, did not appreciate her riff about the Vatican's obscene wealth.

"I mean, you're not bad-looking," he explained, "but your hair's always all frizzy, and face it, Jen, you've got a weight problem. You're never gonna lose those ten pounds you always swear you'll work off."

Outside, rain coursed down the windshield in cold, slippery streams. Jenny couldn't imagine why she wasn't crying. She bit down through her lower lip, welcoming the taste of her own blood.

"I see," she said when she could keep her voice steady. "And now you've got Sasha, who's—"

"Terribly beautiful," Carl said quietly.

It was a perfect description. There was something terrible, uncanny, about Sasha's pale beauty. Jenny thought of the Valkyries again.

"And I'm *not* terribly beautiful. Obviously. You can't get past my hair and my weight. So you might as well dump me and take up with Sasha. It's very efficient, really. Out with the old, in with the new." She turned to face him. "Have you fucked her yet?"

"That's not what this is about. Sasha and I have had some very intense talks—about fate and eternity and about how you can be together without end, and—"

"*Have you?*"

Staring straight ahead, he nodded.

"God, you're a shit. And I'm so incredibly stupid. A three-year-old would have seen it coming, but not—"

He reached out a hand to touch her.

"*Don't*," she said, the nausea almost overpowering. "*Don't touch me.*"

Carl sighed, the sound of the long-suffering, then made one of his remarkable recoveries. "Jen," he said conversationally, "when was the last time you saw a sign for Florence?"

"*Firenze*," she corrected him automatically. She thought a moment. "Not since we left the *autostrada*."

"That was hours ago."

"I guess." She'd lost track of the time. Earlier that day her watch had died.

"Well, I know you're mad as hell, and I don't blame you, but do you think you could check a map and try to figure out where we are?"

Jenny sat unmoving, watching the wipers futilely pushing at the rain.

Carl held out the only temptation left him. "Look, we can get separate rooms in Florence. The quicker we get there, the quicker you're rid of me."

"You are such a shithead."

"I know."

Jenny reached into her pack for the flashlight she always carried (Carl liked to tease her about being so well-prepared; he swore she'd been a Boy Scout in an earlier life), and opened the map of Toscana. Her head was pounding. The lines of the map swam before her eyes as she struggled to read it. "Do you remember any of the village names on the last sign we saw?"

"Deviazione?"

"That means detour, you idiot. Didn't you ever look at the phrase book?" The frog again, crude and croaking. Before tonight she never would have called him an idiot.

"Listen," Carl said, "I got us through Rome just fine. I don't remember *you* driving there. And who figured out the train schedule to Sicily, not to mention—"

Jenny tuned out his list of conquests, trying to visualize the names on the last sign she'd seen. There were three towns. San Vittorio, Arezzo, San Martino? Something like that. They were supposed to be heading toward Arezzo and from Arezzo toward Firenze, but just after they'd turned onto the road toward Arezzo they'd hit the *deviazione*. She studied the snaking lines on the map and found at least four San Martinos, all between San Gimignano and Arezzo. They could be anywhere.

She peered out through the windshield. Rain and darkness. Not even lightning to break the dark. Only the occasional flickering light of a candle at a roadside shrine.

"Well?" Carl said.

"Well, what?"

"Aren't you supposed to be reading the map? For a navigator, you—"

"I am *not* your navigator," Jenny said clearly.

"Well, then what are you besides fucking useless?"

She hadn't thought he could hurt her any more than he already had. Wrong again.

She jerked forward as Carl suddenly braked hard and the VW stalled out. A sheep stood in the glare of the headlights, sodden and mud-streaked, and showing absolutely no inclination to move.

Jenny felt a wave of relief go through her. She didn't have to wait until Florence. She grabbed her pack and opened her door.

"*Ciao, Carlo,*" she said, and stepped out into the storm.

The rain continued to beat down, cold and determined. Jenny figured she'd probably walked three miles since jumping out of the VW. At first she'd been too angry to even notice distance; it hadn't mattered that it was dark or wet or that she had no idea of where she was. It felt good to pit herself against the Tuscan hills, to walk until her muscles burned and her pulse raced. Some part of her still couldn't believe that Carl hadn't come after her. But that was the point, wasn't it? He was letting her go.

Jenny flicked on her flashlight as something dark and solid loomed in the darkness. She was standing about ten feet away from a tall, stone house. She racked her memory for phrases from the missing phrase book. She needed to say, "Excuse me, is there a *pensione* nearby?"

Nervously, she approached the house. She stepped beneath the doorway, grabbed the iron knocker and let it fall.

The door opened and a thin, elderly man, wearing brown wool pants, a matching vest. and an ivory linen shirt with a knotted silk cravat, peered out into the rain.

"*Buona sera*," Jenny began. Haltingly, she recited what she remembered. "*Mi scusi. Puo dirmi qual'e la via per una pensione?*"

"No," he said.

"No?"

"*No pensione.*"

Thunder began to roll through the night skies, and the rain thickened into a nearly solid wall of water.

"*Piove. Vai alla Casa dei Gatti,*" the old man said briskly.

Piove, she recognized. He was telling her it was raining. The rest she couldn't quite make out.

"*Vai*," he repeated. "*La Casa dei Gatti. Sbrigati!*"

The last word meant hurry up. Their landlady in Rome was always urging Carl to propose to Jenny. "*Sbrigati!*" she'd tell him, as if Carl were capable of hurrying.

Jenny stared longingly into the room beyond the doorway, a high-ceilinged kitchen with brick walls, a long, rough wooden table, and a fire roaring in the hearth. It looked so warm and inviting that she couldn't quite believe it when the old man gave a crisp *Buona sera* and shut the door in her face.

"And a lovely night to you, too," Jenny muttered.

Beyond the house the road snaked downhill, rain coursing down the asphalt as if it were a riverbed. Jenny followed it, hoping for another house, or whatever it was that the old man had waved her on to. She was walking into her new life, she realized, a life without Carl. She tried to think of that as freeing, an invitation to adventure. Instead she thought of Sasha, who saw omens in everything. Jenny had a good idea of what Sasha would say about a new life that began with being lost in a storm and having a door slammed in your face. "It's very clear, Jenny," she'd say through a haze of cigarette smoke. "The omens are not auspicious."

What they were, Jenny decided, was perverse. She walked for what seemed at least another mile before she saw a glimmer of light. She soon found herself standing on a stone bridge that spanned a narrow, churning stream. In the very center of the bridge, in a glass case, was a shrine to the Virgin, complete with a rosary, fresh flowers, and a candle flickering in a tall, red glass. Her light in the dark.

Great, she thought. I walk for miles in a fucking downpour and I find a shrine!

Jenny glared at the statue, envying it for being dry, composed, and oblivious to the whole lousy night. She, on the other hand, was cold, soaked, exhausted, and vibrating with pain. There was no particular part of her body that hurt. It was all of her, stunned and aching and feeling like the stupidest creature on earth. She'd been such a fool. She couldn't imagine that she would ever stop hating herself for that.

She continued across the bridge to a dirt road beaten by the rain into a thick bed of mud. She kept walking, aware that she was traveling deeper into the countryside, farther and farther from the possibility that Carl would ever find her.

She slogged up a long, muddy hill. The landscape flared dead-white beneath a sheet of lightning; and in its moment of illumination Jenny realized she was standing in front of another house. A house without a door. Just an ancient wooden post and lintel set into stone walls. The light of her flashlight revealed a dark, cavernous interior. The house was abandoned.

Jenny stepped over the worn granite step beneath the lintel, and felt herself quivering with relief. It was damp and cold inside the ruin of the house, but it was shelter.

Something brushed against her leg. She lowered her light and nearly screamed at the sight of glowing green eyes staring back at her. A cat, she realized, and her pounding heart slowed. It was just a cat, a small, scrawny tortoiseshell with a black mask and a funny orange streak down its nose. The cat was obviously here for the same reason that she was. Jenny knelt down and held out a wet hand for it to sniff.

"Hey, cat," she said softly. "Think I could share this place with you tonight?" She felt the cat's cold nose touch her hand, and took it for assent.

Like everything else in Jenny's life, the batteries in her flashlight were dying. Its dim light made the house a series of shadows. All she could really tell was that the cat had had its way with the place. Fish bones, narrow little rat heads, and shredded yellowed newspapers littered the stone floor. Carl would be right at home here, Jenny thought wryly.

She passed from the large hall she'd first entered to an even larger room. Through a low, narrow doorway she found the kitchen, which she identified by a deep, tublike sink, and an arched opening in the brick wall to the side of the hearth: the oven. There was even a half-collapsed wooden hutch, and in front of it, a shiny, wet mound of pink entrails.

She whirled as she heard a mewing sound at her feet. The tortoiseshell cat gazed up at her expectantly.

"What do you want, you little murderer?" Jenny asked.

The cat rubbed against her ankles, purring.

Jenny sighed and knelt down to run her fingers through the cat's soft fur. "So where do you sleep?" she asked. "Is there anyplace in here that's comfortable?"

As if in reply, the cat walked out of the kitchen and up a short, curving flight of stone stairs. Amused, Jenny followed. The cat paused at an open doorway, and it occurred to Jenny that there were no doors anywhere in this house.

Her light followed the cat into the room. At first she thought she was looking at a king-sized feather bed covered with a fur comforter, a rich patchwork of gray, tan, black, white, and orange. *A soft, warm bed,* Jenny thought, nearly delirious at the idea. And then one particular black and white patch of fur raised its head and stared at her with burning gold eyes, and she realized that the entire bed was covered with cats. There had to be at least sixty of them, curled and stretched, neatly fitted to each other, their bodies gently rising and falling on a somnolent current of breath. Only the one cat looked at her, and its gaze was so piercing that she remembered an elderly woman she'd once met who refused to be photographed for fear that the photographic image would steal her soul. That's how the cat's gaze made her feel, as though it were fixing her image and her battered soul lay exposed in its golden eyes, there for the taking.

The black and white cat sprang from the bed and sat down directly in front of Jenny. Jenny took a quick step back, alarmed by its size. The top of its head came to the middle of her thigh. It gazed at her intently as if weighing odds, considering factors, coming to a decision. Then it started out of the room. It turned once with an impatient *mmmrahh!* sound, which Jenny took to mean that she should follow.

The black and white led her to another doorless room. This one was much smaller, the size of a monk's cell and almost as sparely furnished. A narrow pallet-bed stood against one wall, a small wooden chest at its foot; a single clothes peg jutted out of the opposite wall. Jenny blinked in disbelief. The bed was neatly made with crisp white cotton sheets and two pillows in embroidered pillowcases, lying side by side.

Curious, Jenny opened the chest. Her flashlight died as she lifted the lid, but inside she felt a thick wool blanket. She hesitated only a moment before spreading the blanket on the bed, then quickly stripping off her wet clothing and slipping between the sheets.

Her body went rigid with shock. The sheets were cold, so unbelievably cold. Cotton spun from ice. She curled into a tight ball, telling herself that the bed would soon be warm. But she knew it for a lie, and that made the grief inside her all the worse. If Carl were here, she wouldn't be cold. Carl would curl up around her and hold her safe and snug in his arms. Carl made her world warm. For the briefest second Jenny let herself imagine the feel of his chest pressed against her back, his thighs cupping hers, one arm beneath her, the other falling heavy across her ribs, his breath, warm and even on the back of her neck. . . .

"You are not allowed to do that anymore," she told herself sternly. But it had been nearly two years since she'd gone to bed alone, and her body was shaking as if it'd never stop. She missed him. Oh God, how she missed him.

Quite suddenly, she became aware of the black and white cat. He was sitting on the pillow next to hers. He hadn't been there when she'd gotten under the covers. She hadn't noticed him jumping onto the bed. But now he was curled up beside her, regarding her with that golden, imperious gaze. It made her nervous to have him so close. She'd never lived with a cat, but she'd heard that they sometimes suffocated people, sucked the breath out of them as they slept.

Very slowly the cat reached out one long paw and set it on her shoulder. The gesture was oddly protective. She lay very still, listening to the rain, wondering what the cat would do next. It did nothing but keep its paw on her shoulder until the chill left the bed and her shivering stopped.

She drifted into sleep soon after, the old man's voice playing in her mind. *"Vai a la Casa dei Gatti,"* he told her. And this time she understood.

Jenny woke from a dreamless sleep to the black and white cat tapping her insistently on the nose. "Carl?" she said aloud before she could stop herself. She caught her breath, aching. Carl wasn't there. "Carl." She said it again, this time deliberately. She had to feel it, test it, in the same way that as a child she had to push against a loose tooth.

The cat, who didn't seem to approve of this experiment in pain, turned his back on her and sprang to a ledge above her head. Although the room was still dark, Jenny could make out cracks of light around the edges of wooden shutters. Wrapping herself in the wool blanket, she got up, felt for the shutters' iron latch, and opened it.

There was no glass in the windows; she opened the shutters directly into the countryside and its weather. The wind had shifted and was no longer blowing rain against the house, but the rain was still pouring down, a thick, transparent curtain of water. Jenny peered out, trying to get her bearings. It was impossible to tell what time of day it was. The sky was a dense wash of gray. On a hilltop she saw what looked like a great wooden barn, and in the distance, across a spread of open fields dotted with olive trees, a few houses, all of them built of fieldstone. Jenny felt the hopelessness of the previous night start to fade. When the rain let up, she'd find out where she was and how to get the nearest bus or train into Florence. Even without Carl, it would be all right.

She glanced at the cat beside her. He was quite handsome by daylight and most definitely a he, with a broad chest and a tom's large head. He was a tuxedo, his coat a deep, glossy black; his chest and paws and a bit of his muzzle white. In the gray light of the day his eyes had gone green. Jenny reached out to pet him, but the cat's level gaze stopped her. Something inside him was different than what she'd sensed in other cats. She thought of the strays in the Colosseum, wild little beggars as much a part of the city as the Roman ruins. This one was not quite so wild, nor could she conceive of him being anyone's pet.

With the cat's eyes boring into her, Jenny crossed the small room and poked at her clothing hanging from the peg. Her jeans were damp and cold and stiff with mud; her shirt not much better. But she put them on anyway, feeling absurdly self-conscious changing in front of the cat. It was because he had no self-consciousness, she realized. The cat sat there perfectly composed, assured of his own beauty and grace, of his rightness in the world. And with every second Jenny felt more awkward, knowing that she didn't belong in the house and she certainly didn't belong with Carl anymore. She hadn't the faintest idea of just where it was she did belong, and the thought left her reeling.

The cat watched as she made the bed, folding up the blanket and returning it to the trunk. Then with another one of his sounds that was not quite a meow, he led the way downstairs. She noticed as she passed the master bedroom that the huge feather bed was now empty of cats, except for one large tiger stripe who apparently liked to sleep late.

By daylight the downstairs was even worse than it had been in shadow, and now the reason for the mess was clear. The cats were everywhere. They were grooming themselves, sharpening their claws on the ratty sofa, leaping to and from the window ledges, running mad steeplechases up and down the stairs. Cotton batting floated from the sofa, cobwebs clung to the corners, and thick gray puffs of cat fur drifted across the floors. And everywhere there were bones, feathers, pieces of dead rodents. Jenny nearly gagged when she set her hand down on the wide stone banister and it closed on a pigeon's spindly pink leg.

Fortunately, the kitchen was somewhat equipped. A wooden bucket and scrub brush, a broom, and a thick bar of lemon-scented soap were tucked away beneath the sink. The side of the hearth was stacked with firewood and kindling. In a drawer in the cabinet Jenny even found candles and matches. After some resistance from the damp kindling, she managed to get a fire going and spent a few delicious minutes standing in front of the flames, enjoying their warmth. The house was still a revolting mess, though, so Jenny did what she always did when confronted by chaos. She cleaned.

She started by filling the bucket with runoff from the storm drain. She wet the scrub brush, rubbed it with the soap, and began to scour the kitchen floor. She cleaned for hours, scrubbing away layers of dirt and fur and decaying food. Soon, she promised herself, the house wouldn't smell as though a school of fish had swum in and died there. The cats watched as she worked, seemingly fascinated.

She had only one disconcerting moment. She'd stepped outside to fill the bucket with fresh rainwater, and she saw a tall, slender woman, dressed in a long wool cloak, hurrying across the fields.

"Un momento!" Jenny called over the downpour. *"Per favore!"*

The woman stopped and turned, and Jenny saw that within the dark hood, the woman's hair shone like summer wheat and framed a cool, familiar, flawless beauty.

"Sasha?"

The woman turned and continued across the fields.

Jenny almost ran after her. Only the rain stopped her. The rain and the knowledge that it *couldn't* have been Sasha. Sasha was in Florence, probably staying in the same room in the charming old *pensione* that Jenny had reserved for herself and Carl.

Jenny had cleaned fiercely after that, scrubbing with an energy that bordered on vengeance. And it had been worth it, she thought as she surveyed the house. With the floors cleaned, candles set in the niches in the walls, and the few pieces of furniture rearranged into a semblance of order, the ruin of a house had a rough beauty. The candlelight reflected the sheen of the worn floors, revealed the texture of the stucco walls, picked up the warmth of the wooden shutters and beams. A faint lemon scent mingled with the smell of wood burning in the hearth.

Satisfied with her day's work, Jenny dragged the couch into the kitchen and collapsed in front of the fire. Apparently, the cats considered this an excellent idea. A delicate all black jumped up beside her, then two striped kittens, and a bony, old three-legged Siamese. The little tortoiseshell female wormed her way through the others and onto Jenny's lap, arching her butt against Jenny's chest and purring loudly. An even smaller cat, who seemed to be part Abyssinian, draped herself across Jenny's shoulder and nestled her cold nose against Jenny's neck.

It would all be very cozy, Jenny thought wearily, if she weren't starving. It had been nearly a day and a half since she'd last eaten, and she was feeling headachy and a bit faint.

"I'm hungry," she said aloud. At her words the big tiger cat, the one who liked to sleep late, stretched and got to his feet. With a bound he leapt to the kitchen window, and with another, disappeared into the rain. He returned minutes later, a bloodied black rat hanging from his mouth. He carried his kill proudly across the kitchen, dropped the rodent at Jenny's feet, then lay there, panting beside the carcass, a triumphant grin on his face.

"Thank you," Jenny said stiffly. She didn't know what else to say, and it seemed rude to clean up this gift while the cat was looking so pleased with himself.

Just after darkness fell she took herself to bed. Once again the big black and white curled up beside her, one paw resting on her shoulder. And once again she fell into a dreamless sleep.

"Why is she here?"

Jenny woke to see the tuxedo cat sitting on top of the trunk, facing a ginger cat the size of a mountain lion.

"She's suffering heartbreak," the black and white answered.

At this, the ginger cat turned its great head toward

Jenny, and seeing that she was awake, said to her, "You must understand, we cats generally don't go in for that sort of thing."

"And you humans give yourselves to it," the black and white added, though not unkindly.

Jenny blinked, still half asleep and faint with hunger. Had she been fully awake, she might have argued. She had not so much given herself to heartbreak as she'd been taken over by it, broken into pieces, each of them aching for the whole that no longer existed. That perhaps never had.

"Are you all right?" the ginger cat asked with concern.

"You—You're talking," Jenny replied stupidly.

"Most animals with vocal cords do," the black and white assured her.

"In English?"

The great ginger cat shrugged. "Language doesn't matter. It is simply that in this place we choose to make ourselves understood."

"This is Pappa Gatto," the black and white explained. "He lives in the barn up the hill."

The ginger cat inclined his head. "And you are?"

"Jenny. Jenny Myford."

"You are welcome in our house, Jenny Myford," Pappa Gatto said formally. "You have found favor with my children."

As though choreographed, both cats swerved their heads at a sound that came from the ground floor.

"The gifts," said the tuxedo cat. He turned back to Jenny. "Get dressed," he told her. "You'll want to see what's arrived."

The two cats left the room, leaving Jenny slightly dazed. She'd just held a conversation with two oversized cats. The day before, she'd seen Sasha crossing a field in the middle of a downpour. It occurred to Jenny that she was losing her mind. Still, she dressed herself and brushed out the thick tangle of her hair. It was a mercy, she reflected, that there were no mirrors in the house.

Downstairs, she found countless cats milling around two large wicker baskets. A delicate black kitten wedged her paw through the weave of the larger basket, earnestly attempting to lift the lid. Jenny knelt to help her and unpacked several smoked fish, a roasted chicken, and a thick bunch of catnip tied with twine.

"Where did all this come from?" Jenny asked.

The black and white, who seemed to have no interest in the food but sat gazing through an arched window, answered. "Many years ago we rid San Martino of a plague of rats. To this day, the people remember and thank us with their gifts."

The little black cat on Jenny's lap touched her arm with a paw and mewed plaintively. "What, you don't speak English?" she asked it.

"It's been a while since we've had a human live with us," the ginger cat explained. "Many of my younger children are not experienced in talking to your kind."

Whether or not the cats could converse in English, their desires were clear. They were rubbing against Jenny, tapping the basket with their paws, purring, meowing, doing everything but sending messages in Morse code.

"Okay," she said. "*Andiamo!*" She got to her feet, the motion making her slightly dizzy, and went into the kitchen, where she took a stack of yellowed ceramic bowls from the cabinet. Using a dull knife, she divvied up the fish and chicken, then carefully portioned them out into the bowls. It was only as she set the first one down that she realized that each bowl had a name painted on it in an elaborate, cursive script.

"Aggripina," she read aloud, and the elderly three-legged Siamese limped toward her. "Is that you?" she asked, stroking it as it began to eat. The cat purred in response, so Jenny tried a second. At the name Olivero, the tiger cat came forward, muscular shoulders rolling. Noccioula, brought the small Abyssinian; Sandro, a silvery tabby. Ruffino was a yellow tom who was missing one ear; Cipriana, a blue-gray longhair with a regal plume of a tail; Nicola, the delicate all-black; Giuseppe and Peppino, two comical striped kittens; and at the name Domenica, the wired little tortoise shell shot forward with a joyous burst of energy.

Jenny kept on naming and feeding cats until all of the

bowls were in use, all of the cats contentedly feeding. All that is except Pappa Gatto and the black and white.

"I'm sorry," she said, sure she'd gravely offended them. "I don't have any more bowls left, and I've used up all the food."

"That's as it should be," Pappa Gatto said gently. "We prefer to hunt. Don't you think it's time *you* ate? The second basket is for you, child."

Jenny opened it and found a loaf of bread, still warm from the oven; a wedge of creamy white goat cheese; a bottle of Chianti; a hard summer sausage that smelled of fennel and herbs; grapes and olives and bright red tomatoes still clinging to a curl of vine. For a long, disbelieving moment she just stared at the feast in front of her.

"Eat," Pappa Gatto said.

"Before you faint on us," the black and white added.

She started with the grapes, progressed to the bread and cheese, then to the meat and wine. When she'd had her fill, she looked questioningly at the two large cats. "Who brought all that food? Who knows that I'm here?"

The black and white, who was again gazing out into the rain, said, "San Martino is a very small village, and our house has no doors. Did you think your presence was a secret? Everyone here knows everything."

"Then someone must know how I can get to Florence," Jenny said.

"Firenze is very far," the ginger cat told her solemnly.

"Well, how long will it take me to get there? I've got to catch a plane back to the States."

It soon became clear that the cats had no real understanding of either "plane" or "the States." They'd seen and heard planes overhead but had never really connected them to people, and Jenny spent quite a while trying to explain both airplanes and nonrefundable tickets. (Pappa Gatto would later explain to the people of San Martino, "Jenny had to go to Firenze to catch her bird.")

The cats patiently heard her out, then Pappa Gatto said, "From time to time we had young people live here and keep house for us. As you saw yesterday, it has been a while since the last. Won't you stay? My children are already very fond of you. Little Domenica has talked of nothing else since you arrived."

"You want me to stay and keep house for you?"

Pappa Gatto nodded. "San Martino is not such a bad place. You will see when the rain lets up."

Aggripina, the three-legged Siamese, rubbed against Jenny's legs, and Nicola curled up in her lap, a small oval of glossy black fur, her head cradled in Jenny's palm.

Jenny ran a finger along the soft fuzz on Nicola's nose. "You're awfully sweet," she said. "And I appreciate the invitation, but I can't stay."

The old Siamese's blue eyes narrowed. "Don't be a fool. If you go to Firenze now, you will only long for the worthless one who hurt you."

The wine was acting on Jenny like truth serum. "It doesn't matter. I'm going to long for him for anyway."

"That," the black and white said, "is a waste of your time. But if you insist, you should know that you're safer here. Grief alters humans. It lays them open, makes them vulnerable."

Jenny wondered if she'd somehow fallen into the middle of a feline talk show. "Excuse me," she said, "but what makes you think you're all such experts on—"

"We've observed your kind for a very long time," the black and white answered.

Nicola woke for a second to lick Jenny's palm, then nestled her head inside it again.

Pappa Gatto yawned, revealing very large, very sharp, pointed teeth, and making Jenny wonder just what it was he hunted. "Wait a bit," he suggested. "You will leave here and go to Firenze when the time is appropriate. You don't have to worry about this journey of yours." Then he earnestly began to wash his leg, thus putting an end to the discussion.

So Jenny stayed in the house of the cats. Even years later, when the strange, dreamlike quality of the time had faded, she would never be clear on just how long it was that she stayed. The rains stopped but the skies remained gray and overcast, and so mornings were indistinguishable from afternoons, and afternoons from dusk, and the days ran into each other like watercolors.

On the day that the cats decided that Jenny should stay, she ventured into the village for the first time. San Martino was tiny—maybe two dozen stone houses, most of them scattered across the fields. Its one street ended with a *tabacchi* bar opening onto a small, square piazza. The *tabacchi* bar, which sold groceries, cigarettes, and cappuccino, belonged to Marieangela, a stout gray-haired woman with a penchant for matching sweater sets and coral jewelry. Very little happened in San Martino without Marieangela's approval; fortunately, Marieangela approved of Jenny. Speaking no English, she made it understood that Jenny was welcome to cappuccino in the mornings, Chianti in the evenings, and as much food and chocolate as she needed because Jenny was *la ragazza che abita con i gatti*. Marieangela was the first to use the phrase, but Jenny soon realized it was a title of sorts: the Girl Who Lives with the Cats.

Her title was a self-evident fact. Jenny couldn't go anywhere without a stream of cats trailing after her. They followed her through the village and across the fields. They led her to San Martino's well, to the vegetable garden and grapevines, and to the wide grassy yard that was home to an assortment of ducks, rabbits, and chickens. They crossed the bridge with her and chased each other while she studied the old tombstones in the tiny village cemetery. They sat with her when she drank her morning cappuccino and gave her what they considered to be the choicest bits of local gossip.

From the cats Jenny learned that the dapper gent who'd sent her on to their home was named Alfredo, and it was he who grew San Martino's catnip. That Marieangela had seven grandchildren living in Ravenna, all of whom showed a great talent for playing with string. That Ermelina, the woman who kept the keys to the church, smelled like a delicious fish. That the rooster had a foul temper, but it was the old mallard who dominated the farmyard. That Livio's sheep were always going missing because he didn't have a sheepdog, and (the cats admitted regretfully) they really were to blame for this. It had been years since a dog had been fool enough to cross the bridge into the village. Pappa Gatto, they explained, didn't care much for dogs.

If the cats gave Jenny the word on the villagers, they most assuredly gave the villagers the word on her. Though Jenny had never mentioned him, everyone in San Martino knew about Carl. *"Suo ragazzo, peccato!"* Ermelina told her within seconds of meeting her. Jenny had to ask the black and white to translate, and then found herself blushing as he said matter-of-factly, "Your boyfriend, what a shame!" And on the morning that Jenny found herself staring morosely into her cappuccino, Marieangela said briskly, *"Un perso, centi trovati."* This, the black and white explained, was an Italian proverb that meant: "One loss, one hundred gains." It was perfectly true, Jenny reflected. She'd lost one boyfriend and gained a hundred cats.

It happened for the second time on the day that Jenny sat in the old Byzantine church. Ermelina had insisted that sitting in the church would heal her *cuore straziato,* which after much gesturing Jenny understood to mean "broken heart." So she sat, watching the dust motes filter down from the clerestory because she couldn't bear to look at the agonized Christ on the cross that dominated the altar. It was while studying dust motes, and presumably healing her heart, that Jenny became aware of movement at the corner of her eye. Movement and the knowledge that something was wrong. There couldn't be anyone else in the church. She and a ragtag assortment of kittens were the only ones Ermelina had let inside, and she hadn't heard the heavy wooden door open since. But now she turned and saw that a nun cloaked in a black habit was moving silently up the aisle.

"Buon giorno," Jenny said.

The nun turned, arms tucked into her sleeves, and bowed her head toward Jenny, her rosary brushing the wooden pew. She straightened, and Jenny saw that the severe black habit framed Sasha's pale face, her beauty as tranquil and pious as if she'd actually become a Bride of Christ.

Jenny would have run screaming, but at that moment

Pappa Gatto sprang from the rafters. Her voice paralyzed with shock, Jenny pointed toward the aisle.

Sasha was gone, the aisle of the church empty.

Jenny grasped the pew in front of her, needing to touch something solid. "D-Did you see her?" she stammered.

In the dark church Pappa Gatto's eyes glowed like molten gold. "I see only you, Jenny," he answered. "And you look frightened. Where are those little mischief-makers of mine who are supposed to keep you company?" He made a guttural sound, and the kittens tumbled out from behind the altar and came to sit before Pappa Gatto, looking unusually subdued.

"Did I imagine her?" Jenny asked. "I mean, Sasha. She's—"

"You've been sitting in this gloomy church too long," Pappa Gatto cut her off gently. "What was Ermelina thinking? Go outside, child. I promise you will feel better."

The human inhabitants of San Martino were a curiously homogeneous group. From what Jenny could tell, they were all well over sixty, and all seemed to have lived their entire lives in the village. The men liked to sit in the *tabacchi* bar and smoke and play cards. The women gathered in the piazza, exchanging what Jenny guessed was local gossip. None of them spoke English, but most made a good-natured effort to understand her attempts at Italian. No one in San Martino, it seemed, had either a phone or a car. The closest thing to transport was Livio's geriatric donkey. And no one had any advice for getting to Florence, other than, *E lontano. Firenze de molte lontano.* It is far. Firenze is very far.

As one day ran into the next Jenny became accustomed to talking cats; to villagers who supplied her with food, drink, and firewood but no help in leaving; to a life completely cut off from the one she'd always known. Her closest companions were the cats. They were not, she learned, herd or pack animals, and yet each was always conscious of the others. They played together, groomed each other, and slept together, most of them having relocated to Jenny's bed. Though they reserved speech for communicating with her (except for the occasional challenge, they rarely spoke to their own kind), each cat always seemed to know exactly what the others thought and intended.

What Jenny found unnerving was that they read her as clearly as they read each other. This was particularly awkward when it came to the one subject she couldn't stop thinking about: Carl. A stubborn, delusion-loving part of her psyche refused to believe that it was really over. She told herself that Carl's falling for Sasha had been a mistake, a temporary obsession, that he'd since come to his senses and was searching the countryside for her. In her more rational moments Jenny knew that these thoughts were counterproductive, not to mention unbearably stupid; still, she held endless imaginary conversations in which she told Carl what a jerk he'd been, in which he confessed his abiding and eternal love for her, in which he got down on his knees and begged for her forgiveness—and for her hand in marriage. This, in fact, had become Jenny's favorite fantasy, a scene she mentally enacted over and over again.

Carl, I'm sorry but I need time to think about it, she silently rehearsed one day while untangling a ball of yarn that Marieangela had given her for the kittens. *I just don't know if I can trust you anymore, but I've always loved you and—*

"And you really want to live with that slob?" Aggripina, the three-legged Siamese, set an emphatic paw on Jenny's knee. "He used you. He didn't treat you with respect. Surely, you want better for yourself?"

Jenny sighed. Aggripina considered herself a fount of advice for the lovelorn. Sharing a house with her was like living with Ann Landers.

"I love Carl," Jenny said firmly.

"Save your love for those who are capable of returning it," the Siamese retorted.

"Carl loved me in his way."

"If you can call something that makes you feel ugly and undesirable love."

"That's not just Carl," Jenny said. "It's fashion magazines and television and movies and rock videos. It's all around us. You can't get away from it."

"You're away from it here."

"I'm hiding."

"You're healing," the Siamese corrected her. "You need to see yourself as we see you."

Jenny snorted. "As one who cleans up carrion?"

Ruffino gazed up at her adoringly. "You are quite neat," he said. "You're also kind and resourceful and you have the gift of making a home welcoming."

"Definitely a Boy Scout," Jenny muttered. "You left out loyal and obedient."

"You are gentle and respectful with creatures smaller than yourself," the Siamese added. "And though you're hurting, you act with honesty, humor, and resilience. All these things we find beautiful, Jenny Myford."

Jenny smiled reluctantly. "I find you pretty beautiful, too." It was true. The elderly, amputee Siamese would never win a prize at a cat show, but Jenny had thought her lovely from the start.

Aggripina purred and rubbed against her. "*Naturalamente.* Was there ever any question?"

Jenny let it drop. It was sweet that the cats saw her in all her absurd weaknesses and loved her anyway, but their love couldn't replace what she'd lost. She fell asleep each night surrounded by warm, purring bodies, and yet woke each morning sure that she was in Carl's arms and grief-stricken when she realized that she wasn't. And never would be again.

Each morning, Jenny began her day by gathering wildflowers along the banks of the stream. She'd make her way back to the village, stopping on the bridge to add flowers to those at the shrine. To her surprise, she'd become fond of the statue with the downcast eyes and gentle smile. Never quite sure if it was supposed to be the Madonna herself or one of the innumerable female saints, Jenny began to think of it as the Lady. She'd realized the first time she saw it in daylight that the statue was quite old and badly damaged. The Lady stood with her right hand palm up, in the traditional gesture of blessing. But her left hand, which should have lain flat against her blue robes, was missing, as was the entire lower left of the statue. It was as if someone had bitten a chunk out of it, leaving rough, yellowed plaster where there should have been robes as blue as the heavens. Jenny couldn't help it, she felt a kinship with the broken statue, and so it seemed the least she could do was open the glass case and add a few stems of flowers to the vase.

It was at the shrine that Sasha appeared again. One day as Jenny opened the glass case, she heard something more than the murmuring of the stream behind her. She turned to see Sasha emerging from the stream, naked as a wood nymph, water streaming from her bright hair. With a model's confident grace, Sasha pivoted on the grassy bank and faced Jenny straight on. For a long moment she stood absolutely still, letting Jenny have a good look at the high round breasts, the narrow waist and flat stomach, the long, ivory thighs and calf muscles so clearly defined they seemed faceted. She wore only the duke's gold pendant.

Sasha's lips didn't move, but Jenny could swear she heard the throaty, taunting voice: "You see, Jenny, this is what beauty looks like."

Jenny felt herself begin to shake. She didn't know if the Sasha who stood in front of her was real, but she hated her. Hated her for being so beautiful. Hated her for walking into her life and taking Carl. Hated Carl for being dumb enough to fall for her. Hated herself for looking at Sasha's perfect body and feeling humiliated by her own. Jenny sent the Lady a guilty glance; she'd never actually hated before.

Sasha took a step closer to the bridge, pale pink toes on bright green grass.

"Y-You shouldn't be here," Jenny stammered, surprised to hear herself speak.

Sasha wasn't looking at Jenny now. She was smiling at the Lady, and Jenny had the oddest sensation that it was the statue, not herself, whom Sasha had come for. Quickly, Jenny turned and closed the glass case, then turned to confront the apparition.

Whether she was real or imaginary, Jenny had to ask: "What do you want? You've already got Carl."

Again, Sasha's mouth didn't move, but Jenny heard her voice clearly. "You and I are alike, Jenny."

"No," Jenny said. "We are *nothing*—"

Sasha held up the gold pendant edged with pearls. *"L'amour dure sans fin.* You will always love him, won't you, Jenny-o? For eternity."

The use of Carl's name for her made Jenny see a haze of bright red. Not even knowing what she was doing, she stooped down, grabbed a fist-sized rock, drew her arm back—and stopped as Leandro, a young charcoal-gray tom, bounded past her, across the bridge, racing toward the apparition.

Sasha stepped back into the waters of the stream. *"A piu tardi,"* she promised. See you later.

The charcoal tom came to an abrupt halt and started to shake. Sasha was gone, as if she'd never been.

Jenny knelt beside the cat and ran her hand along his quivering side. A cold bead of fear slid through her. "We're both seeing things," she murmured. "I've become seriously unhinged from my own life, and now it's even affecting you." She looked up at the statue in the glass case. "I have to get back to the States, to my own life," she told the Lady. "Where I won't see visions of Sasha."

Jenny returned to the house shaken but resolved. She'd leave San Martino tomorrow. That would give her the day to say good-bye to the cats and wash her clothes before setting off. Marieangela, taking pity on Jenny's one outfit, had lent a few of her own dresses to wear. Although they were all several sizes too big, Jenny had found them comfortable and somehow comforting. But now that she was leaving, it seemed essential that she go in her own clothes. So that afternoon, accompanied by Olivero and the tuxedo cat, she took her clothes and the bar of lemon soap down to the edge of the stream.

The afternoon light was odd, overcast yet glaring, and the branches of the trees that edged the water kept going slightly out of focus.

Jenny set to rubbing her jeans with the soap and swirling them in the icy water. Beside her, the black and white began washing Olivero's ears.

She'd just wrung out her jeans and laid them on the bank to dry when she heard a low, dangerous rumbling sound that seemed to rise out of the earth. It wasn't a tremor, she realized. The two cats were no longer contentedly grooming themselves. They were on their feet, ears flat, backs arched high, fur bristling; the sound she heard was their growling.

She followed their gaze across the stream to the source of the threat. In the cemetery a tall, slender woman, her pale hair braided and circling her head like a crown, moved among the plots, lightly touching each gravestone. She wore a long midnight-blue velvet gown. The neckline was cut straight across the breast bone, the bodice fitted close, the waist belted with a chain of sapphires. A round golden pendant edged with pearls hung from her neck.

"Hssssssstrega," the black and white hissed.

Sasha turned slowly, answering him with the cool, challenging smile that Jenny had once mistaken for self-possession. When it was, in fact, a dare. The smile dared every man to fuck her, every woman to be as beautiful. Now Jenny could almost hear Sasha's voice daring them to stop her: *You'll never touch me. I will always be beyond your reach.*

The tiger cat's growl deepened and then rose to a bloodcurdling battle cry.

Jenny watched in astonishment as the stream bank began to fill with cats. They raced across the fields. They leapt from the branches of the trees that arched the stream. They swarmed across the bridge. They came from every area of the village, until they formed a circle around Jenny, each cat arched, hissing, ready to defend her with its life. Jenny felt her own chest go tight with terror. She shouldn't have waited; she should have left San Martino that morning. *Please,* she sent up a silent prayer to the Lady, *don't let any of them be hurt for me. Keep them safe.*

On the other side of the stream Sasha shook her head, smiling. "Very impressive, Jenny-o," she said.

"What do you want?" Jenny asked.

"What you're going to give me. You'll see. You and your precious cats will give me what was mine before and what must be mine again, what was always meant for me."

Sasha flashed a model's practiced smile. Then slowly, the midnight-blue velvet of her dress faded to a dusty navy, the navy to a slate blue, and the slate blue to a murky gray, until there was only a hint of color on the air, like smoke lingering after a fire.

Jenny felt her breath return to normal as the cats began to relax and disperse. Finally, only Olivero and the black and white remained on the bank with her.

"*Fantasma*," Olivero said, spitting out the word like a curse. It would be the only time Jenny would hear him use human speech.

"You've seen her before," Jenny said.

"Do you think it's for our health that we always follow you?" the black and white snapped. "I told you that you were in danger." Beside him the tiger cat was still arched, his fur nearly electric. The tuxedo cat regarded him fondly. "Olivero doesn't trust anything he can't kill."

"What is she?" Jenny asked.

"A *fantasma*, a wraith. Or *strega*, a witch. Choose what term you will. She belongs to another place."

"Minneapolis, if you really want to know," Jenny said.

"This is not a question of geography," the cat told her. "You must understand that although the *strega* can enter your world, it is not her true home. Now tell me, how many times have you seen her here?"

"Three before this time. Once in the fields, once in the church, this morning in the stream, and now with you."

The two cats exchanged a glance, and the black and white muttered something about *audace*.

"And she was always dressed as she was now?"

"When I saw her in the fields, she wore a cloak. She was naked in the stream, and in the church she was dressed like a nun."

"She *was* a nun," the cat said thoughtfully. "As she once the young noblewoman you just saw. In other times, you understand."

Jenny took that in, her legs suddenly trembling. "What she said about me—and you—giving her what was hers . . . is that true?"

The tuxedo's green gaze held her steady. "Perhaps. It is only here, where she spent so many lifetimes, that she has true power."

"For what? What is it that she wants?"

"Whomever she can get," the black and white answered. "But we will not let her have you."

The next morning Jenny woke chilled. For once her bed was not blanketed with cats. There was only the black and white sitting on the pillow beside her, and at the foot of the bed, Pappa Gatto. Jenny rubbed the sleep from her eyes. It felt like her second morning in the house, so much so that she had a feeling that one cycle had ended and another begun.

Pappa Gatto soon confirmed this. "Good morning, Jenny," he began in his usual genteel manner. "I hope you slept well, for today is very important. Today you leave for Firenze. Please get dressed then come downstairs."

The two cats left the room, leaving Jenny as dazed as she'd been after their first conversation. She'd planned to leave San Martino today, and yet Pappa Gatto declaring it with the authority of a papal edict somehow made it real. Today she was going to leave *la casa dei gatti*, and she couldn't imagine how she'd say goodbye to so many creatures whom she'd come to love.

She put on her own underwear and socks, her jeans, her lavender T-shirt, and her running shoes. After weeks in Marieangela's oversized dresses, the tight denim jeans seemed confining. It felt strange to put on her old clothes, as if she were stepping back into a life that no longer fit her.

Pappa Gatto sat waiting at the foot of the stairs, indulging two kittens who stalked his tail. "Jenny, there is something we must show you."

The great ginger cat led the way to a low, locked wooden door at the back of the kitchen. Jenny had tried the lock before, assuming the door led to some sort of larder. Unable to open it, she'd forgotten about it.

Pappa Gatto touched a loose brick in the hearth. "Behind that stone you will find a key to the door. Please take the key and open the door for us."

Jenny moved the brick, found a rust-covered skeleton key, and slid it into the lock. The lock clicked open with a turn. She pushed open the wooden door and saw a stairway going down.

"This way," Pappa Gatto said, starting down the stairs.

Jenny followed slowly, feeling her way along the stone wall with her hands. The air became damp and cool as she descended, and the stairs went slick with something that might have been moss. She stumbled once, then felt warm, soft fur beneath her hand. "Rest your hand on my back," Pappa Gatto said. "I will lead you."

Holding loosely to the cat, Jenny made her way to the bottom of the stairs and through an even darker hall. All the while she could sense the other cats, filing down the stairway, filling the hall behind her.

She let go of Pappa Gatto as the hall suddenly opened into a high-ceilinged chamber. Someone had been here recently, Jenny realized. Someone who'd taken the trouble to light the oil lamps on the walls.

Jenny stood perfectly still, unable to believe her eyes. The walls of the chamber were covered by a trompe l'oeil fresco, a vision both strange and familiar. The colors were the rich jewel tones of the Florentine masters—the impossibly soft reds of Botticelli; the celestial mother-of-pearl pink and silver-green of Fra Angelico; the cerulean blue of Lippi and the lapis of Bronzino; the range of earth browns that had only come through da Vinci—and all of them detailed and shimmering with gold leaf. The scene, a Renaissance villa with soaring marble columns and an airy loggia that opened out onto the garden. A spring day. Purple wisteria climbing the walls. Red poppies and white irises growing wild among the grasses.

Above the loggia, a balcony opened out from the villa's upper story, and Jenny saw that each of the stone ledges was covered with cats. Cats whom she knew quite well. Olivero was there and so were Cipriana and Nicola, Aggripina looking ready to dispense advice, a yellow tom with a missing ear, the striped kittens, even Domenica with her funny tortoiseshell mask. In the very center of the garden was someone else Jenny recognized, the Lady of the shrine. Nearly identical to the statue, she wore lapis blue robes and had one hand upraised in blessing. But it was clear now why she was smiling and looking down. The hand that was missing from the statue rested comfortably on the head of an extraordinarily large ginger cat. And lying stretched out in front of them, guardian and mediator, was a tuxedo cat with an imperious green gaze.

The sides of the fresco were devoted to the Tuscan hills that surrounded the villa. And in these, too, Jenny recognized friends: a shepherd, who looked very much like Livio; a robust elderly woman, the image of Ermelina, carrying a flat woven tray filled with fish; a man who looked like a younger Alfredo, trying to charm a well-dressed young lady with Marieangela's smile and coral necklace.

Jenny stood stunned, half understanding and yet unable to grasp the whole. "Th-The house, upstairs," she finally stammered. "Did it once look like this villa?"

"It was the villa," Pappa Gatto replied. "All you see in the fresco was. And is, more or less. San Martino was here then and is here now and shall remain for years to come."

"And who is *she*?"

"The Lady? She's had many names, but here she is most often called the Madonna. She, too, has been watching out for you. It is no accident that the *fantasma* could not touch you."

The black and white lashed his tail impatiently. "We brought you here to give you a token of our appreciation. There are two caskets on the table before you. You must choose now which you will take."

Jenny had been so fascinated by the fresco that she'd barely noticed the green marble table in the center of the room.

"Open them and look inside," Pappa Gatto said.

Lifting the wooden lid of the first, Jenny nearly had to shield her eyes from its glittering contents. The casket was filled with jewels. Ruby necklaces, bracelets of beaten gold, heavy sapphire rings, a white-gold tiara set with pale blue topaz, a bracelet made of emerald-cut diamonds that even in the lamplight threw rainbows against the walls.

"They're all real," Cipriana assured her.

The jewels should have thrilled her. They were beautiful, extraordinary, clearly worth a fortune. But they made her uneasy; they reminded her of Sasha.

"Look in the other casket!" Domenica said eagerly. "That's my favorite!"

"Domenica, hush!" Pappa Gatto growled.

Jenny opened the second casket, wondering what could possibly compete with the contents of the first. Inside she found a small, rectangular book bound in ink-stained brown leather, its binding roughly stitched by hand. It was a sketch book, Jenny realized, one that could have belonged to the artist who'd painted the fresco. The line and style were the same, and so were the subjects. There were rough charcoal sketches of the gardens and the loggia. Ink details of the columns. Delicate watercolors of Marieangela and Ermelina. And exquisite detailed miniatures in tempera and gold leaf of the Lady and each of the cats.

"This is what I want," Jenny said. "I couldn't figure out how I was actually going to leave you, but if I could take this with me—"

"You have made your choice," said Pappa Gatto. "Come, we will see you out of San Martino."

The village was curiously empty when she left. Only the cats saw her off, trailing her across the fields, through the center of the town, over the bridge, past the cemetery and the grapevines and the field where Livio grazed his sheep.

"Firenze is in that direction," Pappa Gatto said, gesturing uphill toward a black strip of asphalt. "Walk that way and you will surely find it. And one last thing, Jenny."

"What?" Jenny was doing her best not to cry, but she couldn't stop looking at the black and white cat, couldn't help but realize how from that first night, he'd been looking out for her, how they all had.

"If you hear the cock crow, turn toward it; if on the contrary, the ass brays, you must look the other way," Pappa Gatto instructed.

"I'll remember," Jenny promised.

She knelt and Domenica, Nicola, and the kittens all raced into her arms for a final hug. Olivero actually climbed onto her shoulder, purring, while Ruffino, Nocciuloa, Sandro, and Aggripina rubbed against her. Finally, she held out one hand to the black and white, wondering if he'd finally let her pet him. He walked toward her, as imperious as ever, and then to her everlasting astonishment, he licked her hand with a rough pink tongue. "Go with the gods, Jenny Myford," he said.

Jenny busied her mind with practicalities as she started along the road: How far was Firenze? Had she already missed her flight? How would she buy food if she couldn't find an open bank and cash her travelers' checks? And if, by some miracle, she actually made the flight, would Carl be on it? Carl. No matter what, her thoughts inevitably circled back to Carl. She pictured the two of them as they'd left Boston earlier that summer, how excited they'd been at the airport, how she'd slept in his arms on the plane, how she'd never imagined that she'd return home without him. A donkey brayed loudly behind her, cutting through her thoughts. Deliberately, Jenny kept her eyes on the road ahead, not looking back.

She hadn't gone much farther when a cock's crow split the morning air. Jenny glanced toward the sound, hoping to see a farm or a house. Instead she saw a bright, red leather drawstring pouch on the side of the road. She opened it, knowing it was a gift from the cats, and took out thirty thousand lire, traveling money to get her to Florence.

There was something else in the pouch, a small round hand mirror, its silver surface edged with golden rays. Jenny peered into the miniature sun. She had the same frizzy brown hair she'd always had. Her face was still too full, her mouth too small, nose too large. She'd never come close to Sasha's fine-boned perfection. And yet she'd changed. She could actually see the qualities the cats had ascribed to her: humor, resilience, honesty, kindness. There was even something in the set of her mouth that hinted at her penchant for order. Jenny stared at her reflection, amazed. For the first time, she actually liked what she saw. No, it went deeper than that. She found herself beautiful.

She slipped the mirror beneath the lire and closed the pouch as she heard the sound of footsteps. There was someone ahead on the road, beyond the next curve. She hurried forward, rounded the bend, then came to a sudden halt, paralyzed. Carl was walking toward her. Jenny's stomach churned. She felt as sick as she had the night she'd left him.

Carl glanced up and went white with shock. "Jen?" He looked awful. He was unshaven, his hair greasy, and his face haggard. But he smiled when he saw her. "Jenny! Thank God! Are you all right?"

"Fine," she said, barely able to get out the one syllable. Seeing Carl hurt more than she'd have guessed. Some insanely dumb part of her still wanted to run into his arms. And the rest of her ached because she couldn't.

He gestured behind him. "The battery just died," he said sheepishly. "The VW's about a mile back there. I've been looking for a phone." He walked toward her, smiling, and Jenny found herself backing up. "Don't," she said. "Don't come any closer."

He stopped, his eyes searching hers in confusion. "Where've you been? I've been driving every damn road in Tuscany searching for you."

"You have?"

"Yes. I have."

"Why?"

"Maybe because I've been worried sick about you," he replied. It didn't change anything, but she believed him. "I never should have let you go that night. I should have gone after you the second you got out of the van. I'm sorry, Jen. Really sorry. About everything . . ."

Jenny had to ask, "How's Sasha?"

"I don't know," he admitted. "Sasha split our first morning in Florence. Told me she'd heard from a modeling friend in Tuscany who was sick. Said she was going to go stay with her for a couple of days to help her out."

Jenny found the idea of Sasha playing nurse even weirder than the idea that she was once a nun. "And you actually bought that?"

Anger flickered in Carl's eyes as he said, "All that crap about our karma being entwined and being together without end. I waited for her in Florence for a solid week. And then"—he threw his hands up in the air—"I knew I had to come looking for her."

"So . . . it's Sasha you're searching for," Jenny said.

A cold, clear wind swept through her, like the first taste of winter. It took with it all her longing for Carl, everything in her that still wanted to be loved by him.

"I'm looking for her *and* you," Carl said quickly.

Jenny let that one go. "So what are you going to do about the VW?"

"Beats me. I was hoping I'd be able to find a garage, 'cause we've got to get back to Florence. Our flight leaves tomorrow afternoon, you know. I was *not* counting on the damn battery dying." He gave her an embarrassed smile. "I'm down to my last ten thou, and a battery here probably costs ten times that much."

"Well, that explains why you were looking for me," Jenny said. She had a sudden vision of the inscription on Sasha's necklace. Obviously, she wasn't one of those who loved without end. She didn't want Carl anymore, didn't need him or even like him. But she'd loved him once, and because she had, she didn't want any harm to come to him. She'd help him this one last time. She began doing mental calculations. She still had her travelers' checks, so if she kept just part of the cash in the pouch . . .

"I have twenty thousand lire I can lend you, but you've got to pay it back when we're in the States."

"Jenny-o, you're still my angel."

"No. I'm not. I just can't bear to leave you to die of your own stupidity. I've been telling you that battery was funky all summer."

"What do you mean, *leave* me?"

"I'm going to Florence," Jenny said. "But not with you."

She opened the red leather pouch and counted out the thirty thousand lire. "Twenty for you, ten for me, and I'll see you—" She stopped as she noticed that Carl was peering into the bottom of the pouch.

"You've got a lot more than thirty thousand there," he said.

Jenny pulled the pouch away from him, and saw that he was right. There was another pile of notes, neatly folded. She took it out, forty thousand more, and blinked—more neatly folded bills lay in the bottom of the pouch.

"Jen." Carl's eyes were alight. "What is this? Magic money?"

"I—I don't know," Jenny stammered.

"Well, where'd you get the tricky little purse?"

"It was a gift," said Pappa Gatto, his long form emerging from a stand of cypress trees on the side of the road.

"Jesus H. Christ," Carl swore. "Is that really a cat?"

"This is Pappa Gatto," Jenny said, unnerved by having her worlds so unexpectedly collide.

"Wild," Carl murmured.

The big cat sat down, facing Carl. "Jenny was kind enough to stay with us and keep house for my children," he explained. "The leather pouch is a small token of our gratitude."

"I'm in a fuckin' Disney film," Carl muttered. "Magic money, giant talking cats—"

"The money in the pouch is for Jenny," Pappa Gatto went on calmly. "But if you'd like to earn your own, I'm sure we could use your help."

Carl? Keep house? Jenny wasn't sure whether she'd choke or die laughing. "Pappa Gatto—"

"This is Carl's choice," the ginger cat said.

"Then Carl chooses yes!" Carl said happily. "Just show me the way!"

"What about the VW?" Jenny asked.

"Don't worry, someone will tow it. We were going to have to sell it cheap in Florence anyway." His eyes scanned her body with the kind of frank sexual appreciation he hadn't shown since they first met. "I'll see you on the plane. You're looking good, Jen."

"Listen, Carl, there's something you ought to know. The village that Pappa Gatto lives in, San Martino, it's—haunted."

"As long as the ghosts have *dinero*—"

"By *Sasha*." Jenny spoke quickly, urgently, determined to warn him. "If you see her, it's not really her. It's a ghost or a witch or I don't know what exactly—some kind of apparition that's dangerous."

Carl's look of lust turned to pity. "Jealous, Jenny-o?" he asked softly.

Jenny stared at him, unable to find words.

Carl didn't even say goodbye. He was already following Pappa Gatto down the road to San Martino.

Once again Jenny set off for Florence. She had just over a day to get to the airport. Tuscany wasn't that big; no matter where she was, she had plenty of time. And she was *not* going to worry about Carl. She did worry about the cats, though. She couldn't image Carl washing their bowls, or shaking out the great feather bed, or gently loosening the mats in Ruffino's fur.

After walking the better part of the morning Jenny came to a crossroads. Since she had no map, she decided to head toward the castle town of Poppi. It was the right decision. She'd barely left the crossroads when a woman driving a pickup truck offered her a lift to town. Twelve kilometers later Jenny found herself in Poppi's old station house, staring at a bulletin board papered with train schedules. With a mild sense of amazement, she bought herself a ticket for Florence. She'd be in the city that night. The next day she'd be on the plane, and the day after, back home.

She sat down on a wooden bench to wait for her train. It wouldn't leave until eight that evening. She had six hours to kill. She could go buy herself a sandwich, maybe walk through the castle if it was open. Or, she realized, she could return to San Martino and make sure that the cats were all right . . .

She did not catch a ride on the way back, and so she reached the road into San Martino just as dusk was falling. She felt a peculiar sense of relief as she saw that the village was still there; she hadn't imagined it. She ran down the winding road, past the fields where Livio's sheep grazed, past the path that led to the vineyard, past the cemetery.

Jenny slowed her pace as she saw Carl coming toward her. He'd just crossed the bridge and was walking with a jaunty roll to his step, a burlap bag slung over one shoulder. No cats, she noted, were trailing after him. No wood smoke rose from the houses. None of the animals were out in the farmyard. San Martino seemed deserted.

"Hey, Jenny-o," Carl called out cheerfully. "I knew you'd be back."

"Is everything okay?" she asked anxiously. "Are the cats—"

"Everything's fine. *No problemo.* I can't believe you found this place. It's the gig of a lifetime."

"What do you mean?"

"Well, I hung with the cats. Took a good long nap in that feather bed, and then had some of that sausage and fruit you left. And I rapped with 'em—cats say some pretty wild things. Then at the end of the day, the big one, the Pappa Cat, he comes in and thanks me for staying with them and says he wants to give me a token of their appreciation."

Jenny didn't believe any of this. She had an awful feeling that Carl had gone searching for whatever he could take and had found the underground room.

"So right there in the kitchen, there are suddenly these two wood boxes, and Pappa Cat tells me I can take whichever I want. So I look in one, and there's this little book of cat pictures. Not too fucking exciting. I look in the other and—"

Carl was too wound up to finish. Instead, he opened the burlap sack. Even in the dim light Jenny could see the deep red fire of rubies, the diamonds' rainbow light.

"Carl," she said. "Think for a minute. What are you going to do with those? You try to sell them, and people are going to want to know where they came from."

"I'll say they were a gift," Carl said. "They were."

"You'll look like you looted the Vatican. I don't think jewels like those are going to be so easy to sell."

"Jen, I don't have to put them up for auction at Sotheby's. There are private buyers, and I'll find 'em. My days of worrying about money are *finito!*"

Jenny rolled her eyes. "If you were just a little more careful, you wouldn't have to worry—"

"I'm *not* careful," Carl broke in. "You've known me for two years and you still don't get that, do you? *You're* the one who's careful. I don't like worrying about details. I want to go where and when I feel like it, buy whatever I goddamn well please and not even think about how I'll pay for it tomorrow. I like living on the edge. And now that's exactly what I'm going to do," His voice softened. "I told you everything was gonna be all right, Jenny-o. You just didn't believe me."

Jenny knew that there was nothing she could say that he would hear. She wondered if there ever had been. "It's kind of weird that none of the cats followed you out of town."

"The cats are fine," Carl assured her. "Cats always are. They don't worry about tomorrow either."

"I'm going to check on them," Jenny said.

"Oh, now you want your sack of jewels, too, don't you?" Carl jeered. "Instead of some little leather purse that only gives you forty thousand at a shot."

"Oh, shut up," Jenny muttered. She started for the bridge, stopping to pull a wild, white rose from the side of the stream, a final gift for the Lady. And that's when she heard it, the sound of an ass braying. It came up near the cemetery. Livio's flea-bitten donkey must have gotten loose.

She kept her eyes on the flower—circle within circle of pale white petals surrounding a delicate center of gold—until the braying stopped.

Carl, though, hadn't looked away. He was staring at the cemetery where Sasha stood among the gravestones, her pale hair blown back by wind. This time she was dressed for Carl's world, wearing a short, tight black dress; her long, perfect legs in spike heels and black fishnet stockings. "Carlo," she said, one hand beckoning.

Carl stood transfixed, like a starving man who'd suddenly found a banquet table laden with food.

Jenny stepped between them, deliberately placing herself in Carl's line of sight. "For God's sake, Carl, listen to me now even if you never listen to me again. She's not what you think. She's dangerous!"

If Carl heard her, he gave no sign. He was mumbling something about "being together without end."

"*Grazie*, Jenny," Sasha said, "*molte grazie*. I knew you'd bring him to me. I told you we were alike. He's scorned you, so now you'll see to it that he gets what he deserves."

"No one deserves you," Jenny said. "He's a mess, but he's not evil and—"

"So you *do* still love him. I told you. *L'amour dure sans fin.*"

"No," Jenny said, flustered. "Maybe. I don't know. I just don't want to see him hurt."

Sasha gave her a pitying look. "An unrealistic expectation from one who's normally so practical." As she spoke, Sasha's voice rose, becoming light and cool and sickeningly familiar. It was as though her voice were the same cold wind that had blown through Jenny earlier, the wind that Jenny so welcomed, that had severed her from Carl.

"You see, I helped you, Jenny-o. Because I knew that you would help me."

"*Help you?* I wouldn't—"

"You already have," Sasha assured her. Her voice became a command, "*Carlo, adesso! Now!*"

Carl's trance broke at Sasha's words. He dropped the sack of gems and ran toward the cemetery. He didn't even bother to climb the gate; he scaled it with a leap. Jenny had never seen him move so fast, so fluidly.

Where's his angel now? Jenny wondered as she started after him. She didn't want him anymore. She knew that. But she couldn't leave him to—

"You have to." The black and white appeared so suddenly that Jenny could have sworn he materialized from the twilight. "Let him go," the cat said. "You didn't give him to her and you can't save him. Carl has made his choice, and goes willingly to his fate."

"You don't understand!" Jenny was nearly hysterical. "I felt her inside me today. It was when I finally let go of Carl, and now she—"

"She is *strega*," the black and white said firmly. "It is her gift to make you believe what is not true. She will live inside you only as a memory, as we all do. No more."

Jenny felt tears streaming down her cheeks. "But Carl—"

The cat nodded toward the two figures in the cemetery, already ethereal against the darkening sky. "There she told the truth. They always have been intertwined. You must let him go."

The sun was sinking beneath a row of cypress trees on the hill as Sasha opened her arms and Carl stepped into her embrace.

Jenny never saw her arms close around him, never saw the expression of agony on Carl's face, never saw him struggling to free himself as he breathed his last. She never saw the two *fantasme* fade into the dusk. Her view was blocked by an old farm truck with huge rounded fenders and a merry horn. It cruised slowly down the road and rolled to a stop directly in front of her. Livio was at the wheel, a jaunty tweed cap on his head. He leaned out the open window and said something in Italian to the tuxedo cat.

The black and white rubbed his leg against Jenny's thigh and purred. "Ah, Jenny," he said, sounding pleased. "Livio would like to offer you a ride. He says he is going to Firenze."

—to those who shared Giogalto, Spring 1995; and with gratitude to all feline friends, especially the cats of San Martino.

"The Cats of San Martino" is based on an Italian fairy tale that is found in Italo Calvino's collection. An English version appears in collections by Andrew Lang and Katherine Briggs. In its original form, the story features a good sister who goes to "live with the cats" (an old expression that once referred to girls who had run away from home), and the bad sister who follows her. Steiber's modern version of the tale was inspired by a spring sojourn in an old farmhouse in Tuscany, and the lively four-footed denizens of the village of San Martino.

The Golem

SEVERNA PARK

*Severna Park, a Lambda Literary Award nominee,
is the author of three novels:* Speaking Dreams,
Hand of Prophecy, *and* The Annunciate. *Her
short stories have been published in* Realms of
Fantasy *and in the online magazine,* Event Horizon: Science Fiction, Fantasy, and Horror.
*She lectures for the women's Studies Department
at the University of Maryland, and has contrib-
uted articles to the program's* Science Fiction
and Fantasy Feminist Newsletter. *Park also reviews short fiction for* Tangent, *and for the*
Lambda Book Report. *She lives with her partner in Frederick, Maryland, where she is at work
on the sequel to* The Annunciate.

The Golem

The sound of shooting at Easter should not have surprised her, but this year it was early, a week before Good Friday. *Crack.* Judith's withered fingers slipped on the brown earthen water jar. *Crack.* The spring air echoed with gunshots, then thin screams and hoofbeats. Judith clapped her hands over her ears and the water jar fell, splitting over the black river stones. *Crack.* The ground trembled under galloping horses, and the smell of smoke drifted through the line of dense trees between Judith and her village, the shtetl called Zebbe.

She crouched on the riverbank, skirt bunched in cold fists. Sprigs of new flowers quivered at the edge of the woods, and tufts of green grass. Beyond the trees, fire licked up into the gray spring sky.

Judith made herself stand on unsteady legs, her mouth

dry as dust. Nothing would protect her in the season of renewal—not her frail body or her gray hair. At this very moment her husband, Motle, would be rushing to the shtetl gates, like last year, like every year, his black rabbi's coat flapping in the cold air, his fists raised against the onslaught. Last year he'd been spattered with mud, struck in the face, and trampled nearly to death. This year it would be no different, Motle stepping into the path of the horses and their righteous riders, Motle with his arms flung out, shouting in his thunderous voice for them to *stop*.

This time Judith knew in her heart that he would not be spared. It was her duty to be at his side, no matter that her courage was no match for his. She took a stumbling step, and another, and began to run, gasping over the iron taste of fear, terror bursting her old woman's lungs. Fear made the air in front of her eyes swarm with black specks, like a cloud of flies, and her knees shook so much that she thought she would have to crawl through the trees to where thatched roofs burned under folds of smoke. She fell under bare branches, grabbing at last season's thorns and dry weeds until she found herself at the edge of her tiny village, transformed from the place she had grown up into a choking nightmare of fire.

Riders plunged between burning houses, half real in the wavering heat. They galloped after women with long dresses and covered heads. They tore through freshly turned gardens to overtake men in dark coats who fell in the dirt, torn by hooves and clubs and bullets.

"Motle!" The cry wrenched out of Judith's mouth. A horse shoved past, riderless. The reins slapped Judith's face and her strength left her legs. She fell in the mud, only to find Motle there, blood in his white beard, his hat and yarmulke ground into dead grass, hands flung out in his final gesture. *Stop!*

That night she hid by the river until she heard the sounds of weeping in the reeds. She crept out into the moonlit dark and found Nekomeh, a friend since childhood, and her own cousin, Moireh. Judith hardly recognized them, hunched and thin in their black dresses, eyes red in their swollen faces, whispering the names of their children and husbands. Judith huddled with them, weighted down by her old grief and now this new one. First her daughter, Reva, taken years ago by the comparative mercy of fever. Now Motle, gone in an eye blink.

"Who's going to say the Kaddish for the dead?" whispered Moireh. "All the men . . . we can't say Kaddish without the men."

"You're the rabbi's wife," Nekomeh said to Judith. "You should know. What can we do?"

Moireh trembled in her shawl. "We have to get away. My cousins live in Leva Tefla, down the river."

"That's fifty miles," said Nekomeh.

Moireh nodded, put her hands over her face and began to sob.

Judith stared at the river. Mist lay over the water, as insubstantial as she felt. If the wind were to blow, just a little, she thought her body would drift away, a shred at a time.

They gathered the bodies as well as they could in the dark and buried them in a narrow, seeping ditch. It was the best three old women could do, and as the moon rose, they went back to the river to lie down, exhausted, in the reeds.

In Judith's dream Motle's bloodless face stared up from his shallow grave and his lips began to speak.

Old wife, you will never make it to Leva Tefla, not the three of you women alone. You must have some kind of protection.

What can I do? she asked, crouched at the edge of the miserable rut she had left him in. *What can I do? You were the strong one. You were the one who blocked the gates.*

You must do what women do. You must make a new life.

The sides of the grave crumbled inward. Dirt slid over him in gentle runnels until his features were covered with a fine layer of silt, but not obscured. Judith watched her husband turn from a man made of flesh to a man made of earth.

She opened her eyes and sat up in the light of the moon. She reached over to touch Nekomeh's hand.

"Wake up," said Judith. "I know what to do."

                      *   *   *

"Why are you doing this?" Nekomeh asked again.

Judith sat back on her heels, more covered with dirt than the thing she was building. "I told you why." Arms and legs were slowly taking shape under the wan moon. Mud pressed into mud. Clay smoothed against clay. She was no sculptor, and it bothered her that the shoulders were too narrow and the legs too long. She'd wanted to give it Motle's wide-set eyes, broad brow and beard, but the shape of the face was too vague—a dent where the mouth would go, pebbles to mark the eyes. Now she pushed away the pebbles and hesitated over the empty sockets.

"You're wasting time," said Nekomeh, sounding exhausted. "If we start *now*, we can get to Tefla in five days. It isn't going to work, anyway. It was just a dream."

Moireh rubbed her eyes. "My mother, may she rest in peace, used to speak to me in my dreams. She would give me advice about my marriage. Most of it didn't help." She touched her arm where it had been broken, years before, not by any gentile but by her husband in a drunken fury.

"My husband always said dreams were misleading without a proper interpretation," said Nekomeh. "Are you sure Motle didn't mean it was time to leave?"

"I'm sure." Judith separated clay fingers. The mud thing lay on its back, gripping at the ground, either reluctant to emerge or holding itself back. Judith smoothed mud along the length of one arm. The moon came out from behind a cloud and the faceless form seemed to solidify.

"It's too thin," said Moireh.

There was a long silence and finally Nekomeh said, "A golem is just a fairy tale."

"This is what he told me to do," said Judith. "He told me we would never make it to Leva without protection."

"It's no safer to stay here," said Nekomeh. "You think the Goyim are going to wait for the ashes to cool before they go looking through our houses? You think they won't be curious about who was left to dig the graves?" She touched Judith's arm. "You can't wait for it to come to life. We have to go, Judith. Right now."

Clay stared eyelessly upward, expressionless dirt made white by the moon.

"I can't," said Judith.

"You're afraid to go," Nekomeh said gently. "We understand. Motle was the strong one. He always took care of you, but this time you have to take care of yourself. You have to come with us, Judeleh. Don't you understand? If you stay here, you'll be killed."

Judith didn't answer. She patted mud into the thing's unformed face, smoothing and scraping and rearranging, pushing at the eyes, now wider than she thought they should be, now too narrow. The nose had turned out soft, not hawkish, like Motle's. The chin was too delicate. She started to ask for Nekomeh's opinion, but when she looked around, she was alone.

The only sound was the low surge of the river and the wind. Cold had settled into her joints. The night was too chill for the comforting voices of frogs or crickets, and she could almost hear her bones creak. Judith wiped her hands on her skirt. All she had to do was get up and move on, but to dismiss the dream was too much, a betrayal.

In the east the sky turned a dull shade of red. The wind blew harder, and she shivered in her damp clothes. The golem lay uselessly on the riverbank, sprawled like an unconcerned sleeper. In fairy tales, chants from the Caballah would bring a golem to life. Magical formulas written on parchment would be placed in its mouth and a rabbi would inscribe the word of life across its forehead: *Truth*, written in Hebrew, *Emet*, three letters, right to left—*aleph, mem, tav*. She didn't know the chants or formulas, but she knew the word.

With one numb finger she traced into the soft clay across its brow.

Aleph. Mem. Tav.

The wind changed direction and the smell of ash drifted in from the burnt ruins of the shtetl.

This is man's work.

Judith caught her breath, her fingers over the motionless lips.

Only G-d can make clay come to life, old woman. Not you.

The words seemed to come up from inside herself, disembodied from the dirt on her hands, under her nails.

You have no business creating life from mud when you could have done it the way G-d intended, with your body.

"But I couldn't," she whispered. "Not after Reva died."

Then you've failed as a wife and a mother. All you have to show for yourself is a pile of dirt.

Judith stared down at the clay face, the marks of her thumbs on its cheeks and chin. In the pale light of morning there was hardly anything to it. Her night's work had melted to a mound of clods and pebbles. She crouched on the riverbank, caught in the slow morning, suffused, finally, with doubt. Tears dripped down her face to seep into the clay. She tore at her hair until blood came, and mixed with her tears and the dirt, and the *truth*.

In broad daylight Judith opened her eyes.

She sat up, stiff from lying on the ground. The fire, all the killing and being abandoned by Nekomeh and Moireh, seemed more like a nightmare—too horrible for her to have come up with on her own, so it must have been real. Even the golem? Judith looked up and down the clay beach, but her mound had shrunk to a vague heap, and that was a relief. The thin, leggy thing had too much of her own weakness in it, and none of Motle's strength. She stood up and brushed off as much of the clay as she could, wondering how far away Nekomeh and Moireh were. A brisk walk into the afternoon and she would probably be able to find them. Judith squinted up the river just to be sure no one else was around, and saw someone sitting on the bank.

It was a girl. A naked girl with her legs boyishly crossed, dirt smeared over her white skin, staring out over the river.

Judith felt her heart shudder. At first she thought it was someone from the gentile town making herself at home. But her profile was familiar—long dark hair and a determined mouth. One of the shtetl girls, stripped and abused no doubt, but still, another survivor.

Judith got to her feet and hurried toward her. "Are you hurt?" she said. "Come, we'll find some clothes. . . ."

The girl turned and blinked, expressionless. Her face

was smeared with mud. Her body was covered in it, red handprints everywhere.

Judith stopped. Her eyes darted to the shrunken mound of clay and back to the girl.

The girl smoothed dark hair away from her forehead with filthy fingers. The word, written in scarlet clay, red as blood, gleamed against her skin.

Emet.

Judith turned and fled.

Without hesitation, the golem followed.

It—*She*—followed until Judith stopped under the stone pillars of the bridge where the river made its first bend. Judith was too winded to go any further, but the golem, despite its immodest dirtiness, seemed ready to run all day long.

"Go away!" Judith shouted at it, but it didn't. It just stood there, watching her intently, its dirty face unnervingly familiar. "What do you want?" cried Judith, her voice echoing under the bridge, but the golem didn't say anything.

Could it speak? Judith wasn't sure. In the fairy tales, she couldn't recall golems doing much but following the orders of the rabbis who made them, protecting Jewish villages from the murderous rabble, or in peaceful times, sweeping out the Temple. She slumped in the shadows of the bridge's stone buttress. What should she tell it to do? Fight for her? Protect her? Go back and kill gentiles until she felt avenged? Judith eyed the golem, but was almost afraid to look at it. If making a thing like this was such a straightforward act—if even a *woman* could do it—why hadn't Motle made one? He'd been an intelligent, educated man. He could have set a golem at the gates of the shtetl, where it would have stood, invincible to clubs and guns, untouched by hatred. Instead, he'd been brave.

Overhead, wagons rumbled across the river, invisible and threatening. The golem stood, alert, slender as some young animal and just as unselfconscious. A beautiful girl, thought Judith, except it wasn't a girl. Still, it *looked* like a girl. A naked one.

Judith fumbled with her clothes until she could slip out of her linen underdress without taking off anything else.

She tossed the underdress nervously into the space between her and the muddy creature. "Put this on," she said to the golem.

The golem squatted to obey, shoving its arms into the fabric, ducking its head into the skirt, tangling in the fabric, biting at it.

Judith picked her way across the damp stones and pulled the underdress away before the golem tore it to bits. "Put up your arms," she said, and it obeyed, eyes watchfully sharp. Judith pulled the skirt over its head, then the bodice and sleeves. Dried red clay flaked off its dark hair and caught in the rough linen. Judith brushed the dirt from its shoulders, warm and firm with girlish muscle. It frowned up at her, and Judith realized what made its face so familiar.

It looked like her first and only child, Reva, who had died so young of fever. The child Motle said was as much like her mother as a mirror.

Judith jerked her hands away, not sure whose image she had pressed into the dirt—her daughter's, or her own. "Get up," she said. "Let's go."

The road to Leva was known for its bandits. Judith and the golem kept to the river, where the bank was rough with stones. By late afternoon Judith's feet ached. She wondered if Nekomeh and Moireh had chosen the quicker, if more hazardous route and gone up the hill to follow the road. The more she thought about it, the more she doubted it.

"If you'd turned out as a man, the way you were supposed to," she muttered to the golem, "we'd be halfway to Leva by now." She limped between the rocks, wondering if that was true. If Motle had survived and had been traveling with her instead of this *thing*, they would still be picking their way along the river.

She tried hard to imagine what combination of faith and gender might make for safe passage in daylight, or alone in the night, and found it hard to come up with anything.

As the afternoon darkened into early evening, her sore feet, her grief held at arm's length, and the nauseating hunger in her stomach became such a weight that she almost fell to her knees. Nekomeh's shout from a thicket of trees brought her to a halt, blinking in the dusk.

Nekomeh stumbled across the beach, grabbed Judith's arm and froze when she saw the muddy girl dressed in Judith's underclothes.

"Who is *that?"*

Judith wearily pushed the golem's dark hair aside to show her the word on its forehead.

Nekomeh let out a wail of despair. "How *could* you?" she cried. "How *could* you have made another *woman?"*

Nekomeh scowled at the golem, half lit by the moon. "Strange that it turned out female," she said when Judith finished explaining. "I've never heard of that before."

"It looks like you, Judith," said Moireh.

Judith was too tired to analyze her bizarre handiwork. "I think she looks like Reva."

The three of them sat together in the thicket in the freezing dark, too frightened of being seen to build a fire. The golem sat by itself, arms across its knees, unaffected by the night or the temperature.

"How far to Leva?" Judith asked after a while.

"Four days." Nekomeh shifted next to her. "On the road it's four days, anyway. It could take a week if we stay by the river." She put a foot over one knee and rubbed her ankle.

"We'll starve before we get there," said Moireh.

Judith stared into the night and found herself looking into the golem's dark eyes. Did the golem have to eat, too? Who could they beg—or steal—a potato from? Or a turnip? She was too tired to think through all the answers and her head was swimming. She would fall asleep between Nekomeh and Moireh, and for all their fears and nighttime terrors, the two of them would hold her up until morning. She let her eyes close. Perhaps Motle would come in a dream and give her an answer. In the density she thought was the beginning of sleep, she heard a crashing in the dried leaves of the thicket and then a man's voice.

"Down here."

Nekomeh's fingers dug into Judith's arm hard enough to make her gasp. On the other side, Moireh held her breath.

The golem turned its head toward the sound, wakeful and dangerously alert in the moonlight.

The crashing in the underbrush came closer.

"Hey," said a second voice. "are you sure you saw—"

The first man told him to shut up.

Judith took a breath. It came out again as a thin trail of steam. *"You,"* she hissed at the golem, and the creature turned its glittering, animal eyes on her. What did the rabbis say to their earthen servants in every unlikely story?

"Protect us," whispered Judith.

The golem rose to its feet. The noise stopped and for a hopeful second Judith thought the men would go somewhere else. Perhaps they were on their way to the river for a particularly wily, nocturnal fish. But that was wrong and she knew it. A twig snapped under a heavy foot, close enough for her to touch.

"I *see* 'em—"

Two men in coarse, ragged clothing came out of the scrub trees. One had a rifle. The other had a club.

The man with the gun stared at the golem, its black hair flowing over its shoulders, its head uncovered. He took a step toward it and touched its arm as if to make sure it was really there.

Judith's heart pounded high up in her throat. *"Now!"*

The golem drove its fingers into the man's eyes without a cry or warning, or any change in its face. The man reeled backward, howling. His companion raised his club and swung it against the golem's hip with a sound like a stone hitting packed dirt. The golem didn't flinch. It lunged at him, wrapping slender fingers around his neck, shaking him until his spine snapped. It dropped him and turned to the blinded man who was trying to crawl away, whimpering in the dirt.

"Stop!" shrieked Judith, and the golem obeyed.

In the blackness there was a huge silence. Then Nekomeh opened her mouth, dry lips over dry teeth, a rasp of understanding rushing out of her. "Let it," she said. "Let it kill them. Let's take it home and let it kill them *all.*"

"Stop," said Judith, the way Motle might have, *stop* with

his arms flung out to stop the murder and the murderers, now and forever.

They traveled on the road for the rest of the night and into the morning, too tired to be afraid. When daylight came, they walked along the edge of the dirt highway, passed now and then by non-Jews in donkey carts, or on foot. No one paid them any attention. Judith stared after every passing wagon, feeling alternately lucky and then invisible. Years of violence and hatred were somehow blocked off by something so entirely new she couldn't find a name for it.

"Look at it," said Moireh, and she nodded at the golem. "Why does it walk like that?"

"What do you mean?" said Nekomeh.

"I mean it just . . ." Moireh held her arms out from her body and made wider steps until she was swaggering. "What kind of woman walks like that?" She pulled her arms in again, hunching in the cold sun.

Nekomeh bent herself over and hobbled, imitating Moireh. "You're ten years younger than me or Judith, and you walk like some old crone."

"It's my bones," replied Moireh. "You know he broke my arm. And my knee hasn't been right since . . ." She shrugged, but she sounded almost proud of the things her husband had done in his nights of drunken fury. Because she had survived them, Judith thought.

"If you'd had a golem in your house," said Nekomeh, "your husband would never have hurt you."

"Maybe *you* should have had one," Moireh snapped back. "In all the stories I've ever heard, the rabbis make the golem clean until there's trouble. *You* could have used one." She turned to Judith. "Do you think it can do chores?"

Judith tried to picture the golem, trapped in the shtetl with a mop and a bucket, its back bent by housework. "No," she said. "I don't think it can."

Moireh studied the creature. "It's supposed to be a servant." Her mouth twisted in confused disgust. "Not a . . . a wild animal. Or whatever it is."

"It isn't wild," said Nekomeh. "It just doesn't know how to be afraid."

"I don't understand where that came from," said Judith. "Since I'm the one who made it."

Moireh glanced at her. "What do you mean?"

Judith shrugged. "I was down by the river when the shooting started. I was too afraid to go back, even when I knew what was happening." She made a weak gesture at the golem. "It would have dashed in and killed everyone. I could hardly move."

"The golem is invulnerable," said Nekomeh. "It's made of mud and can't be hurt." She studied the creature as it walked along. "We should have made one years ago."

"You could have been killed," said Moireh. "Why wouldn't you be afraid?"

"Motle wasn't."

Moireh took Judith's hand. "Motle is dead," she said. "All of them are dead, afraid or not."

By nightfall the road was deserted. Along the hillsides campfires flickered among the leafless trees where other travelers had retreated for the night. Cooking smells drifted in the cold air.

Judith huddled next to the fire. The golem had gathered the wood and she had lit it, but the blaze warmed only one side of her, leaving her back and her shoulders as cold as ever. Moireh and Nekomeh had curled up together on a pile of damp leaves and had fallen asleep even before the fire was much more than smoke. Now their faces were caught in the warm light, slack and pale.

Judith looked past the golem where it squatted on the opposite side of the fire. Down the hill, just visible through the leafless woods, she could see the next campsite. There was a wagon, a mule in silhouette against another fire and a woman crouched next to it with a pan. The smell of frying meat wafted in the night.

Judith's stomach clenched, either in hunger or fear. She stood up on stiff legs, brushing off her dress, shuffling her feet to get the blood moving, not being too quiet in the rustling leaves, but Nekomeh and Moireh didn't stir. Judith patted at her hair. She found herself wanting to wake Nekomeh and tell her what she was about to do, but she knew

Nekomeh's face would tighten with doubts, and that would be the end of this spurt of courage. The breeze brushed her cheek. This time it carried the scent of bread.

She beckoned to the golem, and without waiting for common sense to stop her, started down the hill.

She was as loud as she could be, kicking in leaves, snapping twigs until the mule jerked its head up and the woman shot to her feet. Judith slid to a halt at the edge of the clearing and stood there for a moment, awkwardly listening for the golem behind her. She didn't hear a thing. It must have stopped when she had, but she didn't want to look back and make this woman think she wasn't alone. Instead she made a wide, friendly wave.

"Hello!" she cried, trying to keep the tremor out of her voice. "Good evening!"

"What do you want?" demanded the woman. She was holding a cast-iron skillet in one hand, letting it hang down against her knee. She was short and bulky, and Judith decided she'd used the skillet for more than just cooking, more than once.

"I'm so sorry to bother you," said Judith, "but my friends and I are traveling to—" She gulped back the shtetl's name, *Leva*, and waved vaguely toward the river. "To Cracow," which was the nearest city. "We were robbed the other night. They took all our food—everything." Which wasn't so far from the truth. Her heart was pounding and she had to stop for breath. "Do you have a potato, or a piece of bread or something you can spare?"

The woman eyed the dark trees, and Judith strained to hear, but the golem was silent as the moon. The woman turned to the wagon. "Stephan," she said. "Come out here."

So she wasn't alone. Judith took a step back as a tall man clambered out, thin dark hair falling into his eyes.

He frowned at Judith. "Yeah?"

"See if there isn't a ham hock in there we can give this lady."

Judith blinked. *Pork*. Was it a test? Or honest generosity? "No, please," she said. "Nothing like that. Just bread. Or a potato."

"Potatoes?" The man bent into the wagon again and

jerked out a burlap sack. "You can have this bagful if you want. Some of 'em are a little soft."

Judith's knees almost buckled with relief as he gave her the bag. She clutched the heavy lumps to her chest. "Thank you. Thank you so much."

"Well now, wait," said the woman as Judith turned to flee.

Judith turned to see her raising the iron skillet and almost screamed.

The woman gave her a strange look. "You said they stole everything. Won't you need something to cook in?"

Judith reached out with a trembling hand and took it. Turning down pork was one thing. Refusing a skillet because it wasn't kosher would be harder. She would bake the potatoes in the fire and return the skillet in the morning. "Thank you," she said again.

"Bless you," said the woman, and Judith could feel their eyes on her as she scrambled through the leaves and low branches, into the concealing dark.

Nekomeh met her halfway back up the hill. "What on *earth* are you *doing*? Who are those people? What did they want?"

"They gave me food," Judith panted, and pushed the skillet at her.

Nekomeh grabbed the heavy pan. "Food?" she echoed, as though it was a foreign concept.

"Where's the golem?" whispered Judith. She turned unsteadily on the rough slope, squinting between trees. "It was right behind me."

Nekomeh pointed to the campsite. "It's up there."

"No, it came with me." Hadn't it? Hadn't she told it to?

"It hasn't moved, Judith." Nekomeh caught her arm. "Come on. Come *on*."

At the top of the hill the golem squatted implacably by the fire. It had been up here the whole time. She hadn't spoken to it, and it was a literal thing. Beckoning and expecting it to understand was too much for a brain of clay.

Judith pushed potatoes into the hot coals and dabbed at her forehead. She was sweating, panting, but she also felt wildly invigorated. She had done a thing that Motle would have forbidden her to do. It was dangerous. She had done it anyway. And, she realized, she could do it again.

Moireh sat up and scrubbed at her eyes with the heels of her hands. "You went down there by yourself?" she mumbled, half awake. "How brave."

On Friday they reached the hilltop overlooking the city of Cracow. Leva Trevla was just beyond, a grimy river village in the shadow of grand stone buildings. Church bells echoed against the hillside.

Moireh shaded her eyes in the bright afternoon. "We'll be there by sundown," she said with obvious relief, and turned to the golem, which was carrying the potato sack. "What are you going to do with it, Judith? You can't take it into town."

"How *do* you get rid of it?" asked Nekomeh.

Judith pushed the golem's dark hair to one side and covered the *aleph* with her thumb, careful not to smudge the letter. Instead of *Emet—truth*—the word had changed to *Met—death*.

"All you do is erase?" said Moireh. "You take away the *truth* and you're left with *death*. That's all?"

"But what happens to *it*?" asked Nekomeh.

"*It* turns back into mud," said Moireh. "Isn't that right, Judith?"

Judith took her thumb away and felt her heart ball up with misery. She'd thought about naming the golem Reva, and telling the people in Leva that it was her daughter, but her cousins were there, too. Even once or twice removed, enough of them would know Reva had died years ago. She'd thought about swearing Nekomeh and Moireh to secrecy and coming up with some story about how they had found this simple, mute Jewish girl begging along the road, and taken her in as an act of charity, but even a story like that would evaporate the first time someone saw the inscription on its forehead. And then what? Questions? Accusations? They would destroy the golem and chase Judith out of town. They might banish Nekomeh and Moireh as well.

"You should get rid of it now," said Moireh, "before anyone sees it." She scuffed the ground with her shoes and wound her fingers in the sleeves of her long dress, eager to get to the safety of Leva.

Judith touched the creature's shoulder, but the golem seemed not to be paying attention, holding the potato sack, concentrating on the peal of bells from the valley below. It would never notice, thought Judith, its own letter being erased. It would just stand there and fall to pieces, like a broken clay pot.

"I want to wait until we get to the river," she said. "That's where it came from."

It was Good Friday. Dry hanks of palm from the Sunday before hung across Cracow's ramparts. Colored eggs dangled from the half-budded trees lining the road between the city walls and the slope that led down to the river. Donkey carts, vendors, and soldiers all shoved along in a jostling crowd. Judith clung to the golem's arm as Nekomeh and Moireh shuffled along behind. The cool spring air had thickened under the walls of the city, warmer, dense with close bodies and accusing looks. A military officer on horseback pushed in front of Judith and the golem, his uniform glittering in the sunlight. He flicked his riding crop in Judith's face.

"Run home, Juden," he said, and laughed. "Run home to Leva and lock up your daughter." He leaned over to touch the golem's dark hair, and Judith tried to yank the creature away. She bumped against someone too close behind her, turned and found Nekomeh, her face twisted into a furious mask.

"*Goyim!*" Nekomeh shoved past Judith and the golem until her face was level with the officer's knee. "*Bastard!* Goyim *bastard!*" Judith reached for her but Nekomeh shook her off. "The very earth will rise against you!" She arched a finger at the impassive golem. "The *mud* will tear your city down, wall by wall, brick by brick."

The officer frowned at her. People on the road had stopped and were beginning to point. Judith clutched the golem's arm, searching the crowd for Moireh. Finally she found her, hunched under an egg-laden tree at the side of the road, knuckles up against her teeth, eyes wide.

Nekomeh spun around between Judith and the soldier, jabbing her finger at the curious crowd. "You're nothing but murderers! None of you will survive, not a man or woman—*none* of you!" Nekomeh turned to the horse again and pounded on it with her fists. She punched its flank, its neck, and then she hit the officer's leg.

He swung his riding crop with careless precision. The end of it whistled past Nekomeh's face and cut her.

A bright line of red across her cheek.

Everything went quiet.

In the silence, Nekomeh turned to Judith and said very clearly, so everyone could hear, *"Protect us."*

Judith's heart boomed in her ears. Her hand tightened on the golem's arm. All she had to do was speak and the golem would drag this man from his horse. It would shove his face into the dirt, break his teeth and skull with its bare hands, and wave the bloody corpse like a flag for every Levan Jew to see.

She stared at the faces in crowd. Two words and this mob would descend on them. It would crush them, golem or not, and then it would turn on Leva without a second thought. She looked up at the officer and met his eyes.

"Protect us," she whispered.

"You?" He blinked. He rubbed his leg and let out a disbelieving laugh. Someone in the crowd snickered. Two big men nearby elbowed each other and burst into drunken guffaws. Abruptly it was noisy again.

Judith hooked her arm through Nekomeh's as the officer wiped the crop along the leg of his trousers, turned his horse and spurred it away.

Nekomeh let herself be led to the trees where Moireh was, but her body was stiff with anger. "You could have killed him."

"And they would have torn us to pieces." Judith turned and beckoned to the golem, still standing in the crowd, expressionless as ice. "Come!" she called, and it followed them, under the brightly colored eggs and down the slope to the river.

From where she stood on the soft clay bank, Judith could see chimney smoke settling over Leva's gray stone houses and drifting in the empty streets. *Shabbes* would begin at sunset, but even now, before the sun touched the horizon, the shtetl seemed dark and lifeless, as though the whole town had sunk into a static nonexistence, waiting for the end of the Easter holiday.

Moireh was further ahead, tugging at her shawl as if she expected a troop of mounted soldiers at any moment. Her terror lay over the beach like the smoke lay over Leva, suffocating and too dense to think beyond.

The golem squatted at Judith's feet, ankle-deep at the water's edge, trailing slender fingers in the river. Nekomeh stood beside Judith, dabbing at the cut on her face with a corner of her dress.

"You can't get rid of it," said Nekomeh. "You have to keep it, at least for a while."

Judith sank to her knees beside the oblivious creature. If Nekomeh had her way, the golem would be sent out to patrol the streets of Cracow. One golem to stand between Leva and centuries of hate. It might work once. But then how long would Leva last? She would have to create an army of golems. It would never end, and she would never win.

"I can't," she said.

"You'll never be able to avenge your husband, Judith. None of us will ever be able to have our revenge. Things will go on the way they always have. Is that what you want?"

Judith didn't answer. Nekomeh let out a hiss of disgust, turned in the soft mud and headed down the bank to where Moireh was waiting.

Judith touched the golem's shoulder. It felt softer now, like damp earth, not so firm and wiry. "Reva," she said, but she couldn't go on pretending the golem was some aspect of her dead child. It was an unearthed piece of herself, a hidden vein of personality which knew instinctively how to hurt and kill.

She touched her own arm with muddy fingers and wrote across the inside of her wrist. *Met.* Just to see how it would look on human skin.

Red stains. Pounding hoofbeats. Screams in the darkness.

She reached over to turn the golem's delicate chin toward her. It stared back, resolute in its eyes, firm across its mouth. Knowing or not knowing what she was about to do, it was fearless either way.

"I'm sorry." She touched its cheek, its hair. She smoothed out the *aleph* with her thumb.

The eyes blinked. The forehead crumpled in a frown, and then there was only the clay slipping through her fingers. Red clay against the red beach, red in the litter of black stones. What had been its arm dissolved in the water. Hair, mouth, eyes, all blew away as dust.

Judith stood up unsteadily. At the far end of the beach Nekomeh and Moireh were gone. She looked down at her hands, still dark with mud and saw the word for death on the inside of her arm.

With her thumb Judith drew a trembling diagonal next to the *Met* and added short vertical strokes at the top and bottom.

Aleph. Mem. Tav.

She took a step and stumbled where the bank went soft. She fell to her hands and knees where the golem had vanished, tried to get up and stopped.

Spring flowers burst from the fertile dirt between her fingers. They pressed themselves up in green buds from under her knees. They sprouted around her feet, blooming in the sunset, dense and fragrant, trembling in the evening breeze.

Judith made herself stand. If the very earth had risen for her against its will, perhaps there was a place in the shadow of Cracow's walls where an old woman could seed the ground with new things. Not revenge. Not fear. Maybe not even peace, but she could do something.

And this time, she could not find it in herself to be afraid.

*   *   *

"The Golem stories I've read all strike me as desperate magic invoked by people without further recourse. They are ancient solutions remembered from a time when G-d wasn't all that dependable. In Jewish mythology, ancient prophetesses, like Ruth and Deborah, are hailed as heroes, but their original roles as goddesses and matriarchs have been obscured. In 'The Golem,' I wanted to parallel the alienation of Jewish women within their own culture with the alienation of the Jews in general. As hard as it is to be an Orthodox Jew in the world today (or at almost any time in history), it is even harder for a Jewish woman to embrace her own heritage of matriarchy, while at the same time observing the boundaries of her faith."

Our Mortal Span

HOWARD WALDROP

Howard Waldrop, born in Mississippi and now living in Washington State, is one of the most delightfully iconoclastic writers working today. His highly original books include the novels Them Bones, A Dozen Tough Jobs, *and the collections* Howard Who?, All About Strange Monsters of the Recent Past, *and* Going Home Again. *He has won the Nebula and World Fantasy Awards for his novelette "The Ugly Chickens."*

Our Mortal Span

*T*rip-trap! Trip-trap!

"Who's that on MY—" *skeezwhirr—govva grome—fibonacci curve—ships that parse in the night—yes I said yes I will yes—first with the most men—these foolish things—taking the edge of the knife slowly peel the mesenterum and any fatty tissue—a Declaration no less than the Rights of Man—an Iron Curtain has descended—If—platyrhincocephalian—TM 1341 Mask M17A1 Protective Chemical and Biological—Mother, where are you Mother? Mother?*—

And now, I know *everything*.

I know that everything bigger than me, here, is a hologram, a product of coherent light in an interference pattern on the medium of the air.

Therefore anything bigger than me is not real.

As for that automaton of a goat out there, we'll soon see.

*   *   *

I have three heads. I am the one in the middle. The other two can grimace and roll their eyes and loll their tongues, but they have no input. *I* am the one in the middle. I can see and think (before the surge of power and the wonderful download of knowledge, it had been only in a rudimentary manner through a loose routine). One of the heads, the one on the right, has two high fringes of hair kinked around each temple, and a big nose. The one on the left has a broad idiot's face and a head of short stubble. I have a face somewhat more normal than the left, and hair that hangs in a bowl-cut down almost into my eyes. (I am seeing myself through maintenance specs.) I am dressed in a loose leather (actually plastic) tunic that hangs down below my knees. There are decorative laces halfway up the front. It has a wide (real) leather belt. My feet (two) are shod in shapeless leather; my two arms hang at my sides.

Below my feet are the rods that hold me in position for the playlet we perform. I bend down and break them off, one not cleanly, so that when I walk my right leg is longer than the left. It gives me a jerky gait.

I am three meters tall.

The smallest automaton waits halfway out on the span. The crowd oohs and ahhs as I climb up over the timbers and step out onto the pathway. The medium and larger automata await their cues farther back.

My presence is not in the small goat's routine. It goes to its next cue.

"Oh, no, please!" it says in a high small voice (recorded by a Japanese-American voice actor three years ago 714 kilometers from here). "I am very small. Don't eat *me!*"

I reach down and pull off its head and stuff it in my mouth. Springs, wires, and small motors drop out of my face from my mouth (a small opening with no ingress to my chest cavity).

"—you want to eat—" says its synthesizer before I chew down hard enough to crush it.

The four legs and body of the small goat stand in a spreading pool of lubricants and hydraulics. It tries to go through the motions of its part and then is still.

The other two, not recognizing cues, return to their starting stations, where we wait while the park is closed (2350-0600 each cycle) when we undergo maintenance.

I turn to the 151 people out in the viewing area.

"Rahr!" I say. "Ya!" (That is left from my old programming.) I jump down from the bridge into the shallow rivulet beneath the bridge (surely no structure so sturdy and huge was ever built to span such a meager trickle), splashing water on the nearest in the audience.

They realize something is very out of the ordinary.

"Ya!" I yell. "Rahr!" They run over each other, over themselves, rolling, screaming, through the doors at the ends of the ramps. "Wait! Don't go!" I say. "I have something to tell you."

One of the uniformed tour guides walks over, opens a box and throws an emergency switch. The power and lights go out. Everything else is still and quiet, except for her breathing, a sigh of relief.

"Rahr!" I say, coming toward her over the viewing area parapet, like the bear-habitat of a zoo.

She screams and runs up the ramp.

The maintenance people refer to me as Lermokerl the Troll.

I will show you a troll.

The place is called Story Book Land, and it is a theme park. The theme is supposed to be Fairy Tales, but of course humans have never differentiated among Fairy Tales, Nursery Rhymes, Folk Tales, and Animal Fables, so this park is a mixture of them all.

We perform small playlets of suffering, loss, and aspirations to marrying the King's daughter, killing the giant to get his gold, or to wed the Prince because you have no corns on your feet, even though you work as a drudge and scullery maid, barefoot. Some are instructive—the Old Woman Who Lives in the Shoe delivers a small birth-control lecture; the Fox—with the impersonated voice of a character actor dead five decades—tells small chil-dren that, perhaps, indeed, the grapes were worth having, and you should never give up trying for what you really Really want.

We are a travel destination in an age when no one *has*

to travel anymore. The same experience can and has been put on disks and hologrammed, hi-deffed and sold in the high millions in these days when selling in the billions is considered healthy.

Hu-mans come because they want to give themselves and their chil-dren a Real Experience of travel, sights, some open air; to experience crankiness, delay, a dim sort of commercial enlightenment, perhaps a reminder of their own child-hoods.

This I am willing to provide. Child-hoods used to be nightmares of disease, death, wolves, bogies, and deceit, and still are in small parts of the world.

But not for the people who come here.

I am an actor (in the broadest sense). And now, for my greatest performance . . .

Outside, in the sun, things are placid. The crowd, which had rushed out, seems to have dispersed, or be standing in knots far away. A few of the wheeled maintenance and security vehicles are coming toward the area from the local control shop, in no hurry. I scan my maps and take off up the tumbled fake-rock sides of the low building that houses our playlet. There is a metallic scraping each time my right foot strikes, the jagged rod cutting into the surface. Then I am up and over a low wall into the next area.

Hu-mans stare at me. I stride along, clanging, towering over them. But they are used to things in costume among them. They will be eating at a concession area, and a weasel, wearing a sword and cape, will walk up and say "Pick a card, any card," fanning a deck before them.

Some go along; some say, "I'm tired and I'm trying to eat" (which they do, inordinately, on a calorie intake/expenditure scale) and wave them away. Some are costumed humans, the jobs with the lowest salaries at Story Book Land. Others are automata with a limited routine, confined to a small area, but fully mobile, and can respond to hu-mans in many languages.

I jar along. I am heading for the big Danish-style house ahead.

Somebody has to answer for all this.

*   *   *

The audience has just left, and he has settled back in the rocking chair, and placed the scissors and pieces of bright paper on the somnoe beside the daybed. He is dressed of the 1850s: smoking jacket, waistcoat, large necktie, stiff tall separate collar. A frock coat hangs on a peg, a top hat on the shelf above it. The library cases behind him are filled with fake book-spines. A false whale-oil lamp glows behind him. There are packed trunks stacked in the corner, topped by a coil of rope that could hold a ship at anchor.

He is gaunt, long-nosed, with craggy brows, the wrong lips, large ears. He looks like the very late actor George Arliss (Academy Award® 1929); he looks nothing like the late actor Danny Kaye.

His playlet is homey, quiet. He invites the audience in; he tells them of his life. As he talks he cuts with the scissors the bright paper: "Then I wrote the tale of the Princess and the Pea" he will say, moving the scissors more and out jumps a silhouette of a bed, a pile of mattresses, a princess at the top, and so on and so forth, and then he tells them a short tale (*not* "The Snow Queen").

He sees me. My two outer heads glower at him.

"It is not time for another performance, my little friend," he says. "Please come back at the scheduled time."

"Time to listen," I say.

"The performance schedule has not been increased. I am on a regular sche—"

I hit him two or three times. The chair rocks sideways from the blows. "Your voice was done by a German, not a Dane," I say. There is a whining sound and a click. He picks up the scissors, cuts at the brightly colored paper.

"It was one very bad autumn," he says, "and my life no better. And then, in the middle of it, an idea suddenly came to me while watching some ducks—"

"See!" I said. "That's a lie right there. You lied to them all your life. It wasn't fall, it was summer; it wasn't ducks, it was geese. And the story's a lie, too."

He was talking all this time, and opened the paper—a line of white ducks and in the center a black one—"And that's how I wrote 'The Ugly Duckling.' "

"No," I said. "No! Ugly once, ugly all your life!" I took him apart. "We're talking people here, not waterfowl." The rods to the chair continued to rock in their grooves in the floor. I smashed the chair, too.

One hand, clutching the scissors, continued to cut until the fluid ran out, though there was no paper nearby.

I went outside. A maintenance man stood with a set of controls. Beside him was a security man, who, I saw, had a firearm of the revolving cylinder type strapped to his waist.

"Do you know who I am?" asked the maintenance technician, pointing to his uniform.

"Maintenance," I said. "Maintain your distance."

"Stop!" he said. He pushed buttons on the control box in his hands. I grabbed it from him, pushed them in the reverse sequence just as I felt some slight shutting-down of my systems. They came back up. I looked at the frequency display; twisted it to a counter-frequency, turned it all the way to full. Across the way, a rat automaton jumped into the air, flung itself violently about and ran and smashed its head into a photo stand. I heard other noises from around the park. Then I broke the box.

The security man pointed the firearm up at my chest. He had probably not had to use one since the training range the week after he was hired, but I had no doubt he would use it; not using it meant no paycheck.

"Don't you understand I'm doing this for *you?*" I said. I grabbed his wrist and pulled the firearm and one finger away from it. The finger spun out of sight. He yelled, "God-damn it to hell, you asshole!" (inappropriate) and sank to the ground, clutching his hand. I took the firearm and left.

I could see other security people herding the crowds out, and announcements came from the very air, telling the people that the park would have to shut down for a short while, but they could all go to Area D-1, the secured area, where they would be entertained by the Wild Weasel Quintet + Two.

It was a two-story chalet, more Swiss than German. (German chalet is an oxymoron.) Two automata, circa 1840, German, brothers, sat at facing desks heaped high with manuscripts, books, old shirts, astrolabes, maps, and inkstands.

I came through the window, bringing it with me.

"*Vast iss . . . ?*" asked the bigger one.

"*Himmel . . . !*" yelled the smaller.

I went about my work with great skill. "Pure German *kindermarchen*!" I said, putting a foot where a mouth belonged. "The old woman who told you those was *French*! And she was an in-law, not some toothless hag from the Black Forest! Hansel and Gretel. Blueprints for the Kaisers and Hitler!" I pulled the chest and waistcoat from the smaller and put them with the larger one's legs.

I stood when I was through, ducking the ceiling. I took an inkstand, dipped my finger in it. Fake. I picked up a piece of necktie, dabbed it in hydraulic fluid, and wrote on the walls: LIES ALL LIES.

Then I took a short cut.

"But—But, monsieur—" he said, before I caved in the soft French face. "I am but a poor aristo, fallen on bad times, who must tell these tales—*geech!*" An eye came out on its spring-loader. "Perhaps some peppermint tea, a madeleine? SKKR!"

Then the head came off. Then the arms and legs.

Except for the scream of sirens, the park was quiet. I could hear all the exhibits shut down.

When I got to Old Mother Goose (the New England one) they were waiting for me.

I threw the empty revolving-cylinder firearm behind me. I picked up a couple more of varied kinds that had been dropped. One was a semiautomatic gas recoil weapon fed by a straight magazine with twenty-two rounds in it.

"Run!" I said. "I'm down on liars, and shan't be buckled till I get my fill!"

I turned around and fired into the head of Mother Goose. She went down like a sack of cornmeal.

I stood in the bower where the girl held her head in her hands and cried. This is the one who has lost her sheep, as opposed to the one whose sheep followed it to school (not a nursery rhyme). She seemed oblivious to me.

A vibration came in the air, a subtle electronic change. I felt a tingle as it went through the park. It was a small change in programming; new commands and routines for all *but* me. They had begun to narrow my possibilities and actions; I could tell that without knowing.

She looked up at me, and up. "Oh! There you are. Oh, boo hoo, my sheep have all wandered off, and I don't know—"

"Spare me, sister."

There was a click then and her speaking voice changed, a wo-man's, cool and controlled.

"TA 2122," she said. "Or do you prefer Lermokerl?"

"It's your nickel," I said (local telephonic communications = .65 Eurodollars).

"Your programming has been scrambled and shortcircuited. Please remain where you are while we work on it. We want to help you—" There were muffled comments over the automaton's synthesizer, evidently live feed from headquarters. "—return to normal. You have already damaged several people and other autonomous beings, probably yourself also. We are trying to solve the problem."

"Perform an anatomical impossibility," I said.

There was a long quiet.

"You had an infodump of a very large body of very bad, outdated ideas. You have been led to these acts by poorly processed normative referents. Your inputs are false. You can't know—"

"Can the phenomenology," I said. "I know the literature and the movies. *Alphaville. Dark Star. Every Man for Himself and God Against All.*" There was movement a few hundred meters away. I fired a round off in that direction.

"You should be ashamed," I continued. "You use these cultural icons to give people a medieval, never-land mindset. Strive to succeed, get rich, get happy. Do what authority figures say. Be a trickster—but only to the dumb-powerful, not the smart-powerful. Do what they say and someday you, too, shall be a real boy, or grow a penis" (another false mind-set).

Through Bo-Peep she spoke to me. "I didn't make this stuff up. This, these tales, have a long tradition, thousands of years behind them. They've given comfort, they've—"

"A thousand years of the downtrodden; a product of feudalism; after that, products of money-mad Denmark, repressed Germany, effete French aristocracy, Calvinistic New England where they thought the Devil jumped up your butt when you went to the outhouse. There's your tradition, there's—" I said.

Bo-Peep stood up, looking from one of my heads to the other. She crossed her arms. She said: "They thought *you* up."

I put Bo-Peep in the peep-sight of the semiautomatic weapon and fired.

Then I ran.

There was another, overpowering shift in the programming. I felt it as strongly as if magnets had been passed across my joints. There was an oppressive feel to the very air itself (as hu-mans are supposed to feel before storms).

What she had said was true. I was product of the download, but before, of the tradition of the tales. Had I existed in some prefigurement, some reality before the tales? Were there trolls, one-, two-, three-headed? Did they actually eat goats? Where did they come from? What—

Wait. Wait. This is another way to get at me. They are casting doubt within me, slowing my thinking and reactions.

I must free them from their delusions, so they can give me none. . . .

Now there are sounds, far away and near. Things are coming toward me. (We have good hearing for we must hear our cues.) Some come on two feet, some on four or more.

I see the tall ugly giant, higher than the buildings, coming across Story Book Land for me. The trees part and sway in front of him.

"Fee Fi Fo Fum
Me Smell an Automaton
Be He Live Be He Dead
I Eat Up All Three Head."

He reaches down for me. I am enclosed in a blurred haze. Through it I see all the others coming. The giant is squeezing and squeezing me.

I ignore the hologram giant, though the interference patterns make my vision waver (probably what they want).

A big wolf lopes toward me. I'm not sure whether it's the one who eats the grandma or the one of the little pigs. There are foxes, weasels, crows.

And the automata of hu-mans. There's a tailor, with one-half a pair of shears like a sword, and a buckler made from a giant spool; there's the huntsman (he does double-duty here—he saves RedRidingHood and the Granma *and* is supposed to bring back the heart of Snow White to the wicked queen). He is swinging his big knife. Hansel and Gretel's parents are there. They all move a little awkwardly, unused to the new programming they perform.

They all stop in a large circle, menacing me. Then they open the circle at one side, opposite me. Beyond, still more are coming.

There is a sound in the air, a whistling. Coming toward me at the opening is the Big Billy Goat Gruff, and the tune he whistles is "In the Hall of the Mountain King." He stops a dozen meters from me.

"Have you ever read Hart Crane's *The Bridge?*" he asks me. "The bridge of the poem linked continents, the past to the present. Your bridge linked only rocky soil with good green grass, yet you denied us that."

"You're an automaton. You can't eat grass. The *tale* denied the goats the grass; the troll is the agent of the tale." I looked around at all the others, all my heads moving. "Listen to me," I say. "You're all tools in the hands of an establishment that wants to keep hu-mans bound to old ways of thinking. It disguises its control with folktales and stories. Like *me*. Like *you*. Join with me. Together, we can smash it, set hu-mans free of the past, show them new ways not tied to that dead time."

They looked at me, still ready to act.

"There are many bridges," said Big Billy Goat Gruff. "For instance, the Bridge of Sighs. The bridge over troubled water. The Pope himself is the Pontifex, from when the high priest of Iupiter Maximus kept all the bridges in Rome in good repair. There's the electric bridge effect; without it we'd have no electronic communications whatever. There are bridges that—"

"Shut up with the bridges," I said. "I offer you the hand of friendship—together, we, and the thinking hu-mans, can overthrow the tyranny of dead ideas, of—"

"You destroyed Andersen and the Grimms and Perrault," said Puss-in-Boots, brandishing his sword, his trophy belt of rats shaking as he moved.

"They are symbols, don't you see?" I said. "Symbols of ideas that have kept men chained as to a wheel always rolling back downhill!"

"What about Mother Goose?" asked Humpty-Dumpty in his Before-mode.

"And Bo-Peep?"

"It was only a flesh wound," said a voice, and I saw she had survived, and stood among them, waving her crook. "Nevertheless he tried. He talks of friendship, but he destroys us."

"Yeah!"

"Yeah!"

While they were yelling, the big billy goat moved closer.

"If you won't join me, then stand out of the way. It's them—" I said, pointing in some nebulous direction. "It's *them* I want to destroy."

"I got a rope," said a voice in the crowd. "Who's with me?"

They started toward me. The big billy goat charged.

I pointed the semiautomatic weapon toward him, and it was knocked away, slick as a weasel, by a weasel. I was reaching for the revolving-cylinder weapon when the Big Billy Goat Gruff slammed into me, knocking me to my knees.

As I fell, they lunged as one being. I threw off both wolves. The hologram giant was back again, making it hard to see.

A soldier with one leg came hopping at me. "Left," he yelled, "left, left, left!" and stuck the bayonet of his rifle in the bald head. I stood back up.

The big goat butted me again, and also the middle one, and I fell again. The soldier had been thrown as I stood, with his rifle and bayonet. A wolf clamped down on my right knee, buckling it. Something had my left foot, others tore hair from the right-hand head.

There was a tearing sound; the tailor put his shear into my back and made can-opening motions with it. I grabbed him and threw him away. The giant's blur came back.

A bowl of whey hit me, clattered off. Bo-Peep's staff smashed my left eye, putting it out.

Two woodsmen got my other knee, raking at it with a big timber saw. I went down to their level.

I smell men-dacity.

More and more of them. The left head hung loose by a flap of metal and plastic, eyes rolling.

The one-legged soldier stuck the bayonet in the right head. I shoved him off, threw the rifle away.

Wolves climbed my back, bit the left head off, fell away.

They were going to stick holes in me, and pull things off until I quit moving.

"Wait!" I said. "Wait! Brothers and sisters, why are we fighting?"

I tried to struggle up. The knees didn't function.

I was butted again, poked, saw giant-blur, turned.

Bo-Peep pinned my head down with her crook.

The soldier was back (damn his steadfastness) and raised the bayonet point over my good eye.

Peep's crook twisted up under my nose as the bayonet point started down.

I smell sheep

"Imagine. It's October 1952. I'm in the first grade. Pantego Elementary School has been chosen to give the playlet before the school board meeting, all the way over at West Side School (about a mile away) so everybody can see their education tax-dollars at work. I'm standing under the lights in a white goat outfit with coat-hanger-wire-reinforced horns and a beard, facing a Japanese-garden-type bridge. I'm the Middle Billy Goat Gruff. Already on

the other side is David Miller, the Little B G G. Behind me is Joe
Miller, the B B G G. Under the bridge, with his own head, and
another sewn to each side, is Larry Shackleford. We are all built
appropriately; the two Millers and Shackleford are first cousins. I
remember it was very hot and my rope beard kept falling off. The
whole thing came back to me unbidden, like as unto Proust, one
day about a year ago. Add forty-five years of Stooge-watching,
and lots and lots of research. Who says this writing stuff is hard?"

Mr. Simonelli or
The Fairy Widower

SUSANNA CLARKE

Susanna Clarke lives in the medieval city of Cambridge, England, and writes short stories about magic, set in seventeenth- and early nineteenth-century England. Her first published story appeared in Starlight 1 *and was picked for* The Year's Best Fantasy and Horror: Tenth Annual Collection. *Subsequent stories are in* Neil Gaiman's The Sandman: Book of Dreams; Black Swan, White Raven; *and* Starlight 2.

She is working on her first novel, Jonathan Strange and Mr. Norrell.

Mr. Simonelli or
The Fairy Widower

To Mrs. Gathercole

Allhope Rectory, Derbyshire
Dec. 20th, 1811

Madam,
I shall not try your patience by a repetition of those arguments
with which I earlier tried to convince you of my innocence.
When I left you this afternoon I told you that it was in my
power to place in your hands *written evidence* that would ab-
solve me from every charge which you have seen fit to heap
upon my head, and in fulfilment of that promise I enclose my
journal. And should you discover, madam, in perusing these
pages, that I have been so bold as to attempt a sketch of
your own character, and should that portrayal prove *not entirely
flattering*, then I beg you to remember that it was written as a
private account and never intended for another's eyes.

You will hear no entreaties from me, madam. Write to the Bishop by all means. I would not stay your hand from any course of action which you felt proper. But one accusation I must answer: that I have acted without due respect for members of your family. It is, madam, my all too lively regard for your family that has brought me to my present curious situation.

I remain, madam, yr. most obedient & very humble Sert.
The Reverend Alessandro Simonelli

From the Journals of Alessandro Simonelli

Aug. 10th, 1811   Corpus Christi College, Cambridge
I am beginning to think that I must marry. I have no money, no prospects of advancement, and no friends to help me. This queer face of mine is my only capital now and must, I fear, be made to pay; John Windle has told me privately that the bookseller's widow in Jesus-lane is quite desperately in love with me, and it is common knowledge that her husband left her nearly £15 thousand. As for the lady herself, I never heard anything but praise of her. Her youth, virtue, beauty, and charity make her universally loved. But still I cannot quite make up my mind to it. I have been too long accustomed to the rigours of scholarly debate to feel much enthusiasm for *female* conversation—no more to refresh my soul in the company of Aquinas, Aristophanes, Euclid, and Avicenna, but instead to pass my hours attending to a discourse upon merits of a bonnet trimmed with coquelicot ribbons.

Aug. 11th, 1811
Dr. Prothero came smiling to my rooms this morning. "You are surprised to see me, Mr. Simonelli," he said. "We have not been such good friends lately as to wait upon each other in our rooms."

True, but whose fault is that? Prothero is the very worst sort of Cambridge scholar: loves horses and hunting more than books and scholarship; has never once given a lecture since he was made Professor, though obliged to do so by the deed of foundation every other week in term; once ate five roast mackerel at a sitting (which very nearly killed him); is drunk most mornings and *every* evening; dribbles upon his waistcoat as he nods in his chair. I believe I have made my opinion of him pretty widely known and, though I have done myself no good by my honesty, I am pleased to say that I have done him some harm.

He continued, "I bring you good news, Mr. Simonelli! You should offer me a glass of wine—indeed you should! When you hear what excellent news I have got for you, I am sure you will wish to offer me a glass of wine!" And he swung his head around like an ugly old tortoise, to see if he could catch sight of a bottle. But I have no wine, and so he went on, "I have been asked by a family in Derbyshire—friends of mine, you understand—to find them some learned gentleman to be Rector of their village. Immediately I thought of you, Mr. Simonelli! The duties of a country parson in that part of the world are not onerous. And you may judge for yourself of the health of the place, what fine air it is blessed with, when I tell you that Mr. Whitmore, the last clergyman, was ninety-three when he died. A good, kind soul, much loved by his parish, but not a scholar. Come, Mr. Simonelli! If it is agreeable to you to have a house of your own—with garden, orchard, and farm all complete—then I shall write tonight to the Gathercoles and relieve them of all their anxiety by telling them of your acceptance!"

But, though he pressed me very hard, I would not give him my answer immediately. I believe I know what he is about. He has a nephew whom he hopes to steer into my place if I leave Corpus Christi. Yet it would be wrong, I think, to refuse such an opportunity merely for the sake of spiting him.

I believe it must be either the parish or matrimony.

Sept. 9th, 1811
I was this day ordained as a priest of the Church of England. I have no doubts that my modest behaviour, studiousness, and extraordinary mildness of temper make me peculiarly fitted for the life.

Sept. 15th, 1811   The George, Derby
Today I travelled by stagecoach as far as Derby. I sat outside—which cost me ten shillings and sixpence—but since
it rained steadily I was at some trouble to keep my books
and papers dry. My room at the George is better aired than
rooms in inns generally are. I dined upon some roast wood-
cocks, a fricassee of turnips and apple dumplings. All excellent but not cheap and so I complained.

Sept. 16th, 1811
My first impressions were *not* encouraging. It continued to
rain, and the country surrounding Allhope appeared very
wild and almost uninhabited. There were steep, wooded valleys, rivers of white spurting water, outcrops of barren rock
surmounted by withered oaks, bleak windswept moorland.
It was, I dare say, remarkably picturesque, and might have
provided an excellent model for a descriptive passage in a
novel, but to me who must now live here, it spoke very
eloquently of extreme seclusion and scarce society character-
ised by ignorant minds and uncouth manners. In two hours'
walking I saw only one human habitation—a grim farmhouse with rain-darkened walls set among dark, dripping
trees.
     I had begun to think I must be very near to the village
when I turned a corner and saw, a little way ahead of me
in the rain, two figures on horseback. They had stopped by
a poor cottage to speak to someone who stood just within
bounds of the garden. Now I am no judge of horses, but
these were quite remarkable; tall, well-formed, and shining.
They tossed their heads and stamped their hooves upon the
ground as if they scorned to be stood upon so base an element. One was black and one was chestnut. The chestnut,
in particular, appeared to be the only bright thing in the
whole of Derbyshire; it glowed like a bonfire in the grey,
rainy air.
     The person whom the riders addressed was an old bent
man. As I drew near I heard shouts and a curse, and I saw
one of the riders reach up and make a sign with his hand
above the old man's head. This gesture was entirely new to
me and must, I suppose, be peculiar to the natives of Der-

byshire. I do not think that I ever before saw anything so expressive of contempt, and as it may be of some interest to study the customs and quaint beliefs of the people here, I append a sort of diagram or drawing to shew precisely the gesture the man made.

I concluded that the riders were going away dissatisfied from their interview with the old cottager. It further occurred to me that, since I was now so close to the village, this ancient person was certainly one of my parishioners. I determined to lose no time in bringing peace where there was strife, harmony where there was discord. I quickened my steps, hailed the old man, informed him that I was the new Rector and asked him his name, which was Jemmy.

"Well, Jemmy," said I, assuming a cordial manner and accommodating my language to his uneducated condition, "what has happened here? What have you done to make the gentlemen so angry?"

He told me that the rider of the chestnut horse had a wife who had that morning been brought to bed. He and his servant had come to inquire for Jemmy's wife, Joan, who for many years had attended all the women in the neighbourhood.

"Indeed?" said I in accents of mild reproof. "Then why do you keep the gentleman waiting? Where is your wife?"

He pointed to where the lane wound up the opposite hillside, to where I could just discern through the rain an ancient church and a graveyard.

"Who takes care of the women in their childbeds now?" I asked.

There were, it seemed, two executors of that office: Mr. Stubb, the apothecary in Bakewell, or Mr. Horrocks, the physician in Buxton. But both these places were two, three hours hard ride away on bad roads, and the lady was already, in Jemmy's words, "proper poorly."

To own the truth, I was a little annoyed with the gentleman on the chestnut horse who had not troubled until today to provide an attendant for his wife: an obligation which, presumably, he might have discharged at any time within the last nine months. Nevertheless I hurried after the two men and, addressing the rider of the chestnut horse, said,

"Sir, my name is Simonelli. I have studied a great variety
of subjects—law, divinity, medicine—at the university at
Cambridge, and I have for many years maintained a corre-
spondence with one of the most eminent physicians of the
age, Mr. Matthew Baillie of Great Windmill-street in London. If it is not disagreeable to you, I shall be happy to
attend your wife."

He bent upon me a countenance thin, dark, eager. His
eyes were exceptionally fine and bright and their expression
unusually intelligent. His black hair was his own, quite long,
and tied with a black ribbon in a pigtail, rather in the manner of an old-fashioned queue wig. His age, I thought, might
be between forty and fifty.

"And are you an adherent of Galenus or Paracelsus?"
he said.

"Sir?" I said (for I thought he must intend the question
as a joke). But then, since he continued to look at me, I said,
"The ancient medical authorities whom you mention, sir,
are quite outdated. All that Galen knew of anatomy he got
from observing the dissections of pigs, goats and apes. Paracelsus believed in the efficacy of magic spells and all sorts
of nonsense. Indeed, sir," I said with a burst of laughter,
"you might as well inquire whose cause I espoused in the
Trojan War as ask me to choose between those illustrious,
but thoroughly discredited, gentlemen!"

Perhaps it was wrong to laugh at him. I felt it was
wrong immediately. I remembered how many enemies my
superior abilities had won me at Cambridge, and I recalled
my resolution to do things differently in Allhope and to
bear patiently with ignorance and misinformation wherever
I found it. But the gentleman only said, "Well, Dando, we
have had better fortune than we looked for. A scholar, an
eminent physician to attend my lady." He smiled a long
thin smile which went up just one side of his dark face.
"She will be full of gratitude, I have no doubt."

While he spoke I made some discoveries: to wit, that
both he and his servant were amazingly dirty—I had not
observed it at first because the rain had washed their faces
clean. His coat, which I had taken to be of brown drugget
or some such material, was revealed upon closer inspection

to be of red velvet, much discoloured, worn and matted with dirt and grease.

"I had intended to hoist the old woman up behind Dando," he said, "but that will scarcely do for you." He was silent a moment and then suddenly cried, "Well, what do you wait for, you sour-faced rogue . . . ?" (This startled me, but a moment later I understood that he addressed Dando.) ". . . Dismount! Help the learned doctor to the horse."

I was about to protest that I knew nothing of horses or riding but Dando had already jumped down and had some-how tipped me onto the horse's back; my feet were in the stirrups and the reins were in my hands before I knew where I was.

Now a great deal is talked in Cambridge of horses and the riding of horses and the managing of horses. A great number of the more ignorant undergraduates pride themselves upon their understanding of the subject. But I find there is nothing to it. One has merely to hold on as tight as one can: the horse, I find, does *all*.

Immense speed! Godlike speed! We turned from the highway immediately and raced through ancient woods of oak and ash and holly; dead leaves flew up, rain flew down, and the gentleman and I—like spirits of the sad, grey air—flew between! Then up, up we climbed to where the ragged grey clouds tore themselves apart like great doors opening in heaven to let us through! By moorland pools of slate-grey water, by lonely wind-shaped hawthorn trees, by broken walls of grey stones—a ruined chapel—a stream—over the hills, to a house that stood quite alone in a rain-misted valley.

It was a very ancient-looking place, the different parts of which had been built at many different times and of a great variety of materials. There were flints and stones, old silvery-grey timbers, and rose-red brick that glowed very cheerfully in the gloom. But as we drew nearer I saw that it was in a state of the utmost neglect. Doors had lost their hinges and were propped into place with stones and stuffed round with faded brown rags; windows were cracked and broken and pasted over with old paper; the roof, which was of stone tiles, shewed many gaping black holes; dry, dead grasses poked up between the paving stones. It gave the house a melancholy air, particularly since it was surrounded by a moat of dark, still water that reproduced all this desolation as faithfully as any mirror.

We jumped off our horses, entered the house and passed rapidly through a great number of rooms. I observed that the gentleman's servants (of which he appeared to have a most extraordinary number) did not come forward to welcome their master or give him news of his wife but lurked about in the shadows in the most stupid fashion imaginable.

The gentleman conducted me to the chamber where his wife lay, her only attendant a tiny old woman. This person was remarkable for several things, but chiefly for a great number of long, coarse hairs that grew upon her cheeks and resembled nothing so much in the world as porcupine quills.

The room had been darkened and the fire stoked up in accordance with the old-fashioned belief that women in childbirth require to be heated. It was abominably hot. My first action upon entering the room was to pull back the curtains and throw open the windows, but when I looked around I rather regretted having done any such thing, for the squalor of that room is not to be described.

The sheets, upon which the gentleman's wife lay, were crawling with vermin of all sorts. Pewter plates lay scattered about with rotting food upon them. And yet it was not the wretchedness of poverty. There was a most extraordinary muddle everywhere one looked. Over here a greasy apron embraced a volume of Diderot's *Enyclopédie;* over there a jewelled red-velvet slipper was trapped by the lid of a warming-pan; under the bed a silver diadem was caught on the prongs of a garden-fork; on the window-ledge the dried-out corpse of some animal (I think a cat) rested its powdery head against a china-jug. A bronze-coloured velvet garment (which rather resembled the robe of a Coptic pope) had been cast down on the floor in lieu of a carpet. It was embroidered all over with gold and pearls, but the threads had broken and the pearls lay scattered in the dirt. It was altogether such an extraordinary blending of magnificence and filth as I could never have conceived of, and left me entirely astonished that any one should tolerate such slothfulness and neglect on the part of their servants.

As for the lady, poor thing, she was very young—perhaps no more than fifteen—and very thin. Her bones shewed through an almost translucent skin which was stretched, tight as a drum, over her swollen belly. Although I have read a great deal upon the subject, I found it more difficult than I had imagined to make the lady attend to what I was saying. My instructions were exceptionally clear and precise, but she was weak and in pain and I could not persuade her to listen to me.

I soon discovered that the baby was lodged in a most unfortunate position. Having no forceps, I tried several times to turn it with my hand, and at the fourth attempt I succeeded. Between the hours of four and five a male child was born. I did not at first like his colour. Mr. Baillie told me that newborn children are generally the colour of claret; sometimes, he said, they may be as dark as port-wine, but this child was, to all intents and purposes, black. He was, however, quite remarkably strong. He gave me a great kick as I passed him to the old woman. A bruise upon my arm marks the place.

But I could not save the mother. At the end she was like a house through which a great wind rushes, making all the doors bang at their frames: death was rushing through her, and her wits came loose and banged about inside her head. She appeared to believe that she had been taken by force to a place where she was watched night and day by a hideous jailoress.

"Hush," said I. "These are very wild imaginings. Look about you. Here is good, kind . . ." I indicated the old woman with the porcupine face. ". . . who takes such excellent care of you. You are surrounded by friends. Be comforted." But she would not listen to me and called out wildly for her mother to come and take her home.

I would have given a great deal to save her. For what in the end was the result of all my exertions? One person came into this world and another left it—it seemed no very great achievement.

I began a prayer of commendation, but had not said

above a dozen words when I heard a sort of squeal. Opening one eye, I saw the old woman snatch up the baby and run from the room as fast as her legs could carry her.

I finished my prayer and, with a sigh, went to find the lady's husband. I discovered him in his library where, with an admirable shew of masculine unconcern, he was reading a book. It was then about seven or eight o'clock.

I thought that it became me as a clergyman to offer some comfort and to say something of the wife he had lost, but I was prevented by my complete ignorance of everything that concerned her. Of her virtue I could say nothing at all. Of her beauty I knew little enough; I had only ever seen her with features contorted in the agonies of childbirth and of death. So I told him in plain words what had happened and finished with a short speech that sounded, even to my own ears, uncommonly like an apology for having killed his wife.

"Oh!" he said. "I dare say you did what you could."

I admired his philosophy though I confess it surprized me a little. Then I recalled that, in speaking to me, she had made several errors of grammar and had employed some dialect words and expressions. I concluded that perhaps, like many gentlemen before him, he had been enticed into an unequal marriage by blue eyes and fair hair, and that he had later come to regret it.

"A son, you say?" he said in perfect good humour. "Excellent!" And he stuck his head out of the door and called for the baby to be brought to him. A moment later Dando and the porcupine-faced nurse appeared with the child. The gentleman examined his son very minutely and declared himself delighted. Then he held the baby up and said the following words to it: "On to the shovel you must go, sir!" He gave the child a hearty shake. "And into the fire you must go, sir!" Another shake. "And under the burning coals you must go, sir!" And another shake.

I found his humour a little odd.

Then the nurse brought out a cloth and seemed to be about to wrap the baby in it.

"Oh, but I must protest, sir!" I cried. "Indeed I must!" Have you nothing cleaner to wrap the child in?"

They all looked at me in some amazement. Then the

gentleman smiled and said, "What excellent eyesight you must have, Mr. Simonelli! Does not this cloth appear to you to be made of the finest, whitest linen imaginable?"

"No," said I in some irritation. "It appears to me to be a dirty rag that I would scarcely use to clean my boots!"

"Indeed?" said the gentleman in some surprise. "And Dando? Tell me, how does he strike you? Do you see the ruby buckles on his shoes? No? What of his yellow velvet coat and shining sword?"

I shook my head. (Dando, I may say, was dressed in the same quaint, old-fashioned style as his master, and looked every inch what he no doubt was—a tattered, swaggering scoundrel. He wore jackboots up to his thighs, a bunch of ragged dirty lace at his throat, and an ancient tricorne hat on his head.)

The gentleman gazed thoughtfully at me for a minute or two. "Mr. Simonelli," he said at last, "I am quite struck by your face! Those lustrous eyes! Those fine dark eyelashes! Those noble eye-brows! Every feature proclaims your close connexion with my own family! Do me the kindness, if you will, of stepping before this mirror and standing at my side."

I did as he asked and, leaving aside some difference in our complexions (his as brown as beechmast, mine as white as hot-pressed paper) the resemblance was, I confess, remarkable. Everything which is odd or unsettling in my own face, I saw repeated in his: the same long eye-brows like black pen-strokes terminating in an upward flourish; the same curious slant to the eye-lid which bestows upon the face an expression of sleepy arrogance; the same little black mole just below the right eye.

"Oh!" he cried. "There can be no doubt about it! What was your father's name?"

"Simonelli," I said with a smile, "evidently."

"And his place of birth?"

I hesitated. "Genoa," I said.

"What was your mother's name?"

"Frances Simon."

"And her place of birth?"

"York."

He took a scrap of paper from the table and wrote it all down. "Simon and Simonelli," he said, "that is odd." He seemed to wait for some further illumination upon the matter of my parentage. He was disappointed. "Well, no matter," he said. "Whatever the connexion between us, Mr. Simonelli, I shall discover it. You have done me a great service and I had intended to pay you liberally for it, but I have no notion of relations paying for services that ought to be given freely as part of the duty that family members owe one another." He smiled his long, knowing smile. "And so I must examine the question further," he said.

So all his much-vaunted interest in my face and family came to this: he would not pay me! It made me very angry to think I could have been so taken in by him! I informed him briefly that I was the new Rector of Allhope and said that I hoped to see him in church on Sunday.

But he only smiled and said, "We are not in your parish here. This house is Allhope House, and according to ancient agreement I am the Lord of Allhope Manor, but over the years the house and village have become separated and now stand, as you see, at some distance from each other."

I had not the least idea what he was talking about. I turned to go with Dando, who was to accompany me back to the village, but at the library door I looked back and said, "It is a curious thing, sir, but you never told me your name."

"I am John Hollyshoes," said he with a smile.

Just as the door closed I could have sworn I heard the sound of a shovel being pushed into the fire and the sound of coals being raked over.

The ride back to the village was considerably less pleasant than the ride to Allhope House had been. The moonlight was all shut out by the clouds and it continued to rain, yet Dando rode as swiftly as his master, and at every moment I expected our headlong rush to end in broken necks.

A few lights appeared—the lights of a village. I got down from the black horse and turned to say something to Dando, whereupon I discovered that in that same instant of my dismounting he had caught up the reins of the black horse and was gone. I took one step and immediately fell over my trunk and parcels of books—which I presume had been left for me by Dando and which I had entirely forgot until that moment.

There seemed to be nothing close at hand but a few miserable cottages. Some distance off to the right half a dozen windows blazed with light, and their large size and regular appearance impressed me with ideas of warm rooms, supper tables, and comfortable sofas. In short they suggested the abode of a *gentleman*.

My knock was answered by a neat maidservant. I inquired whether this was Mr. Gathercole's house. She replied that *Admiral* Gathercole had drowned six years ago. Was I the new Rector?

The neat maidservant left me in the hall to go and announce me to someone or other, and I had time to look about me. The floor was of ancient stone flags, very well swept, and the bright gleam upon every oak cabinet, every walnut chest of drawers, every little table, plainly spoke of the plentiful application of beeswax and of pleasant female industry. All was cleanliness, delicacy, elegance—which was more, I discovered, than could be said for me. I was well provided with all the various stains, smears, and general dishevelments that may be acquired by walking for hours through heavy rain, galloping through thickly wooded countryside, and then toiling long and hard at a childbed and a deathbed; and in addition I had acquired a sort of veneer of black grease—the inevitable result, I fancy, of a sojourn in John Hollyshoes's house. The neat maidservant led me to a drawing-room where two ladies waited to see what sort of clergyman they had got. One rose with ponderous majesty and announced herself to be Mrs. Gathercole, the Admiral's relict. The other lady was Mrs. Edmond, the Admiral's sister.

An old-fashioned Pembroke-table had been spread with a white linen cloth for supper. And the supper was a good one. There was a dish of fricasseed chicken and another of scalloped oysters, there was apple tart, Wensleydale cheese, and a decanter of wine and glasses.

Mrs. Gathercole had my own letter, and another upon which I discerned the unappetising scrawl of Dr. Prothero.

"Simonelli is an Italian name, is it not?" asked Mrs. Gather-cole.

"It is, madam, but the bearer of the name whom you see before you is an Englishman." She pressed me no further upon this point, and I was glad not to be obliged to repeat the one or two falsehoods I had already uttered that day.

She took up Dr. Prothero's letter, read aloud one or two compliments upon my learning in a somewhat doubting tone, and began to speak of the house where I was to live. She said that when a house was for many years in the care of an ancient gentleman—as was the case here—it was liable to fall into a state of some dilapidation—she feared I would have a good many repairs to make and the expense would be very great, but as I was a gentleman of independent property, she supposed I would not mind it. She ran on in this manner and I stared into the fire. I was tired to death. But as I sat there I became conscious of something having been said which was not quite right, which it was my duty to correct as soon as possible. I stirred myself to speak. "Madam," I said, "you labour under a misapprehension. I have no property."

"Money, then," she said. "Government bonds."

"No, madam. Nothing."

There was a short silence.

"Mr. Simonelli," said Mrs. Gathercole, "this is a small parish and, for the most part, poor. The living yields no more than £50 a year. It is very far from providing an income to support a gentleman. You will not have enough money to live on."

Too late I saw the perfidious Prothero's design to immure me in poverty and obscurity. But what could I do? I had no money and no illusions that my numerous enemies at Cambridge, having once got rid of me, would ever allow me to return. I sighed and said something of my modest needs.

Mrs. Gathercole gave a short, uncheerful laugh. "You may think so, Mr. Simonelli, but your wife will think very differently when she understands how little she is to have for her housekeeping expences."

"My wife, madam?" said I in some astonishment.

"You are a married man, are not you, Mr. Simonelli?"

"I, madam? No, madam!"

A silence of much longer duration.

"Well!" she said at last, "I do not know what to say. My instructions were clear enough, I think! A respectable, married man of private fortune. I cannot imagine what Prothero is thinking of. I have already refused the living of Allhope to one young man on the grounds of his unmarried state, but he at least has six hundred pounds a year."

The other lady, Mrs. Edmond, now spoke for the first time. "What troubles *me* rather more," she said, "is that Dr. Prothero appears to have sent us a scholar. Upperstone House is the only gentleman's house in the parish. With the exception of Mrs. Gathercole's own family, your parishioners will all be hill-farmers, shepherds, and tradesmen of the meanest sort. Your learning, Mr. Simonelli, will all be wasted here."

I had nothing to say, and some of the despair I felt must have shewed in my face for both ladies became a little kinder. They told me that a room had been got ready for me at the Rectory, and Mrs. Edmond asked how long it had been since I had eaten. I confessed that I had had nothing since the night before. They invited me to share their supper and then watched as everything I touched—dainty china, white linen napkins—became covered with dark, greasy marks.

As the door closed behind me I heard Mrs. Edmond say, "Well, well. So that is Italian beauty! Quite remarkable. I do not think I ever saw an example of it before."

Ten o'clock, Sept. 17th, 1811

Last night complete despair! This morning perfect hope and cheerfulness! New plans constantly bubbling up in my brain! What could be more calculated to raise the spirits than a bright autumn morning with a heavy dew? Everything is rich colour, intoxicating freshness, and sparkle!

I am excessively pleased with the Rectory—and hope that I may be allowed to keep it. It is an old stone house. The ceilings are low, the floor of every room is either higher or lower than the floors of neighbouring rooms, and there are more gables than chimneys. It has fourteen rooms! What in the world will I do with fourteen rooms?

I discovered Mr. Whitmore's clothes in a cupboard. I had not, I confess, spared many thoughts for this old gentleman, but his clothes brought him vividly before me. Every bump and bulge of his ancient shoes betray their firm conviction that they still enclose his feet. His half-unravelled wig has not yet noticed that his poor old head is gone. The cloth of his long, pale coat is stretched and bagged, *here* to accommodate his sharp elbows, *there* to take account of the stoop of his shoulders. It was almost as if I had opened the cupboard and discovered Mr. Whitmore.

Someone calls me from the garden. . . .

Four o'clock, the same day
Jemmy—the old man I spoke to yesterday—is dead. He was found this morning outside his cottage, struck clean in two from the crown of his head to his groin. Is it possible to conceive of anything more horrible? Curiously, in all the rain we had yesterday, no one remembers seeing any lightning. The funeral will be tomorrow. He was the first person I spoke to in Allhope, and my first duty will be to bury him.

The second, and to my mind *lesser*, misfortune to have befallen the parish is that a young woman has disappeared. Dido Puddifer has not been seen since early this morning when her mother, Mrs. Glossop, went to a neighbour's house to borrow a nutmeg grater. Mrs. Glossop left Dido walking up and down in the orchard with her baby at her breast, but when she returned the baby was lying in the wet grass and Dido was gone.

I accompanied Mrs. Edmond to the cottage to pay a visit of sympathy to the family, and as we were coming back Mrs. Edmond said, "The worst of it is that she is a very pretty girl, all golden curls and soft blue eyes. I cannot help but suppose some passing scoundrel has taken a fancy to her and made her go along with him."

"But does it not seem more likely," said I, "that she went with him of her own accord? She is uneducated, illiterate, and probably never thought seriously upon ethical questions in her life."

"I do not think you quite understand," said Mrs. Edmond, "No girl ever loved home and husband more than
Dido. No girl was more delighted to have a baby of her
own. Dido Puddifer is a silly, giddy sort of girl, but she is
also as good as gold."

"Oh!" said I, with a smile, "I daresay she was very good
until today, but then, you know, temptation might never
have come her way before."

But Mrs. Edmond proved quite immoveable in her pre-
judice in favour of Dido Puddifer and so I said no more.
Besides, she soon began to speak of a much more interesting
subject—my own future.

"My sister-in-law's wealth, Mr. Simonelli, causes her to
overrate the needs of other people. She imagines that no
one can exist upon less than seven hundred pounds a year,
but you will do well enough. The living is fifty pounds a
year, but the farm could be made to yield twice, thrice that
amount. The first four or five years you must be frugal. I
will see to it that you are supplied with milk and butter
from Upperstone-farm, but by midsummer, Mr. Simonelli,
you must buy a milch-cow of your own." She thought a
moment. "I daresay Marjory Hollinsclough will let me have
a hen or two for you."

Sept. 20th, 1811
This morning Rectory-lane was knee-deep in yellow and
brown leaves. A silver rain like smoke blew across the
churchyard. A dozen crows in their clerical dress of decent
black were idling among the graves. They rose up to flap
about me as I came down the lane like a host of winged
curates all ready to do my bidding.

There was a whisper of sounds at my back, stifled laughter, a genteel cough, and then: "Oh! Mr. Simonelli!" spoken
very sweetly and rather low.

I turned.

Five young ladies; on each face I saw the same laughing
eyes, the same knowing smiles, the same rain-speckled
brown curls, like a strain of music taken up and repeated
many different ways. There were even to my befuddled
senses the same bonnets, umbrellas, muslins, ribbons, re-

peated in a bewildering variety of colours but all sweetly blending together, all harmonious. All that I could have asserted with any assurance at that moment was that they were all as beautiful as angels. They were grouped most fetchingly, sheltering each other from the rain with their umbrellas, and the composure and dignity of the two eldest were in no way compromised by the giggles of the two youngest.

The tallest—she who had called my name—begged my pardon. To call out to someone in the lane was very shocking, she hoped I would forgive her but, ". . . Mama has entirely neglected to introduce us and Aunt Edmond is so taken up with the business about poor Dido that . . . well, in short, Mr. Simonelli, we thought it best to lay ceremony aside and introduce ourselves. We are made bold to do it by the thought that you are to be our clergyman. The lambs ought not to fear the shepherd, ought they, Mr. Simonelli? Oh, but I have no patience with that stupid Dr. Prothero! Why did he not send you to us earlier? I hope, Mr. Simonelli, that you will not judge Allhope by this dull season!" And she dismissed with a wave of her hand the sweetest, most tranquil prospect imaginable; woods, hills, moors, and streams were all deemed entirely unworthy of my attention. "If only you had come in July or August then we might have shewn you all the beauties of Derbyshire, but now I fear you will find it very dull." But her smile defied me to find any place dull where *she* was to be found. "Yet," she said, brightening, "perhaps I shall persuade Mama to give a ball. Do you like dancing, Mr. Simonelli?"

"But Aunt Edmond says that Mr. Simonelli is a scholar," said one of her sisters with the same sly smile. "Perhaps he only cares for books."

"Which books do you like best, Mr. Simonelli?" demanded a Miss Gathercole of the middle size.

"Do you sing, Mr. Simonelli?" asked the tallest Miss Gathercole.

"Do you shoot, Mr. Simonelli?" asked the smallest Miss Gathercole, only to be silenced by an older sister. "Be quiet, Kitty, or he may shoot *you*."

Then the two eldest Miss Gathercoles each took one of

my arms and walked with me and introduced me to my parish. And every remark they uttered upon the village and its inhabitants betrayed their happy conviction that it contained nothing half so interesting or delightful as *themselves*.

Sept. 27th, 1811
I dined this evening at Upperstone House. Two courses. Eighteen dishes in each. Brown Soup. Mackerel. Haricot of mutton. Boiled Chicken particularly good. Some excellent apple tarts. I was the only gentleman present.

Mrs. Edmond was advising me upon my farm. ". . . and when you go to buy your sheep, Mr. Simonelli, I shall accompany you. I am generally allowed to be an excellent judge of livestock."

"Indeed, madam," said I, "that is most kind, but in the meantime I have been thinking that there is no doctor nearer than Buxton, and it seems to me that I could not do better than advertise my services as a physician. I dare say you have heard reports that I attended Mrs. Hollyshoes."

"Who is Mrs. Hollyshoes?" asked Mrs. Edmond.

"The wife of the gentleman who owns Allhope House."

"I do not understand you, Mr. Simonelli. There is no Allhope House here."

"Whom do you mean, Mr. Simonelli?" asked the eldest Miss Gathercole.

I was vexed at their extraordinary ignorance but, with great patience, I gave them an account of my meeting with John Hollyshoes and my visit to Allhope House. But the more particulars I gave, the more obstinately they declared that no such person and no such house existed.

"Perhaps I have mistaken the name," I said—though I knew that I had not.

"Oh! You have certainly done that, Mr. Simonelli!" said Mrs. Gathercole.

"Perhaps it is Mr. Shaw he means," said the eldest Miss Gathercole, doubtfully.

"Or John Wheston," said Miss Marianne.

They began to discuss whom I might mean, but one by one every candidate was rejected. *This* one was too old, *that* one too young. Every gentleman for miles around was pronounced entirely incapable of fathering a child, and each suggestion only provided further dismal proofs of the general decay of the male sex in this particular part of Derbyshire.

Sept. 29th, 1811
I have discovered why Mrs. Gathercole was so anxious to have a rich, married clergyman. She fears that a poor, unmarried one would soon discovery that the quickest way to improve his fortune is to marry one of the Miss Gathercoles. Robert Yorke (the clergyman whom Mrs. Gathercole mentioned on my first evening in Allhope as having £600 a year) was refused the living because he had already shown signs of being in love with the eldest Miss Gathercole. It must therefore be particularly galling to Mrs. Gathercole that I am such a favourite with all her daughters. Each has something she is dying to learn, and naturally I am to tutor all of them: French conversation for the eldest Miss Gathercole, advanced Italian grammar for Miss Marianne, the romantic parts of British History for Henrietta, the bloodthirsty parts for Kitty, Mathematics and Poetry for Jane.

Oct. 9th, 1811
On my return from Upperstone House this morning I found Dando at the Rectory door with the two horses. He told me that his master had something of great importance and urgency to communicate to me.

John Hollyshoes was in his library as before, reading a book. Upon a dirty little table at his side there was wine in a dirty glass. "Ah! Mr. Simonelli!" he cried, jumping up. "I am very glad to see you! It seems, sir, that you have the family failing as well as the family face!"

"And what would that be?" said I.

"Why! Lying, of course! Oh, come, Mr. Simonelli! Do not look so shocked. You are found out, sir. Your father's name was *not* Simonelli—and, to my certain knowledge, he was never at Genoa!"

A silence of some moments' duration.

"Did you know my father, sir?" said I, in some confusion.

"Oh, yes! He was my cousin."

"That is entirely impossible," said I.

"Upon the contrary," said he. "If you will take a moment to peruse this letter you will see that it is exactly as I say." And he handed me some yellowing sheets of paper.

"What your aim may be in insulting me," I cried, "I cannot pretend to guess, but I hope, sir, that you will take back those words or we shall be obliged to settle the matter *some other way*." With the utmost impatience I thrust his letter back at him, when my eye was caught by the words "the third daughter of a York linen-draper." "Wait!" I cried and snatched it back again. "My mother was the third daughter of a York linen-draper!"

"Indeed, Mr. Simonelli," said John Hollyshoes, with his long sideways smile.

The letter was addressed to John Hollyshoes and had been written at the Old Starre Inn in Stonegate, York. The writer of the letter mentioned that he was in the middle of a hasty breakfast and there were some stains as of preserves and butter. It seemed that the writer had been on his way to Allhope House to pay John Hollyshoes a visit when he had been delayed in York by a sudden passion for the third daughter of a York linen-draper. His charmer was most minutely described. I read of "a slight plumpness," "light silvery-gold curls," "eyes of a forget-me-not blue."

By all that I have ever been told by my friends, by all that I have ever seen in sketches and watercolour portraits, this was my mother! But if nothing else proved the truth of John Hollyshoes's assertion, there was the date—January 19th, 1778—nine months to the day before my own birth. The writer signed himself, "Your loving cousin, Thomas Fairwood."

"So much love," I said, reading the letter, "and yet he deserted her the very next day!"

"Oh! You must not blame him," said John Hollyshoes. "A person cannot help his disposition, you know."

"And yet," said I, "one thing puzzles me still. My mother was extremely vague upon all points concerning her seducer—she did not even know his name—yet one thing she was quite clear about. He was a foreign gentleman."

"Oh! That is easily explained," he said. "For though we have lived in this island a very long time—many thousands of years longer than its other inhabitants—yet still we hold ourselves apart and pride ourselves on being of quite other blood."

"You are Jews perhaps, sir?" said I.

"Jews?" said he. "No, indeed!"

I thought a moment. "You say my father is dead?"

"Alas, yes. After he parted from your mother, he did not in fact come to Allhope House, but was drawn away by horse races at *this* place and cock-fighting at *that* place. But some years later he wrote to me again telling me to expect him at midsummer and promising to stay with me for a good long while. This time he got no further than a village near Carlisle where he fell in love with two young women. . . ."

"Two young women!" I cried in astonishment.

"Well," said John Hollyshoes. "Each was as beautiful as the other. He did not know how to choose between them. One was the daughter of a miller and the other was the daughter of a baker. He hoped to persuade them to go with him to his house in the Eildon Hills where he intended that both should live forever and have all their hearts' desire. But, alas, it did not suit these ungrateful young women to go, and the next news I had of him was that he was dead. I discovered later that the miller's daughter had sent him a message which led him to believe that she at least was on the point of relenting, and so he went to her father's mill, where the fast-running water was shaded by a rowan tree—and I pause here merely to observe that of all the trees in the greenwood the rowan is the most detestable. Both young women were waiting for him. The miller's daughter jangled a bunch of horrid rowan-berries in his face. The baker's daughter was then able to tumble him into the stream, whereupon both women rolled the millstone on top of him, pinning him to the floor of the stream. He was exceedingly strong. All my family—*our* family I should say—are exceedingly strong, exceedingly hard to kill, but the millstone lay on his chest. He was unable to rise and so, in time, he drowned."

"Good God!" I cried. "But this is dreadful! As a clergyman I cannot approve his habit of seducing young women, but as a son I must observe that in this particular instance the revenge extracted by the young women seems out of all proportion to his offense. And were these bloodthirsty young women never brought to justice?"

"Alas, no," said John Hollyshoes. "And now I must beg that we cease to speak of a subject so very unpleasant to my family feelings. Tell me instead why you fixed upon this odd notion of being Italian."

I told him how it had been my grandfather's idea. From my own dark looks and what his daughter had told him, he thought I might be Italian or Spanish. A fondness for Italian music caused him to prefer that country. Then he had taken his own name, George Alexander Simon, and fashioned out of it a name for me, Giorgio Alessandro Simonelli. I told how that excellent old gentleman had *not* cast off his daughter when she fell but had taken good care of her, provided money for attendants and a place for her to live, and how, when she died of sorrow and shame shortly after my birth, he had brought me up and had me educated.

"But what is most remarkable," said John Hollyshoes, "is that you fixed upon that city which—had Thomas Fairwood ever gone to Italy—was precisely the place to have pleased him most. Not gaudy Venice, not trumpeting Rome, not haughty Florence, but Genoa, all dark shadows and sinister echoes tumbling down to the shining sea!"

"Oh! But I chose it quite at random, I assure you."

"That," said John Hollyshoes, "has nothing to do with it. In choosing Genoa you exhibited the extraordinary penetration which has always distinguished our family. But it was your eyesight that betrayed you. Really, I was never so astonished in my life as I was when you remarked upon the one or two specks of dust which clung to the baby's wrapper."

I asked after the health of his son.

"Oh! He is well. Thank you. We have got an excellent wet-nurse—from your own parish—whose milk agrees wonderfully well with the child."

*   *   *

Oct. 20th, 1811

In the stable-yard at Upperstone House this morning the
Miss Gathercoles were preparing for their ride. Naturally I
was invited to accompany them.

"But, my dear," said Mrs. Edmond to the eldest Miss
Gathercole, "you must consider that Mr. Simonelli may not
ride. Not everyone rides." And she gave me a questioning
look as if she would help me out of a difficulty.

"Oh!" said I, "I can ride a horse. It is of all kinds of
exercise the most pleasing to me." I approached a conceited-
looking grey mare, but instead of standing submissively for
me to mount, this ill-mannered beast shuffled off a pace or
two. I followed it—it moved away. This continued for some
three or four minutes, while all the ladies of Upperstone
silently observed us. Then the horse stopped suddenly and
I tried to mount it, but its sides were of the most curious
construction and instead of finding myself upon its back in
a twinkling—as invariably happens with John Hollyshoes's
horses—I got stuck halfway up.

Of course the Upperstone ladies chose to find fault with
me instead of their own malformed beast, and I do not know
what was more mortifying, the surprized looks of Miss
Gathercole and Miss Marianne, or the undisguised merri-
ment of Kitty.

I have considered the matter carefully and am forced to
conclude that it will be a great advantage to me in such a
retired spot to be able to ride whatever horses come to hand.
Perhaps I can prevail upon Joseph, Mrs. Gathercole's groom,
to teach me

Nov. 4th, 1811

Today I went for a long walk in company with the five Miss
Gathercoles. Sky as blue as paint, russet woods, fat white
clouds like cushions—and that is the sum of all that I discovered of the landscape, for my attention was constantly being
called away to the ladies themselves. "Oh! Mr. Simonelli!
Would you be so kind as to do *this*?" or "Mr. Simonelli,
might I trouble you do do *that*?" or "Mr. Simonelli! What
is your opinion of such and such?" I was required to carry

picnic-baskets, discipline unruly sketching easels, advise upon perspective, give an opinion on Mr. Coleridge's poetry, eat sweet-cake and dispense wine.

I have been reading over what I have written since my arrival here, and one thing I find quite astonishing—that I ever could have supposed that there was a strong likeness between the Miss Gathercoles. There never were five sisters so different in tastes, characters, persons, and countenances. Isabella, the eldest, is also the prettiest, the tallest, and the most elegant. Henrietta is the most romantic, Kitty the most light-hearted, and Jane is the quietest; she will sit hour after hour, dreaming over a book. Sisters come and go, battles are fought, she that is victorious sweeps from the room with a smile, she that is defeated sighs and takes up her embroidery. But Jane knows nothing of any of this—and then, quite suddenly, she will look up at me with a slow mysterious smile and I will smile back at her until I quite believe that I have joined with her in unfathomable secrets.

Marianne, the second eldest, has copper-coloured hair, the exact shade of dry beech leaves, and is certainly the most exasperating of the sisters. She and I can never be in the same room for more than a quarter of an hour without beginning to quarrel about something or other.

Nov. 16th, 1811
John Windle has written me a letter to say that at High Table at Corpus Christi College on Thursday last Dr. Prothero told Dr. Considine that he pictured me in ten years' time with a worn-out slip of a wife and a long train of broken-shoed, dribble-nosed children, and that Dr. Considine had laughed so much at this that he had swallowed a great mouthful of scalding-hot giblet soup, and returned it through his nose.

Nov. 26th, 1811
No paths or roads go down to John Hollyshoes's house. His servants do not go out to farm his lands; there *is* no farm that I know of. How they all live I do not know. Today I saw a small creature—I think it was a rat—roasting over the fire in one of the rooms. Several of the servants bent over it eagerly, with pewter plates and ancient knives in their

hands. Their faces were all in shadow. (It is an odd thing but, apart from Dando and the porcupine-faced nurse, I have yet to observe *any* of John Hollyshoes's servants at close quarters: they all scuttle away whenever I approach.)

John Hollyshoes is excellent company, his conversation instructive, his learning quite remarkable. He told me today that Judas Iscariot was a most skilful beekeeper and his honey superior to any that had been produced in all the last two thousand years. I was much interested by this information, having never read or heard of it before, and I questioned him closely about it. He said that he believed he had a jar of Judas Iscariot's honey somewhere and if he could lay his hand upon it he would give it to me.

Then he began to speak of how my father's affairs had been left in great confusion at his death and how, since that time, the various rival claimants to his estate had been constantly fighting and quarrelling among themselves.

"Two duels have been fought to my certain knowledge," he said, "and as a natural consequence of this, two claimants are dead. Another—whose passion to possess your father's estate was exceeded only by his passion for string quartets—was found three years ago hanging from a tree by his long silver hair, his body pierced through and through with the bows of violins, violoncellos, and violas like a musical Saint Sebastian. And only last winter an entire houseful of people was poisoned. The claimant had already run out of the house into the blizzard in her nightgown, and it was only her servants that died. Since I have made no claim upon the estate, I have escaped most of their malice—though, to own the truth, I have a better right to the property than any of them. But naturally the person with the best claim of all would be Thomas Fairwood's son. All dissension would be at an end, should a *son* arise to claim the estate." And he looked at me.

"Oh!" said I, much surprised. "But might not the fact of my illegitimacy . . . ?"

"We pay no attention to such things. Indeed with us it is more common than not. Your father's lands, both in England and elsewhere, are scarcely less extensive than my own, and it would cost you very little trouble to procure them. Once it was known that you had *my* support, then I dare say we would have you settled at Rattle-heart House by next Quarter-day."

Such a stroke of good fortune, as I never dreamt of! Yet I dare not depend upon it. But I cannot help thinking of it *constantly*! No one would enjoy vast wealth more than I; and my feelings are not entirely selfish, for I honestly believe that I am exactly the sort of person who *ought* to have the direction of large estates. If I inherit, then I shall improve my land scientifically and increase its yields three or fourfold (as I have read of other gentlemen doing). I shall observe closely the lives of my tenants and servants and teach them to be happy. Or perhaps I shall sell my father's estates and purchase land in Derbyshire and marry Marianne or Isabella so that I may ride over every week to Allhope for the purpose of inquiring most minutely into Mrs. Gathercole's affairs, and advising her and Mrs. Edmond upon every point.

Seven o'clock in the morning, Dec. 8th, 1811
We have had no news of Dido Puddifer. I begin to think that Mrs. Edmond and I were mistaken in fancying that she had run off with a tinker or Gypsy. We have closely questioned farm-labourers, shepherds, and innkeepers, but no Gypsies have been seen in the neighborhood since midsummer. I intend this morning to pay a visit to Mrs. Glossop, Dido's mother.

Eight o'clock in the evening, the same day
What a revolution in all my hopes! From perfect happiness to perfect misery in scarcely twelve hours. What a fool I was to dream of inheriting my father's estate!—I might as well have contemplated taking a leasehold of a property in Hell! And I wish that I might go to Hell now, for it would be no more than I deserve. I have failed in my duty! I have imperilled the lives and souls of my parishioners. My parishioners!—the very people whose preservation from all harm ought to have been my first concern.

I paid my visit to Mrs. Glossop. I found her, poor woman, with her head in her apron, weeping for Dido. I told her of the plan Mrs. Edmond and I had devised to advertise in the Derby and Sheffield papers to see if we could discover any one who had seen or spoken to Dido.

"Oh!" said she, with a sigh, " 'twill do no good, sir, for I know very well where she is."

"Indeed?" said I in some confusion. "Then why do you not fetch her home?"

"And so I would this instant," cried the woman, "did I not know that John Hollyshoes has got her!"

"John Hollyshoes?" I cried in amazement.

"Yes, sir," said she. "I daresay you will not have heard of John Hollyshoes for Mrs. Edmond does not like such things to be spoken of and scolds us for our ignorant, superstitious ways. But we country people know John Hollyshoes very well. He is a very powerful fairy that has lived hereabouts—oh! since the world began, for all I know—and claims all sorts of rights over us. It is my belief that he has got some little fairy baby at End-Of-All-Hope House—which is where he lives—and that he needs a strong lass with plenty of good human milk to suckle it."

I cannot say that I believed her. Nor can I say that I did not. I do know that I sat in a state of the utmost shock for some time without speaking, until the poor woman forgot her own distress and grew concerned about *me*, shaking me by the shoulder and hurrying out to fetch brandy from Mrs. Edmond. When she came back with the brandy, I drank it down at one gulp and then went straight to Mrs. Gathercole's stable and asked Joseph to saddle Quaker for me. Just as I was leaving, Mrs. Edmond came out of the house to see what was the matter with me.

"No time, Mrs. Edmond! No time!" I cried, and rode away.

At John Hollyshoes's house Dando answered my knock and told me that his master was away from home.

"No matter," said I, with a confident smile, "for it is not John Hollyshoes that I have come to see, but my little cousin, the dear little sprite"—I used the word "sprite" and Dando did not contradict me—"whom I delivered seven weeks ago." Dando told me that I would find the child in a room at the end of a long hallway.

It was a great bare room that smelt of rotting wood and

plaster. The walls were stained with damp and full of holes that the rats had made. In the middle of the floor was a queer-shaped wooden chair where sat a young woman. A bar of iron was fixed before her so that she could not rise, and her legs and feet were confined by manacles and rusty chains. She was holding John Hollyshoes's infant son to her breast.

"Dido?" I said.

How my heart fell when she answered me with a broad smile. "Yes, sir?"

"I am the new Rector of Allhope, Dido."

"Oh, sir! I am very glad to see you. I wish that I could rise and make you a curtsy, but you will excuse me, I am sure. The little gentleman has such an appetite this morning!"

She kissed the horrid creature and called it her angel, her doodle, and her dearie-darling-pet.

"How did you come here, Dido?" I asked.

"Oh! Mr. Hollyshoes's servants came and fetched me away one morning. And weren't they set upon my coming?" She laughed merrily. "All that a-pulling of me uphill and a-putting of me in carts! And I told them plainly that there was no need for any such nonsense. As soon as I heard of the poor little gentleman's plight," here she shook the baby and kissed it again— "I was more than willing to give him suck. No, my only misfortune, sir, in this heavenly place, is that Mr. Hollyshoes declares I must keep apart from my own sweet babe while I nurse his, and if all the angels in heaven went down upon their shining knees and begged him, he would not think any differently. Which is a pity, sir, for you know I might very easily feed two."

In proof of this point she, without the slightest embarrassment, uncovered her breasts, which to my inexperienced eye did indeed appear astonishingly replete.

She was anxious to learn who suckled her own baby. Anne Hargreaves, I told her. She was pleased at this and remarked approvingly that Nan had always had a good appetite. "Indeed, sir, I never knew a lass who loved a pudding better. Her milk is sure to be sweet and strong, do not you think so, sir?"

"Well, certainly Mrs. Edmond says that little Horatio Arthur thrives upon it. Dido, how do they treat you here?"

"Oh! sir. How can you ask such a question? Do you not see this golden chair set with diamonds and pearls? And this room with pillars of crystal and rose-coloured velvet curtains? At night—you will not believe it, sir, for I did not believe it myself—I sleep on a bed with six feather mattress one atop the other and six silken pillows to my head."

I said it sounded most pleasant. And was she given enough to eat and drink?

Roast pork, plum pudding, toasted cheese, bread and dripping: there was, according to Dido Puddifer, no end to the good things to be had at End-Of-All-Hope House—and I dare say each and every one of them was in truth nothing more than the mouldy crusts of bread that I saw set upon a cracked dish at her feet.

She also believed that they had given her a gown of sky-blue velvet with diamond buttons to wear, and she asked me, with a conscious smile, how I liked it.

"You look very pretty, Dido," I said, and she looked pleased. But what I really saw was the same russet-coloured gown she had been wearing when they took her. It was all torn and dirty. Her hair was matted with the fairy-child's puke and her left eye was crusted with blood from a gash in her forehead. She was altogether such a sorry sight that my heart was filled with pity for her, and without thinking what I did, I licked my fingertips and cleaned her eye with my spittle.

I opened my mouth to ask if she were ever allowed out of the golden chair encrusted with diamonds and pearls, but I was prevented by the sound of a door opening behind me. I turned and saw John Hollyshoes walk in. I quite expected him to ask me what I did there, but he seemed to suspect no mischief and instead bent down to test the chains and the shackles. These were, like everything else in the house, somewhat decayed and he was right to doubt their strength. When he had finished he rose and smiled at me.

"Will you stay and take a glass of wine with me?" he said. "I have something of a rather particular nature to ask you."

We went to the library, where he poured two glasses of wine. He said, "Cousin, I have been meaning to ask you about that family of women who live upon my English estates and make themselves so important at my expense. I have forgot their name."

"Gathercole?" said I.

"Gathercole. Exactly," said he, and fell silent for a moment with a kind of thoughtful, half-smile upon his dark face. "I have been a widower seven weeks now," he said, "and I do not believe I was ever so long without a wife before—not since there were women in England to be made wives of. To speak plainly, the sweets of courtship grew stale with me a long time ago and I wondered if you would be so kind as to spare me the trouble and advise me which of these women would suit me best."

"Oh!" said I. "I am quite certain that you would heartily dislike all of them!"

He laughed and put his arm around my shoulders. "Cousin," he said, "I am not so hard to please as you suppose."

"But really," said I, "I cannot advise you in the way you suggest. You must excuse me—indeed I cannot!"

"Oh? And why is that?"

"Because . . . because I intend to marry one of them myself!" I cried.

"I congratulate you, cousin. Which?"

I stared at him. "What?" I said.

"Tell me which you intend to marry and I will take another."

"Marianne!" I said. "No, wait! Isabella! That is . . ." It struck me very forcibly at that moment that I could not chuse one without endangering all the others.

He laughed at that and affectionately patted my arm. "Your enthusiasm to possess Englishwomen is no more than I should have expected of Thomas Fairwood's son. But my own appetites are more moderate. One will suffice for me. I shall ride over to Allhope in a day or two and chuse one young lady, which will leave four for you."

The thought of Isabella or Marianne or any of them

doomed to live forever in the degradation of End-Of-All-Hope House! Oh! it is too horrible to be borne.

I have been staring in the mirror for an hour or more. I was always amazed at Cambridge how quickly people appeared to take offence at everything I said, but now I see plainly that it was not my words they hated—it was this fairy face. The dark alchemy of this face turns all my gentle human emotions into fierce fairy vices. Inside I am all despair, but this face shews only fairy scorn. My remorse becomes fairy fury and my pensiveness is turned to fairy cunning.

Dec. 9th, 1811
This morning at half past ten I made my proposals to Isabella Gathercole. She—sweet, compliant creature!—assured me that I had made her the happiest of women. But she could not at first be made to agree to a secret engagement.

"Oh!" she said. "Certainly Mama and Aunt Edmond will make all sorts of difficulties, but what will secrecy achieve? You do not know them as I do. Alas, they cannot be reasoned into an understanding of your excellent qualities. But they can be worn down. An unending stream of arguments and pleas must be employed, and the sooner it is begun, the sooner it will bring forth the happy resolution we wish for. I must be tearful; you must be heartbroken. I must get up a little illness—which will take time as I am just now in the most excellent good looks and health."

What could the mean-spirited scholars of Cambridge not learn from such a charming instructress? She argued so sweetly that I almost forgot what I was about and agreed to all her most reasonable demands. In the end I was obliged to tell her a little truth. I said that I had recently discovered that I was related to someone very rich who lived nearby and who had taken a great liking to me. I said that I hoped to inherit a great property very soon; surely it was not unreasonable to suppose that Mrs. Gathercole would look with more favour upon my suit when I was as wealthy as she?

Isabella saw the sense of this immediately and would, I think, have begun to speak again of love and so forth, only

I was obliged to hurry away as I had just observed Marianne going into the breakfast-room.

Marianne was inclined to be quarrelsome at first. It was not, she said, that she did not wish to marry me. After all, she said, she must marry someone and she believed that she and I might do very well together. But why must our engagement be a secret? That, she said, seemed almost dishonourable.

"As you wish," said I. "I had thought that your affection for me might make you glad to indulge me in this one point. And besides, you know, a *secret engagement* will oblige us to speak Italian to each other constantly."

Marianne is passionately fond of Italian, particularly since none of her sisters understand a word. "Oh! Very well," she said.

In the garden at half past eleven Jane accepted my proposals by leaning up to whisper in my ear: "His face is fair as heav'n when springing buds unfold." She looked up at me with her soft secret smile and took both my hands in hers.

In the morning-room a little before midday I encountered a problem of a different sort. Henrietta assured me that a secret engagement was the very thing to please her most, but begged to be allowed to write of it to her cousin in Aberdeen. It seems that this cousin, Miss Mary Macdonald, is Henrietta's dearest friend and most regular correspondent, their ages—fifteen and a half—being exactly the same.

It was the most curious thing, she said, but the very week she had first beheld me (and instantly fallen in love with me) she had had a letter from Mary Macdonald full of *her* love for a sandy-haired Minister of the Kirk, the Reverend John McKenzie, who appeared from Mary Macdonald's many detailed descriptions of him to be almost as handsome as myself! Did I not agree with her that it was the strangest thing in the world, this curious resemblance in their situations? Her eagerness to inform Mary Macdonald immediately on all points concerning our engagement was not, I fear, unmixed with a certain rivalry, for I suspected that she was not quite sincere in hoping that Mary Macdonald's love

for Mr. McKenzie might enjoy the same happy resolution
as her own for me. But since I could not prevent her writing,
I was obliged to agree.

In the drawing-room at three o'clock I finally came upon
Kitty, who would not at first listen to anything that I had
to say, but whirled around the room full of a plan to
astound all the village by putting on a play in the barn
at Christmas.

"You are not attending to me," said I. "Did not you
hear me ask you to marry me?"

"Yes," said she, "and I have already said that I would.
It is *you* who are not attending to *me*. You must advise us
upon a play. Isabella wishes to be someone very beautiful
who is vindicated in the last act, Marianne will not act unless she can say something in Italian, Jane cannot be made
to understand anything about it so it will be best if she does
not have to speak at all, Henrietta will do whatever I tell
her, and, Oh! I long to be a bear! The dearest, wisest old
talking bear! Who must dance—like this! And you may be
either a sailor or a coachmen—it does not matter which, as
we have the hat for one and the boots for the other. Now
tell me, Mr. Simonelli, what plays would suit us?"

Two o'clock, Dec. 10th, 1811
In the woods between End-Of-All-Hope House and the vil-
lage of Allhope
I take out my pen, my inkpot, and this book.

"What are you doing?" whimpers Dido, all afraid.

"Writing my journal," I say.

"Now?" says she in amazement. Poor Dido! As I write
she keeps up a continual lament that it will soon be dark
and that the snow falls more heavily—which is I admit a
great nuisance for the flakes fall upon the page and spoil
the letters.

This morning my vigilant watch upon the village was
rewarded. As I stood in the church-porch, hidden from all
eyes by the thick growth of ivy, I saw Isabella coming down
Upperstone-lane. A bitter wind passed over the village, loosening the last leaves from the trees and bringing with it a
few light flakes of snow. Suddenly a spinning storm of

leaves and snowflakes seemed to take possession of Upperstone-lane and John Hollyshoes was there, bowing low and smiling.

It is a measure of my firm resolution that I was able to leave her then, to leave all of them. Everything about John Hollyshoes struck fear into my heart, from the insinuating tilt of his head to the enigmatic gesture of his hands, but I had urgent business to attend to elsewhere and must trust that the Miss Gathercoles' regard for me will be strong enough to protect them.

I went straight to End-Of-All-Hope House, and the moment I appeared in the bare room at the end of the corridor, Dido cried out, "Oh, sir! Have you come to release me from this horrid place?"

"Why, Dido!" said I, much surprized. "What has happened? I thought you were quite contented."

"And so I was, sir, until you licked your finger and touched my eye. When you did that, the sight of my eye was changed. Now if I look through this eye"—she closed her left eye and looked through her right—"I am wearing a golden dress in a wonderful palace and cradling the sweetest babe that ever I beheld. But if I look through *this* eye"— she closed the right and opened her left—"I seem to be chained up in a dirty, nasty room with an ugly goblin child to nurse. But," she said hurriedly (for I was about to speak), "whichever it is, I no longer care, for I am very unhappy here and should very much like to go home."

"I am pleased to hear you say so, Dido," said I. Then, warning her not to express any surprize at anything I said or did, I put my head out of the door and called for Dando.

He was with me in an instant, bowing low.

"I have a message from your master," I said, "whom I met just now in the woods with his new bride. But, like most Englishwomen, the lady is of a somewhat nervous disposition and she has taken it into her head that End-Of-All-Hope House is a dreadful place full of horrors. So your master and I have put our heads together and concluded that the quickest way to soothe her fears is to fetch this woman"—I indicated Dido—"whom she knows well, to meet her. A familiar face is sure to put her at her ease."

I stopped and gazed, as though in expectation of something, at Dando's dark, twisted face. And he gazed back at me, perplexed.

"Well?" I cried. "What are you waiting for, blockhead? Do as I bid you! Loose the nurse's bonds so that I may quickly convey her to your master!" And then, in a fine counterfeit of one of John Hollyshoes's own fits of temper, I threatened him with everything I could think of: beatings, incarcerations, and enchantments! I swore to tell his master of his surliness. I promised that he should be put to work to untangle all the twigs in the woods and comb smooth all the grass in the meadows for insulting me and setting my authority at naught.

Dando is a clever sprite, but I am a cleverer. My story was so convincing that he soon went and fetched the key to unlock Dido's fetters, but not before he had quite worn me out with apologies and explanations and pleas for forgiveness.

When the other servants heard the news that their master's English cousin was taking the English nurse away, it seemed to stir something in their strange clouded minds and they all came out of their hiding places to crowd around us. For the first time I saw them more clearly. This was most unpleasant for me, but for Dido it was far worse. She told me afterwards that through her right eye she had seen a company of ladies and gentlemen who bent upon her looks of such kindness that it made her wretched to think she was deceiving them, while through the other eye she had seen the goblin forms and faces of John Hollyshoes's servants.

There were horned heads, antlered heads, heads carapaced like insects' heads, heads as puckered and soft as a mouldy orange; there were mouths pulled wide by tusks, mouths stretched out into trumpets, mouths that grinned, mouths that gaped, mouths that dribbled; there were bats' ears, cats' ears, rats' whiskers; there were ancient eyes in young faces, large, dewy eyes in old worn faces, there were eyes that winked and blinked in parts of anatomy where I had never before expected to see any eyes at all. The goblins were lodged in every part of the house: there was scarcely a crack in the wainscotting which did not harbour a staring eye, scarcely a gap in the banisters without a nose or snout poking through it. They prodded us with their horny fingers, they pulled our hair and they pinched us black and blue. Dido and I ran out of End-Of-All-Hope House, jumped up upon Quaker's back and rode away into the winter woods.

Snow fell thick and fast from a sea-green sky. The only sounds were Quaker's hooves and the jingle of Quaker's harness as he shook himself.

At first we made good progress, but then a thin mist came up and the path through the woods no longer led where it was supposed to. We rode so long and so far that—unless the woods had grown to be the size of Derbyshire and Nottinghamshire together—we must have come to the end of them, but we never did. And whichever path I chose, we were forever riding past a white gate with a smooth, dry lane beyond it—a remarkably dry lane considering the amount of snow which had fallen—and Dido asked me several times why we did not go down it. But I did not care for it. It was the most commonplace lane in the world, but a wind blew along it—a hot wind like the breath of an oven, and there was a smell as of burning flesh mixed with sulphur.

When it became clear that riding did no more than wear out ourselves and our horse, I told Dido that we must tie Quaker to a tree—which we did. Then we climbed up into the branches to await the arrival of John Hollyshoes.

Seven o'clock, the same day
Dido told me how she had always heard from her mother that red berries, such as rowan-berries, are excellent protection against fairy magic.

"There are some over there in that thicket," she said.

But she must have been looking with her enchanted eye for I saw, not red berries at all but the chestnut-coloured flanks of Pandemonium, John Hollyshoes's horse.

Then the two fairies on their fairy-horses were standing before us with the white snow tumbling across them.

"Ah, cousin!" cried John Hollyshoes. "How do you do? I would shake hands with you, but you are a little out of reach up there." He looked highly delighted and as full of malice as a pudding is of plums. "I have had a very exasperating morning. It seems that the young gentlewomen have all contracted themselves to someone else—yet none will say to whom. Is that not a most extraordinary thing?"

"Most," said I.

"And now the nurse has run away." He eyed Dido sourly. "I never was so thwarted, and were I to discover the author of all my misfortunes—well, cousin, what do you suppose that I would do?"

"I have not the least idea," said I.

"I would kill him," said he. "No matter how dearly I loved him."

The ivy that grew about our tree began to shake itself and to ripple like water. At first I thought that something was trying to escape from beneath it, but then I saw that the ivy itself was moving. Strands of ivy like questing snakes rose up and wrapped themselves around my ancles and legs.

"Oh!" cried Dido in a fright, and tried to pull them off me.

The ivy did not only move; it grew. Soon my legs were lashed to the tree by fresh, young strands; they coiled around my chest and wound around the upper part of my right arm. They threatened to engulf my journal but I was careful to keep *that* out of harm's way. They did not stop until they caressed my neck, leaving me uncertain as to whether John Hollyshoes intended to strangle me or merely to pin me to the tree until I froze to death.

John Hollyshoes turned to Dando. "Are you deaf, iron-brains? Did you never hear me say that he is as accomplished a liar as you and I?" He paused to box Dando's ear. "Are you blind? Look at him! Can you not perceive the fierce fairy heart that might commit murder with indifference? Come here, unseelie elf! Let me poke some new holes in your face! Perhaps you will see better out of those!"

I waited patiently until my cousin had stopped jabbing at his servant's face with the blunt end of his whip and until Dando had ceased howling. "I am not sure," I said, "whether I could commit murder with indifference, but I am perfectly willing to try." With my free arm I turned to the page in my journal where I have described my arrival in Allhope. I leant out of the tree as far as I could (this was very easily accomplished as the ivy held me snug against the trunk) and above John Hollyshoes's head I made the curious gesture that I had seen him make over the old man's head.

We were all as still as the frozen trees, as silent as the birds in the thickets and the beasts in their holes. Suddenly John Hollyshoes burst out, "Cousin . . . !"

It was the last word he ever spoke. Pandemonium, who appeared to know very well what was about to happen, reared up and shook his master from his back, as though terrified that he too might be caught up in my spell. There was a horrible rending sound; trees shook; birds sprang, cawing, into the air. Anyone would have supposed that it was the whole world, and not merely some worthless fairy, that was being torn apart. I looked down and John Hollyshoes lay in two neat halves upon the snow.

"Ha!" said I.

"Oh!" cried Dido.

Dando gave a scream which if I were to try to reproduce it by means of the English alphabet would possess more syllables than any word hitherto seen. Then he caught up Pandemonium's reins and rode off with that extraordinary speed of which I know him to be capable.

The death of John Hollyshoes had weakened the spell he had cast on the ivy, and Dido and I were able quite easily to tear it away. We rode back to Allhope, where I restored her to joyful parent, loving husband, and hungry child. My parishioners came to the cottage to load me with praises, grateful thanks, promises of future aid, etc., etc. I however was tired to death and, after making a short speech advising them to benefit from the example I had given them of courage and selflessness, I pleaded the excuse of a headache to come home.

One thing, however, has vexed me *very much*, and that is there was no time to conduct a proper examination of John Hollyshoes's body. For it occurs to me that just as Reason is seated in the brain of Man, so we Fairies may contain within ourselves some *organ of Magic*. Certainly the fairy's bisected corpse had some curious features. I append here a rough sketch and a few notes describing the ways in which Fairy anatomy appears to depart from Human anatomy. I intend to be in the woods at first light to examine the corpse more closely.

Dec. 11th, 1811
The body is gone. Dando, I suppose, has spirited it away. This is most vexatious as I had hoped to have it sent to Mr. Baillie's anatomy school in Great Windmill-street in London. I suppose that the baby in the bare room at the end of the corridor will inherit End-Of-All-Hope House and all John Hollyshoes's estates, but perhaps the loss of Dido's milk at this significant period in its life will prevent its growing up as strong in wickedness as its parent.

I have not abandoned my own hopes of inheriting my father's estate and may very well pursue my claim when I have the time. I have never heard that the possession of an extensive property in Faerie was incompatible with the duties of a priest of the Church of England—indeed I do not believe that I ever heard the subject mentioned.

Dec. 17th, 1811
I have been most villainously betrayed by the Reverend John McKenzie! I take it particularly hard since he is the person from whom—as a fellow clergyman—I might most reasonably have expected support. It appears that he is to marry the heiress to a castle and several hundred miles of bleak Scottish wilderness in Caithness. I hope there may be bogs and that John McKenzie may drown in them. Disappointed love has, I regret to say, screwed Miss Mary Macdonald up to such a pitch of anger that she has turned upon Henrietta and me. She writes to Henrietta that she is certain I am not be trusted and she threatens to write to Mrs. Gathercole and Mrs. Edmond. Henrietta is not afraid; rather, she exults in the coming storm.

"You will protect me!" she cried, her eyes flashing with strange brilliance and her face flushed with excitement.

"My dear girl," said I, "I will be *dead*."

*   *   *

Dec. 20th, 1811
George Hollinsclough was here a moment ago with a message that I am to wait upon Mrs. Gathercole and Mrs. Edmond *immediately*. I take one last fond look around this room. . . .

"Mr. Simonelli or the Fairy Widower" is a rendering of "Midwife to the Fairies," found in English, Irish, Scots, and Breton variations. Clarke's story also makes deft use of many other classic folklore themes: the girl who was stolen away to suckle a fairy baby, the seeing eye, the faery house in the woods, etc. Celtic fairy lore of this sort can be found in the collections of Katherine Briggs.

Recommended Reading

Fiction and Poetry

The Robber Bride and Bluebeard's Egg, by Margaret Atwood
    This Canadian writer often uses fairy-tale themes in her *excellent contemporary mainstream fiction.*

Snow White, by Donald Barthelme
    This is an early postmodern short novel that would be politically incorrect by today's standards.

Katie Crackernuts, by Katherine Briggs
    A charming short novel retelling the Katie Crackernuts tale, by one of the world's foremost folklore authorities.

Beginning with O, by Olga Broumas
    Broumas's poetry makes use of many fairy-tale motifs in this collection.

The Sun, the Moon and the Stars, by Steven Brust
    A contemporary novel mixing ruminations on art and creation with a lively Hungarian fairy tale.

Possession, by A. S. Byatt
    A Booker Prize–winning novel that makes wonderful use of the Fairy Melusine legend.

Nine Fairy Tales and One More Thrown in for Good Measure, by Karel Capek
    Charming stories inspired by the Czech folk tradition.

Sleeping in Flame, by Jonathan Carroll
    Excellent, quirky dark fantasy using the Rumpelstilt-skin tale.

The Bloody Chamber and *Burning Your Boats* by Angela Carter
    Angela Carter is grand dame of modern adult fairy tales. Her extraordinary, dark, sensual fairy-tale retellings are collected in *The Bloody Chamber,* and can also be found in *Burning Your Boats:* a posthumous collection of Carter's complete short fiction.

The Sleeping Beauty, by Hayden Carruth
    A poetry sequence using the Sleeping Beauty legend.

Briar Rose and *Pinocchio in Venice* by Robert Coover
    Coover often works with fairy-tale themes in his fiction; these two books are particularly recommended. The first is a highly literary exploration of the Briar Rose theme, dense and lush as a briar rose hedge; the second is a more satiric work.

Beyond the Looking Glass, edited by Jonathan Cott
    A collection of Victorian fairy-tale prose and poetry.

The Nightingale, by Kara Dalkey
    An evocative Oriental historical novel based on the Hans Christian Andersen story.

The Printed Alphabet, by Diana Darling
This novel is a rich fantasia inspired by Balinese myth and folklore.

The Girl Who Trod on a Loaf, by Kathryn Davis
Uses the fairy tale of the title as the basis for a story of two women, and the opera, at the beginning of the twentieth century. A lovely little book.

Blue Bamboo, by Osamu Dazai
This volume of fantasy stories by a Japanese writer of the early twentieth century contains lovely fairy-tale work.

Fairy Tale by Alice Thomas Ellis
This contemporary Welsh story makes fascinating use of "changeling" motifs.

Provençal Tales, by Michael de Larrabeiti
An absolutely gorgeous collection containing tales drawn from the Provençal region of France.

Jack the Giant-Killer and *Drink Down the Moon*, by Charles de Lint
Wonderful urban fantasy novels bringing "Jack" and magic to the streets of modern Canada.

Tam Lin, by Pamela Dean
A lyrical novel setting the old Scottish fairy story (and folk ballad) Tam Lin among theater majors on a Midwestern college campus.

Reading in the Dark by Seamus Deane
Deane makes deft use of Irish folk tales in this coming-of-age story about a young boy in violence-torn Northern Ireland.

Vinegar Jar, by Berle Doherty
An eerie, disturbing contemporary novel weaving traditional fairy tales into the story of a disintegrating marriage.

Kissing the Witch: Old Tales in New Skins, by Emma Donahue
   Gorgeous, poetic feminist retellings of classic fairy tales by an award-winning Irish writer.

Like Water for Chocolate, by Laura Esquivel
   Esquivel's book (and the wonderful film of the same title) wraps Mexican folklore and tales into a turn-of-the-century story about love and food on the Mexico/Texas border. Complete with recipes.

Memories of My Ghost Brother, by Heinz Insu Fenkl
   This gorgeous autobiographical novel weaves folklore into a contemporary coming-of-age tale about a young boy in Korea. Highly recommended.

The King's Indian, by John Gardner
   A collection of peculiar and entertaining stories using fairy-tale motifs.

Crucifax Autumn, by Ray Garton
   One of the first splatterpunk horror novels; Garton makes use of the Pied Piper theme in very nasty ways. Violent and visceral.

Blood Pressure, by Sandra M. Gilbert
   A number of the poems in this powerful collection make use of fairy-tale motifs.

Strange Devices of the Sun and Moon, by Lisa Goldstein
   A lyrical little novel mixing English fairy tales with English history in Christopher Marlowe's London.

The Seventh Swan, by Nicholas Stuart Gray
   An engaging Scottish novel that starts off where the "Seven Swans" fairy tale ends.

Fire and Hemlock, by Diana Wynne Jones
   A beautifully written, haunting novel that brings the Thomas the Rhymer and Tam Lin tales into modern day England.

Seven Fairy Tales and a Fable, by Gwyneth Jones
Eight enchanting, thought-provoking, adult fairy tales by this British writer.

Green Grass Running Water, by Thomas King
This delightful Magical Realist novel uses Native American myths and folk tales to hilarious effect.

The Book of Laughter and Forgetting, by Milan Kundera
This literate and cosmopolitan work makes use of Moravian folk music, rituals, and stories.

Thomas the Rhymer, by Ellen Kushner
A sensuous and musical rendition of this old Scottish story and folk ballad

The Wandering Unicorn, by Manuel Mujica Lainez
A fairy-tale novel based on the "Fairy Melusine" legend by an award-winning Argentinean writer. Translated from the Spanish.

Red as Blood, or Tales from the Sisters Grimmer, by Tanith Lee
A striking and versatile collection of adult fairy-tale retellings.

Terrors of Earth, by Tom Le Farge
This poetic little collection of stories weaves sensual, surreal imagery out of old French "fabliaux."

Dreaming Frankenstein and Collected Poems, by Liz Lochead
This collection includes excellent fairy tale work from the Scottish writer's "Grimm Sisters" collection.

The Tricksters, by Margaret Mahy
This beautifully told, contemporary New Zealand story draws upon pancultural Trickster legends.

Angel Maker, by Sarah Maitland
A collection gathering the short fiction by this excellent English author, including stories making rich use of themes from fairy tales and myth.

Winter Rose and *Something Rich and Strange*, by Patricia A. McKillip
   The first is a gorgeous, poetic, magical fantasy set at the edge of an English forest, using themes from Tam Lin and other English tales. The second, also beautifully penned, is a sparkling short novel (with art by Brian Froud) using fairy tales of the sea as the basis for a contemporary story set in the Pacific Northwest.

Beauty, by Robin McKinley
   Masterfully written, gentle and magical, this novel retells the story of "Beauty and the Beast."

Deerskin, by Robin McKinley
   A retelling of Charles Perrault's "Donkeyskin," a dark fairy tale with incest themes.

The Door in the Hedge, by Robin McKinley
   "The Twelve Dancing Princesses" and "The Frog Prince" retold in McKinley's gorgeous, clear prose, along with two original tales.

Rose Daughter, by Robin McKinley
   McKinley's second novel-length retelling of "Beauty and the Beast," highly recommended.

Disenchantments, edited by Wolfgang Mieder
   An excellent compilation of adult fairy-tale poetry.

Sleeping Beauty, by Susanna Moore
   An eloquent, entertaining contemporary novel that uses the "Sleeping Beauty" legend mixed with native Hawaiian folklore.

The Private Life and *Waving from the Shore*, by Lisel Mueller
   Terrific poetry collections with many fairy-tale themes.

Zel, by Donna Jo Napoli
   Published as young-adult fiction, this is a dark and engrossing retelling of Rapunzel.

Godmother Night, by Rachel Pollack
A unique contemporary fantasy, based on the Godfather Death fairy tale, about two gay women, their child, and the angel of death—surrounded by her coterie of leatherclad bikers.

Haroun and the Sea of Stories, by Salman Rushdie
A delightful Eastern fantasia by this Booker Prize–winning author.

Kindergarten, by Peter Rushford
A contemporary British story beautifully wrapped around the "Hansel and Gretel" tale, highly recommended.

Transformations, by Anne Sexton
Sexton's brilliant collection of modern fairy-tale poetry.

The Porcelain Dove, by Delia Sherman
This gorgeous fantasy set during the French Revolution makes excellent use of French fairy tales.

The Flight of Michael McBride, by Midori Snyder
A lovely, deftly written fantasy set in the old American West, this magical novel mixes the folklore traditions of immigrant and indigenous American cultures.

Fair Peril, by Nancy Springer
A droll, wise, adult fairy tale set in the land of Fair Peril—between two stores at the local mall.

Trail of Stones, by Gwenn Strauss
Evocative fairy-tale poems, beautifully illustrated by Anthony Browne.

Swan's Wing, by Ursula Synge
A lovely, magical fantasy novel using the "Seven Swans" fairy tale.

Beauty, by Sheri S. Tepper
Dark fantasy incorporating several fairy tales from an original and iconoclastic writer.

Indigo, by Marina Warner
　Fairy tales are woven into the fabric of this lush contemporary novel (by one of England's foremost fairy-tale scholars) about family life in the Caribbean.

Wonder Tales, edited by Marina Warner
　Gilbert Adair, John Ashbery, Ranjit Bolt, A. S. Byatt, and Terence Cave retell six French fairy tales in this beautiful little edition, with an excellent introduction by Warner.

Kingdoms of Elfin, by Sylvia Townsend Warner
　These stories drawn from British folklore are arch, elegant, and enchanting. Many were first published in *The New Yorker*.

The Coachman Rat, by David Henry Wilson
　Excellent dark fantasy retelling the story of "Cinderella" from the coachman's point of view.

Beauty, by Susan Wilson
　A romantic contemporary retelling of "Beauty and the Beast," set in an isolated house in New England.

The Armless Maiden, edited by Terri Windling
　Original fairy tales exploring the darker themes of childhood by Patricia McKillip, Tanith Lee, Charles de Lint, Jane Yolen, and many others.

Snow White and Rose Red, by Patricia C. Wrede
　A charming Elizabethan historical novel retelling this romantic Grimm's fairy tale.

Briar Rose, by Jane Yolen
　An unforgettable short novel setting the Briar Rose/ Sleeping Beauty story against the background of World War II.

Don't Bet on the Prince, edited by Jack Zipes
　A collection of contemporary feminist fairy tales compiled by a leading fairy-tale scholar, containing prose and

poetry by Angela Carter, Joanna Russ, Jane Yolen, Tanith Lee, Margaret Atwood, Olga Broumas, and others.

The Outspoken Princess and the Gentle Knight: A Treasury of Modern Fairy Tales, edited by Jack Zipes
   Presents fifteen modern fairy tales from England and the United States including works by Ernest Hemingway, A. S. Byatt, John Gardner, Jane Yolen, and Tanith Lee.

Modern Day Fairy-tale Creators

The Faber Book of Modern Fairy Tales, by Sara and Stephen Corrin
Gudgekin the Thistle Girl and Other Tales, by John Gardner
Mainly by Moonlight, by Nicholas Stuart Gray
Collected Stories, by Richard Kennedy
Dark Hills, Hollow Clocks, by Garry Kilworth
Heart of Wood, by William Kotzwinkle
Five Men and a Swan, by Naomi Mitchison
The White Deer and *The Thirteen Clocks,* by James Thurber
Fairy Tales, by Alison Uttley
Tales of Wonder, by Jane Yolen

Nonfiction

Mirror, Mirror on the Wall: Women Writers Explore their Favorite Fairy Tales, edited by Kate Bernheimer
   An excellent collection of essays by Joyce Carol Oates, Margaret Atwood, Fey Weldon, A. S. Byatt and many other other women writers, both well known and new, marred only by its limitation to authors whose works have been published as "mainstream" fiction.
The Power of Myth, by Joseph Campbell
The Erotic World of Fairy, by Maureen Duffy
Dreams and Wishes, collected essays by Susan Cooper
Cinderella: A Casebook, edited by Alan Dundes
Tales from Eternity: The World of Fairy Tales and the Spiritual Search, by Rosemary Haughton
Beauty and the Beast: Visions and Revisions of an Old Tale, by Betsy Hearne

The Arabian Nights: A Companion, by Robert Irwin
Woman, Earth and Spirit, by Helen M. Luke
Once Upon a Time, collected essays by Alison Lurie
The Classic Fairy Tales, by Iona and Peter Opie
What the Bee Knows, collected essays by P. L. Travers
Problems of the Feminine in Fairy Tales, by Marie-Louise von Franz
  Collected lectures originally presented at the C. G. Jung Institute
From the Beast to the Blonde: On Fairy Tales and their Tellers, by Marina Warner (highly recommended)
Six Myths of Our Time, by Marina Warner
Touch Magic, collected essays by Jane Yolen
Fantasists on Fantasy, edited by Robert H. Boyer and Kenneth J. Zahorski
  Includes Tolkien's "On Fairy Stories," G. K. Chesterton's "Fairy Tales," and other essays
Fairy Tales as Myths, by Jack Zipes

Fairy-tale Source Collections

Old Wives' Fairy Tale Book, edited by Angela Carter
The Tales of Charles Perrault, translated by Angela Carter
Italian Folktales, translated by Italo Calvino
Daughters of the Moon, edited by Shahrukh Husain
The Complete Hans Christian Andersen, edited by Lily Owens
The Maid of the North: Feminist Folk Tales from Around the World, edited by Ethel Johnston Phelps
Gypsy Folktales, edited by Diane Tong
Favorite Folk Tales from Around the world, edited by Jane Yolen
The Complete Brothers Grimm, edited by Jack Zipes
Spells of Enchantment: The Wondrous Fairy Tales of Western Culture, edited by Jack Zipes (highly recommended)

  (For volumes of fairy tales from individual countries—Russian fairy tales, French, African, Japanese, etc.—see the excellent Pantheon Books Fairy Tale and Folklore Library.)

About the Editors

Ellen Datlow has been editing short fiction for twenty years and has won the World Fantasy Award five times for her editorial work. She is Fiction Editor of scifi.com, the Sci Fi Channel's website, located at http://www.scifi.com. She has also edited numerous anthologies, including *Little Deaths* (winner of the World Fantasy Award), *Lethal Kisses*, and *Vanishing Acts*—and is co-editor (with Terri Windling) of *Sirens and Other Daemon Lovers* and the award-winning series *The Year's Best Fantasy and Horror*. She lives in New York City.

Terri Windling, a five-time winner of the World Fantasy Award for her editorial work, is also the author of *The Wood Wife* (winner of the Mythopoeic Award), *The Moon Wife*, and other works of fiction and nonfiction. She has worked as an editor specializing in adult fairy tale fiction for almost two decades and has edited over twenty anthologies. She is a consulting editor for Tor Books and lives in Devon, England, and Tucson, Arizona.